MAYHEM

MICHAEL MOLISANI

978-0-578-45070-4 Paperback

978-0-578-45071-1 eBook

Author: Michael Molisani

Content Editor: Athena Driscoll

Copy Editor: Kristen Busman

Cover Artist: Nan Fe

Cover Design: Anita Stefanie

eBook Conversion: Michael Molisani

Illustrators: Karolina Jędrzejak (RinRinDaishi), Audia Pahlevi (Moonarc), LacticWanda & SapFire

INTRODUCTION

Welcome to Veilfall. This is a world that follows the Collapse. I want to thank **Athena Driscoll** for being such an important aspect of the creative process. Besides her role as content editor, she's the one person who I can talk to about Veilfall. I love her for that, and a thousand other reasons. I also want to thank **Kristen Busman** for always being supportive. Her enthusiasm and drive behind these projects have been beyond my wildest hopes. You don't know awkward until you've discussed the adjective "mucilaginous" regarding a sex scene with your copy editor.

This book is self-published. You're probably going to see a typo or two. I'm not even sorry. We spent thousands of hours working to eliminate 99% of all errors, but I'm sure a few made it through. You should probably just get over that. People will like you more.

I also want to thank **Nan Fe**, my amazing cover artist for "*The Bruja*," and "*Mayhem*." Her work is peerless, exciting, and horrific. I consider myself both honored & grateful each time I work with her.

I also want to thank **Delilah Vex, Erin Abid,** and **Melissa Johnson**. Melissa, you may know, is another author who will be working with me on a forthcoming Veilfall anthology. A collection of short stories & novellas which flesh out Veilfall. She's asked me a lot of questions in the last year that I couldn't answer – and when I did, those answers often became part of this book.

Last, but certainly not least, I want to thank my wife; **Kimberly "Gats" Molisani**. She has been, and will always be, a key ingredient in my success. Its hard being an author's wife. I have a day job that requires long hours, and those long hours become *even longer* when I sit down to write, revise, or edit.

Now that I've thanked everyone – how would you like to read a book about a witch named Margaret?

Lady Mayhem by Karolina Jędrzejak (RinRinDaishi)

March 14th, 7 Veilfall

Crafton, Pennsylvania

"Are you," the boy pauses, flexing a fist, thumb knuckle popping, "a witch?"

The two children couldn't have been older than fourteen. The girl is scrawny, her shoulders are misshapen, and one clavicle is slouched down. Her fingers are black, sooty, and her broken nails grind into a lump of charcoal. She sketches flurries on a concrete wall, sweeping lines in monochrome. A spiral of flames pressed and pulled by opposing winds.

"Yeah." The little girl nods, refusing distraction.

"So," the boy flexes his fist again, "can you read my mind?"

The girl nods a second time, "I know how you feel. I know if you're afraid, or if you're happy. If I touch you, I can see pictures."

"I'm not afraid," the boy blurts out, hands pressed to the floor.

There are layers of carpet, woven thin, underneath both children. Each one is a conflicting color or pattern, dusty with age and wear, covered in debris; small twigs, pebbles, crumbs and broken shards of coal.

The little girl stopped. "Yes, you are." Her auburn-red hair tied back in a ponytail with a long strand of paracord. When she nodded, it would bounce on her faded sweater.

The boy knew this was his ruin. His eyes turned murky with all the drama a child could leech from such a moment. He had nothing to hide behind, no *tough exterior*, no biting fury or savage bravery. He was, instead, exposed and naked in front of the girl. All the words in the world could not hide his cowardice.

The girl turned from her umbra flame, laying charcoal down, "I know you're sad. But I don't know *why*. Why are you sad?" What was the boy to tell her? *Because pretty girls don't like cowards*. Before he could open his mouth and stammer out a denial, the girl answered; "You're not a coward. A coward would run away. A coward wouldn't come here."

The boy had spent much of his short life working to be brave. He knew that he could hide *fear* with *noise*. He could shout orders to the younger children and they'd never know how desperate his *fear* was. The little girl with black paracord in her red hair was defiling that notion. Ripping up his rule book, *laughing in his face*.

Except, she *wasn't* laughing. She was smiling at him. Not in a mean, or cruel way. She was smiling at him with eyes that *liked* his compliment. The compliment he'd never spoken. Why wrap up thoughts inside his ribs where no one could find them? *This girl clearly could.*

"I think you're pretty."

The girl leans sideways on her hip, bracing one dirty hand to the rugs and reaching for the boy. "I'm going to touch you, okay?"

The air in the girl's room is thick and musty. Sharp with unwashed clothes and adolescent pheromones. He pulls away, causing her to pause, with a hand suspended mid-stretch, "Why?"

"Because you think I'm pretty." The girl says this as though it was the most obvious answer in the world. It is as if someone has reached into the boy's heart, crawled up his throat and wrapped his mind in warm blankets. The girl reaches forward, her weight shifting as she comes up on her knees. With fingers covered in scabs and scratches, under charcoal stains, she presses a hand into the boy's forehead.

Daniel Hasgard knew his parents had died in a plane crash, a day before the Collapse. His uncle had told him the details, something about a bomb. He didn't remember, it was easier to forget. All he knew of that day was the way his polyester comforter felt after it was hot with tears and snot. Printed in deep blue skies and cartoon airplanes, it felt like a betrayal. He ripped them off the bed, throwing them as far as he could. The sky wasn't harmless. It had killed his mother and father.

The little girl doesn't like this.

Part of her trickles into Daniel Hasgard's skull, a faucet left to dribble across dirty dishes in a brimming sink. Her mind is black and sooty, just like her charcoal, wrapping around his memories. She can't take his pain away, she can't erase his sorrow or loss. She can only *dull* it, as she had *dulled* his fear a moment earlier. She can make him comfortable, give him a respite where he needn't be *the tough guy*. Here, *alone* with her, he was safe.

It's only us, the girl speaks in Daniel's mind. *I won't let you get hurt.*

Daniel feels as if he is floating in that same cartoon sky of his polyester sheets. It doesn't make him angry now, it feels peaceful, and warm. As warm as the little girl's palm pressing into his face. He knows she's kissing him, and he doesn't mind.

The girl pulls him close. Blackened fingerprints cover his skin and clothes, even his dusty blonde hair. Each charcoal stain is an impression, turning his veins the color of night. They bind him closer, as her mind continues to expand across his memories. His loves, his favorite foods, and his most hated chores.

The girl, lost inside Daniel's mind and memories, never heard the door of her room unlatch. Yet, slamming shut, it breaks her focus. The severance is violent, and she can't protect Daniel anymore.

"*What the fuck is this shit?*"

The girl's mother is slim, with a hawk nose and deeply onyx eyes. Her ill-kept hair spills across a tank top that exposes layers of colorful ink across her skin. In one hand she's holding a glass bottle, quarter full of brown fluid.

"*Bruja!*" the boy shouts, pulling away. He *knows* who this woman is. *Everyone* knows who *Maggi Lopez is.* "I'm sorry, we were only talking!"

The little girl stands quickly. She can *hear* her mother's words before she speaks them. It creates a disjointed echo in her mind, "*Only talking,*" Maggi yells, "*Don't lie to me you toe-head fuck!*"

The boy is getting ready to stand, holding his hands out, sputtering and spitting. His terror is a tangible animal in the room, it flits and squeaks like a cornered hare. The little girl can see air bubble and bend around her mother's fingers. She knows what that means.

She's going to burn him. She's drunk enough to burn him alive.

Maggi is pulling from the world around her, *borrowing* flame, summoning it to her free hand. The magic smells of peeling and twisting muscles.

The little girl can't calm her mother when she's this angry, but even an attempt to reach into her mind might shake the older woman's focus and draw her away from Daniel. Even if it only quieted Maggi's flame for a few seconds, the girl would try her best. In an instant, the woman with dark eyes tips her head to one side, favoring the little girl. A look of betrayal darts across her face, lips parting in a snarl.

Daniel was a smart boy and used this opportunity to stand and bolt. He's not fast enough, and his left shoe catches on the rugs, tripping him. When he steadies himself, Maggi raises her left hand, swinging the bottle down to strike.

Although the little girl with paracord in her hair owes Daniel nothing, she jumps up. She's seen too much of his mind to *not* care. She won't break her own promise, she will protect Daniel. Even if that meant placing herself between him and her enraged mother.

The bottle of alcohol strikes the girl squarely in the head. The glass is thick and when it shatters, it covers her in pungent decoction. Broken shards rain, falling down her shirt, and lodging in her auburn red hair. The last thing she sees is Daniel fleeing the room, she's given him safe passage. She'd *told him* that her mother wouldn't be home, the witch that he feared most.

The witch *everyone feared. The Bruja.*

"Who the *fuck* was watching Alexander while you played tongue-twister?" Maggi yells at the little girl who's pulling herself up off the rugs. Maggi has none of it, landing an open palm down on the back of her head, hard enough to create an echoing *thump*.

"He was asleep," the little girl repeats, "*He was asleep.*"

"One *fucking week* I was gone," Maggi yells, her voice husky and sharp with a clipped tone. She shortens all her vowels and bites hard into each statement, "I can't always *fucking* be here. I *have* to fight, and I trusted you with my *fucking* son."

A second time Maggi strikes her with an open palm. This time it hits the girl's face, raising a warm glow from under flesh. Maggi's rage fills the room, acrid and smoky, suffocating. The little girl *could* block it out, but now her own focus has evaporated.

"How *dare* you abandon my son!" Maggi shouts, striking the girl again. The contact with her mother's flesh was like a knife sliding under skin. Prying away at a splinter, wriggling around and bracing nerves. Maggi was *always* a heavy drinker after she fought in the field. She always tasted of bitter medicine and loathing when returning home.

The little girl doesn't answer.

Maggi's *yelling* slips out of English and into *Español*, but the girl is no longer listening. Only after her catatonia became clear does Maggi fall quiet. When she speaks again it is a growl that slips from her throat. Without slur or fumble, she communicates her point with precise hatred. "I swear to *fuck* Margaret, I should have *fucking* left you in that parking lot seven years ago."

Maggi storms out of the room, slamming the door behind her.

Margaret doesn't pull herself up off the mismatched rugs that had worked so hard to trip Daniel. She lies there, still. The blood at her lips is darkening, scabbing, and one of her eyes has begun to swell. Maggi could hit hard.

Margaret wouldn't have cared if her mother beat her every day, if only she would never say those words again. *I swear to fuck Margaret, I should have fucking left you in that parking lot seven years ago.* It was an extravagant wish, pulling and pulling until she felt her organs might rip apart.

It was an irony, of course, that Margaret could ease the pain of others, but could never console her own. The best she could do was retreat to a lumpy mattress and pretend that this had never happened.

8:32 pm January 8th, 39 Veilfall

Stockton, California

The band that performed toward the ballroom rear was made up of two violins, a flute, and a wide hurdy gurdy. The man who slung that heavy wooden instrument from his shoulders wound a crank with rhythmic stops and starts. He was young with brown hair that almost turned gold under gas lamps, nodding his head in time with each tap and turn of his right hand.

Margaret watched him, enamored, and properly drunk. She could lose parts of herself in a musician's mind when she wished, a swimmer at sea, pulled into the wake of a great wave, filling her mouth and ears with freezing water.

Beyond the performers, at Margaret's flank, the ballroom moved with the same predictable rhythm of a hurdy gurdy crank. She could *feel* them shift and turn at the edges of her mind. They weighed the measure of each step, the final template of how others judged them. *Liars,* all of them, presenting their best smiles, perfumed and lascivious. Military commanders chatted, joined by minor nobility, landowners, and various captains of farm and factory; not dancing to Margaret's music, but rather their own pulsing rituals.

This ballroom was part of the former House Owens palace, built into an old university that occupied central Stockton. Paintings, sculptures, row upon row, looked down at a long, narrow dining table from high walls and broad windows. Shining, wooden stairs dipped into a floor of black marble, polish reflecting silhouettes. The air was rich in smoked meats and cheese, pungent vinegar dressing and citrus sides hanging like a fine mist, clutching at Margaret's throat in a casual dance of culinary desire.

It was only with an empty wine glass that Margaret chose to break away from the bucolic calm and return once more to a grander stage. Her mouth was dry, and she was consumed with uncomfortable thoughts about *where* her eyes should land as she stepped, and *who* she ought to greet with a nod. House Owens nobility presented themselves with oblique brocades on jackets and dresses, pandering to the Imperials with understated colors, muted in the wake of occupation. They showed her their respect, tipping formal caps of yellow or white wool, but it was not what she heard them whisper with pursed lips.

Witch. Antecedent witch.

The Antecedent officers; however, gaited about in their white breeches, deep navy jackets, and brown leather sashes, gleeful, antipodal in their grace. They tried to maintain a decorum appropriate to the event, but they were too rough at the edges, chewing sausages on long forks with their mouths open, and loudly regaling each other with sagas of whores, rum, and blood. Unlike the elite Owens society, they *smiled* at her, or perhaps *smirked*, their thoughts a fricassee of respect and lust.

Lady Mayhem looks fucking great tonight.

Margaret was a *very* small woman. She wasn't slender, she'd spent too many years in the field to be fragile, but she was easily the shortest person in the room, glancing up at the Owens wives and concubines. Her dress of red was manufactured from marbled velvet, Georgette, and crêpe wool. She'd chosen a flat front corset this night, without clips or hooks, embellished with complex wool and cotton needlepoint in shades of burgundy and black. It was traditional Antecedent spiral work, the same found on gates and doors back home in Crafton. Although the scallop-lace trim of her neckline was kissing her throat, the gown fell at asymmetric angles, showing off *very* much more of her legs than was *very* appropriate.

From time to time, Margaret would stop and converse with a land minister or wealthy merchant, all certainly important in their spheres of influence. Margaret wasn't so much a Collapse child that she didn't know the fineries of polite society, she smiled and nodded, curtsied and embellished her absolute lack of disinterest for these people.

"Lord Owens," Margaret smiled more genuinely for this man. Unlike the others he was, in fact, *important*. He had light green eyes, and thick lashes threatened by thoughtful brows.

Eric Owens paused, his silence hanging in the air, elbow to elbow with the steamed turkey and barbeque chicken, "Lady *Mayhem*," he said finally. Margaret couldn't decide whether he was intentionally trying to insult her. "You'll forgive me Lady, I don't remember seeing you at these events before." Eric spoke with a rasp at the back of his throat and a light voice that hardly befitted a man wearing a jagged scar across his left brow, around his eye.

Because I fucking hate these events, Margaret thought, "I've been far too busy in recent months to attend them." She did her best to affect eloquent speech.

There was an odd sort of humility about him, his energy, stance, and eyes seemed to laugh nervously. Behind that uncomfortable mirth was a rigid strength, a gleaming nobility that neither his mother nor his sister shared. *Oh*, they were noble for certain, they were used to giving orders, but it felt to Margaret as if Eric Owens was obeyed instinctively.

"Well, it's a pleasure to be graced by your inviolability."

I have no idea what that word means, Margaret nearly choked, visibly.

It was now obvious that Eric *was* looking to insult her, just as quietly as forgetting her name. "That's what I do." Margaret laughed, refusing to display her confusion.

Eric wore the grey uniform that marked him as a member of Antecedent *auxiliary* forces, a role reserved for those soldiers who'd knelt before Margaret's brother. He wore the jacket and slacks smartly, but his awards and ranks were Owens, a lack of capitulation bordering on provocative. "What finally brought you to the Grand Ballroom?" Lord Owens gestured wide, taking in the immense room.

Margaret shrugged, one shoulder moving slightly smoother than the other, "I was invited by The Orders, by *your* sister actually. How could I refuse?" She lied and took secret delight.

"Modus Vivendi," Eric corrected, once again looking for an opportunity to kick down at the smaller woman, "Our father was a brilliant man, but he was none too creative when he named his *witch-cult*, 'The Orders.'"

"Of course," Margaret answered, leaning back slightly, "*Modus Vivendi*."

"I'm surprised she'd not have invited you sooner," Eric favored Margaret with a grimace, then glanced around the room, "I'm also surprised she'd *invite* you to an event that the *Vivendi* themselves chose to ignore, Lady Lopez."

"*Lady Mayhem*, if it pleases. I am not a Lopez." Margaret replied, curtly.

"Oh? But, Emperor Alexander Lopez is your brother?" For the first time since they met, Margaret felt real surprise on those words. Eric's brows also betrayed him, rising slightly as he tipped his head with curiosity. Margaret saw the opportunity, felt Eric Owens open his guard and allow her to enter in the dance with her. She could have used magic now, pressed in just a little, *suggested* he favor her just a bit more, but she'd never *forced* people to like her and she wasn't about to start now.

"I'm *allowed* to call Alexander my brother," Margaret chose her words carefully, the subject prickly on her skin. "Maggi Lopez adopted me as a child, after the Collapse. Her last name did not extend as far as her kindness."

Eric Owens considered, genuinely, before replying, "I remember now, you mentioned that the day you first came before my mother's court. I suppose we're both bastard children then." Lord Owens *finally* smiled, though it suggested no familiarity.

"How so, Lord Owens?" Margaret caught herself showing too much interest when she asked, and a quick jump in Eric Owens's pulse proved it. *Had he assumed this was small talk?*

"I'm the *second* child of Lady Owens, her youngest. My mother's favor of me as successor never sat well with my sister." Lord Owens shrugged, glancing around the room, offering an amused chuckle, "So, what finally brings an Imperial witch to our humble court? *Besides* a fake invitation from *Magnate* Cuttersark?"

"It seemed as good a lie as any," Margaret replied with a sigh, deeply regretting the empty wine glass that she clutched. "In truth, it's because my niece is arriving, soon. She asked me to make her introductions. I can't make introductions for her unless I also introduce *myself*."

"Amy?" Eric's eyes narrowed.

"*No*," Margaret shook her head, "Amihan is still in the south with her father, on campaign. Her twin sister, Ramona, is arriving from Crafton. Two nights from now. Perhaps, we could take dinner that evening?"

Although Lord Owens wasn't actively looking to insult her further, Margaret was aware that he was becoming rapidly uninterested. "Two nights from now?" Eric tilted his head, pretending to consider, but Margaret didn't hear the wheels turn or gears click. "No, *no*, I'm afraid I'm engaged that evening."

With a mother like Maggi Lopez, Margaret had never learned timidity as a trait. Even now, out of options and opportunity, she made one final gambit. "Perhaps *another* evening?"

He's already insulted me; a little extra desperation is fine.

"Perhaps, Lady Mayhem. I'll continue my rounds now." Lord Owens nodded to Margaret, before wandering away, making a show of waving to an Owens landowner, a rotund man who didn't notice that his wine glass was tilted back and slowly dribbling down the front of his brocade jacket.

Does he hate witches? Margaret doubted that, both his mother and sister were incredibly talented. Lord Owens would have grown up around *magic*, ghosts, demons, and ancient gods.

No, he simply hates Antecedent witches.

Exhausted by the effort of playing a role so unnatural for her, Margaret flagged down one of many servants who circled the room, confused as ants. The man was tall and slender with a neat goatee and deep acne scars. He slid a narrow-stem wine goblet off his chrome platter for her, accepting her empty glass.

Margaret up-ended the stemware quickly, chugging the sweet drink, then cleared her throat as the servant had turned to walk away. His legs performed an odd shuffle, and he glanced over his shoulder with a coy smile. Margaret returned that smile, gestured him to return and traded her empty glass for a *second* full one. This time she held up a single finger, warning the man and his weird shuffle to wait for her to finish.

Once she did, she returned the stemware and excused herself politely.

Margaret had already decided to *excuse herself politely* from the entire ball by this point. She'd offer her apologies to Ramona. For now, she simply wanted to escape this world of lies and unspoken rules.

The wide, open halls out of the ballroom were inlaid with pieces of brace tile and dark, polished brick. These were post-Collapse modifications, and Margaret's heels clicked on the floor in oddly rhythmic patterns, reminiscent of a hurdy gurdy crank. Approaching her exit, those echoes were a prelude for two Antecedent officers, who'd been speaking in hushed tones. Both men looked away from each other, their gazes heavy, yearning, kneading at her. She didn't look away, her eyes met theirs, her lips turning up in a smile.

"Keep up the good work boys, these people are savages!"

The first man was younger, bulky under his uniform, testing seams near his shoulders and arms. Uninclined, he couldn't stop his background thoughts as they streamed across the walls, through her skin and bones, his emotions becoming words like *respect, fear, and attraction.*

The second man was older, probably Margaret's age.

"Lady Mayhem." He spoke, and Margaret recognized him. He was Commander of the 3rd Army garrison, serving as a military regent in Stockton. His skull was shaved bare, and his neck grooved with deep lines that had seen too much sun and rain. He wore a bushy moustache so large that it hid his lips and gave him a perpetual frown.

"Lieutenant General Townsend," Margaret smiled easily up at him, her voice relaxed, as though she was welcoming him home, "You should have been in the ballroom to rescue me."

"We're all strangers here, Lady." Townsend's eyes pressed against Margaret and she could feel the heat of tangible desire against her skin. *She's hardly aged, she's still goddamn beautiful.*

Tipsy, with the compliment returning color to her face that Lord Owens had consumed, Margaret placed a hand on her hip and shifted her weight to one side, "I don't recall you and I ever spending time alone. Correct me, commander?"

Townsend shook his head once, "You're not wrong, *Lady Mayhem.*"

Margaret had worn long silk gloves that went far above her three-quarter sleeves. It made it easier to interact socially, without an accidental brush of skin spilling unwanted secrets. Margaret stepped over to Townsend, swaying as she did. The wine, and Townsend's attraction, burned away memories of the ballroom.

"What's your name?" Margaret turned to the second, bulkier man. He blinked rapidly but before he could speak, "Right this moment I don't *care*. Go away. Please?"

She was not cruel when she said it, she didn't wave the officer off like a dog. The bulky man understood and gave her a toothy grin, then winked at Townsend before offering a half-hearted salute in departure.

Satisfied, Margaret turned back to Townsend, examining him. He was tall, appearing more so, next to a short woman. His confidence was a bleeding wound that filled the hallway with the intoxicating odor of copper and wormwood.

"I'd like you to *fuck me*, Townsend." Margaret said, laying a gloved hand on his chest.

Townsend feigned horror, poorly, with a gasp. "I think you've mistaken me. Major Grace and I had been discussing the finer points of small squad tactics, and now you've interrupted us."

"Did I?" Margaret lifted her lips, baring teeth like an angry animal, genuinely drunk.

"Oh yes," Townsend nodded, his right hand reaching out for her and Margaret stopped him. Sliding her palm across his, her fingers caressing his digits, the heat at his skin telling a tale of desire even through her silk. He closed his hand, fingers falling between hers, and his hold was tight. Margaret noticed his campaign ribbons. She remembered more than a few of those battles, including Saint Louis.

"*Tell me the truth*. Tell me to leave, commander." She hissed through her teeth.

"Lady," Townsend's pulse was something like a buzz at his throat, Margaret could *hear* it if she closed her eyes and relaxed. Maybe he was secretly resentful, he was one of the few Imperial commanders who'd never bedded Lady Mayhem. "I'll tell you to leave, so long as I leave with you."

"Good answer," Margaret whispered in reply. Her neck was curved back, showing him her throat, lashes aflutter above dilated pupils and rosy cheeks. Townsend's breathing was deep now, and it felt like he was trying to suck marrow out of the air. Margaret was exercising no magic over the man. This was his own nature, a map of free will, unrolled for all to see.

Margaret offered Townsend her elbow. "Take me to your apartment, Lieutenant General. We'll continue this conversation over more wine."

11:02 pm January 9th, 39 Veilfall

Stockton, California

Under the deep blue jacket, Antecedent officers wore a button-up shirt with a mandarin collar. That last button was typically polished steel, though others may have been bone. Most officers had their own initials engraved here, a kind of *memento mori*, a gravestone worn at the neck. When Margaret ran her thumb across Townsend's shiny steel button, it was smooth and unmarked.

Her fingers wrapped over the mandarin collar, pulling him down to her height, gently.

"You plan to live forever, commander?" Margaret didn't look away from the button, it transfixed her; she could genuinely remember no other officer who wore that button clean.

"It'll be harder for death to find me if he doesn't know my name." Townsend replied softly, and Margaret slid her fingers away from the collar and up his throat to where his jaw hinged. She could feel the prickle of his evening shadow through her gloves, along with the steady, quick, pulse of a man so close to the object of his desires.

"Death comes for us all," Margaret's opposing hand lifted to the buttons of the jacket. These were larger, and concealed under fabric as not to break lines of the uniform, "You suppose you'll escape notice if you hide?"

Townsend didn't answer. The room was *quiet*, and his surface thoughts skittered in the cracks and crevices like a mouse, plain to her keen hearing. *Yes*, he had hoped death would overlook him, he even *feared death*.

"Kneel," Townsend hesitated at the order, his eyes a drama of excitement and apprehension, then he obeyed. Eye to eye now, Margaret slid her thumbs up the sleeves of her marbled velvet gown, loosening the silk gloves at her biceps to pull them off. "You know I'll be in your mind, don't you?"

Townsend did not break eye contact, he only nodded, "I know of witches."

"Do you?" Margaret laughed. It was an honest laugh, at the back of her throat, a sound she made in private when amused, a laugh she rarely shared with others. She meant no cruelty in it, she simply thought it was *funny* that an uninclined would claim any wisdom of her kind, "Do you know what it's like to share a heart with strangers? To *weep* at a loss, you never knew? I'll be able to taste every breath you once took."

Though he was kneeling for her, there was no subservience lingering at the corners of his retina, there was a steel and esprit that Margaret was surprised to see in a man who *feared death*. "I saw you at Saint Louis. Not in battle, but with the sick. You eased the minds of dying men. I know what a witch can give a man."

Margaret didn't *like* that. She doesn't *talk* about that. The smell of those hospitals alone, feces and putrid wounds, flesh turning necrotic, humidity and mud that would never dry, and rain that would never cease. She seized Townsend, fingers running across his face and behind his bald skull, tracing lines and patterns into his flesh with her nails. The kiss was invasive, even violent. She didn't want Saint Louis in the room and she physically used her tongue to press those words back into Townsend's throat.

She didn't *listen* to his mind when she kissed him. It was only the warmth of skin she felt on her palms. When she pulled away, she pressed a small hand against his chest, residual anger expanding out and into his blood, almost a slap in the face.

"Undress me Commander. Take care, this dress is worth a soldier's annual salary."

She wasn't lying. The dress was handmade and fitted just for her. The materials that went into its creation were rare, difficult to come by and time consuming to produce. Even the colors, the darker and more vibrant reds, were made from dyes that required *weeks* of experimentation to capture accurately.

Before the dress could come off, Townsend had to unlace her steel boned corset, worn on the outside. He *did* take care, and his big fingers had no trouble with the metal clasps at the back of Margaret's shoulders. He *also* had the initiative to draw up her hair and rest his lips on the back of her neck, kissing and delicately chewing at her flesh. *Most* officers she bedded feared to do such, refusing to act without her direct instruction.

"Harder," Margaret whispered, a stuttered sigh escaping her lips as Townsend's teeth raked flesh, *fucking draw some blood*, she thought before repeating herself; "*Harder.*"

Townsend did as he was bid, the next bite eliciting a shriek, coupled with a high pitch giggle. The noise paused him, and Margaret felt her temper rise again. "*I didn't say stop,*" she whispered, more for herself than Townsend, then raised her arms, allowing the sleeves on her dress to fall to her shoulders loosely. Townsend followed her lead, drawing the dress upwards and off her body.

Margaret had taken to wearing a wrap of linen around her cleavage as a young woman. It was comfortable and made more sense in combat. It also allowed her to conceal a weapon between her breasts. She withdrew a subcompact .380 and set it aside, turning to face Townsend, mostly naked.

"What do you see, commander?" She spoke to the man the way she would a subordinate in the field. Margaret pointed to her twisted shoulder, and the silken scars down her chest and stomach. The wound at her gut was the ugliest of all, lumpy and pink, as though someone had spilled cottage cheese on her and allowed it to dry, "Do I look like a woman who has a problem with *pain*? If I tell you '*harder,*' don't stop."

When Margaret kissed Townsend again, she pressed her chest into his as hard as her muscles would allow, her breasts compressing into her torso. The sheer sturdiness of another human being so close was an intoxication. Being a witch meant keeping your distance, keeping bare fingers to yourself, restraint from affection, from the simple act of touch. Allowing the lines of her fingers to caress Townsend's skin was nearly as titillating as his nails down her spine or his teeth clamped onto her shoulders.

Slowly, as her barriers lifted, more of Townsend's mind opened up to her. Every minute was a plunge deeper and further into his memories, his dreams and desires. There were nightmares there too, dark recesses guarded by creatures like snakes with glowing eyes of gold and silver. She wasn't a *thing* in his heart now, she was an *idea*, a liquid parcel, invading his blood and marrow, running deep and wrapping around those angry warnings his subconsciousness had created.

Nightmares held their own physical weight, and Townsend moaned in release as each stone fell off his awareness. Margaret was at play in her favorite game now, her nails digging into his chest and fingers pausing to clutch and manipulate his nipples as her mind untethered his fear and ache, giving him permission to offer himself as a divine gift, bone and muscle, dream and sorrow, wrapped in tobacco and soap lard.

"It's a gift," Margaret writhed up and across Townsend, one hand tugging at the knot of linen binding her breasts, the other curling around his shorn skull so she could whisper into his ear. Her lips brushed the lobe and she could feel the warmth of her breath reflected, "You can't be *all mine* when you're tied to pain. *Understand?*"

Townsend understood. He said as much. Perhaps out loud, perhaps in his mind, there was no way for Margaret to know. They were too close, pieces and parts that stitched up their minds had mixed together just as the sweat on their skin. For Margaret, this was a symphony she directed, one instrument at a time. Her hands teased, lips suckling at fingertips or gnawing on the soft flesh inside of his forearms. Her mind; however, pulled Townsend away from the waking world like a small toy stolen by tide. She wanted him to show her all his secrets, this play made from shadow puppets aroused Margaret.

The other boys in the army always made fun of him. Townsend was just sixteen when he first kissed a girl. Old for a Collapse boy, most would have lost their virginity earlier - whether the girl said yes or not.

"I like the way you kiss," Margaret answered the memory, her lips pinching at his, pressing back his thick moustache, as she ran her tongue over and under his, matching the curious explorations of her hand as she reached down past his thighs, between his legs.

The girl was named Katherine. She had freckles across her nose. Those freckles were beautiful and when Townsend kissed her, he didn't close his eyes. He knew he was supposed to, the other boys told him he needed to, but he watched her freckles instead.

Margaret blushed, and realized Townsend still didn't kiss with his eyes closed, he was watching *her* freckles now, they'd swept up at his desires. Margaret answered by sliding her hand to his throat, pressing her fingers around his windpipe to remind him that his memories, his desires, were a manifestation with her.

"Tell me about *Katherine*," Margaret whispered again, her lips brushing on his as she withdrew from the kiss, a narrow strand of saliva falling down her chin.

Katherine was an Ohio girl, her parents worked along trade routes. At sixteen, Townsend held post in the border towns and only saw her every few months. They'd make time, clumsy fingers reaching under clothes, hands exploring nervously, but breaking apart at the last second.

Margaret was pressing Townsend backward, *further and further*, until he was prone on the floor, looking away, breathing heavily. She smiled, pulling herself up, leaning over his bare chest, adorned with his own scars.

She pulled her mind from his, resting only at the ledge of his consciousness, just as she slid her own pudenda close to where a hand still clutched between his legs, viscous humectation dripping down her fingers.

"Why did you always stop?" the words escaped on her long exhale, her body and hands still. Townsend was caught in a moment of tense anticipation. He spoke, and maybe the words were in the air, or maybe the words existed beyond hearing, but he begged Margaret to return. She shook her head, licking her own lips and halting the giggle that tickled at her throat; only for a moment, "Why did you always stop?" She repeated. She could *take* the memory, but it would turn bitter and spoil the presentiment.

It seemed to Townsend that Katherine was perfect, a woman who shouldn't even exist by the covenant of desire. It felt to him as if the moment they crossed over from playful fumbling and slobbery experimentation that the covenant would be broken, and she'd never seem so beautiful to him. Her breasts would never curve the same, and her laugh would turn dull, listless.

"A day came that you *couldn't* stop." Margaret made the bet, promised it to the air around them. Looking away from Townsend, out the foggy glass of his room, she reached down between them to the juncture of their writhing bodies, warm and sticky. She didn't want to rush this, it was her favorite part, *throwing the dice*. Her heart was beating like a hummingbird's wings, darting and weaving, suckling for something sweet.

The day did come that Townsend didn't flee, didn't let go. He thought he loved Katherine in that moment, believing the two would marry and grow old. How could they not? Their bodies pressed together like lost puzzle pieces, each responded to the other in perfect symmetry.

The dice fell, and Margaret won her bet. She shrieked like a feral cat when she forced herself down onto Townsend and came almost immediately. This was the moment, the crescendo she most desired, just as the first clamor of thunder at battle. Just as first blood was spilt. There was no difference in her mind; she was the conductor of carnal desire, both rich and bitter.

"That's sweet," Margaret grinned, laughing, *cackling* as her body responded to the release of tantalization, "But, *I'm* not so sweet."

Margaret *wasn't*. Her hips swayed into Townsend, a hungry, starved animal grinding flesh off bone. She was violent, pouring through his dreams and memories, allowing it to fall across her body, back arched, mouth agape, thirsty for every single ounce of *anger, satisfaction, triumph, loathing*.

Townsend stood at the plains of Omaha, front-left, center-lines, main company ordered to hold pending release order. The antique M1 rifle is braced against his shoulder, he was looking down iron sites at a range of perhaps one-thousand yards. Only a fool would take the shot, only a fool would defy orders. Townsend was that fool. He took the shot and the rifle reported across the open air of tan wheat and dry soil. The Omaha scout took a thirty-ought-six in the chest and exploded like a ripe watermelon. Townsend was the king of this battle. Townsend would live forever.

Margaret's fingers joined at his solar plexus, thumbs crossed. Her hands slid down to where their bodies met, leaning into him, suffusing her own mucilaginous discharge. She couldn't *tell* him with her voice how it felt to know his victory while she drove him further inside her. Her chest felt like it would rip open and her bones would conduct electricity. She wanted to *scream* with laughter and maybe she did.

Or maybe she attempted to asphyxiate him with her tongue.

Whatever remained of his gentle probing had vanished in a cyclone of desire. Margaret and Townsend ceased to be unique people. Though uninclined, Townsend responded to Margaret's embers of emotion and memory, and the two operated succinctly. She wanted him to clutch and tug at her flesh, down the sides of her breasts, wrenching at her as if she was an unseen foe whose castigation was required for survival. *He did,* no words or thoughts exchanged, and it *hurt,* thumb size welts raise along her pale, moist skin.

Lost in lurid, physical ecstasy, memories played out in every fiber of her being. Margaret orchestrated the symphony to its climax. It was such a gray idea that she dreaded the introduction, the climb in tempo, the play of tone and notes across her body. No matter how *good* the meridian was, this was the end, and Margaret hated endings above all else. Her favorite moments were now long past, the gamble, the victory and the raging, ungovernable ferocity of feeling *another inside her for the first time.*

She didn't release him, only ceased the assault of her hips and leaned in. Townsend's breathing was ragged, and his eyes closed. Part of his mind was pulled backwards into sleep, his soul as spent as his body. A piece of him remained, watching and listening, wondering at the small woman that clutches his body to her own.

One last secret, one more box to open. Margaret couldn't resist.

It was not simply that Lady Mayhem's freckles reminded Townsend of Katherine, long in the grave. It was the way she smiled, sweet and vicious, merciless and obliging. This night would be his to treasure.

Margaret, caught in a similar web of exhaustion, put this secret back in the box. She didn't want to hurt him. He'd given her far too much and she'd never been an ungrateful lover. It wasn't the first time a man harbored feelings for her. In his secret dreams and hopes, he imagined Margaret at his side, at the cusp of some great battle, immortal in their dominance over some old, great foe.

She allowed herself to fall asleep on his chest, covered in sweat, dreaming of Omaha and Katherine's freckles. Margaret would never allow herself to visit a partner a *second* time, and at this moment she regretted that.

3:03am January 10th, 39 Veilfall

Stockton, California

Margaret sauntered across Stockton's cobblestone streets. More durable to the elements, they'd long ago replaced crumbling asphalt. Her bare feet trod softly, pebbles and dirt biting between her toes.

Her entire body was bound up in the glow of satisfaction, spent and gazing nostalgically over the memories of Townsend. Consuming so much of another person was intoxicating, better than strong liquor most nights, if she was honest with herself.

"Got a light?"

Margaret had believed herself alone on the street, but a woman a few yards away swung herself outward with one hand clutching a cast iron lamp post. It hissed as it burned, illuminating the street in bounding yellow light and mirror. Margaret's hand clutched the subcompact pistol that had been wrapped up in her cleavage, concealed under the corset that draped over her left arm. Her finger moved to the trigger, and ice water dribbled down her spine.

The woman wore too much makeup, her lips were painted a red that would make flame feel inadequate, and a great deal of time had been spent making her hair appear naturally mussed. Her clothes were expensive, leather bustier and boots, suede skirt, and a fox fur coat. A *whore*, an expensive one at that, not a common street walker or pussy peddler. Her eyes; however, were not *eyes. Her eyes were the ocean*, windows to a clear, blue sea, waves rippling, hinting at unfathomable depths. Margaret could have sworn she heard the cries of seagulls and water lapping at rocks out of sight, lulling her into an uneasy calm.

Margaret blinked, hard, once and twice, a ritual she'd learned as a child. Each blink built barriers, boundaries more intense than the walls which silenced crowded streets. These defenses were active, moving, a latticework of energy that unwrapped like a bow in her mind, spinning up and around her: projected curtains. It didn't matter *how* this *entity* had surprised her, it mattered now that she be prepared for anything.

The woman smiled, and Margaret's chest caught mid-breath. The whore shook her head, "Tell me you've met *gods* before. Tell me I'm not yanking virginity out of your throat."

She smelled like salt breeze and moist genitalia. Pungent with lust, *desire*. At the edge of that sensation was a sharp set of knives that poked and prodded playfully with the ribbons of defense Margaret found herself behind.

"*I have,*" Margaret whispered, barely a sigh.

"Mar-gar-*et*. Mar-gar-*et*," the whore sang quietly, releasing the iron of the gas lamp, head tilted down and a smile creeping across her face. With one hand held out, wrist up and fingers embracing a single, white cigarette. "Got a light?"

Margaret began to stutter. It wasn't a sense of *fear*, it was a physical reaction to being near so much manifest power. Her clavicle and larynx vibrated as the other woman moved and shifted in the air that Margaret shared with her. When she did answer, her voice was clear and the words measured, "I don't smoke."

"Is that *so*?" the whore giggled, "I bet you *want* one now. *Don't you?*"

She was right. Margaret had been craving a twig since she'd woke on top of Townsend, crusted in ejaculate. Townsend *was* a smoker, his moustache smelled of tobacco, and his cravings had been imprinted on parts of her mind, an itch beyond scratching. "I suppose," Margaret nodded, "but I still don't have a light."

The whore withdrew the offered twig and held it up to her lips. When she inhaled, the paper and tobacco burst into flame. Margaret was every bit as *aroused* as she had been picking apart Townsend's mind. "Tough luck, Mar-gar-*et*. Perhaps you need to return to your boy's apartment, wake him again, *say goodbye,* and *steal a stogie*."

Margaret swallowed, "I don't know your name."

The whore cackled, lavishly opening her arms in a wide, sweeping motion. Reality seemed to curve up around her and the cobblestones moved like an undulating ocean. At least in Margaret's *mind*. "You should know me *very well*."

"*Bastet*?" Margaret asked, on a deep inhale.

The whore's eyes turned from a calm sea to the churning of a hurricane gale. Her rage was as solid as a fist, not just as an element or an emotion, but a *violent* anger inside Margaret's bones. The ribbons of defense evaporated like mist on a warm morning and Margaret found herself naked in the face of a storm's fury. She was a child again, the same child who grew up with Maggi Lopez as she bellowed her anger at Margaret for daring to be alive when her partner had died. *"Do I look like a fucking cat to you?"*

The whore snarled, her voice raising gooseflesh across Margaret's body and causing the gas lamp to flicker and flash.

"Okay, *no!" What's wrong with you?* "Aphrodite?" Margaret pulled herself together, pressing away mirrors of her mother and standing fast in the face of her error.

"Did you ever hear the joke about hand grenades?" The angry ocean didn't abate in the whore's eyes. She placed her hands on her hips and tipped a chin up, working her jaw as if she wanted to bite off a piece of Margaret and eat it.

"Close only counts with horseshoes and hand grenades?" Margaret smiled, tipping her chin up in reply, refusing to be intimidated.

"Are you calling me a *horseshoe*, or a *hand grenade*?" The wail of a god could easily have turned an uninclined gray, and even Margaret fought a wave of nausea clawing up from her stomach and pulling her low. This wasn't a *hint*, this was a *demand*.

Margaret had made a point in her life to *never* kneel, at least to the flesh and bone mortals of the world. It was a willing display of submission she could never tolerate. However, she'd insulted a god, and humility was her only path to salvation. *This was Aphrodite*, and if any part of Margaret still knew *how* to fear it would have turned her inside out now.

Dropping to her knees, the elegantly stitched corset fell to stone, along with the click and clatter of her .380. "I beg your pardon." Margaret said.

"I would have *praised* you, offered you a gift for your *fine tribute*, but now I merely find myself disgusted to look at you." Aphrodite answered. *What was she talking about? I didn't worship her, I didn't give her offerings or hold her above other gods.* To be true, Margaret had never *prayed* to any of the old gods.

"I'm sorry." Margaret forced the words out, spittle falling to the cobblestone. Her lips were numb, her face burned hot in rebellion. It was decades since she'd spoken those two words.

Aphrodite's flesh suit sighed, and she answered, "If I wanted to hurt you, I'd rot your *cunt* out with the hatred of a thousand cursed souls. Stand." Margaret did exactly as she'd been told, and when she looked upon the whore's flesh again, Aphrodite's eyes had changed to a cooler, green sea, still churning. "You're not scared."

Margaret wiped the drool from her lips with the back of one hand. She could still smell Townsend on her fingers, "I forgot how to be scared."

"I see that," Aphrodite nodded. "I would have *asked* before, but now you owe me for the insult. You'll need to repay that with a favor." She inhaled the cigarette, hard, but while it smoldered it didn't burn down. Her hands moved and flourished with such grace that it was hard to believe smoking could ever be so *erotic.*

"Never accept wooden nickels, and *never* owe a god," Margaret closed her eyes, waiting for the rage to return.

"You should have considered that earlier," Aphrodite paused, and Margaret opened her eyes again, now as spent as she'd been with her legs wrapped around Townsend. "I will make you a *promise.* The favor I ask will *not* harm you or anyone who you *love.*"

Maggi would be disgusted with me, "Deal," Margaret nodded.

"You should *want* to help me, little Margaret. *I've helped you.*" Aphrodite replied with a whisper that curled Margaret's toes. *I don't dare ask her what she means,* Margaret thought, and Aphrodite followed with a hiss, "Oh, you don't dare ask? The years crawl on, yet you look as elegant and beautiful as the day that *Maggi Lopez died.*"

She wasn't lying. Though Margaret was easily in her mid-to-late forties, she'd never looked it. Gray in her auburn hair was uncommon, lines didn't cut at her eyes, and her breasts had never really sunk as low as gravity would have demanded. She'd considered herself lucky, but a witch ought to know better. "*Why*?"

Aphrodite kept her voice low, watching under brows. She inhaled her limitless cigarette again, chewing on the smoke and exhaled, "How many have you enamored with your graces? How many beguiled and bewildered? You didn't just spend a lifetime satisfying your own lust, you spent a lifetime introducing others to *love*. You think, perhaps, that might escape my attention?" Aphrodite didn't remain at a distance; skin twisted, and bones stirred. When she moved, it was a serpentine act, smooth and calculated.

"I only did what *I* wanted, it wasn't for *you*," Margaret answered, with as level a head as she could muster. The slinking steps by Aphrodite weren't, upon themselves, seductive, but the warbling flow of *power* deep inside her *was*.

Aphrodite was standing next to Margaret now, right hand curling around Margaret's face, her fingertips tracing the most delicate of lines down her cheek, toward chin and throat. She couldn't *quite* control the flesh precisely, and there was a hint of tremor at wrist that matched the pulse Margaret felt in her larynx.

"It's not hard, is it?" Aphrodite whispered, "You're so proud, but I can hear the part of your mind that *wants* to love me, kiss me, *sing to me*."

Once more, she wasn't lying. Margaret closed her eyes, wondering if this was what Townsend had felt under her hands, her energy. Though never a *god*, a witch maintained her own majesty.

"What do you know about Maggi?" Margaret attempted to change the subject.

"*Oh*, plenty," Aphrodite shifted, almost completely behind Margaret now, her fingers weaving lines across her neck and into her hair. By her nature Margaret didn't like *that* kind of subtle or delicate touch, but Aphrodite's fingers left burning trails that prickled skin and elicited a dozen more sensations, each greatly more complex than a simple *touch*. "I know she died with an unpaid debt. I know her grandchildren will *facilitate* a return to the *good old days*. The days when gods could walk as they pleased, free of these stinking meat sacks, free to bend reality and grant favors. Haven't you read the old stories?" Aphrodite's giggle was a viral infection that swam in the air, clutching the gas light and weaving into a tapestry of mischievous loathing, a joke with no punchline.

"Those children are *my* students," Margaret answered, "I won't let them be harmed."

"Do you *love* those two girls?" Somewhere inside Margaret's mind, Aphrodite could sense desires to be plucked out, one by one, and what *felt* like claws raked across Margaret's chest, breaking flesh, demanding the smallest of blood sacrifice. Her body had its own demands and her head shifted back as a low moan escaped her lips. "Would you like to be further reminded of how you are at my mercy and kindness, my *affection*?"

Margaret cringed, a cautious numb and simmering feeling writhing in her belly.

"At *your* pleasure, *Aphrodite*."

Aphrodite's right hand clutched the back of Margaret's skull, left hand slithering up her throat until it reached lips, placing her cigarette near Margaret's mouth so she could inhale if she chose. She did choose.

"At *her* death, your mother possessed a trinket that was not hers to keep. *The eye that does not see.* In her infinite incompetence, she promised that eye to another, for a paltry sum of power. You need to retrieve that bobble, *the eye*."

Margaret exhaled the limitless cigarette. It tasted like finest tobacco, mixed with the sting and caress of clove oil. Her lips and tongue turned numb. "Maggi's grave is a dead volcano."

"Oh, you *think so*, do you?" Aphrodite smirked, licking her lips as though they were made of frosting, "You think all the silly things your silly meat-friends speak is true? Find *the eye that does not see*. You need to be in possession of it." Aphrodite withdrew her hands, shifting her body and taking a step to face Margaret. Every word that Aphrodite loosed was both torturously seductive and infuriatingly taunting.

"Why would you come to *me* on *this* night? Ask *me* to retrieve an *eye* that my *mother* possessed, in order to repay *my* slight?"

Without releasing the twig, her fingers slid up Margaret's arms and chest. "Mar-gar-*et*. Mar-gar-*et*. I'm a god, and gods don't *help* mortals. We merely manipulate them to a path that best suits our desires. We are selfish, and we'll never love you as much as we love *each other*. We only offer kindness when the sweet scent of your soul is required to make the magic *work*, and we only offer suffering when your terror makes the lock turn."

Aphrodite clutched Margaret's face in both hands, her expression turning from sultry to sweet, her lips offering a smile that hinted naught for cruelty. It *sounded* as if waves crashed at rocks, *certainly just a few streets over*.

Margaret kissed Aphrodite.

As a rule, Margaret preferred the company of men if she was to kiss or be kissed. This; however, transcended the cool, moist compact between lips. It was wholly possible that Margaret had never really known what a *kiss* was prior to this moment. Her life felt like a stumbling and sad reflection of blind desire in comparison. It was a glimpse at ancient poems and forgotten songs, a melody she couldn't *quite* hear past the waves that didn't *quite* exist.

Margaret forgot her own name.

"*See?*" Aphrodite whispered as she pulled away, the warmth of breath covering her lips in mania, "That wasn't so hard, was it?"

She wasn't fully aware that Aphrodite had left until her body's perfume faded and vanished, and her eyes could refocus on the physical world. Breathing hard, Margaret looked behind her, then ahead. She was alone. Only now did it occur to her how *strange* that was, that the capital of all Northern California would be so quiet in the youngest morning hours.

She *wanted* to taste Aphrodite's lips again, and she wanted to understand depthless desire. She wanted to return to Townsend, to whisper, "*Wake up*," and run her fingertips across his face.

That was against the rules of course.

Margaret knelt and retrieved her corset and pistol, draping one over the other, and returned to the path she walked.

8:30pm January 11th, 39 Veilfall

Stockton, California

Margaret stood in the shadows, a dwindling cigarette engulfing her with pungent smoke. Lamp light crackled and snapped, illuminating cobble and concrete with a twisting orange glow. San Joaquin Street Station was empty, solitary, except for an occasional ghost, reflected memories caught in the light of her eyes.

Margaret gagged on her cigarette.

She'd *never* enjoyed smoking, but touch was dangerously familiar for a witch, and the act of physical sex was critically intimate. Surface dreams, desires, and addictions leached into the skin like a charcoal stain.

Margaret heard a train whistle, echoing in the distance.

She licked her lips, residue tart on her tongue, and cast aside the butt with loathing and affection. She heard her heartbeat and studied her hands in dim light to distract her imagination. Margaret's fingers were small, short, perhaps even stumpy. The lines that didn't cross her face had accumulated at the edges of her thumbs and wrists. They were ugly hands, she thought to herself, milky white scars raised over freckled flesh, records of a life dedicated to *violence*.

When the westbound train arrived, she was big, black, a steam locomotive. Old rail lines of wood and iron had been restored by House Owens, long before she and her brother came to this place. One company had begun building new steam engines, back home in Pennsylvania, but this one was an antique. Two-hundred years old, her rust scraped off, her iron blackened with grease. She belched steam from her wheels, and a flaming heart washed the night in soot and heat. No machine that old wouldn't find itself an imbued creature after centuries. Not intelligent, not like a person, rather it had more in common with a great old wolf, chest puffed up and paws heavy, acrid drool dripping from maw, feral eyes glancing at Margaret with suspicion, asking her why she slouched in the shadows.

She could hear whispers from a shade near the corner of her eye. A man painted sepia strutted along, smart hat, and briefcase at his hand. He *had to* catch the train, otherwise he'd be late. *Gotta catch the train, can't be late.*

Alone, in places like this, Margaret always wondered what kind of ghost she might become. Would she traipse along walkways in the dim, remembering all the places she had to be? Or would she flutter free and visit locations that life had denied her?

Slowly the iron wolf came to a stop, brakes screeching, cars creaking and groaning as a thousand nails tried to detract from their wooden prisons. Only a handful of passengers disembarked. They were mostly Imperials coming from the east, perhaps here to do business, or make new contracts with various Stockton farmers. They were dressed in the mottled grays of east coast fashion, one lady's long dress embroidered with Antecedent spirals, black leather stitched onto stone cotton.

The last to depart the train was a young woman, only a teenager, *alone*. Her head was held high. Margaret waited for other passengers to walk past, then tip-toeing in their minds, reminded them that they shouldn't glance into the shadows, perhaps *the shadows might glance back*. No one gave her away, not one eye quivered or darted. Her barriers were stout, clean, and wrapped tight against her skin with all the subtlety of carbonation on a warm, summer day.

The girl's skin was glowing with youth and vigor. Her sable hair was pulled back in a ponytail, and she was wearing a black knee length pencil skirt with a deep gray jacket cut to flatter her wasp waist and accentuate her bosom. She *walked* like nobility and worked her hips with a sauntering grace. When Margaret turned to chase the girl, her own feet were bare and black with street grime, shadows pulled and tugged like taffy around her, cool on her neck, forgiving. She didn't raise her hands, snap fingers, or flail her arms. None of her mother's theatrical tricks. Instead, she quieted the world around her, and faded into the forgotten moments.

Margaret already had her hand on the 9mm pistol lodged in her cleavage. Bigger than the subcompact, there was no concealing it. The weapon was drawn and out, pointed at the back of the young girl's ponytail.

The night around Margret twisted open, a flower greeting morning sun. Ink drew up from the station concrete, a black secretion wholly void of *any* energy or power. There was no warning. Margaret had not the slightest flutter of ill in her sternum. One moment she was alone, quiet as death, scampering on naked toes; the next she was captive between four obsidian silhouettes, blurring, sharpening, and taking manifest shape.

The girl and her ponytail spun on a heel. Lithe and acrobatic, her barriers snapped awake around her, flutters of green and yellow reflect off flesh and tarmac.

She was holding her own pistol, leveled directly at Margaret.

"*Pinche perra,*" the girl swore, shrill, nasal. Her sidearm tilted to the ground.

Lower your weapon. The liquid shades around Margaret were *ghosts*, but they felt more like hollow shells. Their impact on the physical world felt lonely, as if she'd entered an empty home to find family photos left on the walls, but no furniture or belongings. They didn't smell like the man who had to catch the train. Eyes watched with pulsing nerves, *nerves long dead.*

"You've gotten quick." Margaret smiled, replacing her weapon in tightly wrapped linen that kept her bosom *up* and *out of the way*. She tried to ignore the shades. They looked like old-world soldiers when they flickered or sharpened, their gear part and parcel of a lost era.

"*Yes*, I remember," The girl was replacing her weapon at the small of her back, up and under her dark jacket. "*One good bullet, that's all it takes.*"

"No witch can take a gunshot to the skull." Margaret quoted her mother, "Come here."

Ramona Lopez jumped forward and wrapped her slender arms around Margaret, then pulled her off the ground, past tip-toes. Margaret remembered when *she* would lift Ramona, a child of no more than four or five years old. She smelled like the Atlantic Ocean, sweet wine, and crisp peppers. Her eyes were big and dark, with thick lashes and brows. Her lips were a little too full, and the shade of her skin was much like a summer beach, the same as her mother. Unlike the last time Margaret saw her; however, there was a magnetic draw, a deeply planted foundation somewhere in her spine that latched around Margaret. It felt *familiar*.

"Bodyguards?" Margaret turned away from her niece to study one of them. This was a puzzle that defied all of Margaret's education, they were *souls* wrapped up in a non-corporal specter. They weren't mirrors, or mimics of lost memories, there was no anchor about them, they simply felt *empty*, devoid of history.

"Father calls them *poltergeists*," Ramona gestured to the one closest to Margaret, "They've been *enhanced* beyond the bounds of any conventional ghost, their bones are engraved and painted in the Chaldean sigils."

Margaret couldn't *see* the soldier's eyes, but *he* was *watching her*, something like pupils drilling into her mind. "Free will?"

Ramona laughed. It was not her childhood laugh, it's more mature, self-centered and cynical, "Of course *not!* Why would dead men protect the living? All of us, father, Amihan, and myself, have them."

Ghosts couldn't *impact* the physical world, they couldn't do more than lay a cold hand on the living or cast objects about. *How dangerous could these poltergeists be?* Margaret wondered to herself, then forced a smile, "I've been away a while, I suppose."

Ramona smirked, "You tucked me in bed and left for Saint Louis, if I remember."

Margaret had trained Ramona and her sister, until her brother's first push pass the Mississippi river. As a young girl Ramona's energy poured across her skin like a warm rain. There was something *different now*, something colder and *tighter* at the edges. Her mind, closed as it was, clicked in a rhythm that the girl previously never exuded.

"Let me grab my coat," Margaret withdrew. As she did, the four guards evaporated in a thick, black mist. It was ice cold on the skin, dry rain falling back to the ground. The soldiers had followed a procedural guide, an operating schedule, but there was also a memory of sorrow that crossed Margaret's mind.

"You're still barefoot," Ramona shook her head, almost laughing, sputtering a sound like a hiccup as she waved off Margaret.

"Stockton's streets aren't as dirty as Crafton's," Margaret answered, returning to her niece's side, pulling the coat over her shoulders. The exterior was bright yellow tweed with black fasteners and cuffs.

"It's snowing back home. In Crafton." When Ramona spoke, it was not *just* her voice that echoed across the lonely train station, it was a distant sound like a spring yawn following a bleak winter, a trait she'd carried since she was a baby. "How can you wear a coat out here? It's *hot!*"

Margaret didn't answer.

Instead, she removed a magazine from a back pocket of her pants and loaded it into the 9mm withdrawn once more from her cleavage. She racked the slide once, chambering a round, and replaced the weapon between her breasts. "Stay with me. I have a guest bed, and I *have* missed you."

Ramona stopped, mouth half-open and looked at Margaret for a second, beads of sweat at her forehead. "I have a room reserved at the Grand California, near Old Downtown. I suppose I can stay there tomorrow night. We should catch up on the years."

Stockton was a city unlike most. Great walls rose up around her, a concrete tidal wave, every inch painted in murals and works of nationalist art. After sundown a hundred types of illumination brought the city to life. Gas lamps, electric sodium, torches and moonlight, mixed to make the paintings dance, giving the city a strange illusion of fluttering movement. "This was once the capital of House Owens," Margaret gestured. "I can show you around."

Tiny varmints, *something* like goblins, or half-dog creatures, rustled through the garbage, raced with rats in the gutters, all intent on stripping the world bare of forgotten refuse, cast offs, sewage, and horse shit. Buildings rose from wooden sidewalks, leaning at suspicious angles like drunk men holding themselves aloft. Many stores were closed, though street vendors peddled boiled cabbage or slightly *off* sausage sticks, red and yellow from a deep array of fried spices.

"Stockton is much more *civilized* than I had anticipated," Ramona nodded at the streets, "I'd heard House Owens was a proud place."

"It still is," Margaret chuckled, "the former heir actually turned *me* down."

"*You*?" Ramona replied, her shock genuine.

"*Me*," Margaret shrugged and stretched her back, "I'm getting old, I suppose."

No wall, no entryway, no fence or facade lacked an expansive mural, and in the flickering shadows, even the most cheerful painting evolved into a grim sideshow, just like Ramona's face now. "Old enough to consider retirement, I'm told."

Margaret paused, head tilted back, watching the sky above. Stockton wasn't bright enough to drown out the stars, which gazed back, waiting for her to speak.

"I *am* retiring."

Ramona didn't answer, but her eyes carved into the smaller woman like a hungry child might cut up his roast beef. Margaret returned her gaze to the Earthly world and shook her head, "We set out to conquer a continent, and didn't we do that? My brother and the 1st Army are in the southwest now, unifying what's left. I want to *see* this land we captured. I want to walk on the dirt and mud with my *bare feet*, and I want to get *drunk on silence*."

Margaret had already sent word to her brother the autumn before. By 40 Veilfall, she planned to step down as lead battlewitch of the Empire. There were a *thousand* reasons that she was done being the creature Maggi Lopez groomed her to be, and she supposed that Ramona would understand none of them.

"You always had Aphrodite's favor." Ramona didn't stutter or pause, she blurted the words out like a foreign phrase that she'd been told to repeat as part of a practical joke.

"*Aphrodite*? What do you know about Aphrodite?"

Ramona turned, a few feet away, showing Margaret her back. "*Nothing*, I suppose."

The words were cool and hollow, *intentionally* stripped of all emotion. Ramona may as well have been a child again, hiding her face, caught in a fib.

"I didn't become an *old* witch eating lies up like sugar," Margaret's voice lowered, and she wanted to scold her former student for playing such a juvenile game, "If you'd like to *tell* me something, turn around and say it like a *Lopez* would."

"*Fine,*" Ramona threw her hands up, "I chose to worship Aphrodite last year. It was *hard* after mother died, you *and* father on this *endless* campaign. I've been my own woman for a while, and it was *my* choice to make."

"You took a *god* just because you were lonely?" Margaret shouted, more in exasperation than rage. "A fool favors one god over others. The queen of *damn fool witches worships* that god!"

Avoiding contractual ties with the ancients was in the first page of *The World According to Maggi Lopez*, core principles that she'd hammered into Margaret's head since she was old enough to listen.

"*Mayy,*" Ramona answered in her best attempt at a *woman's voice*, "Father expects me to rule *with* my sister one day, but I don't have the freedom to offer *myself* to a god?" In all this, Margaret struggled to take her seriously. How many times had she shrieked like this, refusing to eat her porridge, as a child?

"What did you promise her?" Margaret asked slowly, once Ramona had a moment to vent her impotent anger.

Ramona didn't answer. Instead she pursed her lips, crossed her arms, and a new wall of barriers erected themselves around her person.

"Perhaps I *should* stay at my hotel, after all."

No part of Margaret treated Ramona like the heir to an empire. She was simply her niece and a child still, in so many ways. A child she hadn't seen in *years*. "No, I've missed you. I've missed having someone about. My time in Stockton has been lonely."

"Lady Mayhem? *Lonely*? Do you still take an officer to bed *every night,* or is it now *every other night?*" Ramona laughed at the older woman, and Margaret was amazed at how deep the chuckle cut. It didn't hurt *right away*, there was a pause, just like a knife opening taunt skin, air biting at the exposed nerves. "Maybe you should reconsider your views on patronage. It's a big, *bold,* new world that we live in."

Margaret had no desire to quarrel with her niece, she had no desire to be *Maggi Lopez*, to push everyone away with an undisputed set of black and white laws, a code that no one else had a copy of. It was easier to capitulate now and return to the subject later.

"Maybe after so many years, I can't tell the difference between what's best for *someone I love*, and what's best for *myself*."

Margaret offered the peace too late. Ramona was stubborn, too stubborn to let go and too stubborn to take notice of how deeply she'd hurt her aunt. The ignorance of youth blossomed inside her, "I *only* told you about Aphrodite because you *smell* like her." Ramona spun to talk as she walked backwards, "*You* met with Aphrodite, didn't you?"

"*Yes*." Margaret only replied with a whisper.

"What did she want?" Ramona latched on. "What did Aphrodite want from the *soldier-slut* of the Antecedent Empire?"

That was something her brother had called her, back when there was only *one* Antecedent army. It *did* get under her skin, but Alexander had always prodded roughly, just like his mother.

Now, Ramona sounded just like him, and it was a *step past* what Margaret could take.

"I'll see you in the morning, Ramona."

Margaret turned to walk away. She all but erected combat barriers around herself, layers and lattices of formless energy, hollow and empty, denying another witch any data. In this case, denying Ramona the satisfaction of knowing she'd made her aunt cry.

11:02 pm January 11th, 39 Veilfall

Stockton, California

The door to Townsend's apartment was old. It was old before the Collapse, painted in untold layers of lead, the most recent shade was a deep mauve. Chipped and nicked, asperously under the lines on her fingers, Margaret imagined she was the needle of an old victrola, caught in the spiral of a wax record, a melody whispered in the distance; just beyond the edge of hearing. These were all memories, a resonance left behind for centuries and Margaret did her best to focus on that song.

The rack and *crack* of the lock jarred Margaret from her catalepsy. She had no time to move, or shift, or jump back, the door was simply open, and a very disquiet Townsend was watching her. His right shoulder was pressed forward at an incline, and she knew he was holding his sidearm, barrel pressed to the layered wood.

Of course, if he'd fired, he would have missed the top of her head by easily a foot.

"Lady," Townsend withdrew a moment, and she watched him lower his right arm.

Margaret had already committed to this action, she was already here, there was no way to turn back, so she decided to amend his verbiage, "My name is Margaret."

Townsend opened his mouth to speak, then stopped himself. He wore black slacks of wool and a gray undershirt tucked tight across his broad chest. He was a boiling pot of confusion, bordering on real anxiety, clear as the paint on his own door for a witch to hear.

"*Lady*, what can I help you with?"

Does he not know? Margaret had never considered what Townsend *wanted*, and the concept of *fearing rejection* may as well have been as distant as the moon. "May I come in?"

"Of course, Lady." Townsend backed away from the door and allowed her entry. He returned to the night table to lay down his antique .45 caliber ACP.

The apartment was opulent by military standards, complete with a small welcoming space, a kitchenette and private bathroom. The wallpaper was sun faded, and long before the 3rd

Army requisitioned the building, someone had painted clusters of purple and red flowers at random points on the walls.

Townsend leaned back, then sat himself at the foot of his bed, produced a twig and struck a small wooden match. The hiss of flame filled the air, along with sulphur, shading his face in hues of bright orange.

"Why are you here, Lady?" Townsend took a second drag off the twig.

She repeated, softly, "My name is Margaret."

When Townsend smoked, he held the cigarette between his middle and ring finger, pressing palm to face. "Lady, when a commander brags that he's shared a bed with you *once*, no one calls him a liar. Until the moment he claims it was *twice*."

Margaret was neither shocked nor repulsed. Vehicles of the 3rd Army bore paintings of her, clad in nothing but a colloquial witch's hat. Margaret was proud of this, despite enduring decades of disparaging remarks from her brother.

"It's a rule I wrote for myself, after *The Bruja* died in California," Margaret reached over and ran her fingers up the back of Townsend's hand, the touch reminding her how much she wanted to *only* be here. "Do you know what it's like for a witch to *lose* someone she's shared a mind with?" Margaret slid Townsend's cigarette from his hand and took a small drag. She nearly choked, then handed it back.

The musty smoke changed and became something like rotten copper and gunpowder. Margaret reached for Townsend's free hand, fingers wrapped around his wrist, body pressing into his. The film unraveled in her mind, flickering behind blinking lids and ebbing about with motion she couldn't familiarize herself with.

The ground is thick with snow, and snow could be painted in such vivid colors. The man lying next to Townsend is dying, a stream of blood pouring off his lips like a spring thaw cascading down rock and dale. He reaches out for Townsend, but before he can touch him his eyes turn dead and the arm sinks to the ground.

"You never knew his name, did you?" Margaret asked.

"No," came the reply, as he stood, pulling away from her, tugging free his wrist and crushing the twig out on an ashtray.

Margaret approached behind him and pressed her whole body into his back and buttocks, the 9mm in her cleavage biting into her chest, the rail pressed into her sternum with a sort of comfort that made her feel familiar and *happy*.

Townsend liked *puns* and had memorized many, but would never share them for fear of what others would think. He also loved broccoli. The bold memories of masticating it at meal, between his teeth, the flavors flooding across his tongue and throat were a flashing edifice in Margaret's mind. Her chest was heavy and chilled as she remembered his eyes watching a particular desert sky, one night in northern Nevada. She must have seen that same sky, maybe even that *same night*, but it hadn't captivated her the same way. That had been a moment which he considered unique in his life, something undeniably perfect.

"Why are you here, Lady?" Townsend repeated, his head tipped down. As Margaret ran her hand up his chest, she could feel the syllables vibrate down his throat.

"Would you like to spend a *second* night with me, commander?"

Townsend didn't move or flinch. This close he smelled of sweat and cotton, memories crossing his skin and shoulders, something like burning diesel and blood. Margaret *liked* that, and she inhaled deeply even if her nose could never perceive with the same clarity as her mind.

"More than anything else," Townsend answered.

11:21am January 14th, 39 Veilfall

Stockton, California

Although former Heart Aurora Owens was no longer allowed to call her old palace home, the dwellings she now occupied in south Stockton, near McLeod Lake, remained stately. The exterior was manicured and watered, surrounded by carefully tended rose bushes and red brick paths laid surreptitiously through high and vividly green grasses that flitted in the breeze.

"Mayy," Ramona greeted Margaret at the threshold, dark hair pulled back in three braids that ran from her temples and forehead to the back of her neck, "A *word*?"

"A *word* then," Margaret nodded to her niece.

"I'm sorry," Ramona began. She was wearing an Antecedent uniform. Where Townsend graced himself in blue woolen jacket with white slacks, a *witch* and her bullfrog ancillaries had a black jacket. Ramona's was tailored around her hips and shoulders, presenting herself far more licentiously than other officers.

"I regret our words. I *regret* talking to you the way father would have."

Margaret, at this second, desperately wanted a cigarette. She'd declined keeping any on her for the moment, but this emotional intensity picked at scabs she'd already forgotten with her legs wrapped around Townsend.

"You *are* your father's daughter."

Ramona reached forward, laying a glove of dark, brown leather onto Margaret's shoulder, squeezing, "I'm a Lopez. We bite before we bark. Just, *please*, accept the apology. It was unworthy of *you* and *me*." She was right. Her family *did* bite, and bite hard, but the apology was genuine, and Margaret accepted it with grace. It didn't mend the narrow cuts that stung with a breath of air, nor did it fill Margaret with false affection. That's what an apology was, after all, a selfish action to relieve a person of their own guilt.

Ramona opened the tenant doors for her senior, and both women entered the lobby of Aurora's home. The floor was pre-Collapse, black and white marble, with carefully drawn patterns of green and gold inlaid across parts of the entryway. Arches that supported a steel and glass frame had been painted in deep shades of gold and blue. Block flowers and clouds were sewn together in a canvas of thick oils and dried, layer upon layer, creating a tangibly contoured surface.

"Lady Mayhem," a guard nodded to Margaret. He was old, as was his counterpart to the left, both easily in their sixties, with cleanly shorn beards of gray. Both still wore outlawed uniforms of the House Owens army, post-Collapse campaign ribbons, and roughly hewn medals of silver blossoms. These old men remembered well the glory of *Aurora the First*, the witch who once helmed much of Northern California.

"Derrick," Margaret respected the old man enough to tolerate his illegal uniform. She approached him, gloves of silk, ivory white, on his arm. Drawn to tip toes, she offered him a kiss on the cheek. Derrick obliged her and bowed forward so she could reach his face. The kiss shared a quick snap of Derrick's past, not enough to frame or read like a book, merely sights and sounds. "My niece and I seek an audience with Aurora Owens."

Derrick nodded, standing up straight and returning to his watch, eyes on Ramona, "*Lady* Owens is expecting you."

Margaret's hair was drawn up with a pomade of boiled honey and beeswax, twisting and braided above her ears. It smelled of thyme, lavender and almond. Her scent was all over the old man as she reached up to run her fingers down his face, offering him a final wink before the second guard pulled wide the double doors.

"You're quite familiar here," Ramona leaned in, whispering with hands clutched behind her back. The two stepped into a narrow vestibule, tile changing, now set in deep shadows of red and sorrel, mixed with veins of faux gold.

"Aurora and I have dined together since I came to Stockton," Margaret shrugged.

The former *Lady* Owens herself oozed a sly, matriarchal tone that comforted Margaret. In her darker moments, she had wondered how different things *might* have been if it was Aurora who had found her as a child, *not* Maggi Lopez.

Aurora kept a house butler by the name of Cyrus. He was an old man, and Margaret had often wondered at the way Aurora treated him, above the station of a servant. He greeted them, dressed in muted gray and white, and introduced both Antecedent witches, seating them across from Aurora, offering lunch and tea.

Despite her failing health, Aurora Owens sat straight on a deeply upholstered sofa of red velvet and enameled cherry wood. Gone was the crown she had worn when Margaret first met her, but the adornment of her vast jewelry remained. So, too, did the workmanship and opulence of her gowns, flowing red and black, in silk and velvet.

Ramona sat, crossing her legs politely, bullfrog uniform tight across her chest in all the right places. In the foyer, her perfume was bold and smoky, but in Aurora's apartment it was drowned and swept aside by lemongrass and pine smoke, so thick that a fine fog hung across the room itself.

"This is the niece?" Aurora watched Ramona, eyes calculating. The older woman was also *listening* to the air around Ramona, a polite, though aggressive, review. Margaret could *feel* Ramona bristle, "That's quite a ward you're wearing, child."

Margaret remembered the magnetic draw about Ramona from the night before, *familiar*, yet an energy spoken in another language. Ramona simply shrugged, a mischievous smile creeping across her lips, matte red ribbon.

"She's more pleasant than her father," Margaret attempted to change the subject, concerned that the two would snap at each other.

"And you've brought *ghosts* to my home," Aurora grimaced, ignoring Margaret, "That wasn't part of the arrangement I had with your aunt."

Ramona's smile grew larger and her lips part. Her teeth were crooked, overlapping in misshapen places, but they were clean and white, "You have your guards," she gestured behind her, past the foyer, "I have mine."

"*Mm-hm,*" Aurora's disdain was barely veiled, "that ward you're wearing would have any uninclined guards with *blood and bones* lusting for you in a matter of minutes." Although

Margaret couldn't solve this particular ward, she wasn't offended or slighted that her elder had. Aurora Owens was a pre-Collapse witch of no small skill.

"Not *all* witches are battlewitches." Ramona's smile did not abate.

Margaret nodded, again hoping to cool the mood, "Like her mother, Ramona has a knack for *understanding*. Even as a very small child."

Aurora showed a hint of disdain for the interruption, "I remember your father well. He was an unpleasant man with little mirth, and a hunger that I don't see in you," It was Aurora's turn to smirk, nodding her head side to side, "*Oh,* you're hungry. Just not for land and prestige. The game is different for you."

Jokes were one thing, but to speak ill of Ramona's father, back in Crafton, *back east*, was a sin that guaranteed unhappy tidings. Alexander Lopez was a well-loved dictator and Ramona had enjoyed much for that.

"My father is a man of single purpose, I've known that since I was young."

Margaret cleared her throat, "We came here, today, for the court of Aurora Owens, *The First*." Aurora's ego *needed* to be stroked. At the end of her life, feeble and crippled, stripped of power, she remained no fool. Her eyes prowled like a wolf, but kind words would calm her ill ease and satisfy the respect that she'd earned. "We also hoped that you might offer a tale, or two, of Ramona's grandmother. You knew Maggi Lopez, briefly."

Glowing with regal pride, Cyrus returned with small plates at hand, full of little sandwiches made from fresh bread, smoked meats, and cucumber slices. Aurora thanked him and Margaret was once again reminded of their strange relationship.

Nobility never thank the help.

"Do you know your *aunt's* name?" Aurora didn't lean in to eat immediately, instead she favored Margaret's niece, her smile as constant as when it first unfolded.

"I've only ever known her as *Mayy*." Ramona answered, grabbing one of the sandwiches with thin fingers, delicately gluttonous.

Chuckling, Aurora finally reached for one of the sandwiches, no longer than her thumb, "'Mayy' is a name she gave herself. Her real name is *Margaret*. Maggi and I talked about her. She held a great deal of regret for the way she treated *Margaret*."

Margaret's jaw clenched, fingers curling into fists. She had come to visit Aurora, weekly, for close to a year, and had never been told such a thing. Part of her wondered if it was true, and part of her questioned why she'd share that *now*.

Ramona, through a mouthful of food, inquired, "Why did you call yourself Mayy?"

"Your *mother* thought it was just a silly phase. Didn't she?" Aurora watched with a smirk, "The drama of a girl at puberty?"

Her face dour, Margaret had no interest in discussing her name. Her tone fell low and her lips barely parted when she spoke, "When I learned to read and write, I tried to pen my own name. *Margaret Lopez* is what I wrote."

"Maggi didn't much care for that did she?" Aurora didn't look away.

"*No*." Margaret sneered, spitting with unveiled aggression, "She broke my nose."

Ramona chuckled at this, a few crumbs of bread spat across her knees, and Aurora nodded, taking another bite. Chewing before she spoke, "Maggi, I believe, regretted those choices, late in her life."

Margaret bit her lower lip, speaking with a bit less vitriol, "Regardless of what she did *or didn't* regret, I never wanted to hear my name after that day."

Before Ramona could interject, Cyrus returned with a silver tray and three, small cups of tea. The ceramic was dull and cracked, but enameled in complex hues of green and black, likely antiques *long before* the Collapse.

Aurora Owens accepted her cup first and said, "You wanted me to regale your niece with stories of her grandmother. Did you only wish I tell her of the day she brought me *Dread Harvester's* mask?"

Yes, that's exactly what I hoped you'd tell her, Margaret worked to hide her sigh.

Ramona was a mottled painting of sympathy and amusement, her eyes tipping kinder than Margaret had seen them since she arrived in Stockton, "Mayy, I'm not an idiot. *The Bruja* wasn't known for her kindness. I've seen that in my sister. I can't change the past, but I will always think of you as family, *a Lopez*. You raised us both after mother's passing."

Reaching for her tea, Aurora's thin brows rose, "The suggestion of Margaret being a legitimate Lopez could be *provocative*. The *granddaughter* of Maggi Lopez saying that, out loud, could be dangerous to Margaret."

What the hell are you playing at, Aurora? Margaret was the stiffest person in the room when she answered, "It's why your father never allowed it," *He also never saw me as a real sister.* "A wise witch doesn't name themselves."

"Like Amy?" Ramona giggled.

"*Plague Dog*," Margaret relaxed for a moment, her fists unclenching, her shoulders lowering, "no one calls her that."

Aurora sipped her tea from the antique ceramic. "In my youth I believed I could force people to respect me with a slick name. I was angry at losing the use of my legs, angry at my husband, *angry at everyone*. Perhaps your sister is simply *angry at someone*."

Happier now that the conversation had shifted away from her youth, Margaret reached for her own sandwich, "I've heard the older people call you *Aurora the Bloody*, I never heard *why*."

Aurora Owens leaned forward to place her tea back on the table, folding forearms on her knees, "Dread Harvester crippled me for life, when I tried to capture San Francisco. I had to flee, crawling, dragging my legs for miles. By the time I returned to our operating base, I was covered in my own blood."

Margaret held no ill will for Aurora, but she was very comfortable turning the tables and reminding the older woman of her defeat. "Dread Harvester must have been a terrifying witch, to have wounded my mother *and* you so grievously."

Aurora offered the ghost of a smile, unwilling to show her discomfort. "Your mother didn't believe in *random happenstance,* and neither do I, *Margaret Lopez*."

Margaret tossed her sandwich back to the plate. She disliked cucumber, and her stomach was jumbled. Hearing the name *Margaret Lopez* bandied about so easily in this room made her queasy. "Speaking of my mother, I was told recently that Maggi Lopez had an unpaid debt. She was in possession of an '*eye that does not see*.' I was also told that I needed to visit her grave."

Aurora Owens didn't answer right away. She sniffed at the air once or twice, probing at Margaret as far as she could, politely. When she replied, her tone had changed. She had ceased to be *Grandma Aurora* and was now *Heart of House Owens*.

"Who told you this?"

Margaret's tone changed as well, a battlewitch emerging. "I don't think it's important."

A younger woman sat in Aurora's place, years washing away like caked mud in the rain, wearing wrinkled and spotted skin. "Maggi came into possession of a glass eye shortly before she met Dread Harvester. Not just *any* glass eye, *something special*. Something I couldn't identify. Magic more completely concealed than anything I'd seen before. My *dearly departed* husband was a surgeon, he installed that eye in Maggi's face. She would use it to defeat the Ifrit at Carbondale."

"Xanthous Mine," Margaret swallowed hard at the memory, "It's a dead pit of lava rock. There's nothing there, no hint of Ifrit. No hint of my mother." *Not entirely nothing*, Margaret thought, remembering the cold air and violent wind when she visited. Something happened there, something that had damaged reality. It felt like swallowing a needle, inescapable, maddening.

"Xanthous Mine isn't the grave of Maggi Lopez," Aurora Owens closed her eyes. "It's the birthplace of The Beast, but *not* the final resting place of your mother."

Frustration was clinging to Ramona, steaming like stew on the stove. It was common knowledge that Maggi had died for her *son*, for the *Empire*. Her fight at Carbondale was nothing short of legend now; half-truths, exaggerations, and total lies. In death Maggi was remembered a true hero, a witch who'd faced down ancient powers and defeated them with good old-fashioned Antecedent know-how. To suggest *The Beast* was born from the same struggle would have been alien to any Antecedent citizen.

"So *where* does my mother's body rest?" Margaret's reply was curt, truncated as the half-eaten corpse of her sandwich.

"I will tell you both a secret." Aurora's hands were free when she spoke, and the air twisted around them from heat. Aurora Owens never *stopped* being a fire eater. The very rhythm of her heart was flame, and a thousand kinds of control could not contain that, "I was there when Maggi died. I sent my soldiers down, after her glass eye. My men died, *every one of them.* Save Cyrus, who stayed up top with me. That night *The Beast* was born. I will promise you, *both* the eye *and* your mother's remains rest with The Beast."

Many had believed The Beast to be a myth, others swore they'd been so close as nearly to be crushed. Some said it was a garbage golem, made of scrap and refuse. Others claimed it as the very ghost of *America*, an industrial banshee that walked on two legs and cursed all who fell before it. Stories said it was a hundred feet tall, or perhaps a thousand feet high. Many claimed it breathed fire, others said it was clad in sooty smoke. Margaret herself doubted those stories until she personally saw the cold ruins of Federal bases it had battered and beaten into ash.

"When I first came to Stockton, you offered to take me to San Francisco," Margaret breathed deep. "Was this why?"

"You never took me up on that offer." Aurora Owens cooed, not chiding the small woman, just smiling sadly, "A slumbering giant watching the Pacific. Maggi Lopez rests inside. It was a manifest extension of her love, and her *rage*. When The Beast crossed House Owens, my generals told me it was the end, that we must evacuate. I knew they were wrong. I knew it was only a tired, old *mother* on her way to a long nap."

Nap? Margaret thought this was an odd choice of words. It implied The Beast could wake. *How could Aurora possibly know that?*

Ramona interrupted, her voice a shrill caterwaul, "How can that even be possible? The Beast was a demon."

Aurora Owens favored Ramona with a disdainful glance, "Did you almost die in the birth of The Beast? Did you watch it wreck destruction on the Federals? Don't speak when you have nothing intelligent to say. That goes *double* for pretty girls and *triple* for noble ladies."

Margaret took some delight in Ramona's expression. Back east *no one* would have dared speak to her like this. "Is your offer, for San Francisco, still good?" Margaret spoke in the void, softly, carefully.

Aurora Owens shook her head, an enormous flood of sadness cooling her hands and drawing back the fire that was burning in her chest, "I can no longer travel."

"Mayy," Ramona pretended she'd sustained no insult, "to whom did Maggi owe this debt?"

And what does Aphrodite have to gain in satisfying that debt?

Margaret had no intention of answering Ramona's question, rather she deflected, "My mother made plenty of deals with old gods, who could guess?"

Aurora Owens chuckled, "The Beast isn't hard to find, you know. It still stands hundreds of feet above the Bay, in San Francisco. The two of you could visit together, make a day of it. I think you'll find the city herself to be a charming vacation."

Margaret had known Aurora long enough to never trust *old-lady Owens'* smile, a twinkle in her eye that promised fresh baked muffins and perhaps a sugar tea for dessert. The days were not far past when she was the most dangerous witch on the west coast.

"That doesn't sound like a bad idea, we'd have some more time together too."

Ramona's smile was far more insidious. It reminded her of the little girl she'd once raised, and the woman that Margaret all too often forgot *wasn't* her daughter.

"Yes, I think it's time we visited San Francisco."

Antioch Queen Sunrise Special, California

"So, Grandma broke your nose?"

Ramona asked the question in a chirping rhythm, as if this was a funny anecdote that she could enjoy and cherish. It surprised Margaret and she slowly rolled her eyes away from the window to favor her niece. "*Yeah.*"

"What's the story behind that?" Ramona's lips parted upwards, she was showing the smallest hint of her front teeth and it was hard to find her *rude*. Margaret felt her chest flutter for a moment as her own memories rose up, a tide groping at the world she'd built for herself.

"Your *grandmother* was drunk. She drank to *forget*, and she was a mean drunk." Margaret hesitated, second after second, counted and timed by the *click-clack, click-clack* of *Antioch Queen's* roll. "She didn't just break my nose when I wrote my name, she *kicked the shit out of me*. I ran away from her that night, I sought help from the *only* friends Maggi had, the *only friends I* had. Her assault team, hard men, soldiers and mercenaries. They took care of me, asked me *who did this*? They were angry. I lied, so I could spare them the ache of betraying me when they realized they could never raise a hand to the immortal Maggi Lopez."

Ramona nodded, as if all this was fodder for a grand biography she planned to scribe. It rubbed Margaret the wrong way and she regretted speaking.

"Did you *hate* Maggi?"

Margaret shrugged, "Yes," then quickly bit back, "*No*. I hated her at the time, but I still crawled back to her. She saw my face in bandages, and black eyes and then *she* demanded I tell her who had done this. She didn't even *remember*. I had to sit through *hours* of her schooling me on self-defense. I let her keep that." This too had stung, being reminded of her own physical inferiority. Margaret knew she could never brawl like Maggi, it wasn't a lesson she needed.

"Why didn't you tell her?" Ramona challenged, an elbow braced on window seal. Black lacquered wood flexed and shifted around her as the passenger coach flowed, twisting to follow the engine, nails and joints breathing with the beast's pace.

"Tell her what?" Margaret laughed, "You didn't know Maggi Lopez. There's nothing you could *tell* her about anything, especially if you were a child. The next day I decided to become *Mayy*." It was a shrill and aggressive name, a wordless poem dedicated to all of Margaret's rage. When *Lady Mayhem* walked the battlefield, she allowed that rage to slip loose, tied tight to her fingers and toes, a marionette allowed to sing and dance for her audience. Mayy was the woman who tamed that rage with a smart little smile, and a twist of her hips. Mayy was Maggi's student, a textbook battlewitch modeled after her mentor.

"'Mayy' is a better name. 'Margaret' sounds like an old spinster from Cleveland, someone irrelevant, *someone who doesn't matter,*" said Ramona.

Margaret smirked back at the younger woman, "It means '*pearl*,' and it's *not* for old spinsters. It's a *pretty name*." Margaret remembered glimpses of her childhood. She could hear the voice of her father, reading a book to her, laughing about her name, and stroking her hair.

"All right, *Pearl*," Ramona gestured, "are you mad at Maggi?"

Margaret sighed, a deep press of oxygen in her throat, more like a growl than anything else, "What is there to be mad over?"

Ramona offered up her hands, sunlight dancing off her wrists and the fine hairs of her forearms. "Amy is still mad at *you*."

"That's a *fine sack of shit*," Margaret laughed, licking her lips, "She was a darling until the age of five, then she couldn't be contained. If she wasn't your sister, I'd have disowned her."

"That's a *bit much*, Mayy." Ramona's playful expression faded. Her brows furrowed and her eyes told a story of disapproval, "I seem to remember all the times she begged for your attention, how often you *ignored her*."

Margaret didn't want to discuss this, and after matching Ramona's gaze, let her eyes wander back to the world outside their coach.

Antioch Queen Sunrise Special was beginning to slow. Lush greens of the Bay Area Reach began to thin, trees and shrubs falling away, offering glimpses of the bay itself, deep blue and gray water flirting with a sky the same color. Even inside the passenger cars, the ocean scent was thick and heady with salt.

Another passenger sat across the center aisle with bunked bags and a book. The sound of his thoughts, repeating printed words, etched a strange melody into the air that Margaret could *hear,* no different from a droning hurdy gurdy.

They had traveled close to one-hundred miles west of Stockton, rolling into the growing metropolis of San Francisco, perched like a crown on the Bay Area Reach's northern tip. With no functioning bridges to cross the Bay, train, petrol and wagon lines ran south to San Jose, almost the full length of the Reach. The city had spent much of the Collapse as the desolate, abandoned, home for a mad witch known to travelers and scavengers alike as *Dread Harvester*. Children's rhymes warned of her brutality, and tales around countless camp fires recounted the terror she inflicted on any visited her city. In all these old tales, Harvester had never spoke with her own voice; she sang and rhymed her threats through the lips of dead, croaking corpses.

After Dread Harvester's death, Lady Owens had committed unreal resources to the restoration of San Francisco. New iron tracks were laid, stations built, and vast construction up and down the peninsula was commissioned. The city was a key hub of commerce and trade, connecting southern territories along coastal sail and steam routes. From Mexico and the Southern Americas, into the cold clutches of Canada and Alaska. A city *had* to exist here, if House Owens was to flourish.

Disembarking from the train, Margaret and Ramona waited on the station, deep in a massive pre-Collapse excavation. They were surrounded by towering concrete and steel supports, covered in scaffold, as construction teams built new structures up and down the tracks and carved platforms for disembarking cargo. The air was cool and dry, full of swill smoke and wet steam. Several other locomotives waited nearby, all of them antique, all of them a unique personality of their own evolution. These were mirthful, fitful, and even an adjacency to madness.

A flowing torrent of humanity threatened to drowned Margaret, a sizzling flux of living traffic, *so very loud* in the great pit. Their voices churned up to a hum, random words popping in and out of the noise. Many of the laborers spoke a kind of low-English, as if they mumbled, their words caught in their mouths like too many bites of mashed potatoes, syllables dull and lazy. Their *minds* whipped up a froth of different energies around Margaret and her stomach moiled to maintain equilibrium. She was forced to bar and reinforce her barriers, block harder and harder against the press.

For certain, a city was *loud*, but the impact of open and clumsy uninclined minds was spread out, a veneer that existed only at the back of the eyes. This was *chaos*, like falling into the center of a vast ocean, hopeless and helpless on waves as steep as moving buildings.

Margaret licked her lips, mouth full of cotton. Her ears rang with clatter. Ramona's barriers snapped a few sparks of red light as she struggled to keep footing in the crowd.

"Back off a little," Margaret spoke, her words almost lost, "keep it hidden." Ramona nodded, knowing full well that she'd exposed herself as a *witch*.

It took little time for Margaret's valet to join them on the platform. He was pushing a hand truck with two small trunks. Both belonged to Margaret, made from thin steel and brass, painted red and white, locked and wrapped for transit. Ramona had traveled light from Crafton, choosing to purchase most of her clothing and toiletries in Stockton.

"The Occidental Hotel, Lady?"

Margaret's valet confirmed. He was a stout boy in his mid-twenties with a big mouth and narrow eyes the shade of a dead fish.

"Yes, check two rooms, Antecedent accounts. Both under Margaret, no last name." Margaret was best known as *Mayy*, in the former House Owens, so it was easier for her to hide. *Ramona Lopez* was another challenge entirely. She was the daughter of a tyrant, walking free in the jeweled city of a conquered state. Bandying about her identity invited no end of trouble.

Margaret's valet nodded and departed towards the western cargo ramp. Passengers on foot could disembark and climb many sets of stairs to the southern highways, seeking their fortune and fame in San Francisco. Closer to the surface a chilly breeze cut to bone, a silver and heather sky pressing down into the heart of a city that erupted.

San Francisco lacked the expansive, colorful, murals of Stockton. Art still wound against plaster walls and wooden doors, but with nowhere near the capitol's intensity. Wide, long, cursive words etched across wooden fences and tall brick facades, advertising everything from *Doctor Dick's Flu Remedy*, to the *Wanton Ladies of Wade House*.

A boy of perhaps twelve or thirteen, rushed past Ramona and bumped her left hip. Margaret could smell the machinery about him, a clockwork of fingers, hands moving, his energy a quick summer breeze against the frigid kiss of San Francisco. Margaret's mind spun out, curling around the boy's brain, pressing deep and seeing glimpses of his breakfast and a litany of all the girls he'd ever had a crush on. She was inside every crevice, and if Margaret wished it, she could show him horrors beyond reckoning. This wasn't a battlefield; she didn't want to harm the child.

Instead she simply froze him where he stood, casually approaching him.

"Tell your friends, your smart-boy gangs," Margaret leaned in to whisper, making sure her lips brushed his ear, "Stay clear of us both. I won't be so kind next time."

Margaret's hand, tightly clad in shiny, black leather, removed Ramona's coin purse from the boy and released the urchin. A flow of people swirled around the scene, horseshoes *clicked* and *clacked* on cobbles, wagons squealed and whined, rolling on uneven pavement and the child vanished into the storm.

"What happened?" Ramona looked confused.

Margaret extended her hand, coin purse offered in return, "You and your ghosts are so worried about someone who wants to kill you, you never noticed someone who wanted to *steal* from you."

The surface of San Francisco was a thrusting current of progress, but underneath all the fresh construction, fishmongers, dock workers, and whores, there was an even deeper array of magic currents that wound up and down the streets. Ripe with curious danger and ringing lust, this place was alive in its own way. Ghosts clamored with the living, and creatures Margaret had never seen outside of Maggi's old books lurked in shadow. She could understand why *Modus Vivendi* kept their headquarters here, and *not* Stockton.

"I'll pay attention." Ramona nodded.

Finding The Beast was *easy*. By the time Margaret and Ramona came into view of the eastward San Francisco coast, it towered perhaps *four hundred feet* above the city. There was a quiet belonging that it exuded. Margaret's eyes didn't pop out of her head, her jaw didn't drop, it simply felt as though the monster had *always* been a part of the city and *always* would be.

San Francisco was a small city, less than ten miles ocean-to-bay. It was mid-afternoon before the two women stood in its shadow. This close, Margaret realized that The Beast was partially submerged in the bay, its legs, perhaps near the knee, were underwater. It was impossible to guess how much taller it would have been on open land.

Margaret understood that the name was aptly given. The monstrosity was indeed *a beast*. It was hewn in a shape like a person, as *if* the sculptor had never known how a person *ought* to look. The arms were far too long, knuckles licked by cool bay waves. The head erupted like a broken bone from its hunched shoulders, above a pinched, narrow chest. Dreary and loathsome, with a wide maw, crossing nearly shoulder to shoulder, grinning at San Francisco, past her, and into the great Pacific.

Margaret's eyes went mad trying to identify all the pieces that bent and shaped it. Wrecked engines, shredded automobiles, varied shards of heavy I-bar. A wheeled excavator seemed to comprise the bulk of its misshapen torso, made of whole broadened blades. Articulated shovels larger than a house bulged from discolored, rusty hands to become fierce fingers. If metal was turned soft and rent apart, shaped, molded, and formed like clay, a god could have perhaps created this creature, a defiant act against natural order. It was a grand mess, dead and cold, a dreadnaught bogeyman, forever laughing at a joke to which only it heard a punchline.

"*The Beast*. It could be named *nothing* else," Ramona swallowed, her neck craned back as far as her ligaments would allow.

A series of wooden piers reached out toward The Beast, and metal scaffolds wrapped around its thighs and torso, climbing high on the gargoyle. Enterprising locals had invented an attraction, charging entrance for a chance to climb the dread terror of America's west, violator of dreams and dominator of the Federal military. Every Imperial knew the stories, *knew* how city-states laughed in private and said it was easy to conquer a continent if you had The Beast to clear a path for you. Perhaps that was so, but Margaret had watched many a young man die under the pretense of *easy*.

Margaret and Ramona paid their dues, a few coins each, and silently hiked up into the wide variety of stairs, rickety superstructure, metal algae and moss for a monument. Grates and steps creaked, and the two witches passed other visitors. Married couples held hands and looked up in reverence. Several teenagers crouched on broken decks and chairs, sketching in detail the grand jumble of wreckage that bound up every square foot. The Beast held nothing in common with any part of the world Margaret had understood before this day, a fairytale manifest, a thousand nightmares made flesh.

Margaret tugged away her gloves and ran both hands across the exterior. Dusty, sooty, her fingers were black before long. Streaks of grease and memories of flame darkened her jacket and crossed her face like swatches of paint telling a story. She held her forehead against broken axles, tethered sinew, listening to a rhythm of forgotten battles, the screams of those who wept and fell. The metal was full of memories that played together as one dire symphony, falling into a low melody that made her marrow itch.

Margaret's flesh puckered with goose pimples at these tastes and sounds, sweat ran down her back no matter how cold it was. She pulled off her yellow coat and tossed it to Ramona before diving in so close that she lay her lips on a spiderweb of safety glass, bent bolts and twisted rebar. She found a ghost, a young soldier who'd been caught in The Beast, a tumbleweed begging to be set free.

Her kiss released him, and his screams fell quiet.

Margaret possessed something unique, an extremely powerful empathetic nature. She could tune that power to push the tiniest nerve in the mind of a young street urchin, or she could spread *her terrible wings* across the field of war and educate *thousands* on the true meaning of terror. A woman, gifted as such, needed to love sad songs and tragic poems. She needed to revel in chaos, rejoice in the storm and allow waves to consume her.

That's what The Beast is, Margaret thought, *it was the storm*. A gift of total strife, seductive ataxia that whispered all the right *dirty words* into her ears, clutched at her throat until she giggled, and her breath quickened.

"There was no way Aurora Owens could have made it up here," Margaret heard Ramona's voice behind, tangled in the wind.

"I *wish to the gods* I'd come sooner, when she invited me." Margaret's answer wasn't for anyone but herself, blackened and filthy hands captivated her, the soot and grease moved like blood and semen as light refused to refract correctly.

"Armor plate, god of hate."

Did Ramona say that?

Margaret turned from her hands and looked back at Ramona. Her jaw was quivering, her eyes watered from the cold, scarring her cheeks with tears. "What did you say?"

"I'm scared of heights." Ramona answered, her voice small in ways Margaret realized could not be her own perceptions. For a moment she *hated* the young woman, her smooth features and sparkling eyes were as fetid and disgusting as sewage left in the sun to rot.

"As a child we introduced you to fear, and you became so fluent in the language of terror that you betrayed your friend to die." Margaret snarled in reply, her voice no longer her own, deep and angry, a painting of hatred that warped the air at her lips. Margaret forced focus upon herself, breaking away, taking *control*. "Memories. Just memories. I'm sorry."

"I'm scared of heights." Ramona repeated, eyes closed.

"Let me in," Margaret nodded, "let me into your mind."

Her niece had followed her up these gantries, *hundreds of feet* above the bay, never uttering a word of protest, never hesitating. Only now, under the weight of heady and dark magic, did she lose her grip. *Old things* lived here with The Beast, memories of smokeless fire, forgotten kings, and hate that defied all imagination.

Margaret took a step forward and ran her fingers through Ramona's hair, skin sparking on skin, barriers surrendering to the touch. It smelt of cinnamon and peaches for a moment and Margaret could step in as easily as she had walked into Ramona's nursery as a baby, hushing her to sleep when she was sick, calming her after a nightmare. She was older now, and stank of a *god*, but it was nothing for Margaret to calm her once more, to wrap around her terror and sing it to sleep, a lullaby she saved for her favorite niece.

"Better?" Ramona's eyes opened again as Margaret withdrew her fingers. She nodded, slowly, and Margaret turned away from her to gesture at The Beast. "Ghosts of djinn haunt this place. Even faded, they are terrible in their hate."

"Someone else is in there," Free of her fear, free to simply pay attention to her gifts, Ramona could sense the *other* entity, dreaming, inside the monster.

Margaret nodded. "That's old, older than the Ifrit. Older than the oceans, the mountains, *older than the gods*."

"Primordial." Ramona's eyes focused far away, and her voice was not quite her own.

How would you know something like that?

Margaret turned back to The Beast, seduced by the memories of chaos, pressing upwards and onwards, past Ifrit ghosts, toward misshapen shoulder blades. In the recesses of The Beast, dark places no one looked, Margaret could smell *cigarette smoke*. On broken metal beams and impaled motors, she caught the odor of *her* cheap perfume; Maggi Lopez wasn't just lurking, hidden, inside The Beast, her soul *slept* here, merged with the metal limbs, thin in some places, gluttonous in others. Breathless, close to hyperventilation, further up the metal steps and frame than any tourist *dared*, Margaret almost collapsed to narrow walk below her. The grates wobbled as she panted, frantic to express herself.

"Maggi's soul is bound to this monster. This really *is* her grave."

Ramona closed her eyes, and the air chilled quickly, whistling around The Beast's wreckage skin. Margaret could feel her chest turn inside out and fought a wave of nausea. She knew Ramona had allowed another *in*. Allowed, *or* permitted, she wasn't sure, but her barriers were long gone.

"Dirty, *dirty* girl." Ramona's lips parted in a smile, as did her teeth. Her big, brown eyes were windows to a cool, green ocean.

"Aphrodite."

Margaret offered her own smile, but it was disingenuous. Concern pressed at the back of her neck, worry for her niece, as Margaret tried to remember that Ramona had cursed herself with this affliction.

"You look like an oil spill, and twice as ugly." Ramona stepped forward, eyes darting and jumping all over Margaret, surveying her, *sensing her*, pressing deep into her mind.

"What did my niece promise you?" Margaret's voice was quiet as she watched Aphrodite move around in the skin of Ramona, the girl she'd helped raise, helped teach, the girl she *loved*.

"What do gods *always* ask for? Eternal service in my name." Ramona laughed with Aphrodite's cackle, grinning wide, "*Mar-gar-et, it's a big, bold, new world that we live in.* I've given your little witch power that you'll never dream of, I'm in her blood, her very bones, she is *blessed* with favor that *you* couldn't fathom."

Margaret shook her head, sadness sinking deep in her chest, pulling her words down, a sense of *defeat*. "Gods aren't supposed to have *that* much power, not over mortals."

"Who taught you that, Mar-gar-*et*?" Aphrodite laughed again, falsetto and melodic, rain on a tin roof, "The dead *witch* who merged with a *primordial titan*? A time once existed where power knew no limits."

Only now did Margaret realize how cold she was, shivering far above San Francisco in the sharp breeze. Something in Aphrodite's words flooded up through her hands and arms, clutching deep inside her, questioning her very grasp of *power*, the meaning and nature of it. She didn't have words to reply, and Aphrodite pressed on, stepping closer with Ramona's body.

"*Mortals* aren't supposed to command the power of elemental *witches*, yet they do. You imply that *power* is an unethical thing. Yet, you control your lovers' hands across your hips and breasts. How many times have you whispered in their minds, *harder, please, harder*?" Ramona's lips dripped a provocative tone, as though her very syllables were delicate fingers that teased at Margaret's flesh, tweaking her nipples and biting at the soft skin near the back of her neck where auburn-red hair grew thin, "You would command *such power*, yet deny me the same? Perhaps *you* are crueler than any god, Mar-gar-*et*."

Margaret trembled at the words, "What the *fuck* is a primordial titan?"

Aphrodite narrowed Ramona's eyes. "Clever apes like *you,* worship *us*. We once worshipped primordials. As we gift *you* power now, so too did they once gift us the same."

Something like revulsion ran down the back of Margaret's throat. Ramona's body was just feet away, eyes set open to see, lips moving with supple ease. Aphrodite's words grappled along the nerves of Margaret's shivering fingers, reminding of her what it felt like to run her hands across the slick conclaves of her own genitalia. It was one thing for Margaret to feel that dark and seductive draw from the body of a prostitute, it was disgusting for her to suffer the same lascivious afflictions at the vibrato of her niece's voice.

"I haven't found the eye yet," Margaret lifted her cold palms, pressing incongruous desire far from her mind, forcing the subject to change.

Aphrodite looked bored, "I thought you were trying to crawl back into your mother's womb down there. I'm sure you've got screws and lug nuts shoved *everywhere*. Maybe even a glass eye." Ramona's hand reached out and pointed to Margaret's chest. She paused, looked down, then reached for her own blouse, black linen oily and torn after her escapades.

She felt something smooth, rounded, caught at her cleavage. Margaret groped aimlessly for long seconds, fingers pressed down to where her breasts met, and she withdrew exactly what Aphrodite had predicted was there.

The eye that does not see.

"*Thank you*," Margaret responded, quietly.

"Your *mother's* womb," Ramona's voice cackled for a second, and Aphrodite spoke again, raising her eyebrows, "Maggi isn't your *real* mother. Do you even know what your mother's name was? Or do you only remember what she smelled like, after she was on fire?"

Margaret swallowed hard, fingers no steadier, the eye swallowed up by her fist. Her breathing turned ragged. She had hidden her own worst memories away in a place she could forget. Alone with Aphrodite; however, Margaret had no secrets. Whatever barriers she kept, the goddess had found, and *knocked* at that door.

"Not anymore," Margaret whispered.

"Your *real* parents burned on a pyre, Mar-gar-*et*, and you never even pause to remember them? None of *my* children are so terrible as to forget me." There was *nothing* sexual in the air now, eyes of merciless anger watched from Ramona's face. Aphrodite needed to do *nothing* more to Margaret than pick on a wound that had *never* healed, nibbling at her nerves.

"Don't *wet my cunt* and twist a screw, under the flesh of someone I *love*, when calling *me* cruel." Margaret pushed the words through clenched teeth. Her face was covered in sweat and sooty black grease.

"Someone you *love?*" Aphrodite smacked Ramona's lips as if she was checking her lipstick in a mirror, "Our bargain is met, if you *love* this one, no harm shall come to her. I never promised I wouldn't introduce you to splendid pain. Cruelty has more flavors than the wind blows, don't assume us the *same*."

Margaret could *smell* her mother burning.

With eyes closed, tight, she did her best to excise the odor, block it far from mind and lock those memories away where they belonged, but it was to no avail.

Aphrodite pressed the lips of Ramona into Margaret's and there was a snap of ozone. Perhaps some rogue element of energy that the two witches shared, or just an expenditure of

Aphrodite's capricious nature made manifest. Margaret's stomach turned up and twisted, the smell of crisp skin prying open her mouth and tangling her tongue.

When Ramona's face pulled away, Margaret's stomach heaved up, bile and saliva running down her lips, hot against chill wind, her throat pulling in quick, successive, contractions.

"What's wrong, Mar-gar-*et*? Ramona isn't your *real* niece. That's only a gentle lie you tell yourself to forget how badly you want your *own* child."

Margaret was unable to answer right away, her free hand groping at her stomach as if she could command it calm, "I found the eye. *Why would you do this?*"

If she could still fear, Margaret would have flinched from Aphrodite. Her question bore no weight of presentiment, nor did she beg for mercy. She simply sought to understand.

How have I angered her?

Aphrodite shrugged, "Mar-gar-*et*, Mar-gar-*et*. This isn't *anger*. This isn't even *real* cruelty. I *told you*, we only offer suffering when the lock must turn."

Aphrodite stepped out of Ramona's body, without another word, as if this had explained to Margaret everything she needed to know. She had no threat to offer, no promises to make or deals to broker. It seemed to Margaret as though Aphrodite *only* wished to see the eye to safety and offer some kind of twisted *thank you*.

A thank you that would have broken most people, Margaret thought, bitterly.

Ramona collapsed a moment later, laying off the side of rusted, steel gantry steps, almost *four hundred feet* above San Francisco's bay. Her body, a limp sack of produce.

Trying to keep her safe, Margaret had pulled her a few steps back to lay her down on the flat cat walk. Pressed up next to her, it'd be harder to fall, and her head could rest in the older woman's lap. This meant Margaret was resting her back on a single, narrow handrail with nothing but the bay behind her, legs dangled over the other side.

Most people would have found the position terrifying, but Margaret considered it merely *comfortable*. From this angle Margaret could watch the metal skin of The Beast, running her fingers through Ramona's hair. Her yellow jacket was gone, as were her gloves. Now the bitter bay wind caught her slick skin and bit hard into her bones, corset and linen blouse offering no warmth.

Her stomach did not calm, and the memory of Ramona's kiss became an abject horror that needed to be locked away, just as the odor of her parents' burning flesh. It wasn't the physical intimacy, or the scent, that rattled Margaret so badly, it was her own unique satisfaction in the experience. Every ounce of her mind *promised* this was a *hateful* thing to be inflicted on her, her body demanded she *weep*, and *cower* behind this violation.

Margaret did not weep or cower. She didn't hide *this* feeling. It was a loss of control, an exotic tryst that left her stirred and excited beyond the simple act of *fucking*.

A thank you, Margaret repeated, *that would have broken most people.*

5:40pm January 17th, 39 Veilfall

San Francisco, California

Part of Margaret was *there*, in the flesh, watching over her niece, *shivering*.

Some of her drifted through Ramona's surface memories, her dreams, and the flavor of her mind, like saltwater taffy. Another part, a very small part, drifted in and out of the world that wrapped around The Beast. Reality had been broken, bent, and betrayed for this monster to walk the earth. There were layers beyond layers to pull apart and pick through. Every mangled component had a story, a collection of memories, shades of the Collapse, a dusty remembrance of a world that came before. Margaret would not have possessed the tenacity, or constitution, to dive so deeply into The Beast, if Aphrodite hadn't reached into her with uniquely rousing abuse.

Residual power that a talented witch could turn to their own needs.

When the Veil shattered and society collapsed, the world was plunged into years of barbarism. People like Maggi Lopez and Aurora Owens had fought that lawless descent. To imply *either* of them did it selflessly was a lie, but they changed the world. The Beast was a representation of their life's work, their struggle against man's feral nature, constructed to remind the world how hard they fought, how much they lost, a broken doll sewn up tight with hatred.

Armor plate, god of hate.

Below the broken machines, beyond the rust and grime, a bitter black soup of blood and heat, there was a symphony inside The Beast. A *million* souls sang, a turbine of loathing that powered The Beast with a molten heart. Margaret's mother did not sing in that choir, she was the conductor, a flowing well of memories caught in a second of time, the moment of her death. That was her mother's voice, *Maggi's voice*, unfolding in her head, open like a can of rotten meat.

"Offer the dying woman immortality? Threaten me with a good time."

A smooth, melodic rumble under the skin, spiders in Margaret's hair, spindly arms wrapped around her. "*I will construct a golem, a beast made from bones and blood, I will even make sure our might protects the hopes and dreams of your son.*"

"He doesn't need his mama anymore. He's got the world now. I'm ready." Maggi answered the primordial.

How dare she, Margaret's mind clamped down on Maggi's words like a rat trap. Her physical body heaved a wretch of anger.

How dare she. Where was Alexander right now? Did he fight for his mother's grave, did he visit her? Was he covered in filth, freezing in the Bay Area Reach to say his goodbyes?

"Speak my name." Margaret heard the primordial.

When Margaret's eyes opened, her legs were covered in spiders, black and sooty, crumbling as dust when caught by the wind, a hymn of longing.

"Anapu Weita," Margaret's spoke the name with her mother's memory. The words were cast far and wide into the waking world.

The Beast howled.

This wasn't the howl of an animal. This was the howl of dying cities, crying out for mercy; or revenge. The sound filled Margaret, calming her stomach and unclenching angry muscles. The whole of San Francisco seemed to quiver at the sound, even lights dimmed behind The Beast's great silhouette, and air gusting harder than before.

"Don't speak with *her*. Don't speak with the primordial."

A new voice spoke near Margaret. Not a shadow of the past set to replay on an old Victrola, this was a *living thing* sharing her gantry, close enough to touch.

Perhaps not *living*.

There was a *ghost* crouched at the opposing handrail, her back to The Beast. She was opaque and her body blurred in and out of focus, through a collection of lenses refusing to work properly. She was cast in hues of sepia and chestnut; thick hair draped across her shoulders and wore pre-Collapse clothing. What looked like jeans and a dark sweater. The air filled with wormwood, orchid, ginger and sandalwood.

"I'll speak to who I please, *specter*," Margaret lashed back, soaring on the wings of rage, anger dripping from her lips along with drool. "Begone."

The ghost with thick hair laughed. She had a narrow mouth and bedroom eyes that smirked, "I'm not *that* kind of ghost," she looked around, eyes flailing wildly for a second, and face blurring out, "I'm not *that* kind of ghost either."

She can see Ramona's bodyguards, Margaret realized.

"Just leave us alone, go back to wherever you came from."

The ghost's voice sounded healthy, *worldly*, but her laugh was a flat clap, a noise overheard from another room, "This *is* where I'm from! This is *my* city."

"Oh!" Margaret nodded, "I'm *sorry*, I didn't realize this was *your* city. What else would you like to declare to the *lead battlewitch of the Antecedent Empire*? Do I owe you a tax?"

The ghost's brows rose, and her grin skipped from a smirk to a proud smile, "Is that so?"

If this specter had been of flesh and blood, the answer given might have been driven with terror. The kind of terror Margaret could unleash in the minds of those who *had* minds. A specter's existence was a flimsy thing, something she could neither *touch* nor be *touched by*, and it would take far more than a *kiss* to dispel.

"Leave us alone. This is a city of thousands for you to haunt."

"I suppose," the ghost shrugged, patterns on her sweater shifting, "but none of them are wearing *the eye that does not see*."

Margaret paused, her blood cooling, and looked around. The sun set, casting the world in shades of copper and ink. "What do you know of the eye?"

"I know many who wish to possess it. I know an ancient spirit who it's owed to. I *know* that Maggi Lopez wore it the last time *we* met."

The ghost and Margaret watched each other, seconds ticking by. *Some* ghosts, a very rare few, could travel of their own volition beyond the places they died. Margaret had met one such spirit in her life. It was unlikely she'd meet *two*.

"You met Maggi in San Francisco? There were only *two* living souls here, and you're *not* Aniceta Lopez." The ghost tilted her head down, spread her arms wide and gave a nod with her chin. As she moved the air blurred, shifting shades and color. "Dread Harvester."

"Call me *Aubriana*," the dead woman nodded her chin again, "I haven't been the Ferry Mistress in many years."

For the first time in many long moments Margaret overcame her rage, a bubbling fury under her skin, receding like the tide. When she spoke again her voice was even, focused, "Ifrit ghosts, a primordial, my *mother*, a goddess and now Dread Harvester herself. The Beast is *the* place to be."

"*Mother?*" Aubriana asked as her face blurred and the expression was lost. Her voice took on a rigid tone, laced with accusation.

"Maggi Lopez was my mother. Not by blood. She adopted me as a child." Margaret shrugged, her neck suddenly sore, "I came here to claim the glass eye and say my *goodbyes*."

Aubriana's face came back into focus, scornful now, lips raised and angry. There was something *off* about her, the way her jaw rested, as if it was not quite connected. It didn't shake Margaret, but the conversation's tone changed, "Maggi was an *unrepentant cunt*."

Margaret reached out her hand, dirty palm facing the ghost, "Easy, *easy*. She was my mother, *not* my friend. Whatever the two of you had going isn't my concern."

As she spoke, Aubriana's eyes turned dark, her hair twisted into dreaded branches and flesh started to fall from her jaw, exposing hazel bones and teeth. "Is that so? What if I told you I *killed* Maggi here? At bay's edge, decades past."

"I'd say you *didn't*," Margaret raised her eyebrows, watching Aubriana twist into something unrecognizable, maybe something closer to the Dread Harvester of myth. "She went on to kill Ifrit at Carbondale, a month later."

"*Oh, honey*," Aubriana hissed, her voice no longer a soft ribbon drug along the skin, she sounded like radio chatter in the distance, "*When* Maggi died is irrelevant. I spread decay through her flesh, her bones and organs, I rotted her from the inside out. When she cut my throat, she was *dying*."

Margaret closed her eyes and questioned her sanity at keeping council with a ghost. Aubriana may have kept her memories intact but was likely insane.

"They called you a necromancer. The *only* necromancer to ever exist."

Aubriana's exposed jaw *fell* away from her throat, vanishing in the air, exposing her

pharynx and throat as her tongue fell limp. "It's amazing what you can do when you refuse to die,"

the distant radio crackled at Margaret.

Margaret licked her lips, tasting bitter soot and bile, "What *did* my mother do to you?"

It was only now that Margaret found herself rattled, even repulsed. Dread Harvester

could not harm her, but she was a visually disturbing creature, hunching forward on all fours,

knuckles pressed down, her sweater and jeans giving way to leather and tattered fabrics.

"At the Collapse your '*mother*' left me for dead in a San Jose hospital. I was in a coma,

starving to death, my lower face ripped off. She knew I was alive, she *knew* she was damning me,

and she took her son and *boyfriend* and left. She *lied* to herself. She told them I *died*."

"But, you didn't."

Aubriana shook her head slowly for Margaret.

Watching Margaret like a rabid animal, Aubriana's eyes darted, skipping from

Margaret's hands, to her mouth, to her hands again, waiting, watching.

The specter no longer blurred, she was crystal clear, and Margaret could *feel* rage radiate

from her. The hate bound up in The Beast was a force of nature, a tidal wave. *This* hate was

concrete, and very human, it could have turned milk sour and wilted leaves. Margaret realized that

for the first time in her life she was talking to someone who *didn't worship* the almighty Maggi

Lopez. This was someone who didn't want to hear war stories, who didn't balk when she spilled the

truth, and now, alone with The Beast and a sleeping Ramona, Margaret could speak *anything*.

"If Maggi ever regretted how she treated me, she hid it well," Margaret swallowed, and

the words came easy. "She was an alcoholic all the years she raised me. I could deal with her fists,

pain doesn't scare me. But, every time she told me how she wished she'd *never* adopted me, how

she *wished* I was dead, how I was never worth her lover's life, it was the most painful thing I knew.

I never learned to forget Maggi's cruelty. I wish she was here, right now. I'd call her an *unrepentant*

cunt too."

There it was, all the cards on the table, everything that Margaret had wanted to say. She could have told a hundred stories, talked for hours, but none of it *really* mattered now.

Minutes passed, and Dread Harvester did not move, save for her eyes. They locked on Margaret's and changed from a washed-out chestnut color to ivory and deep beryl.

"What was your name?"

Harvester spoke finally, her head twisting up. As she did her tongue fell sideways, a thick and languid rope.

"I'm known as Lady Mayhem. You should call me *Margaret*."

From her lap Ramona coughed, squirming like a child waking at a start. Margaret turned away from Dread Harvester and laid her hand at Ramona's back to keep her from accidently rolling off the gantry.

"What's going on?" She asked.

Margaret glanced back to where the specter had knelt, perhaps a few feet away, but she was gone, lost in the shadow of The Beast. "Nothing."

"*Mayy,*" Ramona turned, looked up, watching with her big brown eyes, "don't lie to me."

"Witches lie. *Good* witches lie."

Margaret offered a thin smile, dirt and grease streaking her face where sweat had dried. She had begun to shiver again in the chill air.

Ramona pulled herself around and crouched next to Margaret, wiping at her eyes, "I can feel your anger, it's like a fireplace."

Margaret weighed Ramona's words, then pulled herself to her feet, one hand gripping the rail tightly. "Do you know, Ramona, that I *love* you? Do you know, that I think of you as my own child? I taught both you and your sister since you were old enough to touch and *taste* magic, but you were always my favorite."

Ramona reached her hand out for help. Her fingers were impossibly soft on Margaret's. "Why didn't you have your own children, Mayy?"

"I *can't,*" was all Margaret answered.

"I know that you love me," Ramona nodded. She was spreading her calm across Margaret now, helping her. The press of rage, the ascent of The Beast, her mother and Harvester, all of it had been exhausting. "And we *all* know that I'm your favorite."

Margaret was surprised at that last part, but her voice faltered. "I'm going to talk to your father, when he comes back from campaign. I'm going to tell him something he won't like."

Ramona nodded, knowingly. Her dark hair was pasted across her face, her skull, "You'll tell him you're *Margaret Lopez*." Margaret didn't answer; she simply let out a deep breath. It was not so much a sigh, but the exhalation of a diver coming up for air. "You know he'll hate it. So will my sister."

"I'm a little too old to take a smack across the face." Margaret's jaw tensed.

"I've spent the last few years studying Antecedent politics, and our servant states like House Owens." Ramona released Margaret's hand, stepping down a few stairs. "You'll shake the hornet's nest for sure, but maybe I can help."

Margaret was watching Ramona when she spoke, and as she turned away there was something different about her. The young woman so petrified of heights earlier had vanished. Ramona moved on the steps confidently, her barriers sound.

The same barriers she'd *dropped earlier*. Margaret had never considered diving further into Ramona's mind when she'd offered her calm; it never occurred to her that Ramona would have *lied*.

Margaret's own words bounced around her skull, "*Good witches lie.*"

"Let's get down from here. I need a drink."

Margaret and Townsend by Karolina Jędrzejak (RinRinDaishi)

10:35pm January 17th, 39 Veilfall

San Francisco, California

"What do you think would happen, if you were pregnant with a no-name child? If a johnny decided to play for the Lopez name?" Margaret's voice was a careening hiss as she stumbled over her words, weighted by inebriation.

At the center of a roughhewn table, stained a thousand times over in beer and hard spirits, was a collection of off-white candles, burning down. The lot of them had melted into a series of sharp peaks and valleys, casting a flutter of yellow light across Margaret and Ramona. The soft glow erased some of the lines at Margaret's lips, stealing a few years away from her face. Ramona, on the other hand moved in and out of her own shadows, eyes playing across the room like a billiard ball.

"I don't want to be Empress." Ramona answered, quietly.

Margaret leaned back, her head spinning. She eyed the antique tumbler made of green glass in her hand and considered downing her drink but thought better of it.

The two witches sat toward the rear of a fishmonger tavern, perhaps a half mile north of where The Beast stood. It was narrow, cramped, and the walls were made of mismatched wood and lacquered heavily, creating patterns of red and brown, caked in the dried flow of laminate. The bar had been decorated in a collection of old-world trinkets, faded painting prints of lilacs and brass letters mismatched to read words Margaret had never heard, like "*malacy*" and "*rasale.*"

The tavern smelled of salt and musk, warm beer and pungent liquors. Mostly men drank here, save a few women who were burly in the shoulder and tan of face. Several games of cards played in hushed tones, while fisher teams discussed the day's work and netters chatted filthy descriptions of their latest conquests. An old man, older by far than anyone else there, played concertina near the bar. His face was cracked like asphalt and his eyes were pale like an ocean sky before a storm.

"You don't get that choice," Margaret shook her head, releasing the green glass tumbler and crossing her arms. "A Lopez child can't just become a *prostitute* and abandon the blood she was born to. You don't get a *common* life."

Ramona showed her teeth, sneering. They were devoid of decay, a blessing of her station. "Do I look like one of these *fishmongers*? Do you think a holy whore of Aphrodite skulks in the shadows of Crafton offering *blowjobs for a dime*? *Do you think that, Mayy?*"

Margaret blinked for a second, then threw caution to the wind, knocking back the last of her drink. The quality was maudlin, it burned going down.

"I don't know *what the fuck* to think."

"I'm a woman grown, Mayy." Ramona leaned in, "A servant of Aphrodite, I don't turn tricks, I'm *Hetairai*. I *choose* my consorts, and they pay me as I *demand*. It could be coin, it could be favor. *All* of them must love me and their love is tithe for Her Lady of Desire."

Margaret was, to a certain degree, resigned that Ramona's world would be different from her own. She'd kneel at the whims of gods and make her own magic. The gospel according to Maggi Lopez didn't have to be *absolute* rules of the post-Collapse world, and Margaret wouldn't live to see where Ramona's path took her.

How can I tell her that? How can I tell her that I'm jealous?

Not jealous of whatever boon had been granted Ramona, rather Margaret found herself profoundly jealous of the regard that her niece now bore Aphrodite, affection she had always coveted, quietly.

"I'm sorry, I didn't understand," Margaret's intoxication bled through her words. "The men I took to my bed were *paid* for what they gave. When it was dark, *quiet*, I needed them."

There was a desperate *sorrow* as Margaret spoke, memories consuming her, stroking her hair and cooing in her ear, syllables rolled off her tongue and spread into the tavern. So too did her melancholy. The chatter and gossip dulled, and men who played cards fell quiet. Not one could have answered *why*, but their thoughts drifted to times long past, the people they had kept close, who they had *loved*, and lost.

Ramona, in her immunity, offered a smile. She wasn't prodding at Margaret, she was genuinely admiring, "We're not so different, I guess."

On the verge of tears, too drunk and lost in a ballad of hazy memories as beautiful as they were horrible, Margaret realized her niece no longer needed her. As a friend, maybe an ally, perhaps. Ramona had found her path in this world, something greater and more majestic than Margaret ever knew her to be. She was truly a witch in her own right now.

Looking to the floor, coated in something glossy, Margaret nodded to no one in particular, "It's a big, *bold*, new world that we live in."

"It is, at that." Ramona reached forward and bumped her glass against Margaret's empty tumbler. "Father's throne holds no seduction, but I have my own aspirations."

Forgetting the russet floor, Margaret met Ramona's eyes and pursed her lips for a moment. *What would those aspirations be?* When she spoke, it was with care, "I had hoped you could protect the Empire from Amihan."

"*Plague Dog?*" Ramona chuckled, finishing her own drink, "Perhaps *you're* the one who needs to save her from herself. She always looked up to you."

"*Ha!*" Margaret barked, a loud yelp that snapped the tavern denizens out of their sorrowful stupor, back to their games and conversations, "She's too much like my mother, with none of her kinder traits. She's a *daddy's girl*."

Ramona lowered her voice to whisper, "You worried about *me* getting pregnant? Amy is the one who had a child. Before she left on father's southern campaign. I helped her find an adoptive mother for the boy."

Margaret's jaw lowered and she was too stunned to reply. The information sobered her for a moment, and she *wanted to* answer, a thousand things running through her mind.

I'd have raised her son. Amihan simply walked away from her own flesh and blood?

Margaret's simmering rage was caught in a quivering moment of confusion. A chill cut across the room, twisting at humid air. It was as though a crystal goblet hit the floor of the fishmonger tavern, spilling shrill contents of magic everywhere. Margaret could see it in Ramona's eyes. Her lashes fluttered, then pupils dilated, darting around the room.

Turning in her chair, Margaret looped an elbow over the misshapen wood, exhaling long and slow as she unpackaged all her senses and focused on *control*. It was one thing to flood a room with sorrow or wistful dreams, it was another to expose strangers to the rage that Margaret *wanted* to express.

Focused on her breathing, regaining her senses, Margaret nearly missed the cloaked figure who had entered the tavern, waving off a waitress with sun bleached dreadlocks.

"We have company."

Ramona's voice dropped, throaty and low, her defenses locking tight, then evaporating in the rapidly cooling air. They were barriers, *quiet* ones, unseen to anyone around them.

Margaret merely nodded, erecting her own subtle boundaries. The cloaked figure was likely a woman, wide in the hips, chest, and shoulders, but she carried herself with willful grace, not unlike the stride of Eric Owens. Beyond her own eyes, parts of Margaret slithered across the room, slipping into the mind of each of the tavern denizens, waitresses, barkeep, even a dishmaid. She was everywhere at once. In this broad connection, their lives blurred together, and dreams became an ugly gray pallet.

Each one of them ceased their drinking, cards falling impotently out of their fingers, sliding across tables, bets ruined. Swayed to Margaret's will, a hundred fingers tickling their minds, wrapped around vertebrae, nervous systems, kissing souls, shushing them to sleep. With *one* blink of her eyes, *one* thought, Margaret could set them against each other with primal terror and bloody-minded greed. Quiet, all who kept company in the tavern watched the woman tossing back her hood of crisp jet.

"Lady Mayhem."

The cloak was covered in *white* flecks. The woman's face was pudgy, with a wide jawline and chin that curved slowly down into her neck. She had deep set eyes, black as ink and long lashes, upon which more ivory powder sat.

I know you, Margaret realized, her inebriation pressed back to quiet recesses of her mind. *Aurora Owens, The Second, eldest Owens child, and one-time heir.*

"The *other* Lady Owens." Margaret nodded, lips suddenly dry and mouth full of cotton.

"May I seat myself?" Aurora's voice was clear, like her brother's, biting down on her syllables, no hint of lazy tongue, or slang in her vernacular.

She burns like salt.

"Any member of the Owens family is welcome at my table," Margaret replied, attempting to hide her own dingy accent, just as she'd attempted with Aurora's younger brother. "Ramona, please meet Lady Owens, *The Second*."

A dusty haze of chalk swept over their table, and Margaret did *not* release the patrons of the tavern, their eyes glazed, hands lethargic, absent desire.

Aurora scoffed from her sternum, "I no longer take my mother's name. You may regard me as *Lady Cuttersark*."

Lady *Cuttersark* stepped past Margaret and jerked free an empty chair with unexpected aggression. Ramona gestured with her chin, her own voice taking on *airs of court*, a form of speech that Margaret could only emulate unsuccessfully, "Magnate of *Modus Vivendi*, I believe?"

Aurora nodded to Ramona, fingers steepled, as she sat. Her cuticles were dried and torn, her long nails cleanly shorn despite a layer of abrasion that crossed them. Margaret licked her lips, her tongue like sandpaper.

What the hell are you? You didn't bite like this the day we first met.

"Modus Vivendi was my father's ambition, an ambition I *shared*. They look to me now for leadership, and I avow myself as such."

"What circumstance blesses us with your company, Magnate *Cuttersark*?" Ramona chirped in reply, but Aurora ignored the younger woman, eyes rolling across the table and falling on Margaret like a great boulder sent to survey a hillside. She drew up one leg to cross the other, cloak falling away to reveal a black dress of lace and lacquered wicker, coated in pale talcum.

"Lady Mayhem, do you normally avail yourself an Alviso gutter whore, or have you been up to visit The Beast?"

Aurora's words tasted like spoiled fruit. If she wished to break the rules of *polite* society, Margaret would meet her on equal ground, "Maybe you should speak to the *lead battlewitch* of the Antecedent Empire as something other than an *Alviso gutter whore*?" Margaret's voice turned to a growl as she let slip venom. "If we were men, we could *measure our dicks* right now. I can promise you, *mine* is longer than *yours*."

Ramona burst out laughing with that final remark and reached to pour herself another finger of whiskey.

Aurora did an excellent job not reacting, "As eloquent as ever, Lady Mayhem," she replied at last.

Margaret relaxed, if only for the sake of Aurora's pride, and did her very best to mimic the immaculate court speech of her table companions, "*Yes*, Lady Lopez and I *graced* The Beast with our lustrous…" Margaret clenched her jaw, searching for a word and failing, "…*grace*."

Aurora looked away, running her tongue across her teeth. It was sallow and white like some kind of albino slug. Margaret had to fight herself to *not* recoil in revulsion.

"Modus Vivendi take care to watch and listen to the world around us. San Francisco is a key hub, a port among ports, and we make certain it's safety. In this, you would not be surprised that we *heard* The Beast screech in slumber."

So, that's what you're after, Margaret thought, scolding herself for not realizing sooner, "The Beast is property of my family, Lady Cuttersark. What interest do you have?"

Aurora rolled her eyes, "*Yes, yes,* House Owens capitulated to the Antecedent Empire, The Beast is your right, your property. Do you *think* I actually *care*?"

Well, yes, actually, "If I misunderstand, enlighten me." Margaret bit out in return.

"My father understood that the world of *states* and *maps* had come to an end with the Collapse. The *only* power in this world is *magic*. Magic doesn't serve petty tyrants like Aurora Owens or Alexander Lopez. *They serve magic*. Do you really think I care *who* owns the land on which The Beast sleeps?" It was only now that Margaret could *see* the old Owens woman in her daughter. Her spine straightened as she spoke. "*We know* you whispered to The Beast."

Okay, now I'm interested.

"Why forbid it?"

Aurora's lower jaw jutted forward as she spoke, "The Beast is the grave of Maggi Lopez, her spirit exists somewhere in that *thing*. It's the will of ancient power. A will that can *awake* as readily as it can *sleep*."

Ramona leaned back, arms crossed, as she spoke, "It's not *dead*?"

"Far from it, Lady Lopez," Aurora never looked at the younger woman. Margaret was favored wholly by her grim look, "The Beast is *alive* and well, no matter how quiet it seems. If that monster *walked* across the city, it would be devastating. If it stepped deeper into the bay, the displacement of water would drown thousands."

Margaret laughed despite herself, running a finger across the table, painting an arrow in the pale film that had accompanied Aurora Cuttersark. "You thought we were here to take command of that thing? How do you know that's even possible?"

Aurora seemed annoyed, working her jaw side to side with frustration. She sighed, paused several seconds, looking between Ramona and Margaret before answering, "Because, I once tried to master The Beast, when Alexander's army crossed the Sierra Nevada."

Margaret was satisfied now. Aurora had doffed her pride and humbled herself as much as a noble child could. It was all the victory that Margaret craved.

"Poor Lady Cuttersark," Margaret looked over to Ramona, glee on her lips, "she wonders what it is that an Antecedent *whore* like me possesses, which she does not."

Aurora Cuttersark closed her eyes, accepting the slap in the face, knowing full well she'd earned it. "What *do* you possess that I do not?"

This was all too much for an inebriated Margaret. Her stomach boiled for a second, and she fought off a wave nausea. She had known a hundred people like Aurora Cuttersark in her life, all of them looking down on her, *including her brother*. The sweet taste of redress had never lessened over decades.

"Why *the fuck* would I would tell *you*, Cuttersark?"

4:08am January 18th, 39 Veilfall

San Francisco, California

In her small fingers, Margaret held *the eye that does not see*.

It was such a diminutive thing, so simple, a glass stone cast in creams, blues and black, looking back at her. There were no ghosts, no stories, *nothing*. It was a quiet, serene artifact that Margaret would have assumed worthless, had gods and noble witches alike not sought its possession.

Margaret closed the eye in her right palm and turned to the man on a barstool next to her. He was wide in the shoulders with upper arms wrapped in vines of thick sinew and muscle. He smelled like cigars and gunpowder and hummed with aggression.

"I'm not familiar with the *Maul*," Further intoxicated, Margaret's lips were numb, and she lisped through syllables with imagined ease.

The man looked up from his glass tankard, warm froth at the edge, "You didn't seem that interested *b'fore*. You just stared *at'cha* glass eye."

He favored her with a glance, a stream of beer glistened at his mouth. Under his low brows were two tiny eyes that fumed in his skull, *angry* for the sake of anger. Margaret *liked* that anger, that concrete rage. It was an intoxicant, a proxy expression of things she could rarely emote. Absorbing that enmity was as freeing, *liberating,* as the alcohol that saturated her blood.

"Jealous, *Sammy*?" Margaret asked, reaching down into her cleavage to hide the eye.

"*Naw*," the big man with wide shoulders scoffed, "Just didn't seem like you cared."

Returning to the Occidental, Ramona had called the evening short after the departure of Lady Cuttersark. Margaret had accepted this and was even grateful. It gave her a chance to skulk at the edges of San Francisco's peregrine vulnerabilities. Each step told a new tale of the city's nature, and Margaret would have been a poor conqueror to leave well enough alone. Early in the morning hours many taverns and bars kept their doors open, brothels buzzed and street whores plied their trade under stuttering light as storefronts readied for the morning business.

Margaret had crossed perhaps a half mile before she found *The Metal Hammer*. Like the fishmonger tavern, this was a narrow haunt, bent up and thrust between two larger structures. The sign outside was etched aluminum, weathered and bent, hanging from chains thicker than required. Inside was a long hallway, covered in antique photography, stained and faded under yellow plastic. Stools lined the rail bar, and two older men tended drinks, colorful bottles scattered about them, lining dirty and cracked mirrors, a century unkept.

I don't care, Margaret thought, watching her reflection shift in scuffed glass. She'd washed off much of the grit and oil from her face, but she didn't present anything more than a common peasant.

"Tell me."

The words flowed free, and in those words were hooks that dangled above Sammy, bounds of energy and lust, intended to *lure* and *control*. Sammy shrugged, took a chug off his beer, then looked down at Margaret, "You *ain't* no Owens daughter. The *Maul* was *wance* pride *a'* the Owens military. Vanguard! We was always on *a'* front lines, each of us born *an'* bred for war."

Margaret ran her nails up Sammy's back, over his cotton tunic, dyed a deep shade of green. When she reached his neck, she lay fingertips into his flesh and slid her hand into his shortly shorn hair. His skin was sticky with old sweat and maybe a little grease.

Sammy is just a boy, no older than thirteen. He was always big for his age, and when it was time to spar an older child, he'd been eager to try his skill against a more experienced combatant. The brawl didn't last long, and Sammy was brutal. His opponent got a few good hits in, but the fight was over quickly, and Sammy was beating his face so savagely that he could have drowned in the warm copper of fresh blood.

"Mmm," Margaret's moan was audible. She caught her breath and continued to explore the creases in Sammy's neck and his lumpy skull with bare fingers, "You're right, I'm no Owens daughter. I came west with the Antecedents."

Sammy threw his head back and hacked up phlegm, spitting it across the counter, onto the floor behind the bar. The two older men who tended drinks either didn't notice or wished to make no quarrel with Sammy.

"*Fuck* Antecedents. *They's* just guests, the *Maul'll* drop on them someday."

Give me all your anger, Margaret stood up from her stool, left foot braced on a rung, her other on the rail. Standing off the ground, Margaret was just tall enough to press her lips into Sammy's big neck. She could taste the blood on his teeth in childhood memories, burrowed so deep in him now that no nerve twitched without her approval. He was too drunk to realize that a witch ensnared him

"They're not *so bad*, Antecedents. You'll learn to love them, *to kneel for them*."

Give me all your anger!

Sammy did. He twisted on his stool, a hundred stones pressing down, his rage was no less tangible than the bar or tankards.

Sammy's heavy hand reached out for the small woman, dirty behind the ears. She smelled like grease and carbon, and it titillated him. He wanted to break her neck, but not so much as he wanted to fuck her, fuck her mouth closed, fuck the disrespect out of her. He grabbed her throat, pressing her spine to his palm, constricting her breath, slowing her blood flow. If he could just strike her with the glass tankard, right across her skull, that would shut her smart mouth, teach her to come to an Owens bar and talk about kneeling for Antecedents.

Margaret tugged at her hooks, all her threads deep under his skin. He was a ponderous creature, he never felt the tickle of her needles, never imagined the web she was weaving around him. His left hand released the beer and slammed down onto the sticky bartop. His right hand clutched her throat, tightening around her neck just as hard as he wanted to.

Just as hard as she wanted him to.

Margaret bared her crooked teeth, snarling at Sammy, inhaling desperately for whatever air she could pull through her compressed windpipe. Adrenaline chattered in her blood, faster than the alcohol, lifting her away from the marrow of all responsibility.

"It's too bad the 3rd Army never met your *Maul*," Margaret rasped, her voice a squeak, each syllable and vowel forced. She could lighten his grip, but it would bore her, "My boys would have eaten you alive."

No part of Sammy held the reins, he was angry beyond imagining. For Margaret it tasted like she was drinking the sun and swimming naked in moist, humid grasses of a summer field, drunk on the odor of deep, rich soil. There was no drug in existence that could compare to that spiraling lust, no whiskey sweet enough, nothing so wicked and provocative. This was where Margaret lived, in the raging human mind. This was between her and Sammy, and when she was done with him, they'd both have taken something they desired.

Rather than allowing Sammy to land endless closed fist impacts on her face, Margaret released the tension in his hands and allowed him to slap her, once, twice, even three times. She was choking on her own spittle and was only content when he split her lip. The blood in his mind became a tangible thing in her mouth. She didn't allow him to smash her skull into the bar, instead Sammy found himself shoving away the barstools and hammering into her back with his elbow. Her torso was pressed down, forcing her into the bar top, pressing her breasts painfully against ribs. She gasped at air for the first time in many minutes. Her vision was a haze, she'd allowed him to choke her to the edge of blacking out.

She didn't care what the half-awake denizens of the bar thought. They were no more interesting than crabgrass. This was her private world and if anyone cared to *watch*, or *walk away*, that was their own business.

Sammy pressed Margaret's face down into the bar. It smelled pungent like alcohol and vomit, a million jumbled memories sparked and sputtered around her, and she lost herself as Sammy ripped into her clothes and undergarments. She forgot her safety for a few seconds; he hurt her more meaningfully now, his nails digging into her flesh and carving out bloody grooves.

Margaret allowed Sammy to *fuck her with all the hate he could muster*. For long minutes she was the personification of everything he truly loathed. She was the Antecedent Empire, she was Alexander Lopez. She was the girl that broke his heart when he was seventeen years old, and the wife that cheated on him. The wife he loved too much to harm for that infraction, the wife he *still* loved. She was even Aurora Owens, the liege he'd sworn himself to as a child who betrayed his trust with surrender.

I would have died for you, his mind erupted like a volcano, *I would have fought them to my death. My father, my mother, my sisters would have fought their Empire until we were no more. Why would you have denied us such a glorious death? We loved you. We loved you!*

When Sammy erupted inside Margaret, she took this as a form of *payment*. It wasn't a physical climax she sought, it was the final confession. It was his darkest secret, a part of him buried so deep that it would fester for a lifetime.

Margaret, satisfied, wasn't about to steal from Sammy. He wasn't an *evil* man, just a broken creature she'd provoked beyond reason. He'd offered her everything she wanted, he'd given her what she most needed to survive *a day like today*.

Now, he'd take his remittance.

"*Pull me up and hold me close.*" Margaret said the words, and there was power in her voice. Any bystanders would have known now that she was a witch. She didn't simply command the uninclined Sammy, she verbalized her will.

Sammy obliged her, pulling her up and pressing her back against his chest. She's covered in sweat, semen dripping down her legs. His big arm pressed her chest in, and she found herself panting for long moments before she could speak.

"*Aurora Owens betrayed you,*" Margaret's voice still vibrated and warped the air around her lips. She was bending energy, *raw magic*, flowing from her loins to throat, filling her lungs and opening her mind to see not merely the bar around her, but the city block and even the whole of San Francisco. "*She was unworthy of your love. I am not. Love me and I shall never betray you. If you walk with me to hell, I will give you such a glorious death that your Maul shall sing of your deeds for a hundred years to come.*"

Margaret could feel the big man heaving his breath behind her and pulled his arms away, turning to face him. Tiptoes still balanced on the rail below her, she was exhausted, spent in emotional and physical ways that went far beyond something as simple as *sex*.

Sammy was calm now, voice still stout, full of pride, but also a strange sort of awe. As though he spoke directly to the god of his forefathers. Margaret was letting it leach into her bones now, locking it up, saving it for later. It'd never be as effluvious as this moment, but in a dire place or time, she *could* call upon it.

"I will keep my promise if we meet again."

Margaret reached up and ran her fingers down his fleshy, moist face. Stubble prickled at her fingers and she could feel serenity in his mind, a release from the pain he'd known.

With that, Margaret offered him a sincere smile and stepped down from the bar rail. Half of the patrons had left during her *hatefuck*, the other half worked hard to ignore their conversation. She pulled her clothes back together as best she could, tattered and ripped, and availed herself as lead battlewitch of the Antecedent Empire.

Despite her small size, despite the stains she was caked in, Margaret strode back to the streets of San Francisco easily ten feet tall.

Stockton, California

The original seat of government for House Owens had been built on top of a college campus just north of downtown. When the Antecedent Empire came, they built further upon that seat and provided most of their senior officers dwelling in nearby buildings, many of which had once been hotels before the Collapse.

For Margaret, she had desired a more private abode. Regardless of her affection for the 3rd Army, she simply had no desire to be a part of the crude Antecedent dismantling of Owens' city-state. She could *feel* what Aurora Owens had built, she could hear men with hammers and nails raising a new world from ashes of the old. They whistled and sang, and as Antecedent office displaced those memories, so too did the music vanish.

Margaret had taken up a home on Atherton island, a small lump of land connected to Stockton, huddled against the blue and brown San Joaquin River. On the other side of that river was the great city wall of Stockton, shadowing her residence most of the day and keeping it cool in all but the noon hours. She had hired local gardeners to keep grounds, along with the two servants she'd maintained in her years on campaign. One was a lady's maid, the other a cook. The maid was a woman a few years younger than Margaret, named Janet Lécuyer. Her parents had been French, tourists stranded in a foreign land during the Collapse, and first citizens of the Antecedent States. Back in Crafton, Janet had tailored several dresses for Margaret, though her talents extended beyond stitchcraft, to general housekeeping. Margaret *could* dress herself without help, she very much preferred *not* to. Janet was well paid, and the two were as close as a battlewitch and stitchwitch could be.

"My Lady, you have a guest." Janet spoke with a *puckered* accent, as though she was holding her lips in preparation for a kiss that never came. She pronounced her own name *'Gee-nette,'* and referred to her Lady as *'Mar-gar-uete.'*

Margaret turned away from her dining room wall. She was wearing black pantaloons, drawn up at her waist and calves with golden cord. The fabric was a thick cotton that wrinkled a thousand times, crisp from drying in the sun. Her feet were bare on a stonework floor, and above the waist she only wore a bra to offer support up and over her shoulders, animal bone lined with lace. Both garments were hand manufactured for her alone by Janet: seamed, cut and assembled.

"Who is it?"

Janet shrugged. She was tall and her furrowed brow was a poor missive for her welcoming, brown eyes. "I know not, Lady. They wear Antecedent uniform."

"Is it a gentleman?" Margaret asked, despite herself, considering Townsend more often than she wished.

"No, Lady, it is a woman." Janet swept her hands up from her waist, drawing an underline of breasts in the air with index fingers.

It's for the best, anyway.

Margaret's face flushed for a moment. She had rules, molded like clay over the years, a fluid sculpture. *Never* return to a lover's bed. You could also forget their faces, once *you fucked* them. *You could walk away from the tethers, bring them no harm, allow them no power, and best of all, never weep when they died.*

"See her in, Janet." Margaret nodded, walking away from the blanched and textured wall she'd been working.

With her index finger and thumb, Margaret gripped the largest piece of charcoal in her right hand while her left held a collection of smaller flakes. Each shaped and worn differently, allowing her to apply different styles and volumes in soot. Her hands were pitch black for several inches above her wrists.

The wall behind her was swept up in an ocean of atramentous monochrome, moving and dancing like leaves caught in a river as the light shifted and struck at different angles. This was the most recent in torrent of murals that stretched from the wall where Janet stood, perhaps ten feet away, across the dining room and towards the window on Margaret's right. They were all memories, trinkets she'd purchased and bartered for.

She was creating the boy's face that Sammy had pummeled in his childhood, but in her creation the eyes had swollen shut and blood had become a flowering wreath upon his brow. She wasn't merely sketching memories, she was expressing the emotions she *felt* in those moments. It was a habit she'd kept her whole life, even as a girl she'd etched the world as it tasted on her lips in midnight black, grinding colors in so deep that the walls changed texture; or delicate hints of shades, each darker than the one before.

When Janet returned, she gestured toward the dining room and a slender woman entered. She was easily over six feet tall with a long, narrow, neck. Platinum hair shaved close on the sides and a braid ran down the zenith of her scalp. Her dress uniform of blue slacks and white jacket was dusted and stained from travel, but her face and hands were clean.

"Lady Mayhem," the adjunct, based on her patches and collar pips, nodded briskly.

"Lieutenant," Margret didn't return a nod or a bow.

"I bring a private message from Lady Manticore, 2nd Army," the tall officer glanced over to Janet, scowling.

"*Yes,*" Margaret chuckled, "I know Geraldine well. What does she wish?"

Janet was no fool; as servant to a battlewitch, *lead battlewitch of the Antecedent Empire*, she commanded more authority than a young officer could dream of. She simply crossed her arms and smirked. The officer turned back to Margaret after a moment, her nose wrinkled, and replied, "It's private."

"*Yes,*" Margaret answered a second time, blinking slowly. The servant knew this game well, Margaret would never allow anyone else to command her about a room. When their eyes met Janet nodded, turned and exited the room. Only upon her departure did the blonde Lieutenant stride toward Margaret, a walk so quick, and intense, that Margaret briefly considered this an attack.

Once the officer stopped, she reached into her jacket and removed a small slip of paper, holding it out, waiting for Margaret to accept.

She *did* accept, but only after nearly a minute of holding eye contact. The young woman was doing her *best* to maintain military standards, and clearly didn't *intend* to step on Margaret's nerves. This didn't change the fact that she *was*, nor did it change the fact that Margaret was inclined to step on *her* nerves in return.

The slip of paper was wrinkled at the edges and looked like something torn from an old and yellowed notebook. In graphite was a single word, *'windtalker.'*

Margaret knew what this was and closed her eyes a moment.

As the syllables formed out loud, the young officer's eyes rolled up into her head and her arms went slack, shoulders low, while her head dropped forward as if her neck could no longer support the weight.

"*Margaret,*" the voice that came out of the officer's lips was Geraldine Bianchi's surly rasp. In person, she was a lifelong chain smoker, her voice a contralto dragged through gravel, stumbling through one of various east coast accents. She hammered on her "r's" like nails, and cast "d's" to the wind like a fly fisherman. "*I hope yuh' fuckin' great up there in tha' redwoods an' shit. Tucson fell to tha' 2nd Army this afternoon. Shitlicking cuckolds fucking folded like a fuckin' lawn chair. Yuh' brother is on his way with tha' 1st Army, a detached a command element. Half of tha' 2nd Army will remain inna' south, garrison against tha' Republic of Texas. Tha' rest'll head for Stockton. I'm sending yuh' this fucking message because I know yuh' stepping tha' fuck down. I'll see yuh' in Stockton soon, to relieve yuh'. Then we'll relieve a few bottles of whiskey together, amiright?*"

When the officer's lips stopped moving, she didn't return to her senses immediately. It was a mind recording. An experienced witch could leave an impression of themselves in another's memories, hidden behind a spoken trigger that *they* themselves implanted. It was a difficult task, but also far more private than anything like a letter.

Margaret's eyes were heavy with tears.

Geraldine was a pre-Collapse witch, like Maggi, older and kinder, despite her language. She'd been, more than once, a fantasy stand-in as mother, just like Aurora Owens. Geraldine would take no joy in assuming her command, but she'd also never let a friend down.

As the blonde officer started to regain her wits, Margaret spun on her toes and pressed away the urge to wipe at her tearing face, smearing carbon everywhere.

"Lady Mayhem?" Margaret heard the officer say, to her back.

She was disgusted by her clean accent, even pronunciations; it was an insult to Margaret's aural sensibilities after Geraldine's message.

"When did Manticore give you this message?" Margaret asked, coldly, crossing her arms up under bra with her chin tipped down. From this angle there was a glint of white stone, from where *the eye that does not see* hid between her breasts.

"Shortly after the new year, Lady."

The officer answered the question, curtly, promptly, so keen to impress. The 1st Army wouldn't arrive for a while yet, but if Alexander and Geraldine traveled with fast vanguard, they'd be in Stockton by perhaps a week distant, two at the latest.

Decades of service to the Empire, and *this was it*. Just a few more weeks.

"Please, leave me," Margaret told the officer. She didn't want the woman to see her tears and she didn't want to explain herself. More than anything else, she just didn't want to be near this polished creature, this denizen of Alexander's new world with her perfect Imperial English.

Good riddance, she thought, and allowed her pulse a moment to relax.

Her mind was playing a game of toss ball, and before she had fully puzzled out her words, she decided to act without further consideration.

"Janet!" Margaret shouted, turning and looking for a towel to wipe at her face, "Fetch me a day dress. I'm going out this afternoon. *Low in the tits*, if you please."

2:01pm February 20th, 39 Veilfall

Stockton, California

Margaret had forgotten Janet dressing her, all snaps and laces, as the servant muttered to herself about measurements, cooing. She'd also forgotten her carriage ride toward the former Owens palace, and the center of 3rd Army command. She *knew* she'd nodded and waved politely as officers paid her respects, welcomed her, or questioned her. She may have even spoken to them, answered those questions, or made cheerful small talk. Perhaps a wink here or a blown kiss there. Try as she might; however, those details were cast aside in the blinding light of her own disbelief at what she was about to do.

You're a grown fucking woman, you're a battlewitch feared across North America, and you will not be defeated by a door.

"I'm going to be defeated by this door," Margaret whispered to herself.

Lieutenant General Townsend's secretary had waved Margaret past, and into the small waiting room which opened into his office. Outside the main hall were a half dozen such doors, each employing a separate assistant, banging away at steel typewriters, making notes, filing folders, or transcribing documents by hand. Townsend kept the largest of these offices at the end of a wide hallway. He also had the prettiest secretary, the most impressive door, and a waiting room with leather stitched sofas and a disintegrating bear rug. The animal's head had been chewed at over the years by rats, and its glass eyes were missing. Despite this, it still provided a menacing welcome.

At Margaret's *will*, Townsend's secretary, with her pert breasts and upturned nose, did *not* tell him that she arrived. Neither of the two women had spoken, but Margaret *had* rummaged briefly through her mind, wondering if Townsend had taken her into his office before. Laid her across the table, one hand gripping at her wrists while the other drew up her linen skirts, palm crossing her buttocks. The notion didn't *anger* Margaret, far from it; she found the notion titillating.

She would have enjoyed watching Townsend, through another woman's eyes, free of the control that Margaret herself maintained with any lover.

The secretary had been a disappointment, and so had Townsend. She had a mind full of rosters and troop rotations, and today she was making hand copies of a dozen records that catalogued 3rd Army debauchery in the bars and brothels of Stockton.

A few feet from the wooden door, stained deep mahogany with a steel nameplate, bolted a foot above her eye level. She studied the engraving, wondered who'd done the work, a blacksmith from the Empire or a local businessman? Or maybe it was manufactured for Townsend years ago, and he brought it with him to mark whatever office he held?

You're just stalling.

"I'm just stalling." Margaret whispered again.

She closed her eyes and reached her right hand for the doorknob. Her leather gloves squeaked on the brass, the catch released, and she walked directly inside.

"Lady Mayhem?" Townsend's voice cracked when he spoke.

Margaret opened her eyes after three steps into the room. Townsend's office was once a sprawling suite with a lowered tile floor, appointed seating, and a huge desk; likely antique even before the collapse. The wide windows that looked out onto the bustle of Stockton spread deep yellow light across the room and shadowed parts of Townsend's face. He was much more impressive here, stiff and squared away in his chair, all his attention drawn up, a kind of armor no different from the sort of magic Margaret kept.

Margaret's jaw fell open for one second, then two, before she replied to him, "Lieutenant General."

Townsend paused, placing his palms on the table, watching her. His moustache seemed more robust, and his tone bordered on angry, "*What are you doing here?*"

Townsend had *not* been the first man that Margaret was drawn to so intimately. This wasn't the first time in her life that she'd *wanted* to see someone more than *once*. This was; however, the first time she'd ever acted on these desires, and she found herself stumbling like a fool, crippled by a life of granite rules and personal self-discipline. She was now anemic in her talents and confidence.

"I've come," Margaret swallowed, holding in check all the carbonation that threatened to burn away her esophagus, "to speak with you."

Townsend's gray eyes watched her. He tilted his head and she noticed the little wrinkles above his ears, and the lines on either side of his mouth. He was concerned, *confused*, on guard as though she wished to harm him.

"What can I do for you, Lady Mayhem?" He replied.

"Do you remember the night, at the gala?" Margaret began, taking another step forward. Townsend smoked in his office, the odor of stale tobacco was thick, an embrace, and Margaret yearned for a twig suddenly. "*Tell me the truth*. Tell me to leave, Commander."

Townsend did not reply. Rather, he reached for a tin of cigarettes on his desk and withdrew a heavy lighter that seemed to act as a paperweight. It was stout and cylindrical, made of a dried clay that was set with hundreds of broken mirror shards. He leaned in to light the twig, inhaled deeply and exhaled. The smoke was caught in afternoon light and told stories.

Margaret continued, shaken, but determined, "I'm a *witch. I can smell a lie,* I can see your words and taste your emotions. You're confused right now, on guard. There's a gun in your desk drawer, maybe two. You're afraid you may have to shoot me. You're afraid you've done something to offend." Margaret stopped, her voice dropping low as she spoke. "I can't *stop* being what I was born, I can't stay *out* of your mind, I can't stop bending the world around me. If that's too much for you, tell me to leave, commander."

Townsend relaxed to some degree, but she admired his dedication, his discipline. He was no fool, and when he answered, he spoke with great care.

"I don't wish you to leave."

To Margaret's mind this was no different from battle. The enemy had been sighted, and her forces were on the move. She could *see* them, *feel* them, and she waited for her moment to strike when all around her was fire and mud. The worst of it was over now, it was time to *engage*.

"No matter how hard I try to find offense, no matter how much I try to laugh at your moustache, or *forget* you, I keep failing. I find that I *like you* and want to learn whether or not that's something we have in common."

Townsend answered quicker than Margaret had expected, and she realized she shouldn't have been surprised, "You're a *witch*. Wouldn't you be happier with someone… *else*?"

"Witches are *cruel*," Margaret replied, just as easily, dropping her hands, palms to hips, "We are by nature competitive, *mean*, we like to revel in our power. I've never bedded one, as rare as male witches are. I've spent my *entire life* in service, I've only known soldiers, only *loved* soldiers. We have more in common than I could share with another inclined."

Margaret could no longer read Townsend, his fret was gone, his worry, but she couldn't dig past his eyes or smell his intent. She honestly had *no idea* what he was about to say next. That was a rare experience for her, and Margaret's pulse snapped at the thrill of it.

"Is this a joke?" Townsend replied slowly.

That's not what I expected.

"I don't care for jokes. I have a younger brother who *did*, and I'm quite satisfied off *that* experience." Margaret closed her eyes, cracked her jaw with one hand, "When Alexander was a boy, he convinced me to take him past the tank traps of Crafton. He knew of a place our mother went, to be alone, and *swore* that she'd be happy to see us. We got *lost* of course, Alexander had made the whole thing up. Maggi didn't appreciate the risk. When she caught up with us, she *beat the shit* out of me while her son laughed his handsome little head off. So, *no*, Lieutenant General, if you think I'm the sort of person who'd get a giggle out of *fucking with you*, you're mistaken."

No one alive, save Alexander Lopez, knew that story. It was a difficult memory to repeat. Maggi's rage was legendary, and it was one more reminder that Margaret wasn't Maggi's *real* daughter. One more reminder that Alexander was the boy who would be king.

When Townsend answered he spoke softer, in a tone Margaret had not heard before. In their intimate moments, he'd spoken almost submissively, but now he regarded Margaret as a peer, an *equal*.

That was all that she wanted from him.

"Thank you," is all he said, and she could feel it press into her flesh and raise the short hairs on the back of her arms.

"At home I'm no more than the woman who stands before you."

Townsend stood, pulling another cigarette from the metal tin, and stepped around his desk. He seemed larger now, a towering master of his domain here in the office he kept.

"A secret for a secret, then. I've *desired* you since the siege of Saint Louis. I was just a junior commander then, and you walked the formations in a *yellow* ball gown, train covered in mud, wearing your plate carrier. It didn't fit right because of your breasts. Your hair was full of flowers, and I swear to this day *I could smell those flowers*. You told us that if we marched at your side we would live forever, a history that you would personally carve in granite."

Margaret giggled, feeling her cheeks flush, "You *did* smell the flowers. I was projecting that into your minds, the minds of a thousand men. I didn't want you to be afraid, I didn't want you to believe you were *fodder* for me. I wanted each and every one of you to know I would be there, *with you*. You needn't face the nightmares alone."

Townsend met Margaret's eyes, taking another drag off his cigarette. He extended a hand, offering her the second cigarette he'd withdrawn, "The next time I saw you, your flowers were gone, your dress was tattered. A *lot* of men fell for you at Saint Louis, Lady Mayhem."

Margaret's frame was but a child before Townsend. True to her request of Janet, the sleeveless doublet she wore dropped low, her breasts pale and veined blue in sunlight. The doublet itself was manufactured from velvet, in a damask flower brocade.

"I never lied. *I loved each and every one of you*."

Margaret accepted the cigarette and allowed salted tears to trickle across her cheeks. She *wanted* Townsend to see that, she *wanted* to be an ordinary woman, here and now, for his eyes.

Townsend retrieved another lighter from his slacks and offered a flame to Margaret. She accepted, leaning in, purposefully so he could better see her cleavage.

"I suppose we have some ground rules we'd need to cover," Townsend said.

Margaret nodded, her eyes burning, as she straightens up. The twig was hot when she inhaled it, and she'd lost her taste for tobacco since last the two had slept together.

"First, you're not to call me *Lady Mayhem* in private. My name is *Margaret*, and it's what I'd like to be called." Margaret coughed on the cigarette, raising back of hand to her lips before she spoke again, "Second, you're not to speak *up* to me again. You speak to me like an *equal*."

Townsend audibly ground his teeth and corrected himself, "A battlewitch is *always* the ranking commander at war."

"We're not at war, are we?" Margaret smiled, inhaling another puff of the cigarette, "I never chose to overrule a good commander, we were always a team. To be honest, that's the closest I've ever known to a *real* relationship."

Townsend turned, raising his brows, and stamped his own twig out in one of the two ashtrays sitting on his desk, "I ask for privacy. Whatever *we* share, we share together. We don't exist for my men, we don't exist for morale, we're not *the flowers in your hair*."

Margaret understood why he requested this, and she couldn't blame him. A witch always played the crowd, a witch was *always* a showman of the circus. "You're not my *pet*, you're someone I *like*, and I don't treat people I like poorly."

Townsend turned his gaze back to Margaret, and his brow was heavy and grim. No mask between them now, there was something unveiled in his eyes.

The twig burned down to Margaret's fingertips. She felt hot cherry next to her flesh, and she didn't move to put it out yet. "I'm also going to ask you to accompany me to a banquet. I haven't a day yet. It's a *date*. A public date. *All* of your junior commanders will hear of it. *All* the garrison soldiers will know that you're the man who *fucked* Lady Mayhem twice and took her to banquet. A first among nobles and *scoundrels* alike."

Townsend seemed to bristle at this, then tilted his head, a smile creeping across his face. No matter how serious he could be, behind his bushy moustache, a boy was peering out at Margaret with the understanding of a secret joke between them.

Margaret's cherry was burning her index and forefinger. It hurt, but not enough to drop the embers on Townsend's tile. She quietly leaned forward and placed the remains of the tobacco in his ashtray.

"You'll meet me, in my home, the day of that banquet. At sunset."

With that, Margaret turned, walking away from Townsend. Her wake pulled at his energy, entangled his desire and his adrenaline. *The flutter in his chest* may as well have been fruit she'd picked directly from a tree, branches laden low. She *was* giving him a gift to pay for the golden treasure she stole from him now.

"*Wait*, Margaret," *That's the first time he's spoken my name,* "why is there a banquet being thrown?"

"In celebration," Margaret studied the blisters on her skin, red and dirty, her back arching toward Townsend, "my brother and Lady Manticore return from the southwest, in triumph. The Empire is complete, the *wars are over*."

8:18am February 25th, 39 Veilfall

Stockton, California

French Camp Gate was the southernmost entrance into Stockton. The wide highway that drove north narrowed under Stockton's great walls, with multiple sub streets branching off across the arena. Smaller farms made a living at the outskirts of the city, along with hundreds of warehouses, some of which dated back to before the Collapse. Trade goods coming north from the port of San Francisco would offload caravans and wagon trains, while steam engines from the east divested their properties, north of Stormair; the largest military base west of the great Sierra Nevada.

Stormair had been an airport prior to the Collapse. Aurora Owens herself was said to have led a siege against Federal forces that occupied the area. Nearly four decades later it had become a sprawling fort that housed at least a one-third of the 3rd Army's total infantry and mechanized units, along with virtually all engineering and support corp.

Margaret stood just outside Stockton's walls, on the West Side Highway, where the Arch banked east toward Stormair. The concrete branched up at a wide angle and curved away, toward some of the smaller warehouses. Part of the Arch was still pre-Collapse, but it had been widened, allowing the former House Owens army to deploy their armored vehicles, double-wide in case of a siege.

There were no trees or scrub here, only tan and beige concrete, stained yellow and sooty by rubber and motor oil. Beyond the wall's tank traps the air was low and hazy with diesel smoke and cattle excrement, thick, humid and burning away the cool ease of night. Margaret could smell livestock fields to the west, and alfalfa farms to the south, a palpable nebula which harassed her sinuses and made her eyes weak for sleep, puffy and red. Dust devils gathered, spun up, and fell, as countless vehicles, line by line, rolled across the Arch.

This was the command element that Lady Manticore had spoken of, mechanized troops, returning from the south. Roughly *eight-hundred men*, riding close to *two-hundred* vehicles. It was a mix of old-world military transports, MRAPs, HMMWVs, conventional trucks and 4x4s converted to technicals, mounting belt fed machine guns or autocannons. Smaller vehicles with seven-slot grills had Antecedent infantry hanging off their side doors, while large vehicles contained their soldiers inside. None of the trucks ran clean, *all* of them heaved a thick tidal wave of black soot, engines choked for fresh air, running loud with exhaust leaks or straight headers. Their tan and brown desert camouflage had been highlighted black and sometimes only grill lights could be seen through the smoke, a looming haze that rambled and twisted like some giant snake, a creature of its own awesome dread.

Burning petrol and oil were a lover's kiss at the nape of Margaret's neck. She'd always traveled with a fast, mechanized unit, light armor and fire support. She'd ridden on the outside of the smaller trucks a hundred times to let the wounded or sick take seats, her arms aching after eight hours on the road, her goggles black with grime and her lungs choked and burning.

I'll never ride to war again, she ruminated, wistfully. She would *miss this*.

Hungry, *sleepy*, Margaret waved down one of the rolling cart vendors who sold their wares outside the walls. As the day progressed closer to noon, this highway would become packed by cart and wagon, petrol transport and pedestrian. Stockton's streets were mostly post-Collapse, too narrow for traffic, and limited to day-permits. Hundreds, *thousands,* would wait on the highway into late evening. It was no surprise that plenty of entrepreneurs found themselves heavy in coin, catering to this never-ending flood of humanity.

The peddler was in his early seventies and wore a dark orange tunic stained by the same engine carbon that covered everything else at the gates. His glasses were oversized, with a wide crack through the left lens, and a long beard that was more salt than pepper. He greeted her politely, nodding once and twice, then accepted the hand she offered, her *naked hand.*

Before the Collapse this man's family owned a restaurant in north Sacramento. Margaret pressed other images away, along with memories of the Collapse, the dead and dying. For a moment, for a *very brief moment*, she thought she could smell Sacramento ablaze. The *memory* was more violent than a punch to the gut, a wave of heat she thought might burn her flesh off.

Margaret watched the man in his orange tunic prepare brightly seasoned meat on a stick over his makeshift rattle cart, burning wood and kerosene. She noticed his hands and wrists were burned, long ago.

Though she wished the old man no ill, she paid him and brushed him off. These were memories for days far darker. The Collapse was a demon she kept locked far away from her waking existence. There were *millions* of sad stories, just like the vendor's, that could be found in a handshake, brushed flesh, or a kiss, all emoting screams in the night. Allowing the crushing sorrow of those dreams to break and pull apart your bones did *no one* any good.

The meat was likely chicken, but perhaps mixed with pigeon or something else stringy and lean. It was good, the seasoning bit back in Margaret's mouth. When she'd eaten it all, her fingers were red and yellow, gleaming with grease and lard, pieces of skin and fat buried under nails. She suckled at each digit, licking as a happy puppy might greet its master, chewing at her nails, and running her teeth under to dislodge any remaining food. She paused before pressing her hands down her cotton skirt. The dark yellow fabric was smeared with grease and spittle.

By now soldiers of the northbound battalion were walking past her, groups of friends, lance buddies, and fire teams mixed together. Filthy from the road. Their fantigues were covered in carbon and dust, mud, and even the tell-tell hue of dried blood. Most wore scarves or masks, to breathe on the road. They smelled rank, a vulgar mix of body odor and stale urine. They'd be on their way into Stockton, checking in with Townsend's command and getting bunk assignments before questing into bars and taverns, bath houses and brothels. Judging by their unit patches they were 9th Battalion, 1st Army. Alexander's own troops. Some wore painted logos of a snarling Doberman Pinscher, a few had leather patches naming them, *Dogs of War*.

Although they weren't *Margaret's boys*, they *felt* like her soldiers. They were buzzing from the road, amped up on the freedom of solid land and stirring with hunger. Margaret could *hear* the low jumble of their background thoughts, cursing across a spectrum of tawdry remarks. Undressing Margaret with their eyes or lost in visions of their own personal fetishes, to be pursued later tonight. It was a warbling yammer that tasted, *sounded*, like no other group of thoughts Margaret had ever known in her existence.

She would *miss this too*.

A young man, maybe sixteen or seventeen, charged up to Margaret, grabbing her waist and lifting her off the ground. She let him, and she *giggled* for it too. His arms felt like rebar and he planted a kiss on her lips before running off at a shout; "Stockton is one beautiful city!"

His lips felt like corn husks, his mind a firecracker held to her bosom. He was a young man, *burning with life*, the kind of energy that could wake up a sleepy old witch, or tempt her to cavort with the 1st Army tonight.

I'd shine poorly on Townsend if I fucked them, but no harm in a few drinks.

Before she could consider the possibilities further, Margaret's stomach turned. It wasn't her chicken-pigeon breakfast either. There was a high-pitched vibration around her, something that the uninclined 1st Army could never notice. It fractured the air and made her skin crawl as though her own sweat had been sucked inward, allowing it to fester and boil above her muscles.

It *was* a familiar sensation for Margaret. This is what Maggi Lopez had felt like to other witches. Unsettling and invasive, it was always difficult to spend time near her. Her jaw set and her brow furrowed as she remembered the time she spent near The Beast, the words of Aubriana, and even Aphrodite.

That contempt was exaggerated further when Margaret spotted Ramona's twin sister in a pack of rowdy soldiers returning from the Arch, vehicles parked and ticketed at Stormair.

She was a wider woman than Ramona, but Amihan Lopez had the same face, same features, same jawline and brows. She was bulkier, stronger in the shoulders and neck. Her short hair was a mad array of windswept havoc, bleached with potassium lye and stained deep red with various shades of henna. From ear to ear, across her face were two red lines, permanent tattoos, just like messy and colorful blemishes that ran down her neck, under scarf and goggles. Regardless of the face she shared with her sister, Amihan walked, gestured, and *smelled* like Maggi Lopez.

There was no avoiding her. Just as Margaret had sensed Amy first, so too had the young woman found Margaret. She was looking around, eyes wandering concrete and dust, blinking back at carbon when she noticed Margaret.

Amy shoved aside one of her companions, leaning into stride, and rushing for Margaret. As tall as her sister, she engulfed Margaret in a firm, almost painful embrace. No different from the rest of 9th Battalion, she reeked of rotten sweat and dirty fabric, her face beaded with sweat.

"*Aunt Mayy*," Amy laughed, careful to keep her skin off Margaret's skin, but running her hands down the older woman's grey blouse, "I'm sorry, I'm filthy from the road, I'm *so sorry*."

Are you sorry you gave a child up for adoption?

Margaret's face turned, no matter how hard she tried to hide it, and Amy noticed. "It's fine. They're just clothes, they'll wash."

"We're ahead of the 1st and 2nd Army." Amy turned, her tan cheeks a shade of rose, gesturing out across the soldiers returning down the Arch, "This is *my unit*, the 9th Battalion."

Amy was pressing for a compliment, as if these road weary men and women were somehow sacrosanct because they reported to *her*. Margaret did her best to satisfy the need for approval, placing hands on her hips, "They're a fine group," Margaret paused for a moment, squinting into the sun, "Geraldine isn't here, with you?"

Amy laughed, "No, I'm the command element. Father sent me to relieve you."

And just like that, Margaret's rage was a creature lose in company, a mongrel dog allowed into the dining room. Chomping at hands, yanking meat from the table and defecating in the corner. Her face screwed up in anger, lips peeling back to show her crooked, yellow teeth.

"*You?*"

Amy recoiled, stepping back with her hands up and palms out. They were black, save for the horizontal lines that ran down her palms and joints, "Dad told me you were going to retire. You're *retiring*, aren't you?"

Margaret's fists were clenched, shaking, her neck tensed, and her tongue was thick with a thousand words she wanted to yell. Amihan Lopez was a *junior battlewitch*, unable to command her powers any better than Ramona. "*Manticore* is our secondary battlewitch, it's her role to accept, not yours."

I coddled you when you wept for your mother, I taught you everything you know.

Margaret worked to keep her thoughts to herself, maintaining a degree of decorum. Soldiers of the 9th Battalion began to detour around the two women. They knew that Amy was now at odds with another inclined witch. The acrid air around them was choler and tasted like old pennies. It spun up into a wide, shallow, dust devil that was carving a thin circle around them in soot.

"It wasn't *my* call Mayy," Amy's nose wrinkled, along with the ink on her face, "you act like this is beneath you. Wouldn't you be *proud* that I was chosen to take your place?"

Margaret was at a loss for words. She huffed out an aggravated note, back stiff and chin upturned defiantly at the taller woman, "I served twenty years as your father's lead battlewitch, and when I decide to retire, he installs his *daughter* to replace me? What have you done to make *me* proud?"

Amy stepped back, putting roughly a yard between herself and Margaret. There was no hint of anger in deep brown eyes, but for a second it seemed to Margaret like she might run.

"I just wanted your respect, Mayy. I wanted to be a battlewitch like you *and* my grandmother."

Just like your grandmother.

Breathing heavy, chest falling and rising, Margaret poised as if she was about to take a swing at the larger woman. No amount of control could keep Margaret's temper in check, and her eyes were wide with rage, a smile stretching her face with foul sarcasm.

"Congratulations, you're *just like* Maggi. A self-centered and self-interested *bitch*."

It was a shout, and once it escaped Margaret's lips, she couldn't take it back. The 9th Battalion soldiers around them all heard it.

I shouldn't have said that.

Amy's eyes turned dark, and her mouth parted. She looked as if someone had slapped her, and though she'd never trade tears for insult, *hurt* crossed her face. Margaret *felt* something in Amy crack and recognized the sound of splitting wood.

Looking around her, Amy turned back at Margaret, aware that she was now on display for her unit to see. They'd remember this, they'd talk about it, they'd gossip later.

"I'll take it as a compliment, if you say I'm *just like The Bruja*."

"Her name is *Plague Dog,*" one of the 9th Battalion sneered at Margaret, moving to the side, and standing directly behind Amihan Lopez.

"She's *the Plague Dog,*" another one said, younger by far, a patch worn over his eye, face red and swollen from injury, "and she saved my *life*."

One by one, more 9th Battalion members joined her. They felt the trade of hostility between Margaret and Amy, no matter how uninclined they were. It was a siren call, the smell of fresh baked bread or the hum of a mother's lullaby, "Maybe I deserve your title after all, Mayy. I've been in the field fighting with the 9th. When was your last battle?"

Reno, I last fought at Reno. Two years ago, before the fall of House Owens.

"We should talk privately," Margaret realized what this had become, she could feel searing hate, and there was no way she could communicate *anything* to Amy here, with her men.

"Why not here?" Amy shrugged, cinching her lips, her face moist with sweat and grime, "Why don't *you* tell my men how *you* inspire loyalty?"

"We should talk privately," Margaret repeated, it was her turn to take a step back, separating herself further from Amihan. The confrontation was out of their hands, and Amy was placating a crowd.

I need to leave, I can win nothing here, Margaret thought.

"*Dogs of War,*" Amy shouted to roughly two dozen 9th Battalion soldiers, each one as dingy as her, "this is *Lady Mayhem* of the 3rd Army. You might have heard of her, the legendary *soldier slut*. Her regiments follow her because she's *fucked* most of them."

The 9th Battalion erupted in laughter, energy shifting once more. Amy was wielding it as a weapon now. As she moved her hands, each finger was trailing edges of string and tether. It wasn't the same as Margaret's magic, but the mob was at her control, and the taste had turned to sour oil, stale pepper and rattled *lust*. They were eyeing Margaret with loathing, a base need to cause *pain* for the sake of pain. Oozing animus and avidity, the Dogs of War wanted to rip Margaret's face off, rape her to death and light her on fire, *just because*.

What have you become, Amihan?

"*Fuck you*," Margaret showed her teeth, not willing to flee with her tail between her legs. She was backing up, toward the gates of Stockton, her hands down and ready to wield *real* magic in her own defense. She wouldn't show them barriers or let them know that she considered them a threat. They'd mistake it for *fear*, and Margaret would never have displayed such tawdry emotion.

Amy didn't answer her, and her mind was locked too tight, but at the edges of her energy, in the shadows of greasy hair, and stained fatigues, Margaret could taste the familiar hurt. It was the same bitter chew of Maggi's relentless regret.

"I should have fucking left you in that parking lot."

Margaret wanted to be *angry* at her niece. As angry as she'd always been, for her impulsive nature, but the only one she was angry with now was *herself*.

6:02pm February 27th, 39 Veilfall

Stockton, California

"Let's skip the red and yellow gown, Janet," Margaret whispered, her voice no more than a spring mist on window panes, "in fact let's skip all the gowns and dresses. I don't wish to present like an Owens aristocrat."

Margaret studied the charcoal paintings of her boudoir, fingertips drumming softly on a marble top vanity. It felt cool, forgiving, oil light causing her own sketches to be free and withering in a stage act.

Janet inquired, "Perhaps, Lady, I can make a suggestion?"

Nodding, Margaret acknowledged her, turning to see what she'd return with. To her surprise she'd gathered a molle corset and a *very* short, burgundy skirt, made from velvet and chiffon. The corset was field gear, practical and black with D-hooks and elastic fasteners.

"I'm not sure how I feel about that," Margaret blinked, leaning back, crossing her legs. "No, *maybe* I do know. This is an Antecedent banquet. *Only* officers from the 3rd Army garrison and the 9th Battalion will be there. I'm a *battlewitch*, not a *real* Lady."

When was your last battle?

Amihan's words bounced around in Margaret's head. It wasn't that she doubted herself, it was that Margaret genuinely believed Amy was *right*, the implication that she'd become soft and pampered behind Stockton's walls, that she'd lost her edge, and her taste for blood.

Margaret studied her reflection as Janet fixed the skirt and began lacing her corset from its center. Her hair had been styled, *puffed* out and full around her face, held with a mixture of alcohol, sap, oils and attar. Violet shadow crossed her eyelids, moving out toward her temples, and her lipstick was made from paraffin wax, olive, lard and ground roots.

Margaret *absolutely wanted* to stand out as much as the outfit suggested she would. She relished the idea of turning heads *away* from Amihan, even Ramona.

What would Townsend's subordinates think when the woman of their dreams sauntered in, at his arm, dressed like this?

No matter how *excited* she found herself, the confrontation with Amy did not subside in her mind. She could not let it go or move on to more pleasant thoughts. Amihan was *not* the woman she'd been. There was brutality in her eyes, clutching at her lashes and crawling across her rosy-tan cheeks.

"Fetch me the brown-suede boots, the ones I like, loose around the ankle," Margaret nodded to Janet once her corset was fully trussed, an overbust sweetheart, black coutil cotton with velvet bias strips, and a series of leather panels binding the molle.

The skirt *was* too short.

Janet returned from one of Margaret's closets with the suede boots when there was a knock at the front door. A silky cool tone stole at Margaret's mind, and she *felt* her niece close at hand, a familiar vibration in the air that only Ramona left behind. One of Margaret's other servants would offer admission.

"Get yourself some dinner. I'll want a few moments of privacy," Margaret told Janet as she finished tightening the straps at the back of each boot heel.

"Of course, Lady," Janet rose, before leaving the boudoir. Waiting for Ramona, Margaret withdrew her 9mm from a table. She dropped the magazine, checked it, then slapped it back into the pistol before racking the slide to chamber a round. The weapon fit neatly in one of her midsection holsters, latching snugly into the molle web of her corset.

Ramona's dress was supported by her own sweetheart corset, like Margaret's, strapless, exposing her narrow, curved shoulders. Her skin was a glistening bronze like windows catching dusk light, and her perfumes were an escort of their own device, arm in arm with her, sauntering through the room, lilac, cloves, benzoin, and storax. Her shadowed eyes didn't menace, they were deep pools of still water and storied ecstasy.

"*Always* with your damn *tit-holster*. It's not nearly as attractive as you think." Ramona shook her head, eyeing Margaret's pistol for several seconds.

Gods be fucked, she's beautiful.

"Putting your aunt to shame?" Margaret saw no point in suggesting otherwise, Ramona was every bit the *Hetaera* she claimed.

Ramona didn't answer, rather she smirked and glanced around for a place to sit. Margaret gestured to an over plump chez lounge near her northward window. It was green and gold, embroidered by hand, a gift to Margaret from one of the 3rd Army officers after the fall of Reno. It wasn't nearly as comfortable as it was *gorgeous*, a humbling piece of art that she loved.

"You've made Amy *quite* angry," Ramona sat, bent forward and fingers clutching down towards her bare shins, "she spent *hours* lamenting the southern gate."

Margaret bit her lower lip, then remembered her lipstick and waved both hands out furiously, "I'd speak with you, about that, if you'd listen."

For a moment Ramona examined Margaret, oil light dancing off her eyes, the twinkle casting her as something more innocent, "My sister and I have rarely been of the same mind, but Amihan *adores you.*"

Margaret didn't choose to avert her gaze or cower, she'd considered these words well and repeated them in her mind, "It's been a long time since you and Amy were my charges, *together*. How would you say I've treated your sister?"

Ramona's face changed, and when she spoke, it was slowly, with chosen tones, "If I only ever told you lies, the one truth I'd like you to believe from my lips is that Amihan has worshipped you since she was a child. You were her battlewitch hero, she followed all your teachings, *she* never took a god as her own. While I'd never trade your favor for the world, *she and I both know* that you never cared for her as much as you did me."

Margaret's pulse was a rhythmic surf, her tongue dry and thick. As she considered her reply, a second knock at the door came, this one louder and firmer. It was almost certainly Lieutenant General Townsend.

"Seat the commander in the dining room, I'll be out shortly." Margaret shouted past her hall, unwilling to leave this conversation immediately.

Ramona shook her head, and her tone returned to its more natural clipped, sing-song rhythm, "You wanted *me* to save the Empire from Amy. The only one who can save *anyone* from Amy is you. She's not Maggi. She's the witch you trained her to be."

She's not Maggi.

"She's not Maggi," was all Margaret could say, a dull victrola of her thoughts spat back to the air, for no benefit besides her own hearing.

Ramona's slender lips narrowed, barely smiling, "You've treated her as the *unwanted* child her entire life. What did I ever do to make you love *me* so much more?"

It was truer than Margaret wanted to admit. All these years she'd looked at Amy as a resurrected Maggi Lopez, a young fire eater who loved brawling. The girl had been impossible to discipline as a child, and while Ramona had sat quietly for meals, Amy had been the monster, pressing every button Margaret had to offer. She had fought on *everything*, challenged every lesson, deliberately went out of her way to anger her aunt. It seemed a forgone conclusion that the child took after her grandmother, that she'd end up a hard-drinking misanthrope who *no one* really loved.

Margaret's lips pressed tight, slowly shaking her head, before words erupted from parted lips, "She *always* got under my skin."

Ramona shrugged in reply, separating her palms as though she held a delicate vase of antique ceramic, "I wonder how often *you* got under your mother's skin."

Left to an endless sea of her own imagining, Margaret realized *she* had also been *that child*. She too had challenged *every* lesson that Maggi set forth, she'd disobeyed her mother's instructions, and for every time Alexander tricked her into a sadistic trap, *Margaret herself created plenty more trouble without anyone's help.*

"What have I done?"

Margaret didn't speak the words, but her lips moved regardless.

Ramona didn't answer that question. Rather, she unfolded her legs and stood, a fluid motion, both graceful and sensual. "I won't see you tonight. That was the other reason I came to visit, to wish you well in your evening."

Pulled away from a revelation, Margaret looked up to her favored niece, genuinely disappointed, and working to hide it from her face, "Oh? And where are you headed?"

"Lord Owens and I have dinner." Answered Ramona.

On any other night, Margaret could have bristled at the idea of her junior winning over Lord Owens. Perhaps even an *hour ago*, she would have been pricked by the casual rejection.

Margaret offered a smile every bit as warm and supple as buttered bread, fresh from a wood burning oven, "I'll see you another night, then. You can join me here, and you can drink to my retirement."

Ramona's returned smile was not nearly as warm, nor did she answer.

I deserve that, I suppose.

Before Margaret left her boudoir with Ramona, she unlatched the holster at her corset, squarely mounted under her breasts. For a rare moment she was self-conscious, considering the beautiful *Hetaera*, and she sat the pistol down from where she'd retrieved it.

6:44pm February 27th, 39 Veilfall

Stockton, California

Returning to the dining room, Ramona offered polite excuses to the Lieutenant General, gathering a coat from near the door to see herself out. Margaret followed, offering a goodbye, but Ramona only answered with a blown kiss. Not even a wink, or nod.

At her departure, Margaret took a moment to gather emotions and truss them up neatly about her mind. She didn't want to betray Townsend's grace with an ill temper.

Turning in her suede boots, she spied Townsend standing at the dining room table, eyes lost in shadows, examining Margaret's artwork that consumed every inch of wall. His hands were clutched at his back and he was still, in both mind and body.

"Townsend," Margaret smiled, for only herself, "am I allowed to promote you? *Lieutenant General* is an awkwardly long rank. *General* is so much easier on the tongue."

"*Ahh,*" Townsend looked around the room, stepping cautiously, as though he was watchful of traps, "That's a bad idea."

"Probably," Margaret nodded, "I have poor impulse control."

Townsend seemed uninterested in the banter, his voice trailing for a moment, as he studied the murals behind Margaret, "*What* are these?"

"Nothing." Margaret shook her head, glancing over to the etchings, then back to Townsend, larger than life in his blue and white dress wool. His cap was pushed sideways at a clever angle. By *rank*, he was allowed to wear the ribbons of every battle he'd commanded, whether or not he *fought*. Judging by the narrow collection over his heart, he'd chosen to disregard that privilege and wear only what had been earned in blood.

Don't lie to him, idiot, he's interested.

"No, they're *something*." Margaret corrected herself in a soft stutter.

"Is this your work? You're an artist?" Townsend approached another wall, this one an entirely different vantage point. Margaret had painted these a year earlier; they were memories of the Nebraska plains, unending fields of golden grass and a sky that seemed large enough to swallow her army whole.

"All of my life." Margaret's cheeks heated, and suddenly she was embarrassed.

You don't need to pretend you care, I'll fuck you all the same.

Margaret would have slapped herself, if it wouldn't have made the scene even more uncomfortable. The thought annoyed her, second guessing herself in Ramona's wake. That was another one of her rules, set in granite, a rule that she wouldn't allow to be broken: no one commanded her confidence.

"I had no idea." Townsend gestured at the deep onyx sketching, visibly lost in the art.

He's not pretending.

"I started sketching as a kid," Margaret squared herself away, approaching the man, much more confidently now, "I used my mother's eye shadow at first, then found charcoal. When I moved out on my own, Maggi and I stopped talking the way we used to. When I asked her things, when I tried to share with her, she didn't listen. She always said a good witch doesn't *paint the room with her emotions*. I was a teenager, and angry, and I wanted to do just that. I painted all the rooms."

"You never stopped." Townsend whispered.

The sketches he fixated on are a vast symphony of snakes spilling from a corpse, half buried in mud. The blonde wood behind was so heavily shaded in black and grey that even the strokes themselves took on a new texture.

Margaret shook her head, "Some are my memories, and some of them are memories I watched. I don't want them to be lost."

Townsend turned slowly and favored Margaret with eyes as warm as they were piercing. He didn't fear her, not the way the uninclined *always* did. Rather, he seemed to admire her, just as he had the charcoal murals. It felt like warm summer grass on bare feet to Margaret, a place she never knew she wished to visit, under a sky she didn't dream existed.

"Are you sure about this? Tonight?" Townsend asked her, pointedly, "I'd not be offended if you changed your mind, if you decided this was unwise."

Shaken free from her daydream, Margaret cinched up a polite grin and turned back to the dining room table, withdrawing gloves that Janet had left for her. They ran to the elbow, black velvet with square seams on each finger, tailored *only* for Margaret's hands. "What should I be unsure of, *Lieutenant General*? After tonight I cease to be lead battlewitch. I'm a free woman, and I wish to keep your company."

On the dining room table was a small wooden box, an inch wide, maybe an inch tall. There were no bevels, and the hinges were merely grey steel. It could have been the most ordinary thing in Margaret's home.

"What is that?" Townsend inquired, moving between the walls around them, closer to Margaret's side. Inside the box were loops of narrow, gold chain, held at either end by clasps. She wouldn't let *anyone* touch it, and she fastened it on her own, under stiff puffs of hair.

"Just an old piece of my mother's jewelry," Margaret replied, not giving Townsend the whole story, but also telling him the truth.

It took a moment before the necklace finally sat correctly. She'd commissioned it the morning after her confrontation with Amy Lopez, and she'd spent much of the day with an old-world jeweler as he crafted the item, refusing to leave it alone, refusing to be parted with it, even for a few hours.

Behind her, she heard Townsend say, "*Margaret.*"

Less a collection of syllables and more of a growl, an evocation of her very essence. Margaret blinked slowly, holding a hand to her midsection, "I like the way your voice sounds, speaking my name. You should let me ruin my lipstick on you."

Turning around, Margaret braced her palms down, onto the table, pressed her body up, scooting her buttocks across the lacquered wood, her knees pressed together, and her suede boots *tap, tap, tapping.* "I can't keep calling you *Townsend.*"

"Townsend is my family's *last* name, and I'm sure I once had a first name." The large man reached up to the leather buckle under his chin, fidgeting.

"You just don't remember?" Margaret offered, slowly, quietly. She shifted and spread her knees several inches. Her intimates were bright red silk. "It's okay. I don't remember my *last* name either. The one that belonged to my parents."

"Townsend is a good name," He nodded, looking down at Margaret, stepping forward, "it's been my name for plenty of years, it'll be my name for plenty more."

"As you wish," Margaret replied, and Townsend leaned in to kiss her. A few inches from her lips, a single index finger pressed into his chin, sliding up his lower lip. With her other hand, Margaret reached forward, groping for Townsend's pressed, white trousers, loosing each button.

"When I said I'd like to ruin my lipstick, I didn't mean by making out with you."

9:30pm February 27th, 39 Veilfall

Stormair, California

The banquet for returning 1st Army soldiers was not held in the House Owens palace. The grand ballroom of Lady Aurora Owens was dark this night. Rather, the banquet had been hosted at Stormair, just outside the city walls.

One of the old hangers had been partially emptied of the 3rd Army's armor rotation in order to host the small gathering. Only officers of the Antecedent Empire, currently in Stockton, had been invited. Perhaps fifty men, and a few women.

There was no band of violins and flutes. Rather, a field bard on raised steel, sawed away at an aged fiddle. He was young, his fatigues clean and his face shorn. His fingers darted and jerked around the faded fingerboard, playing old songs from before the Collapse along with Antecedent melodies. The strings warbled and vibrated at his whim, echoing across the hanger.

Two large dining tables were set close to him, each one accompanied with metal chairs and simple white plates. Wax candles burned and danced as a breeze interviewed the flame before fleeing away. Large rolling doors to the hanger fore were open by perhaps twenty or twenty-five feet, and night flooded oil stained tarmac.

This was the world that Margaret felt most comfortable in, these were men that she'd fought and died with much of her adult life. They didn't skulk about, perfumed and pretty, planning their next machination. Nor did they work hard to impress people they didn't like. Townsend's senior officers nodded and smiled, hiding snickers and holding their tongues when he led Margaret in. She had wrapped her own elbow around his forearm, free hand close to her pale chest, running an index finger across her collar bone.

I guess we all know what's down Townsend's pants for sure, Margaret heard from one officer, and *Luckiest son of a bitch this side of the Mississippi.*

She could choose whomever she wished to bed, but Margaret had never allowed herself to be displayed this way. Least of all near those she spent years traveling and fighting with.

As soon Amihan takes up my role, I'll never see them again, Margaret thought, gesturing Townsend down to brush his clean-shaven cheek with a genuine kiss, whispering, "As you make the rounds, remember that I can still taste your *cock*."

She didn't take the time to see his expression, she didn't *want* to. If he'd blushed, she'd have lost respect for him. If he'd shrugged it off, she'd have been wounded. It was best simply to set the comment down and walk away.

Several small carts, field service wagons for mess and coffee, had been rolled in to serve drinks. The service wagons were as clean as they could be, wheels encased in a permanent film of dust, the drawers and handles rusted dark red and worn smooth. Bottles of whiskey and bourbon had been neatly arranged, along with glass tumblers of a dozen different designs, so that those at the banquet could serve themselves. Between the clusters of alcohol were brass and copper chargers, full of local fruits and vegetables. Carrots, peaches, and even cherries, along with odd apple or orange.

As Margaret filled her chosen tumbler, a simple design, cylindrical with a star inlay on the base, she bumped someone's elbow. As she turned, she caught a stout woman in her late twenties grinning, biting into a red apple, juice running down her chin.

None of the 9th Battalion officers wore their blue jackets, rather they were dressed in black cotton button-ups, the undershirt of the Antecedent uniform, a contrast to their white wool slacks. Her skin was a deep shade of tan, and suspenders arched across her breasts, brows bushy, and hair had been braided into four separate rows across her skull. Each knot decorated with live 9mm rounds, giving her the look of a great horned creature.

"I'm sorry," Margaret nodded, politely.

"*I'm not.*"

When she spoke, her voice was a rasping, hushed tone. It made Margaret feel like a slab of meat had been thrown onto her sternum to sizzle, boiling fat down her corset, burning and exciting her intimate parts.

One of the tumblers, an inch or two from the wagons edge, tipped over and rolled, directly off the side, shattering on tarmac with a pop.

Margaret took a step back, all her attention on the woman who watched her under unkempt brows. She blinked and her eyes glazed gold, moving like pools of liquid, reflecting Margaret's slack jaw expression. With one hand she held her garnet apple, index finger and thumb at zenith and nadir. She spun the fruit with a single flick from her opposing hand.

When it stopped rotating, it faced Margaret with carefully carved cursive.

'*Legitimate Daughter.*'

"Try a bite!" The woman with golden eyes snapped, "*It's delicious!*"

Margaret took a second step back. "Who the *fuck* are you?"

The woman shook her head, holding up an index finger to waggle in Margaret's face. The air around the two smelled sweet, fragrant with citrus blossoms and salt.

"You can't guess?" With deft fingers she rolled the crimson apple around her wrist, then behind her back, grabbing it with her opposing hand. Upon its return, it was made of solid gold, fissured with a carved stem and leaves protruding from the top. "How about now? Should I ask your paramour if he prefers *power, beauty, or fame*?"

Which one would I be to him?

Margaret glanced at her tumbler, raising it to her lips and chugging away uncut whiskey. Liquor ran down her chin, across her throat and between her breasts, chilly in the night air. When she tilted her head down, the apple was gone and the woman with golden eyes shrugged, a maniacal grin stretching at her face.

"*Eris.*" Margaret's voice steadied.

The 9th Battalion officer cackled like a dying animal, gasping at the air, *snorting*, then she reached out to hammer a balled fist into Margaret's shoulder hard enough to bruise, "I *love* that you had to up-end a fifth of whiskey, just to say my name!"

She wanted to be anywhere else but with the golden-eyed flesh costume worn by a *chaos god*. Eris, like Ares, Tyr, and The Morrigan was worshipped by Antecedent soldiers the night before battle. Some claimed that they knew who would die in the morning; offered a vision of heads clutched by the fists of The Morrigan. Others carved in blood, begging favor of the Chaos Queen, that Eris may see them worthy of survival in the coming light. On campaign there was no room for gods like Aphrodite with her ocean breeze eyes.

"Say it for me. *Say it with those beautiful lips*, Margaret. Tell me there's no place for *fucking Aphrodite,*" Eris snarled answering Margaret's thoughts.

Margaret, remembering her failures, did exactly as she was told.

"On campaign there's no room for gods like Aphrodite."

Eris bit at the air, her teeth cracking loudly. The officer slid her left foot back, bowed gently to no one, and swung herself into a solo minuet, arms garishly waving over open tarmac, waist spinning and wrists fussing as if she groped and held an invisible partner. Margaret's gaze crossed the room, looking at the other officers, *all of whom were utterly ignoring the insanity that had unfolded.*

When Eris grew bored of whatever music played in her head, she spun around and crashed into Margaret, violently. The tumbler in Margaret's right hand flew loose, bounced off the wagon, and fell to the ground, another *pop* echoing in the hanger.

"You had Aphrodite's favor because you *love* unconditionally. That, and all the *fucking*." Eris moved gracefully behind Margaret, grinding her chest into the spin, hands groping upward and cupping the witch's breasts. "Didn't you ever get any diseases? I mean, *seriously*, you basically *fucked everyone*."

"*No.*" Margaret replied, less offended by the question itself than the fact that no one else had ever been brave enough to ask.

When the officer's fingers reached up, past Margaret's corset, roughly floundering against her chest, she found herself drowning in a feeling she'd known only in moments before a battle was waged. The moment when *everyone's* breath was held, when fear ceased to exist, and men had become immortal. It was a sibilation of pure anxiety, twisting up every muscle, a voice crying out against adrenaline and lust, *run away now, for all that you love, run!*

The sensation bled out from Eris, spreading through Margaret's bones, filling her wholly with the purest sense of anticipation she'd ever imagined.

Eris whispered down into Margaret's ear, "I was *there*, every time you walked into the fray. Tell me, *tell me Margaret,* what do you call it when you extend your mind across a thousand men who don't know they're dead yet?"

The savory piquancy of chaos was a sort of elation that dwarfed sexual forays. Margaret didn't hesitate to speak the words, "I call it *spreading my terrible wings over the battlefield.*"

Eris pulled her fingers back, shoving Margaret away from the mess wagons and pushing past her. As she did, two more tumblers fall to the tarmac, *pop, pop,* "Those aren't your wings, are they? Do you know what *I* look like free of this flesh and bone I wear? Free of costumes and lies? Those are *my terrible wings.*"

More than anything Margaret felt hungry now, free of Eris, broken from her touch. She was hungry for *battle*, for *blood*, and most of all she was starved for *chaos*.

A thousand men who didn't know they were dead yet.

Margaret had swept across their minds, a tidal wave, wrapping them close to unleash their primal fears, their instinctive paranoia. She couldn't control individuals on that scale; imparting a particular derangement was impossible. Each one *saw* something different. They would descend on each other, feral animals, clubbing brothers with rifle butts, ripping faces off, beating their commanders, shooting wildly.

Absolute chaos.

"*Thank you,*" Margaret moaned, one hand clutched to her chest, the other braced down on a wagon to steady herself. She bumped *another* tumbler, sending it skittering, bouncing once on the tarmac, and then shattering, *pop*.

"Don't thank me Margaret," Eris reached out and pulled Margaret's hands into her own, "I'm here to *fuck you.* You'll soon have your fill of chaos. The old gods seek to emerge, and they don't care who is broken in their wake. Maybe you'll die, *maybe you'll live.* I don't *really* care. I never sat at *their table*, I never *painted by numbers.*"

"*Fuck me?*" Margaret was lost in a hazy stupor of ataxia, her thoughts as tangled as a web of vines, coated in thorns, "I think I won't like that."

Eris smiled beyond Margaret's fluttering eyelids, a private smile, toothy and wild. Eyes of liquid gold ran down her face forming tears that reflected fruits, whiskey, and Margaret's lavender eyeshadow.

"You won't. But you've worshiped me for *so long*, how could I destroy you without a parting gift? Tailored just for you, the same as all your pretty dresses and corsets."

Eris wrapped her fingers around Margaret's hands, pressing them between each of her digits and pulling hard. From the sleeves of the officer's shirt oozed thick, *black oil*. As crisp and pure as a starless night. It was viscous, running up into Margaret's wrists and fingers, wrapping around her hands, flooding each pore, traveling her arms, her chest, down her breasts and into her throat, coating every inch of her pale and scarred flesh until she'd turned thick sable.

Time *probably* still existed beneath the ebony asphyxiation, but Margaret ceased to care.

After the long breath, when melee truly was unleashed, Margaret had almost *always* climaxed. It wasn't a sadistic glee in the wholesale slaughter, rather a unique side effect of alluvion chaos, an undeniable surrender that promised *anything*. She would have screamed, had she any connection left to her physical body.

This is what it must feel to be a god.

Only the necklace she wore was free of the liquid charcoal, *the eye that does not see.*

Eris pulled Margaret close, comatose in her strange mummification, whispering to her ear, "Don't worry too much. *He won't choose beauty.*"

Margaret barely heard the words, and if she did, no functioning part of her mind could have parsed them intelligently. The liquid charcoal was the calmest she'd known in life, it was a kind of mirror that absorbed her nightmares. It freed her of a thousand vile words and bound her up in the cool place between snow thaw and spring bloom. When it evaporated, consumed by her hungry meat, Margaret was left exposed, wrapped in her *human* garments.

For long seconds, or perhaps minutes, she'd known what it was to be *loved* by a god, embraced beyond the monochrome hues of an uninclined world.

Blinking back tears, Margaret stood alone, surrounded by broken glass, devoid of the power and discord. Her heart was broken, and the world suddenly fit into neat categories again.

It startled Margaret when Townsend stepped up next to her, a big, strong hand falling on her shoulder. The flesh connection betrayed his serious tambour as he imagined her lips pulling tightly on the shaft of his *cock* and her nails biting into his testicles.

"Amihan Lopez is arriving with her adjuncts. Are you all right?"

Are you all right? Margaret repeated the thought in her mind.

I can't ever be all right again.

10:23pm February 27th, 39 Veilfall

Stormair, California

Margaret recognized one of Amihan's adjuncts. He was the young man who'd worn a patch over his left eye. His face was less swollen and red, and his hair had been cut slipshod, as though he'd taken a large knife to it and then slicked it back with engine grease. Like the others, he wore a black button-up and suspenders, sans woolen coat. He was almost certainly fifteen years old, *sixteen maybe*, easily the youngest officer in the hanger.

Amy's other adjunct was a burly man with hands too large for his body, a square jaw and tiny eyeballs. Where the one-eyed boy seemed unable to dress himself in uniform, the larger man's clothes didn't even fit. His cuffs ended three, maybe *four inches* too short of his wrists.

When Margaret approached the three, Amy turned. She gestured with thumbs toward the two men, then made quick hand motions for them to leave. The big man did as he was told, but the one-eyed boy sneered at Margaret and only backed up slowly.

"Little young to be an officer," Margaret raised her eyebrows, as the boy slipped away only ten or twelve feet, watching like an angry child who'd been denied supper.

Amy shrugged, her expression a mix of boredom and apathy, "Did you need something?"

I didn't think this would be easy.

Margaret still felt a tingling under her flesh and a vertigo that pulled at her head and ears. Focusing on Amy was a challenge, but she needed to do this.

"Can we talk? Maybe outside?"

Amihan shrugged a second time, then gestured toward the hanger doors. Margaret took the invitation and began walking with Amy at her flank. She didn't *look* over her shoulder, but she could feel the one-eyed boy skulking back and following them. Margaret didn't want to dive into his mind for fear Amy was watching, but he was simply *odd*. Utterly uninclined, he recalled a particularly brave rat following a fat barn cat, fearless and curious.

Stormair didn't *sleep*. Outside there were vehicles rotating between shop and roster hangers, along with patrols and mixed operations. The air was cool and sharp, and raised goose flesh along Margaret's arms.

"Only you would show up to a military banquet dressed like a *whore*," Amy said, reaching the tarmac that Margaret occupied, her arms crossed, face set in stone. Over her black shirt and ivory slacks, Amy wore an overcoat made of dyed and cured leather, a shade of red darker than blood. It was frayed at the lapels and shoulders, but not faded.

"Let's call truce," Margaret sighed, palm pressed to her temple as she turned and stepped closer to Amy than the two had stood at the southern gate a few days earlier, "I'm *apologizing*."

Amy's eyes narrowed, but her expression didn't change, "What would you have to apologize for?"

Margaret glanced up from Amy's eyes, back at the one-eyed boy who stood by the hanger doors, watching, then back, "For my behavior, at the gates."

"What would you have to apologize for?" Amy repeated herself, dropping her arms, lifting palms to the sky and offering a smile, if a disingenuous one, "You changed my *diapers*, that means you have the right to speak to me, *treat me*, as you please."

The whiskey she'd hammered earlier was at her head and Margaret fought against slurring, "If you'd just *listen*, Amy, I'm trying to fix this."

Amy laughed, then shook her head, pausing, and letting her granite expression fall away, part of the little girl Margaret raised was looking back at her again.

"You know, when we were kids, you'd just *look* at me. As if *looking* at me was the worst thing you had to experience. You smiled when you *looked* at Ramona, you laughed with her, played with her, brushed her hair. Is it *any wonder* that she grew up to be a *whore* just like you?"

Margaret didn't have an answer. Amy's smirks reminded her *so much* of Maggi, and despite everything, it made Margaret's skin crawl, "At least Ramona didn't get knocked up and give away her own *child*."

Why did I say that?

Margaret bit down on her lower lip, taking a half step back, her anger only mitigated by inebriation.

"What the *fuck* are you talking about, Mayy?" Amy didn't even look offended, as though the accusation was lost on her like a bad joke, "Ramona had a child when she was sixteen. Dad made her give it up for adoption because her son would be an illegitimate Lopez."

"What the *fuck*?" Margaret's jaw slipped and she shook her head, "That can't be right."

Amy raised her hands, "*Yes*, it's *right*. Ask dad, when he gets here. *Ask him*. Your favorite niece is the only one who ever let you down."

How many times had Margaret thought it? How many times had she said it? The moments came back in a flash, every time she'd disparaged Amihan and called Ramona *her favorite* in the same breath.

Amy laughed, looking down at the ground, "You know what, Mayy? I know my grandmother wasn't a *good* person, dad told me stories. He told me about the time that she *beat you* for taking him beyond the walls of Crafton. He thought it was *funny*. He *laughed*, and he laughed so hard, that he never noticed *I* didn't. When I went to war with him, I wanted to prove to you, that I was *better* than Maggi Lopez, and better than my *father*." Amy looked away, and to Margaret's surprise her eyes had welled up with tears that flickered with reflections of Stormair. "That wasn't enough, was it? You could only see Maggi when you looked at me."

All the tumblers that had fallen earlier shattered in Margaret's heart. One by one, *popping* in a cascade of shattered glass. *Regret* wasn't something Margaret did, she never looked back, she never dreamed of doing *anything* over.

Except, that was, *right now*.

"I'm sorry," Margaret whispered, arms extending, to embrace Amy.

Amy retreated this time, grinding the palms of her hands into her eyes. She wore heavy shadow, *charcoal*, just like her grandmother. The pitch was now smeared downward.

"Too late. *Years* too late."

Amy stopped, and her face tensed. She sniffed back mucus and pulled her coat straight. The two watched each other for a moment, then Amy turned to walk away.

"*Wait,*" was all Margaret said, the most impotent word that she'd ever let slip.

I should have kept my mouth shut.

"*No,*" Amy repeated, pausing in her turn, words dripping venom, "I'll be a better person than you. I won't mock Ramona again for her choices, her *whoring*. At least I can trust her. At least she told me about *you*."

The footfalls of Amy's boots were soft and certain, her hands relaxed, she wasn't *angry* or *hateful*, she was simply done with her aunt.

To that degree, Margaret was *done* also. There was nothing left to discuss. She could spend the remaining years of her life regretting the way she'd treated Amihan Lopez, and what would it change? There was no making this right, and if there had been, Margaret had washed away that opportunity at the gates of Stockton.

I hope she succeeds, Margaret thought, sadly, *I hope she is a better person than me.*

Margaret waited for Amihan to reach the hanger doors, hook and lure for her one-eyed adjunct. Dinner would be served shortly, and Margaret would formally retire her title in front of the 3rd Army and 9th Battalion officers.

It was only as Margaret reached the doors that she wondered what it was that Amy had meant when she said, "*At least I can trust her. At least she told me about you.*"

11:00pm February 27th, 39 Veilfall

Stormair, California

"*What was that?*" Townsend spoke softly, below anyone's hearing as Margaret stepped into the hanger.

"It was me being a fool," Margaret answered, her head swimming and her chest wracked with the weight of Amy's words, "I'll explain later."

Townsend wasn't happy with that answer. Margaret saw his jaw clench, then he looked back to the officers in the room. Dinner was being set to the tables by several civilian servants. They wore white slacks like the Antecedent officers, but their shirts were simple affairs of cotton with shoulder stitching and naked arms. There were large platters full of seasoned and stuffed hard-boiled eggs, at least two roasted boar, and smaller plates with boiled pheasants. Even for Antecedent officers, this level of opulence was uncommon.

As she walked away, Margaret heard him again, "*Lady*," his voice louder, deeper. His eyes were serious, more than at any time he'd looked at her prior.

"*I'll explain later.*" Margaret bit back, lower lip fallen, teeth exposed.

The two watched each other, testing their wills, refusing to blink or glance away. Townsend's pulse was elevated, Margaret could feel it at her temples, and he was on edge, vigilant. Something had unsettled him.

Fuck. He wouldn't talk to me this way for no reason.

Margaret offered an open palm to Townsend, "Give me a twig. I'm listening."

Townsend stepped closer, hands fumbling in his jacket pockets, withdrawing his cigarette tin and lighter, "The 9th Battalion officers aren't acting *right*."

Margaret didn't move closer, but as Townsend spoke, she spun up thin, azoic defenses around him. Amy would hardly notice, but it would keep his thoughts from broadcasting around the room, as intense as they were.

"I don't know what that means," Margaret took the offered twig and allowed Townsend to light it for her. It was also a modest peace offering, she'd *almost* walked away, almost dismissed him outright. A poor witch assumed she knew more than a trained, veteran officer. It seemed to Margaret, this was true of paramours as well.

"Antecedent officers follow basic old-world military protocols. They're not saluting their superiors in the 3rd Army. They're *rude*, in a way that a commander would never abide."

"Okay," Margaret tipped her head side to side, inhaling the hot tobacco, "Amy and I are having a *family tiff*. Maybe she asked them to be rude?"

Townsend surveyed the room, chewing at the air, but not withdrawing his own cigarette, "That's not how *we* work. Those officers *know* something."

"They know I'm about to retire, and they know their boss and I are at odds." Margaret inhaled again, "*But,* take whatever precautions you consider appropriate, Lieutenant General. Consider it my final order as lead battlewitch of the Antecedent Empire."

Margaret reached down for Townsend's left hand, feeling it relax, gloved fingers running across his palm. She pulled his arm up and carefully placed the partially smoked cigarette between his fingers.

"We'll watch your back," Townsend said, softly, as Margaret turned away.

The only individuals gathered around the banquet tables now were setting utensils and food. Some of them were lighting oil lamps, positioned every other plate. Margaret slipped between them, and several women backed away, noticing *what* she was, if not *who she was*.

Grabbing a plate of lacquered china, along with a heavy steel spoon, Margaret held the two over her head, hammering the spoon to dish, hard enough to create an echoing *ding, ding, ding* sound in the hanger.

One by one, officers of 3rd Army and 9th Battalion turned to watch Margaret.

Some held tumblers, filled with liquor. Others nibbled at pheasant wings that they'd torn off preemptively, excited for dinner. Their eyes scrubbed up her legs, and skirt, all the way past her corset to her arms and the plate she held. Margaret could see the same 9th Battalion officer who'd contained Eris earlier. She stood near the back, looking as if she was in a great deal of pain. Both Amy's adjuncts watched, along with Townsend's, who was skulking low, ignoring her, talking to his own people.

"Officers!" Margaret shouted, "Officers of the 3rd and 1st Army, *pay heed to me now!*"

With their attention focused, Margaret slowly lowered dish and spoon, chewing at her lower lip. She didn't *want* it to be over, she didn't *want* to stop serving; but far more than that, she didn't want to keep fighting. The ways of Stockton, the comfortable life of House Owens had spoiled her, and the idea of *settling down* was every bit as seductive as the eyes Townsend held for her under his brow.

This is it.

"Tonight, we celebrate the end of an era. My *mother* helped found the Antecedent States, and her *son* founded the Antecedent Empire. For two decades we fought to conquer a continent, and we *succeeded*. With that success, I am formally announcing my resignation as lead battlewitch to Alexander Lopez and his generals." Margaret's voice projected around the room, sturdy, calm, and strong. "I've fought next to you. I've buried your brothers. I've laid in hospital beds near you. All of that's over now. The war engine of the Antecedency is quiet tonight, and for the first time since the Collapse, real *peace* may be known in this land."

With hands raised, the hanger began to applaud her. Even the 9th Battalion officers joined them, sincere in their offerings. But, as the room's cheering grew silent, one man stepped forward, hands low, and his *one eye* watching with disparagement.

"That's a false speak there, yeah?" Amy's adjunct asked, "Your *mom*, our Emperor's *mom*, she's not likewise blood as you, yeah?"

Silence.

"No," Margaret swallowed after a moment, answering the one-eyed boy, "No, I'm not the true born daughter of Maggi Lopez."

The adjunct nodded, smarmy and insolent with both youth and arrogance, the big rat turned from curious, to predator, "No likewise blood, no likewise at all. Why would you false speak?" The boy was using a modern form of English, rough and mumbled, he was a step below Margaret's own lazy pronunciations.

"*Shut up pop-eye*," a 3rd Army officer shouted. He was a Captain, a few years younger than Townsend and one of the Saint Louis veterans, "Lady Mayhem has earned the right to call *anyone* whatever she pleases. With her blessing I'll call *you* to the ground now and feed you that *other* eye." He was pointing to the tarmac as he spoke, so angry that his mouth was sputtering.

The one-eyed boy raised his right hand and gestured for the older man to come forward, his chin jutting out. Before the situation could become more heated, Amihan herself moved forward, grabbed the dinner plate from Margaret's fingers and smashed it the concrete floor with both hands. Green and white shards exploded, flying so far that little of the plate remained visible.

The hanger was silent again, servants backing off, sneaking away toward the shadows.

"Lady Mayhem has *always* called Maggi Lopez her mother," Amy's voice was louder, rawer. She'd been educated to speak *above* boys like her one-eyed adjunct, "There's no crime here, no *false speak*. Maggi Lopez raised Mayhem since she was a child."

Surprised at this Margaret spoke, "*Thank you*."

When Amy turned to Margaret her hand was raised, finger pointed down. Her face was twisted up into rage, and her eyes didn't register Margaret as a flesh and blood person anymore, *least of all* family.

"That *never* gave you the right to call yourself *Margaret Lopez*."

Margaret pressed herself back toward the table, mouth open, stammering, "I *never* said that."

"You *did*," Amy fulminated, and Margaret realized that the young woman's hands were free of gloves, "You told the former Owens queen that you wanted to be *Margaret Lopez*, you told her you would make your brother call you that. Make *me* call you that. My own *sister* is your confessor!"

All the plates may as well have been smashed.

Each word at Amy's angry report was a hammer strike. She remembered Ramona nodding, her dark hair pasted across her face, "*You'll tell him you're Margaret Lopez. You know he'll hate it. So will my sister.*"

The one-eyed adjunct reached for his sidearm, thumbing latch free and raising it for Margaret's skull. Every single 9th Battalion officer did the same, no racks to slide, rounds already chambered, holding weapons on the 3rd Army. Margaret could no longer see Townsend, and she didn't have time to worry about him now. He hadn't become a Lieutenant General through an inability to *plan*.

Every officer held their breath and weighed their actions. Margaret was cycling barriers up, green sparks whipped off tarmac as walls erected themselves around her. Some of those barriers bounced off Amy's, they stood so close.

"It's true. I *wanted* to be Maggi's legitimate daughter but drawing a gun on me for a *childhood fantasy I shared in private* is how your adjunct will *die*."

The look on Amy's face was one of intimate hatred, "You told Aurora Owens you'd displace my *father* for the throne."

"*No!*" Margaret shouted back, pressing her molars together painfully.

"Call my sister a liar," Amy nodded, holding hands away from her coat. The air was beginning to heat at her fingertips. Margaret could see her caramelized nails and blistered fingers, scarred just like the hands of Maggi Lopez, "Call Ramona a liar. Say it. *Tell me* my own sister lied when she cried and asked me to protect our father. *Call her a liar when she begged me to spare your life!*"

The situation was now beyond anyone's control. Had Amihan spoken with Aurora Owens? Was Aurora Owens even *alive* now? Who else had Ramona talked to? *What the fuck was Ramona doing?*

"I *will* call your *whore-sister* a liar!" One of the 3rd Army officers stepped forward, a tall man in his early thirties with blazing green eyes and dusty brown hair, ignoring the two guns leveled at his skull, "I will call out *anyone* who cries traitor of Lady Mayhem, the only *true* battlewitch the Empire has known!"

Amy's eyes rolled to meet the officer, her head never shifting from Margaret. She didn't raise her hands, or snap fingers like Maggi, she didn't speak words of power or perform any rituals.

She simply *stared*.

The officer was Captain Henry Francs, he'd joined the 3rd Army in Omaha. During the siege of Fort Collins, he'd found his squad stranded behind enemy trenches. Just like Amy had saved her adjunct's life, so too had Margaret walked *into* suppressing fire to spread her terrible wings and save Captain Francs, as well as his men. That night she'd *fucked him* to taste the wild gratitude on his lips. She'd walked his mind, and knew he'd lost his virginity to a *step-sister*, that his father had run him from their home and into the Antecedent military for it.

The Captain's eyes had gone wild with insanity, he clawed at his lips with curling fingers, ripping off skin that Margaret had kissed the night after Fort Collins. The saliva in his mouth was superheated, boiling, steam erupting from his mouth and nose, burning his cheeks from the inside out, scalding his lungs, eating away the inside of his throat. His face had begun to blister, red lesions turning pustule. Yellow syrup leaking down flesh, twisted and pinched like pork chops set before flame, sizzling in fat.

He groped for his throat, trying to breathe, leaning forward, and vomited forth his own tongue, twisted red, and half a foot long. It hit the tarmac like cooked liver, steaming and bubbling, jerking from the heat.

Amy turned back to Margaret. Henry Francs wasn't dead *yet*, but he couldn't even cry out in pain as he slowly suffocated.

"You came to me, tonight, asking me to forgive you. Did you think Ramona loved you so? That she'd keep your secret? That you could convince me to back your scheme, against my father?"

Both Amy and Margaret were using battlefield defenses now, sparks dancing across concrete, and patchwork lines of energy emerging from unseen magic into a tangible field around them both, lit windows covered in dust and grime. Margaret's world had fallen out from under her, she hadn't even mourned for Henry Francs when she began to consider how she was going to kill the niece who looked so much like her mother.

One by one, 9th Battalion officers fell out of focus, watching a horizon that no longer existed, their jaws hanging free, tshoulders slouching. It was only four, five, then finally six and seven that Margaret could *fully* control. Among them was Amy's one-eyed adjunct boy, all of them shifting their slumberous gaze on Amy, turning with the same ease Margaret might offer as she filled a plate with food or opened a door.

All of them leveling weapons on Amy.

"Amihan," Margaret's voice was certain, "I don't want to do this, but I'm no traitor."

Pop, someone fired a pistol in the room. Margaret could hear screaming, followed by two more concussions, *pop, pop!*

"Funny story," Amy nodded, calm, unblinking, and it seemed to Margaret, unbreathing, "You're not a traitor, yet you have the guns of my men trained on me now. And you'll shoot me? If I don't release you?"

Margaret nodded, "*Yeah*."

Her shields offered her a modicum of safety against Amihan's fire; she couldn't reach past them as easily as she'd boiled Henry Franc's saliva.

"*No*," Amihan replied.

Where are Amihan's poltergeists?

Margaret realized the ghostly bodyguards had manifested when Margaret pointed an unloaded pistol at Ramona. Amy's twin claimed those guards protected *both* her sister and father. Right now, there were *seven chambered bullets*, aimed at Amy's skull, it should have triggered them.

What the fuck was Ramona Lopez doing?

Amy proved herself the granddaughter of Maggi Lopez and lunged, a brawler uninterested in the limitations of magic. Their defenses erupted in mottled glow, grinding, shattering embellished fields, Amy physically slammed into Margaret with her full weight. The corner of a banquette table stabbed Margaret's lower back, her knees gave way and both women toppled to tarmac.

Amy struck her aunt in the face with a balled left hand, so hard that her knuckles cracked under the force. Margaret was clutching at the other woman's neck, pressing her away with all the strength she could muster. She'd never grown as large as the daughters of Alexander Lopez, she'd never been strong, nor had she been good at fighting. It was no matter at all for Amy to overpower her, left hand bloody at the knuckles, forcing Margaret's face to the concrete and her right knee pinning her leg. With focus broken, her attention spread, Margaret could no longer maintain control over the 9th Battalion officers.

Weapons fire filled the hanger like a flooded pitcher, cascade reports became a jump of messy *cracks* and *pops*. From her vantage point on the ground, Margaret could see bodies cast apart, blood erupting from wounds, men screaming.

Chaos, Margaret thought, remembering Eris.

Amy braced her weight on her right hand and struck Margaret in the face again, and again, *and again*. Each impact was hateful, her maw snarling, a stream of drool reaching down.

Despite Margaret's best efforts to fight back, her body refused to press. An impact dropped down on her exposed temple, stunning her. Amy's left hand opened, grabbed Margaret's face, thumb across her lips and fingers spread wide.

"I *loved* you."

Amy seethed, her voice raw, chin quivering, and her throat enfeebled to produce the degree of rage that Margaret could feel burning in her chest, white hot, blistering.

Blistering, like Margaret's face.

Margaret didn't feel the pain immediately. Whether that was a side effect of the temple strike, or whether it was her own nerves rebelling at the notion. It took seconds to realize that she was *on fire*. Her chest, ribs, and shoulder, flame was eating her alive, a hungry animal falling upon an injured prey. Flesh twisted and turned black, pulling away from the muscle. Oil and sweat sizzling, grease on a griddle, as her ligaments began to burn. The *hiss* and *pop* of meat, fat loosed from bounds, charring her skin, dripping toward the floor. She'd heard men burn before, *she'd watched her own parents burn alive*, but nothing prepared her for what it would feel like, *or sound like*, as her own body was caline and ablaze.

For the first time since she was a *child*, Margaret was afraid.

Margaret began screaming, something like a caged animal, guttural, no longer human. She was thrashing under Amihan, pushing her hand away as flesh began to tear lose, cooking under a fire eater's embrace.

This was the Collapse made manifest, the day *they* came to her parents' home. Beating her father, raping her mother, *holding her down and demanding she* watch as her parents burn on the pyre of furniture and clothes.

For the first time in *years*, Margaret could remember their faces, screaming, *screaming, screaming so loud*, as flesh fell from bones turned black. They didn't cry out for her, they begged for mercy, and finally they *begged for death*. They wanted to escape torture, and in their final moments, the daughter they left behind was inconsequential.

In all her years of abuse, Maggi had never considered Margaret *inconsequential*.

Somewhere in those memories, in hysteria of scalding pain, Margaret *knew* that Amy was shot. She'd heard two rounds empty, the *pop* of hammer on primer, and the keening dance of brass on concrete. She *felt* Amy's blood, freezing on her burns, *sizzling on fire*. When her face was released, she looked up to see Amy's coat was tattered at the shoulder, and she clutched her own neck with a hand of rose red, face twisted up in a cauldron of loathing, falling, standing, stumbling as she withdrew.

Blood was in Margaret's eyes, blood across the tables, the floor, everything that Margaret could see was coated in thick cruor.

This isn't the Collapse.

Margaret began to retreat, crawling toward the shadows, out of the madness that was unleashed. She *knew* she'd been on fire, so it confused her now that she was *freezing, shivering*.

I'm in shock, Margaret thought in a haze, *I've seen dying men shiver. I'm dying.*

Lady Mayhem by SapFire

December 4th, 32 Veilfall

Saint Louis, Missouri

The wave that swept over Eads Bridge was ugly, so swollen with mud that it became a tangible force of will, a great claw rising from the Mississippi River, dragging down perhaps a hundred 3rd Army soldiers.

One of those pulled under the river's surface was Lady Mayhem.

Oscillating sludge wrapped around her, flowing like a spigot, whipping at her armor. She was being wrenched deeper by coiling liquid and silt. It was dark, void of light, freezing and hollow. She wanted to scream, to gasp for air, but there was none. As others drowned, they radiated bright needles of terror, clutching and swimming against the current, desperate for breath and sky. The Mississippi was a living gullet, yanking at her ankles and wrists, ravenous as a starved animal.

It wasn't fear that inspired Lady Mayhem. That was something she couldn't feel. At the back of her mind was an angry woman screaming, "*I swear to fuck Margaret, I should have fucking left you in that parking lot seven years ago.*"

Lady Mayhem's barriers were manifest, bright orange lines twisting around her, withering and dimming, illuminating the mud as it thinned and parted. When she breached the Mississippi's spiteful surface, the barriers exuded an auditory *crack* before they dimmed, quiet.

A poor swimmer, bound in armor, Mayhem had barely escaped the great hand of mire and loathing. Clinging to the soft and dingy shore on hands and knees, her gown of yellow tattered, coated in sludge, plate carrier loosened. Her combat helmet had vanished, and her hair was slathered around her face and shoulders, glued in place as she retched up blood and fine rocks. Hungrier than the river had been, Mayhem bit at the air, filling her lungs as best she could, feasting on a broth of simmering sewage, freezing rain, and black smoke, hanging in her throat like a chicken bone.

My brother will never forgive me if I lose, here and now.

Behind her was *abject insanity*. The 3rd Army fought with bayonet and pistol across Eads, a direct assault that Ozark troops contested each step of the way. She could hear their screams, and she could *feel* the fray expand, breathing, undulating with sour fright and lascivious cruelty.

"*Surrender.*" Came a shout, from ahead.

Lady Mayhem looked up slowly, wrists and knees sucked down into pregnant Mississippi banks. An old woman stood before her, flanked by a great golem.

She was The Missouri Witch. Brown leathers and green fatigues soaked, her hair was pulled back in a silver-white braid. Her arms bled from a hundred cuts, washing pink farrago in heavy rain. Diminished by years, her face was scrunched up, her neck skinny, yet she still cast a wholly robust form. A woman of great strength and total confidence in the powers that she had wielded since the Collapse; an aquaphilia, a *water witch.*

The golem was wrapped in mud and steel, a dozen feet tall, a giant ape, dragging its knuckles. Old rubber tires created gnarled maw, jerking up and down, belching fallow algae. Molding meat spilled across its broad chest, as it sang a loathsome wail of hatred with every seizing step.

I should surrender, the 3rd Army will be lost, thought Lady Mayhem, but she did not give reply. Instead she stood, slush sucking at her boots with each step, knees quivering.

The Missouri Witch stepped forward, a few paces, flexing her fingers, lips curled up in a gawking grin, front teeth missing. "*Surrender.*"

I can't reach into her mind. I can't kill a golem. My mother would be ashamed of me.

A golem required a complex and dedicated series of rituals to raise. Once summoned, they existed *forever*. One golem could walk through a thousand trained soldiers, *her* soldiers, rending them apart like wet tissue, swallowing blood and bone whole.

The Missouri Witch rolled her tongue out, cackling in a stuttering rasp. She was bursting with unquestioned faith.

"*Surrender.*" The old woman shouted, a third time.

Swallowing cruor and sludge, Lady Mayhem shivered.

"*No.*"

Launching into a languorous stride, Mayhem reached for her plate carrier's breast, fingers groping at a pistol or knife, only to find them stolen by the Mississippi. The old witch saw the fumble, and *laughed*, her throat gasping for air, braying like a donkey. With one arm, she directed the abomination behind her, and the golem tripped forward into a run, using knuckles of broken stone to carry its balance forward. Each apathetic blow to the river banks was a vibration resounding up Mayhem's knees and ribs, toward her larynx and uvula.

It had launched itself toward Eads Bridge.

They can't stop it. My men can't stop it.

Lady Mayhem had *nothing* to throw at it. No flame or muddy waves, no spinning tornedos. She was crippled against the power of such creation.

Turning away from the monster, Mayhem extended her mind out, seizing for The Missouri Witch, raking down her barriers as blade on granite. The lurid terror that she could command bled in a weary drizzle. Ink turning opaque and kissing mud with impotent splatters. Against a witch *this* powerful, Mayhem could not call herself *nightmare mirror*, she was just a cold little girl with bloodied gums.

Fuck you, fuck this river, fuck it all.

Unable to break the old woman's defenses, Lady Mayhem allowed nightmares to consume her. That chilly, primitive magic, fetid paint on hide canvas, she turned her *own magic* inward. Her proto-human instincts begin to take over. Reason was now an abstract concept that she could no longer fathom, as she launched into a keening charge, screaming.

Eyes dripping with glee, The Missouri Witch pulled a switchblade from her belt, and began to slough forward. Drawing first blood, angling her knife up, and under Mayhem's plate carrier, she planted steel between ribs. Skin parted with little effort, ruby drizzles spiraling to the wind, a silk scarf drifting for a lost love.

Mayhem only felt a hard *tug* at her side and cared little. She answered The Missouri Witch with a small fist planted into the old woman's face. The blow was backed with a rage most people could never feel, a deep apoplexy summoned from her stomach.

A tooth tumbled from the old witch's mouth, followed by another gurgling cackle.

The knife still planted in her side, Lady Mayhem grabbed The Missouri Witch's face, jaws driven for her throat. Whatever nobility this fight had held was gone. Mayhem could taste loose and drooping flesh against her tongue, feel teeth wail against tendons, and flexed her jaw to *bite,* again and again. Mayhem's mouth was awash with copper syrup, choking her. Like an axe felling a rotten tree, she gnawed against a jugular, cruor in her nose and eyes.

She ate mouthfuls of The Missouri Witch, raw.

The old woman fought back, trying to press Mayhem away, driving the switchblade into her ribs, repeatedly, but no dominion was found. Eyes darting with madness, Mayhem stood awash in sanguine treacle, shreds of skin and muscle dripping off her lips, down her plate carrier, and into her cleavage.

The Missouri Witch lurched forward, a sack of organs and bone, falling limply, and her face pulled across Mayhem's plate carrier, fusty lips bouncing along molle web.

Lady Mayhem's eyes rolled back into her skull, and she was racked in seizures. Her hands vibrated, and her jaw scooped at the air impotently. She could *hear* the siege of Saint Louis, each staccato dance of automatic weapons tossing her nerves, flashes of powder and fire causing an involuntary jerking in her fingers.

Ankle deep in mud now, her stomach retched, angry at what she'd consumed. She vomited *corpus delicti* and flesh, colored a shade of dead roses. She wanted to force her fingers back into her esophagus, pry out the bitter gristle. Adrenaline and memories of primordial anguish gnashed against her flesh and puckered her eyes. It was more than she could tolerate, and the Mississippi demanded penance for the murder of her mistress.

Falling forward, the impact vibrated up Mayhem's spine and caused her head to tilt back until she was looking up, *up and up.*

She could see the golem standing over her.

"I suppose I'll die now," the words passed between her lips, a mumbled curse.

To neither her expectation, nor surprise, the golem began to melt. Although the rain was slowing, offering a quiet capitulation, droplets slid down the monster's broad chest and bulbous shoulders. Wrought iron bars that twisted up into the creature fell. Shattered stone and broken rocks trickled, a thousand rough tears. The creature was collapsing in on itself, folding up, bit by bit, returning to the bank.

It occurred to Lady Mayhem that this was *impossible*. A golem would live a hundred lifetimes after its creator turned to dust, an automated memory.

Unless it was never a golem.

"You shall not die." It was a collection of noises and chirps, clipped and glued together to become real syllables. Whatever was left of the golem had boiled to a shivering bipedal. Not *quite* human, arms a little too long, legs a little too squat, and only a bit taller than Mayhem herself. She could make out no eyes, no mouth, no face. It spoke with the drizzle of rain and splatter of river rocks, tumbling into soft mud. *"I was bound to this place. This river. You bested the old Bête Noire. Killed her. Butchered her. You freed me."*

Lady Mayhem watched the creature stumble towards her, perhaps a yard away. "Now what do we do?"

"I owe you a favor. The favor of a god."

"You don't seem much of a god." The small witch answered, her chin tilting back to her sternum, words flavorless on tattered tonsils.

"Is not your belly empty? Are you not weak? So may a god be."

"Name yourself." Mayhem accepted.

"I name myself Condatis. I will see you again. I will repay this debt, and we shall part ways forever after. I speak no more, Bête Noire."

The god calling himself Condatis fell into mud. All that he had been was nothing more than a pile of tide pool wreckage, flotsam and run off.

Unable to move or shift her aching knees, Mayhem felt ballast drag at her jaw and breasts. Gods didn't *belong* to the waking, they pressed apart Veil scraps as children might kick aside prized paints or sculptures to make merry.

It was a long time before the little witch with auburn-red hair could shake heft and sorrow. She'd never unlocked the madness of her own hindbrain before, and she had no idea the physical toll it created. Her eyes darted about the saturated ground and festering rain, hypervigilant to peril. The base of her skull ached; her shoulder blades burned, and she wanted to peel apart flesh to tend sore muscles. It wasn't the traditional kind of fear she knew as a child, the trepidation and recoil that had burned out of her soul. It was an earthen terror, a rusted trinket buried in deep forest and stained tawny. There was no place in the world for that primal horror, a leftover from her prehistoric ancestors, a place full of secrets and forbidden knowledge.

Limping away from the river, Margaret clutched a bloody hand to her lips and forced back an overpowering weight of regret. Summoning up primordial panic was a weapon that carried a grave price tag. She wanted to *scream* at the gray skies, she wanted to end this awareness that seemed to drag at her heels like a great stone.

Only in its absence did she realize the peril offered by her blood loss, and only in its wake did the world begin to feel like a place she wanted to live.

Margaret's mother had told her the stories, of why men created fire; kept it burning at night and slept close to its glowing kisses. Out there, in the darkness, were *things* that no mortal could fight with stick or steel. Out there were *things* that taught humans the true meaning of fear, an imprint so deep, so twisted in scars, that eons would not see it erased from their minds.

More than she worried for blood loss, Margaret prayed to any power who heard her, an unspoken hope, that she would never need to turn to that awful weapon again.

12:02am February 28th, 39 Veilfall

Stockton, California

"*Fuck me.*"

The ragged cry came out, half choked.

Margaret attempted to roll over, off her back, but her right shoulder didn't respond. She took a moment, blinking at the dreary rafters, to take inventory of her limbs. She could drum the fingers of her right hand to thigh. They *worked*. Her wrist rotated, and she could feel muscles twist, yet the shoulder remained silent.

After some struggle and kneeling, Margaret groped with her left hand for a table, pulling herself upward, to her feet. Standing for long minutes she studied forks and spoons, still arranged with care, nicks glistening on polished silver. When Margaret leaned forward, pressing herself to the table, a thick flag of bloody mucous unfurled from her lips, draping across flatware, painting them in red so deep that it could have been black.

Why is it so fucking cold in here? Why didn't I bring a coat?

Margaret's mouth fell open and she inhaled hard, aching at temple and jaw. One of her eyes was swollen shut, and skin across her face sang a graceless cry of pain, flushing her cheeks. Frustrated, she stumbled and kicked a chair back so that she could sit. Her mind had begun to wind around questions, and her eyes drifted across the deserted hanger.

Woolen jackets of blue had turned dark with drying claret. Skulls broken open, and contents stretching like tanned leather. These men were dead or *dying*. She could *hear* the rattle of their breathing, but she couldn't *feel* them. The hanger was quiet, as if her senses had been blinded in a great flash.

My niece set me on fire. It was a phlegmatic thought, Margaret couldn't rally her wits around the notion, it felt as though someone else had burned. Not her.

Those were *her* officers on the ground. Their disgorged organs crusting in a chilly night breeze. She'd known many of them for *years*, and of course *fucked* more than a few. They had places in her heart, each was a miniature altar she'd erected in their memory. Moments of their lives, their loves, and even their fears. They each had names, and eyes that no longer twitched or pulled at her bust or legs. They weren't ghosts, *as such*, it was simply that their absence played like a rat in her stomach.

Margaret's right hand rested in her lap. She tipped her head down and watched it shudder, leaves on an autumn breeze. Soot painted her chest in ethereal wisps, curling up, beautiful from the raw, incarnadine, meat of her breast. Skin had curled away, exposing layers of muscle and fat like a tawdry hooker lifting her panties for a wayward Johnny. The skin was covered in melted molle web, corset liquified, running together with flesh.

How could I sketch that? Those patterns, from the fire.

Slowly, with a detached sense of curiosity, Margaret surveyed the damage at her ribs and right shoulder. Yellow pools of pus and ragged skin were braided by blisters. Singed *bone* had turned black, and fat boiled away, drying as thick lumps where tendons had once been.

"They're going to cut my arm off," Margaret spoke to her shoulder, pausing briefly as she waited for a reply that never came. "What am I going to do with one arm?"

I'm right handed.

The pain she'd suffered under flame was unfathomable affliction, but now, as bad as those wounds looked, they didn't *hurt*.

"Is this how they felt, mom?" Margaret looked away from her shoulder, across the hanger, talking to only herself, "All those people you burned."

Standing, Margaret realized her skirt had rolled up, around her hips. With care she tugged down on the fabric, pressing it over her undergarments again.

How ridiculous must that have looked?

Margaret decided to make her way to the hanger doors. She needed to shuffle across gore dispatched tarmac, *aware* that some officers still squirmed, writhed, and waited for death. There was nothing she could offer them. Her tendrils, the aspects of her mind that allowed her such deep connections, felt as mussed and uneven as her skirt had been. She couldn't *feel*. They were a whisper just outside of hearing.

At the hanger doors, her good hand pressing up to dusty aluminum, Margaret looked to a sky devoid of stars and wonder.

Ramona, gods be fucked, what have you done?

12:22am February 28th, 39 Veilfall

Stormair, California

It was a long press of minutes before Margaret realized someone was calling her name. She'd begun to walk, one foot in front of the other, toward Stockton's southern gate. Where else could she go? Perhaps she could walk home. Janet would help her, and she could lay down.

"*Margaret!*"

Who calls me that?

Margaret stopped, listening to the wind move around her. It stung the burns on her face, and upended her skirt, again. She'd forgotten to care about that. She could hear horseshoes beating tarmac, a metallic echo crawling across her skin. A sound that had always set her on edge, no matter how much she liked horses or riding.

It occurred to Margaret that she wasn't armed. Hand to sternum, directly below her breasts, she found nothing. She'd remembered the pistol in her boudoir. She'd second guessed herself. Because of a beautiful *Hetairai*.

Why would I do something so stupid?

The horses separated as they approached, one moving to her left arm where she clutched her corset, the other facing her directly.

The first rider dismounted, oil lantern held up, dress uniform illuminated in flickering peach. She tried to reach out, seep into the rider's mind, wield some sort of control. It was a lecherous invasion, clumsy awkwardness, a virgin boy falling into the window of his quarry, bumbling and lost in thoughts of *what could be*.

Townsend. The rider's mind was a familiar one.

Though she wasn't afraid or even under duress of pain, she began to weep. The tears came and she gasped, with a low whimpering that seemed to start at her sternum.

"*Gods be fucked,*" Townsend's voice was a broken window at slumber, a single act of audible shock. Even under lamp light, he lost color, his jaw dropped open. Margaret could see revulsion in his eyes, and this time *feel* his discomfort, his need to look away.

"Hello, Lieutenant General." Margaret said, pretending she was stout and healthy, bare shoulders quaking under sobs.

"Lady Mayhem," the second rider, still mounted, stuttered, "are you okay?"

Townsend looked up to his adjunct in shadow, face turning concrete, "Did I *fucking* train you to ask stupid *fucking* questions?"

"*Sir!* No, sir!" The other man replied, stammer erased.

"Pull the best combat doc in Stormair," Townsend bellowed orders, "Bring them to the hanger, and assist anyone who may be alive, then wait for me to return. You tracking, Captain?"

Margaret had never heard this tone in Townsend's voice. He wasn't flirting or jesting about Owens nobility, he was deploying a shout from deep in his chest.

"*Sir!* Yes, sir!" With Townsend's dismissal, the Captain pulled on reigns. His horse, a gray and black beast, whinnied and reared back before leaping into a turn and crashing forward, full gallop.

I don't know if I can trust him, Margaret thought sadly as Townsend turned to face her again. His temples throbbed with pumping veins.

"We're alone, Lieutenant General. Do I get a kiss, or a bullet?"

Maybe both?

Townsend's broad chest heaved a sigh and his brows pressed down, "I've already dug my grave tonight, Margaret. I won't shoot *two witches*."

Margaret couldn't drop her jaw, the burns across her cheek had puckered the skin, "You shot Amy? You shot *Amihan Lopez*? Heir apparent to the Antecedent Empire?"

Townsend didn't reply.

"*Fuck me!*" Margaret tried to shout, but her lower lip split, delivering cutting pain where Amy's thumb had burned, "Amy names me a traitor, and *you* shoot her."

"She was going to kill you," Townsend didn't speak to Margaret with soft affections, his face was a mess of anger and discipline, and what thoughts ran through his mind remained Margaret's mystery to solve. "I know what I did, and I have no regrets. I watched you in rags, weak as a kitten, tending to my men after Saint Louis. The 3rd Army remembers."

Faint in the head, blind in the mind, Margaret stepped forward and ran her left hand up Townsend's chest, gripping his uniform tight, "Did you kill her?"

In reply Townsend shrugged, "I have no idea. I clipped her in the neck. She was bleeding. There was fighting in Stormair, but most of the 9th Battalion members surrendered. She likely fled into Stockton."

There's still some hope then, we don't have to kill each other.

Her tears abated, Margaret felt her lips move, and thought her voice had drifted between them. Uncertain if she'd spoken her thoughts aloud, she replied, "Who am I kidding? Even if she and I make peace, she'll demand your head for drawing on a Lopez."

Angry, Margaret was tired of *looking* at Townsend, watching his moustache twist, alert to what his unyielding face was holding back. Standing up straight again, Margaret placed the fingers of her left hand in her mouth and bit into gloves. She jerked at the delicate fabrics around her thumb, a wild coyote ripping apart a rabbit who'd run just a little too slow.

Her hand naked, free, she grabbed Townsend's face, thumb under his lips, fingertips roughly stroking his upper jaw, flesh greasy with old sweat.

The fighting will start tomorrow. 9th Battalion will turn on us. Margaret must be hidden.

A weight of anxiety lifted, she could *hear* him, his thoughts, and Townsend knew it.

Margaret's shoulders slouched low. The right one had always been misshapen, and now peeled like the skin of a pig left to cook on a spit. She wondered if his adamant focus on holding an expression of martial rage was the way *he* coped with stress, just as Margaret needed to *listen* to the moving parts around her.

"Tell me what it means. When your mind sounds like an engine?"

Townsend didn't *look* surprised, he only *felt* it, as if she'd played a game with a stranger who'd actually guessed the number imagined, "It's easier in combat, when it's *quiet*. Like right now. I look at the world like I would look through a rifle scope. It's a little easier."

Margaret couldn't manage a smile, not with burns fighting every muscle movement, "You're looking *through* me, commander. Maybe I'm your rifle scope."

You are, Margaret heard him.

"Amy will also be down with a doc, so we won't need a witch tomorrow. It'll be a good old fashion door-to-door. Shake the rust off, that's all. If you eat dirt, all of this was for nothing." *Sadness* drizzled down Margaret's fingers, off Townsend's skull and into her bones. It spilled across her skin, cooling burns.

"Hush, hush," Margaret said, almost as if cooing a baby asleep, "3rd Army sticks together. I won't let the *bitch* come for you. They can bury us together, *traitors*."

"They'll dump our bodies in a ditch, actually."

For some reason, this made Margaret laugh. The action was involuntary, and it caused an eruption of pain across her right cheek and jaw, raw flesh illuminated in agony. It was then that Townsend's face shifted, *ever so slightly*, as he examined her, eyes darting over every detail. He seemed to be examining her *quality*, a farmer checking teeth and hooves of livestock. Margaret found herself hurt, until he leaned forward, crouching down, to press his lips and bushy moustache into her left eye.

My lips are burned, she realized, *he was searching for where he could kiss me.*

He held the kiss there, for seconds, just as he might have on her lips. When he brought himself to full height, his face was stone once more, "I'm going to *hide* you where no one will look. As the night grows old, I'll return with a combat doc to perform surgery. You're as wounded as I ever saw a man who died, and I can't allow that."

Margaret, exhausted to her bones, had no desire to argue, and no desire to doubt Townsend's plan. This was his chance to *take care of her* and there was no sense in fighting. He would be right, or he would be wrong. Only time would tell.

For now, Margaret just wanted off her feet and out of the cold.

3:18am February 28th, 39 Veilfall

Stockton, California

Although Aurora Owens had never been friends with Townsend, the two were familiar. He had been altruistic in his appeal to Aurora's sense of mercy when he established the need to hide Margaret and had gone so far as to beg.

The ride to Stockton had been exhausting and painful. Back against Townsend's chest, one hand wrapped at her stomach, the rhythmic jostle of a hard gallop was excruciating. By the time he helped Margaret inside Aurora's apartment, she struggled to stand. Where her corset melted into blackened flesh, the skin itself was *ripping*, flaying Margaret. Fading between the conscious world and a dimly lit agony, she was aware that Townsend dismissed himself, promising he'd return by morning with a combat doc. In moments of clarity, Margaret could see Aurora, a mind of wooden sticks, sharpened, jabbing at her temples and forehead.

"I offered your mother solace, once. I suppose it would be fitting that I offer the daughter safe harbor as well."

The words sounded like a threat, and even her wealth of kind regards as she departed for bed seemed like a menacing hum, the sound of something gnawing at her mind from behind stiff and sound walls.

Only her servant, her *friend*, Cyrus remained.

He sat next to Margaret, where she laid on a chaise lounge, upholstered in velvet and carved from cherrywood, enamel dark and smooth when her hands or calves brushed it. The room, as before, carried a corporeal weight of lemongrass and pine smoke, thick, and almost claustrophobic.

"You *need* aloe. You *need* a lot more than this," Cyrus said, smearing grease across her shriveled, red, flesh. His fingers moved in circular patterns, above her right breast, crisscrossed by narrow ridges of dried blood. Flesh had begun to separate from muscle tissue. "Petroleum jelly will only do so much."

Margaret's eyes scrunched shut as she inhaled sharply. The ramifications of her injuries were no longer a grim curiosity, they'd become a much more vivid affliction.

"I'll take what I can get, doc."

"*Captain*," Cyrus answered, "and I'm not a doc, I was Eleven-Charlie."

Margaret opened her eyes, blowing several breaths out and looking at the man who was easily a decade older than Aurora Owens. His hair was white, and thin on top. His left eye was blue, but the right was milky-gray. He smelled like aftershave and rubbing alcohol.

"I don't know that designation, *Eleven-Charlie*."

Cyrus shrugged, "It's not an Owens designation."

"Federal?" Margaret winced as Cyrus applied another mirthless slather of jelly across her chest, this one curving into her armpit.

"*Mhmm,*" Cyrus grunted in affirmation, "I was Mortars, back in the old days. When no one lit things on fire with their minds."

The pain subsided and Margaret worked on her breathing, pausing to exhale, "Tell me, Mortarman, how did you end up a house-servant for Aurora Owens?"

Cyrus laughed, pausing to meet Margaret's eyes, red and irritated, "*Eleven-Charlie*, please. 'Mortarman' is Marine Corp. And, I'm not her house-servant."

"Okay, okay," Margaret panted for a moment, then regained some of her calm.

"I'm going to put this on your shoulder. I'm not sure how much good it'll do. Dollars to donuts, that arm comes off," Cyrus pointed at exposed bone. In plentiful candlelight, the wound looked so much worse.

Dollars to donuts?

"I'm as *wounded as any man who died*," Margaret reminded herself of Townsend's words, then laid her head back, silently, ignoring the shoulder.

Cyrus replied after a moment, greasy fingers groping about bone and crusted tissue, "I'm Aurora's friend. Been her friend for close to two decades. Since the day The Beast woke. After her husband, Lord Cuttersark, died, I was her social accompaniment."

Margaret found Cyrus's tone to be surprisingly open, and his emotions obvious. She blinked once, astounded, and felt a familiar weight on his wrinkled skin.

"I didn't notice before. I didn't *pay attention*. You love her."

Cyrus nodded, running his fingers along Margaret's ruined arm. She feels *nothing*, "I do, and after a fashion, she loves me back."

"But, it's not the *same*," Margaret finished his thought. Aurora loved him as a *companion*; Cyrus loved her far more extravagantly.

Cyrus nodded again, smirking, "*Hole in one*, we used to say."

Hole in one? Is that a euphemism? Margaret didn't understand, but pressed on, somewhat more comfortable now, "I'm sorry *Captain*."

"Don't be *sorry*, Lady," Cyrus winced, focusing on her arm, eyes painting a portrait of dismay that rattled Margaret, "I'm happy here with her, and she's happy with me. I've done my *best* to live the last forty-odd years right, make my amends for what we did to the Bay Area, back in the Collapse."

Voice stuttering with disquiet, Margaret asked, "What did you do to the Bay Area? The Bay Area *Reach*?"

Cyrus stopped spreading jelly and fell quiet. Like Townsend, his face betrayed nothing more than a gaze that looked far past Margaret's arm. She could have pressed harder, dug into his mind, but she chose to allow an old man his secrets. For a moment though, Margaret thought perhaps she heard something in the distance.

Thump, thump, thump.

"Love," Cyrus looked away, and picked up a white towel to wipe his hands, "is the closest I can ever know of your *magic*. Aurora has told me, over the years, what it's like to not just *see* the world. I envy her sometimes, but I have my own kind of magic. She's always beautiful to me, no matter how old, or sick, she gets. She makes the world stop and *dance*, and I'm happy to dance with that world *for her*."

Gods be fucked, that's beautiful, Margaret thought, licking at the edges of her mouth as Cyrus dug between his fingers with the towel.

"That man who delivered you, your knight in shining armor? He loves you."

Knight in shining armor? Why would you want armor to shine? That's sniper-bait.

"Townsend?" Margaret asked.

"It's a hard thing to love a witch, Lady." Cyrus ignored the question and leaned forward, clasping his hands. It seemed to Margaret that he was no longer speaking *for* her, but rather himself. "You warp gravity around you, and either weigh a thousand pounds, or *nothing*. Light as a feather. Do you know what the skin of a witch *feels* like? For someone like *me*?"

Margaret shook her head, mystified by Cyrus. She liked the sound of his voice, it was deep, comforting, and made her forget about the pain.

"When you touch a witch, her skin *vibrates*. You can feel all that energy in your fingertips. The hairs at the back of your neck rise, and your *teeth hurt*. Like you'd eaten a bite of *candy apple*. It's not all sweet, it's terrifying. Knowing someone so close could swat you like a fly and maybe your life isn't worth notice."

That was, to Margaret's mind, more like her *mother*. For Maggi Lopez, people were a collection of tools. She'd never really understood those tools, she'd simply collect them and *hammer* away at problems until those tools *broke*.

"That's why I always take such care," Margaret answered herself, "you're so fragile."

Nodding, Cyrus chuckled, "Grant a fragile old man a favor, Lady Mayhem?"

Margaret didn't hesitate, "Of course."

"Losing her House broke Aurora's heart," Cyrus leaned forward, braced his fingers on his knees, and slowly stood up, bones creaking, "I'd like her to be happy, *really* happy, before she passes on. If it's ever in your power, I hope that you restore House Owens."

Margaret averted her eyes, unwilling to share her own broken heart, remembering Amihan, hand pressing her face to the tarmac, "I'm not sure how I could help you *or her*."

Standing, Cyrus straightened his linen jacket, tugging at fabric. Coughing for a moment, he said, "What do you call us? *Uninclined*? I'm uninclined, not *stupid*. There are *two* fire eaters on the west coast. One is asleep in our bed. The other is heir to the Antecedent Empire. If she burned you, then you stand against her *and* Alexander Lopez. You could run, I suppose, but you don't seem the type."

Margaret's eyes shot back to Cyrus, jaw clenching, "I'm not," *and neither was my mother,* Margaret thought proudly.

"Then, I suppose you'll need to fight Alexander *and* his daughter. Either you crown yourself queen of the Empire, or you shatter it to survive. Whatever happens, a day is coming that the restoration of House Owens will be within your power."

I need to fight the other Lopez twin too.

Margaret didn't answer Cyrus.

This seemed to be enough for the old man. Simply that Margaret listened to him, that she heard him. Perhaps he understood witches were *not* to be begged or threatened, perhaps after years with Aurora Owens he trusted a woman like Margaret to weigh the words of her own volition and see his logic.

"Get some sleep, Lady Mayhem. You'll need *all* your strength."

Cyrus turned and walked away, leaving Margaret alone with the lemongrass and pine smoke that threatened to suffocate her. There was a portrait, woven through the old *Eleven-Charlie's* words, a story of desire and terror and how the two could be mistaken for each other. Margaret desperately wanted to tell that story across empty wooden walls with sticks of broken charcoal.

How can I sketch without my right hand?

Margaret wouldn't have closed her eyes to the pain, but *that* thought was somber enough to press her to slumber.

11:30am February 28th, 39 Veilfall

Stockton, California

Margaret *would* need all her strength for the morning.

Bones were cut out of the corset. Removing the remaining molle web required skin to be pulled *up* and away, falling under steel's edge. For a moment Margaret had watched this, and against polished blade, an eye looked back at her, drowning in tears, stained pink and swollen. White willow bark would only thin her blood for surgery, and peyote couldn't be taken by witches. Although it was used as a painkiller in many parts of the southwest, Nevada, and the former House Owens, it also contained psychoactives. If Margaret lost her grip on reality, she could easily destroy her surgeon's mind.

Or drive Stockton mad.

This was all she could hold onto now. A monomaniacal control over her waking mind, counting through memories and dreams, a catalogue of things that had won her heart. The treasures of blueberry moonshine on her lips or teeth breaking the flesh an inch below her left ear. These trinkets became steps in an uphill stride, a breathless race between screams, phantom songs to drown out the nearly incomprehensible pain of being *flayed alive*.

Her chaise lounge was now covered in blood, pus, and charred flesh. Her bottle of scotch was three-quarters empty and when Margaret took swigs, she'd become sloppy; much of the liquor ran down her chest, into crushed and yellow fat of her right breast, curled up and lumpy, a malformed teat remnant.

How can I sketch without my right hand?

Cascading memories cut and ground at Margaret's eyeballs as if she waded under a waterfall of diamonds. The hold that kept her mind *aware* and *harmless* under such duress now turned into a jabbing anxiety. *Fear* would have been easier; its absence was a vile poison that turned her blind and deaf against what her own raw cries must have sounded like.

She was breathing heavy through her nose, jaw clenched, blinking hard. She'd already cried all the tears she had, her face stained in salt. At first it had been easy, cutting dead skin off her right arm. The doc had explained that these nerves were gone, and necrosis would likely take hold. Less severe burns required more care, more cleaning. Margaret had, at this juncture, lost consciousness a few times. The pain unfolded like a long and monotonous book where all the sentences read the same. Just as she believed she could take no more of the repetition, something would get *cut off*, or pulled, or tugged in a way that created a new variation of agony. She would weep with all the precision of a rabid animal.

The doc was absolutely a professional. He wasn't afraid to work on a witch. In fact, there was nothing about him that didn't feel like a neatly ordered toolkit that had fallen open on her lap, creating a warbling din of Latin jargon around Margaret's mind. There was something soothing to be found in this, but only in a way that hinted further towards madness, a kind of itching distraction that only served *to annoy* her beyond suffering.

Doc Rosso.

He was an old man, perhaps in his early seventies. A pre-Collapse surgeon who had served the 3rd Army. His head and face were clean shaven, along with his *eyebrows*, and even hands and arms. Townsend had delivered him, then vanished as the morning sun carved up the world into servings of percolated *fear*.

Fear. It wasn't her own, it was a flood that ran in through windows and slipped under the door like river water. It filled Aurora's apartment and spread across the whole of Stockton. *Thousands* of people were afraid, whispering, quivering. The machine of commerce didn't wake easy this morning, there was no hum or burgeoning bustle from Stockton's great gears. *Fear*, for Margaret, was a better painkiller than single-malt scotch would ever be. It was a warm bath in the privacy of a hostel, after a week eating petrol, dirt, and bugs. It was the first bite of masticated steak to reach her stomach, after days starving. It was a wild and feral friend, a creature she'd *never* kept on a leash. Rather, for Margaret, fear was a loyal animal that washed across her foes with a whisper and slept at her feet by night. It calmed her mind, made her dream of better places, *happier times*, a distant lullaby in her ear.

When Margaret was young, sometime after her mother had defeated the witch Vix, the two had spent weeks away from home. In those days, Maggi was a broken heart with teeth and eyes. She'd allowed Margaret to sleep on her chest. The old nightmares, the *terrors* that Margaret had long since locked away, still owned her. She'd wake, screaming, sobbing into her mother's chest. Maggi would simply wrap her arms around the little girl and sing her back to sleep. She had no magic that would have helped, she couldn't calm minds, or soothe nerves, but there was something deeply maternal in that action.

> "*A la nanita nana*
> *nanita ella, nanita ella*
> *Mi niña tiene sueño*
> *bendito sea, bendito sea.*"

Maggi wasn't a particularly good singer, but Margaret could remember her ear pressed to Maggi's chest, listening to the words resonate behind her clavicle. No matter how cold or hungry she'd been, there was a solace in that song. Solace behind Maggi's skinny fingers, clutching her so tight that it hurt.

To a young Margaret, Maggi Lopez was the personification of *fire*. Somewhere in her young mind she would pretend that an ancient god had sent this merciless creature, *The Bruja*, to rescue Margaret from the *smell* of burning skin. Her parents' burning skin.

Margaret hadn't realized, but she was singing the song aloud. Never turning away from his work, Doc Rosso asked her, "What does that mean?"

"I don't know," Margaret exhaled, her voice ragged, "my mother never taught me."

Doc Rosso grunted, and for a second before he ran his scalpel across Margaret's lower breast, she realized she wasn't in *pain*.

It was a blissful respite, no matter how few seconds it lasted.

6:37am March 1st, 39 Veilfall

Stockton, California

"Tick, tick, tick."

Margaret was caught between waking rest and dreaming sleep. Her skin was screaming, *itching* under bandages, and her head felt packed full of lard. She knew that the chaise lounge velvet was soft under her left cheek, and that she was inhaling long dried vomit, crunchy on her lips. But, behind this, she was also in the dark. *Running.*

Not running *from* something, running toward it.

Perhaps, Margaret thought, it was decades on campaign. Radio transmissions had etched a channel in her mind that still buzzed. Perhaps, instead, she was simply connected with her paramore; that was Townsend's voice in her head, speaking calmly.

"Tick, tick, tick."

Margaret opened her eyes. She knew what was coming.

"Troops in contact," Margaret whispered, left hand forcing herself up and off the lounge. Aurora Owens' apartment was quiet, swaddled in the first rays of morning light, orange and yellow playing off embroidered tapestries and luxurious couches.

The first *crack* came from the south. It was a 120mm cannon, a main line battle tank. The big, thirsty bitches that drank endless petrol.

Seventeen pounds of propellant.

One of Margaret's first jobs, as a child, was helping reloaders. Amihan's troops didn't have heavy armor, which meant those were 3rd Army guns.

Seventeen pounds of propellant, Margaret thought again, "I need to get to work."

Crack. This one came from the east. Townsend would have split his forces, entering the city from both gates.

"*Captain* Cyrus!" Margaret shouted, doing her best to sit up straight. Her right shoulder, which had always rested a little low, wouldn't square back correctly. Likewise, the bandages across her chest restricted movement, pulling her into a rigid and uncomfortable mass that made even simple tasks slow and taxing.

"*Captain* Cyrus!" Margaret shouted, a second time, her voice a choking rasp that sounded like a broken hand mixer trying to grind up wet rocks.

"Lady Mayhem." Cyrus said from behind her.

"Do either you, or Aurora, still have field dress?"

Cyrus paused for a second. Margaret could hear his mind rattle off a list of possessions, where they'd been stored, or if they'd been sold off. "A few vests, some shotguns and my old service pistol."

Margaret nodded, mostly for herself, and attempted to turn her head. This caused shrill pain across tugging flesh. It was a strange sensation, like a steel spring pulled open then snapping tight across skin. She was forced to shift all her weight to her left arm and buttocks.

After a quick gasp, she slowly croaked, "Bring me your pistol and a vest. Wake the Lady Owens as well. I need to negotiate the Antecedent Empire's surrender, in exchange for one of her old gowns."

Cyrus was wearing a pressed white shirt, cuffs rolled to his elbows, and a kitchen apron that was sprinkled with bits of flour and oil. He didn't answer immediately, and the two locked eyes across the room.

Crack.

The silence between Margaret and Cyrus was such that the sound, preceded by chirping automatic weapons, was a tangible exclamation point. Cyrus slowly smiled, understanding unfurled as a flag in his mind.

"Of course, Lady Mayhem."

Margaret returned his smile, then turned back, hiding her face. When she'd heard Cyrus leave the room, she allowed a pained groan. The more *awake* she became, the more it felt like some great dog had locked his jaws onto her breast, gnawing the flesh like a supple chew toy.

She wasn't hiding her pain from Cyrus. He *and* Aurora had certainly heard her lamentations. This was part of her dress for battle. The 3rd Army, *her* troops, could never see her cry or cringe, they had to know that their battlewitch was alive and strong.

While she waited for Aurora, and her clothes, Margaret began ripping the bandages off her face. She didn't *want* those, they felt constrictive, like a hobble or a crutch that kept her from moving freely. Standing up was the easiest thing she needed to do, and despite herself a triumphant giggle escaped Margaret's lips. She was wearing the same underclothes she'd had on the previous night, but the skirt and corset were gone. Linen bandages on her arm and chest provided some cover, but her left breast fell free and Margaret briefly considered whether she cared, before dismissing it.

On a table, just a few feet away from Margaret, was the necklace she'd commissioned to hold *the eye that does not see*. It had been tossed there, unceremoniously, its thin chain of gold scattered about and hanging off tan wood. The eye was mounted by clasps on a basic setting, nothing more than a dull looking piece of glass, ovoid and imperfect.

"I wanted to *steal* it while you slept," Lady Owens said, lurching toward her on antique crutches, painted in rich, orange, enamel. It was obvious that she was struggling, elbows jittering and her shoulders trembling.

"You should be in your chair," Margaret gurgled a placid reply.

"*Should!*" Aurora Owens cackled, "I hear you'd like to negotiate with me."

Margaret looked back to the necklace and pressed her left palm into it, fingers closing on the chain, "I need to dress. My commander has begun an assault on the 9th Battalion in Stockton. They'll need me"

"*Oh, I see,*" Aurora snickered, but Margaret didn't turn to watch her, "the mighty Empire begins to fragment. Turning on each other. Do you plan to lay claim to your brother's throne?"

For a second, with her hand on the eye, Margaret was certain she could hear voices. One of them was her mother, "*One day, after I'm dead, Mayy will replace me.*"

"Mom?" Margaret turned, her back to Aurora, and then felt foolish. Her mother was nearly twenty years in the grave, the *eye*, whatever it was, had played a dirty trick on her.

"Maggi is dead." Aurora *heard* her, and continued speaking to her back, "Your brother rules and Amihan Lopez has turned on you. *Why?*"

Margaret pulled the necklace off the table, puzzling how she'd wear it with only one hand. The answer was, *she couldn't*, she'd ask Cyrus for help. Even now, Margaret couldn't summon the anger this betrayal deserved as she remembered Ramona's reply, "*You'll shake the hornet's nest for sure, but maybe I can help.*"

Aurora Owens answered Margaret's silence, shuffling closer on crutches, "*Oh*, is this a guessing game?"

Before Aurora could finish, Margaret interrupted her, "Ramona told her sister that I planned to take the *Lopez* name and assume my brother's crown. She told Amy I would betray her father."

When Aurora answered, her voice was serious, clean and hard, like a blade, cutting to the heart of this matter, "Look at me, Margaret *Lopez*." Margaret did, but only after allowing her face to twist up in pain. The surname hurt, every bit as much as the blisters on her right cheek. "You've spent your entire life at war. You told me of your childhood, at Maggi's side and your years after her death. You don't understand the machinations of men; or in this case, a *very clever* young woman."

When Margaret licked her lips, she could taste jelly and aloe vera; it was greasy and turned her tongue numb. "She's an heir to the Empire, she's already got *power*. Why betray *me*?"

"Are you going to kill Amy Lopez?" Aurora leaned in, raising her eyebrows with the question. On her crutches, clawing for disquiet balance, she was still taller than Margaret.

"*Yes*," Margaret hissed.

Aurora nodded, smirking, her eyes every bit the polished silver of a monarch, "Ramona has betrayed you *and* the Plague Dog. Why is that? You're smart. Figure it out, my dear."

Some days Margaret would hate to admit it, and others she'd swear it proudly; but she was the product of Maggi Lopez, and right now it was Maggi that snapped back with venomous rage, "She wanted to *fucking* eliminate her rival, *her fucking sister.*"

Aurora's lips were thin, puckered down to her chin, and etched deep with fine wrinkles. Her answer held the same grit as her question, "Ramona has already won whatever game she wanted to play. Chances are, she's met with my *son*, under *her* conditions. If you bring Eric a *better* deal, he'll side with you. I'll make sure of it."

Margaret exhaled, anger choking her, "A better deal?"

"Total independence. The restoration of House Owens." Feeble and sick, Aurora may have well been an immovable statue when she spoke.

"All of it," Margaret nodded, "Total restoration. And after the smoke clears, I want a home here. No bullet in my skull, no exile. I want asylum for myself and the Antecedent soldiers who follow me."

Aurora Owens studied Margaret for a while, so long that Margaret was becoming concerned that the older woman might topple on her crutches. Finally, she leaned sideways, shifted her weight to the right. Looking at Margaret's good arm, then back to her eyes, extending her left hand, "My home is your home. My House is your House. I offer you the protection of Stockton, San Francisco, Santa Rosa, the Owens Army, and the Maul. We'll back you against Amihan, Ramona, and your brother. There's a price of course."

Margaret didn't answer. She didn't take her eyes off Aurora Owens, nor did she accept her hand, she merely *waited*, listening. Aurora took this deal seriously enough to stand on broken legs one last time, using her crutches. There was a wall of silence around her, rigorous, passive defenses, one layer after another, no stray thoughts, no emotions could fly free. Margaret had done the same. Partially to disguise her own pain, partially out of respect.

"When this is over, I want *the eye that does not see*."

It's not mine to give you, Margaret thought, but she didn't hesitate to extend her left hand to shake Aurora's. Clutched between their palms was the golden necklace.

"Deal." Margaret said, her voice stern.

Just as her favorite niece had feigned terror on The Beast, just as she'd promised Margaret aid in legitimizing her as the daughter of Maggi Lopez, Margaret lied also. There was no shame at the back of her throat, no regret. She'd given *twenty years* in service to the Antecedent Empire, and there was no way that she'd be rewarded with *death*.

Margaret's words bounced around her skull again, "*Good witches lie.*"

10:44am March 1st, 39 Veilfall

Stockton, California

"You've a handprint on your face."

Margaret turned to look down at the boy who was studying her. She'd been aware of him at her heels through Stockton's alleys. He smelled of warm bread and apples in the sun, traipsing building to building, evading her eyes as best he could.

"And your face is dirty, so I suppose we're even." Margaret offered a smile, affectionate and calm under her hood. The rain cloak that Aurora gifted her had an exterior of matte black, coated in hard paraffin and boiled oil; the inside was lined in crushed velvet and animal fur. It was an extravagant garment, and one that Margaret would almost certainly destroy.

"Why are you so close to the fighting?" The boy asked her. He couldn't have been more than eleven or twelve. His brown tunic was stained at the wrists and chest, black with an amalgamation of colors, leaving hands tinted yellow or orange. His family did well for themselves judging by his proper boots and clean teeth.

Margaret sighed, and turned away. He reminded her of someone she'd known as a young girl, a boy named Daniel Hasgard. Perhaps it was the way his eyes moved across her, or perhaps it was the scent of his rising fear that he was biting back so hard.

Pretty girls don't like cowards, she heard him think.

"This is my job. You're a calico printer. I get close to the fighting."

Planning to move up and into the smoky streets ahead, Margaret turned her back to this alley wall. It was covered in antique street signs, most of them upended squares, symmetrical diamonds. Each one had been hammered into place, laid down like tile, creating a checker pattern of white, black, blue and red in antique symbols and numbers, meaningless to anyone but those who'd been born before the Collapse.

"You don't dress like a soldier."

Frustrated and a little afraid for the boy, Margaret stopped sliding down the alley and turned to face the young man. Her eyes fell *past*, watching stories unfold a thousand yards away. She had set up a picnic in his mind, a checkered towel stretched out on the grass, and she'd begun to unpack her basket. There were things in that basket that she would *never* share with a curious lad, but she wanted him to show *one* memory in particular.

It was Daniel Hasgard's body, seen through *her* eyes. It wasn't merely the savage desecration of his chest at the hands of several well-placed shots, it wasn't the five feet of intestines he had trailed, dragging his body to safety. She was sharing the *smell* of stale copper, dried *shit*, and burnt hair. The vision blurred and faded, as her own tears had ejaculated into field of view, blinding her.

"*You're no coward boy,*" Margaret was speaking with her lips and her mind, creating a tandem echo across his awareness, "*but if you follow me, you will die.*"

The boy's jaw fell open and a sea of fear surged up and across his expression. He closed his mouth a second later, whispered a single word, and then ran. He ran so hard and fast that his body was bent, driven by legs that hammered in a perpetual spiral to keep him upright, barreling forward.

Margaret couldn't hear the word with her ears, but her mind was none so deaf.

Witch.

Turning away, pressing herself against the wall of tin and bolt, Margaret began to sidestep forward. The air smelled like ashen wood, oil, and gunpowder. There was no wind, not in the shade of Stockton's walls, and hanging smoke diffused sunlight. Small arms fire sounded like chirping pops, the cries of morning songbirds, greeting a new day, only to be punctuated by a violent hammer. Heavier weapons, a kingdom of bees unleashed on an unsuspecting world.

As she got closer to the main street, she could see shadows running in the thick haze, moving with purpose, crouching or striding, shouldering weapons. No one shouted or yelled, no orders could be heard, only begging from the wounded.

They're so close now, both sides can hear the other. Margaret thought, resting tongue on her lower lip where she could feel ragged blisters. This was door to door fighting. She couldn't simply focus on a mass of enemy soldiers, she couldn't see her foe across a battlefield, she had to *listen*, choose her targets, *take her time.*

The silence of the wounded and dying was nearly immediate, creating a void in the battle, pausing weapons fire.

Hush, hush, be still my beautifuls. Be still now and we'll forget the pain.

If the body or the mind bled, she was powerless to effect repairs. All that she could do was distract, offer a parallel reality, devoid of agony. She could feel *every* mind that lay prone in the streets under a canopy of lead. She could feel the men pressed against barriers or clinging to cover, under the care of a doc, heads cradled in the arms of their brothers. All of them burning hot, venting suffering.

She sang to them, holding their thoughts, memories. She was a ghost, faceless and quiet, their hands pressed to her bosom as she reminded them of things, they loved so much more than bleeding out, punctured organs, or burned flesh. There were no promises to be made for the dying, Margaret wouldn't lie *that way*.

This branch of the battle turned dead, quiet and quivering. Waiting for *something*, anything to shift. Stockton was a familiar partner for Margaret, unfolding around her, enveloping *her* *guests.*

Perhaps a few seasoned men of the 3rd Army knew what was happening.

Perhaps they know I'm here.

Margaret's right arm still hung limp at her side. With her left she swept the hood off Aurora's rain cloak and tipped her head back, inhaling deep. Acrid smoke was stinging at her sinuses. Her fingers clawed at the air above her head, and anyone watching her would have seen blue and white pigment dripping from nothing, then vanishing before falling to her forehead. She seemed like a dancer about to fall into an elaborate prance, her body stiff, and her eyes twitching behind lids. A single spark snapped off the metal signs next to her, creating an arc of harmless power, excess energy, shunting into nothing. A hundred tendrils swept out around her, diving for the warmth of beating hearts, latching around bone, tunneling into minds, *one after another* until Margaret had created a web across her city sprawl, linking one soldier to the next, regardless of what side they were on.

One of these men, not even twenty years old, sat on the second floor of a bakery, covered in flour. A stray round had exploded bags near him. He was listening to the silence, right eye a few inches from his scope, looking for *anyone* in range of view.

This could be a witch, he thought, *and not Amy*.

Margaret seized on the young man. He'd identified himself as her *enemy*. At the expense of her body, motor functions, and all others she was connected to, her mind leapt into the flour-covered soldier, possessed his nerves and bones, and all the winding electrical wires that powered his meat skeleton. With no hesitation the man leaned back, away from his rifle and scope, and withdrew a sidearm from his right hip; an old 1911.

I'm sorry you chose the wrong side. What's your name? Margaret asked the man as he cocked the hammer on his antique pistol and lifted it to his skull, barrel on his ear.

"Calvin. My name is Calvin."

Crack.

The connection was broken. A .45 round shattered Calvin's skull, and Margaret was thrust back into her own body, eyes open, alert, ignoring the drool that ran past her ragged lips and onto flak vest.

What the fuck? That was Calvin's window!

Margaret heard that next, and her eyes fall deep into the streets of soot and fog. This man was drowning in fear, Margaret could feel it all around him and her senses lapped at the choking dismay no different than a kitten would lick up a bit of milk. He was on the opposing street, behind a brick and mortar pillar, and he'd seen the muzzle flash. Calvin had just waved to him a few moments earlier.

I'm sorry you chose the wrong side. What's your name?

Margaret severed threads that connected this man's mind and body with a cuspate aspect of herself.

"Andrew Yates," the man said. She was letting him stay awake, his consciousness fully aware that *someone* or *something* else now owned his body.

Back in her own skin, Margaret convolved and nearly doubled over, grinning. Lips pursed tight, to keep the moan in her throat. She was *absorbing* the terror of Andrew Yates, gobbling at it as an upended soup bowl, potatoes and clams flooding her throat. Unable to *feel* her own fear, Margaret found the visceral reaction in others to be an intoxicant, an unfettered *power* that was euphoric. She was a flower open in the sun, absorbing nothing but fuel she needed for her terrible engines to *burn*.

Show me your friends, Andrew Yates.

Andrew Yates did as he was told, turning away from the pillar and shouldering his rifle. He swept the barrels across muddy air, and Margaret could see a boy through his eyes. Shaved head, missing his left ear, and a visible 9th Battalion patch on his shoulder. Margaret giggled as the boy turned to see Andrew, just for a second, wondering why his friend was aiming a rifle at him.

That was as far he got. The boy with a missing ear was now dead, a *five-five-six* round opening a hole in his throat, tearing apart his arteries, windpipe, and shattering his spine.

Andrew Yates *laughed* as he turned the rifle on his companions, his lungs *chortling* with Margaret's glee as he shot a second and *third*. Margaret could hear *nothing* with her own ears now, she was deep in the mind of Andrew Yates, and as *fear* spread around the man, so too did a complete understanding of her enemy. This was a tool Margaret could use to tell friend from foe, and even if she didn't possess the knowledge of *all* 9th Battalion soldiers, she knew where enough of them were now.

Crack-crack, two rounds hit Andrew Yates in the chest. Neither Andrew nor Margaret felt the pain, or even the pressure, save that Andrew's body stumbled backwards. The rounds had missed his spinal column, and his arms still worked. The arms Margaret owned. With fingers and hands, she brought the rifle back up to Andrew's shoulder, sites locking with eyes, nothing but windows for Margaret.

It was a *woman* who shot Andrew. He knew her name, *Angel McNally*. Originally from Texas, she was a *firecracker* in bed. Margaret wondered if Angel loved Andrew? Perhaps that's why she hesitated to deliver a fatal shot to Margaret's puppet. Or, perhaps, she was simply dumbfounded as Andrew's body moved so easily after consuming two rounds of lead.

It didn't matter because Angel McNally took a *five-five-six* in her right eye. An eye that had been such a bright green, the green of sea foam and beach lichen.

Margaret executed a total of *seven* 9th Battalion soldiers before Andrew Yates had his body crippled. It was a round to his stomach that separated his spinal column, dropping the man to his knees.

I'm sorry you chose the wrong side, Margaret whispered in Andrew's head as she withdrew her claws from his nerves and motor functions.

Awake, *aware*, in her own skin, Margaret's chin was coated in shiny saliva, and her body was hunched against the alley wall. She stood up straight, reaching a palm up to wipe at her mouth. As she did, she also realized that her left hand was coated in something like black ink, thick and viscous, liquid charcoal dripping off her fingers, oozing from the pores of her forearm and falling down her velvet sleeves.

What? Margaret was pulled out of the fray for a second, until dusty morning light crossed her palm, turning the oily residue reflective and allowing Margaret to see her own face. The flesh where Amy's hand had pushed her skull into tarmac was angry, punctuated by fatty, yellow blisters.

Whatever shock Margaret *felt* in looking at this umber liquid washed away, swept aside in a tsunami of rage that cradled around her heart.

"*I loved you.*" Amy had told her, jaw quivering, when she lit her aunt on fire. Not an aunt by blood, but the aunt who had changed her diapers as a baby, the aunt who had taught her the tenants of magic and told her tales of the gods.

Amy had delivered an intimate understanding of what it felt like to fall under the hands of a fire eater. She could not have told another with words, but there was a certain kind of horror to feeling bones glow hot as embers, melting flesh from the inside out. This was a memory that Margaret would walk with for the rest of her days.

This was also a memory that Margaret shared with the 9th Battalion.

Every one of them that she'd located with Andrew Yates. Men she couldn't see, or Andrew barely knew, each one of them had their skulls drilled open and a boiling pot of Margaret's agony poured in.

This was what Margaret called *spreading her terrible wings*. Showing them all a glimpse of her pain, distracting them, swelling up in their emotions, a soft and sallow balloon, pressing them to their limits of sanity and inducing waking terror.

Waking terror that existed *only* in their minds.

The streets of Stockton fell into a second maelstrom of violence. This time the 9th Battalion soldiers began screaming, *begging*, letting out cries of pain not hitherto known in this place. The 3rd Army held post and turned on their enemy as they fell to the ground, rifles clattering on cobbles, small arms fire bursting forth and igniting the streets anew with heat and glow. Men with bayonets and squad automatic weapons ran past Margaret's alley, she heard a grenade fly and *pop,* the 3rd Army was descending on Amy's men like a vulture on flesh carrion, drunk with hunger and bloodlust boiling hot in their loins.

An officer strode past the alley, easily *six-foot-two* or *three*, gaunt, his chin-to-toes may as well have been a flat board under armor, and kit. He stopped, turning to look at a tiny woman in the alley, covered in something like motor oil, her face burned with a *handprint*.

"Lady Mayhem," the officer nodded, turning. He wore chainmail sleeves over his thickly woven shirt, blackened by flame to reduce reflection.

Margaret recognized him. He was another one of Townsend's Captains. *Jared?* Margaret would never insult one of her men by forgetting his name, so instead of fumbling a reply she nodded smartly with a face covered in slobber, "Captain. How's your day?"

The tall Captain smirked, looking around, understanding, "Better, now that *Pups* of War are falling all over themselves to retreat. What are your orders, Lady Mayhem?"

Margaret glanced down at her left hand, then dropped it below her cloaks, listening carefully to the tall Captain. His chest was stiff with pride. He *knew* quite well this was the work of Lady Mayhem, *his* battlewitch, *his* 3rd Army. There was nothing in his soul but total loyalty.

"Hunt down every member of the 9th Battalion. No prisoners, *no quarter*." Her voice cracked as she growled a reply. Manic glee surfaced once more as a nasty smile spread across her face, cracking the scabs at her lower lip.

The tall Captain's smirk became a grin. There was a sense of satisfaction about him now, a hammer with nail to strike, a wrench with bolt to turn. His imagination also fell to the spittle coating Margaret, a symptom of not fully commanding her own functions. He was imagining *cock and balls* in her mouth, the image as clear as a photograph in hand and as loud as the battle around them.

Margaret wasn't sure if that was a *compliment* or not, and she replied with the same awful glee resonating in her tone, "You should probably raise your standards, Captain."

If the tall Captain was embarrassed at the notion of his fantasy on display for the very *object of his fantasy*, he didn't show it, "Never been my experience that a *blowjob* could be ruined by a few scars."

She was pleased that at least one man didn't find her burns as disgusting as *she did*, but Margaret had always used sexuality as a form of *control*. Its unleashed impact on this Captain made her uneasy and stole away confidence she never knew she possessed.

Margaret's eyes rolled across smoky streets, down toward the 3rd Army lines. In all the world, right now, it was only Townsend who offered a sense of wholeness, belonging, something else it seemed which Amy had stolen.

"Escort me to the Lieutenant General."

2:20pm March 1st, 39 Veilfall

Stockton, California

Townsend helped Margaret remove the rain cloak, tossing it to wooden chairs and tables of the abandoned tavern they occupied. Across the bar, sans stools, were dozens of maps, layer upon layer, with measure and leaden pencils. Most of the maps were views of Stockton's street-level planning, but some also showed sewer mazes, and the internal structures of her city walls.

"I can't tell if you're in pain," Townsend didn't immediately look back at Margaret from her coat. What *he* could not read in her eyes, *she* could read in his. He was repulsed by the blisters along her lips and up her cheek, and she didn't *actually* blame him. The wounds were gruesome, and she hardly wanted to look at them herself. Under bandages, and the black gown that Aurora loaned her, she could easily forget the extent of her injuries. It didn't make her *feel* better physically, her face still cried out, and her chest ached savagely as she moved and twisted, warbling along cobbled streets and sidewalks to meet Townsend. She was physically exhausted, her eyes heavy, and mind drowsy. She wanted to just *rest for a while*.

"I am," Margaret frowned, sighing heavily.

"Is there anything…" Townsend's voice fell off and she heard his thoughts, *there's nothing that I can do.*

Margaret closed the yard that separated them, pressing herself into Townsend's plate carrier and armor. His gear prodded and pushed her, invading her body in uniquely impersonal ways. Her left arm reached up, fingers wrapping around his neck behind collar and chainmail, dusty with charcoal. She was embracing him as best as her body would allow, and Townsend pressed her left side closer.

"Thank you," she said, "for the other night. For Stormair."

Townsend didn't answer and she wished for his beating heart against her ear. She could always feel his pulse, but it wasn't the same as pressing her face against his broad chest and just *listening*.

After a moment Margaret pulled away, heavy on her feet. She started to pull a chair out, with one hand, but Townsend reached over to help her. Leaning down and across her shoulder. Margaret couldn't smell him. The smoke of Stockton's ruin hobbled her sinuses. Yet, she could *feel* a unique vibration this close, the clockwork connections that made up a soldier, the woven tapestry of both his strength and concern, a thick wall betraying little.

As she sat down, Townsend offered his hand and she accepted. Looking up at him, she smiled, blinking several times, long and slow, then waggled a finger at him, inviting him closer. He extended one leg and dropped to a single knee.

"Do you still want to be a traitor with me?" Margaret asked softly.

"I think that train left the station," Townsend grunted, looking away from Margaret's ragged face, eyes scanning across the empty tavern, "The 3rd Army garrison of Stockton showed their loyalty when they attacked the Dogs of War."

"What of Amy?" Margaret replied, eyebrows high as she leaned back in her wooden chair. It wasn't comfortable, and her back mumbled in disdain.

Townsend shook his head, eyes still distant, "No one has seen Amihan Lopez. I was concerned she'd close Stockton, so we rallied the heavy armor and entered the city. The Dogs didn't make it easy."

Margaret realized her neck ached from where one arm simply hung down from her collar bone. She used her left hand to pick up the forearm and place it in her lap.

Townsend continued, voice hushed and low, "The east gate offensive was turned back. Casualties were high. Our southern gate offensive was stalled, fighting across a dozen city blocks. We broke them thanks to you."

Is Amy dead? Margaret wondered, before answering Townsend, "Did you send for the other garrisons? San Jose and Santa Rosa?"

Townsend refocused his eyes on Margaret, doing his best to ignore the crumpled flesh around her eye, where Amy's finger tips had pressed, "Dogs of War sent riders north. The 3rd Army is in disarray. Some are loyal to *you*. Others consider you a traitor to the Empire."

She lives, Amihan ordered that.

Margaret found the knowledge of Amy's health oddly satisfying, though not out of any concern for the young woman, rather a hard and weighty rage in her own stomach. "So, we're on our own against Amy."

Townsend turned his head to the side, chin up, and brows furrowed, "I want to tell you that's not a problem, *but...*"

"*But* the 3rd Army has been *fat and happy*, eating and fucking the heart of House Owens for nearly two years," Margaret didn't need Townsend to lay it out for her. Life was *easy* here in the west. The garrison had grown soft, *complacent.*

"The Dogs fight *hard*." Townsend leaned forward and stood. As he paced away from Margaret his boots made the wooden floors keen and creak. Reverence turned to anger when Townsend spoke, and to his credit Margaret could feel him press and fold it, like a starched shirt, hidden away in a suitcase. "We've also lost track of Ramona."

Looking to Townsend's bald head, broad wrinkles of muscle and fat at the back of his neck, Margaret replied with a hiss, "Ramona Lopez is the reason we're in this *shit show*. I confided in her, *I trusted her*, and she lied to Amy. Tell your men to *flee* her on site. She's not a battlewitch. She might be worse."

"Worse?" Townsend looked over his shoulder.

Blinking slowly, Margaret lifted her filthy left hand to hold it against her chest. This had begun to ache in a new way, as muscle being pried up, and off her bones, "There are *three* tenants of magic," Margaret quoted her mother, "one of which is *reveal*. Certain witches can get to the truth of a thing. Ramona, she can see to the *desires* of a person, and can control their motivation. She may be *better* at it than any I met before."

This reminded Margaret of the times her mother had issued such stern warnings about the other divinations, their insidious lures, and created a litany of ridiculous exercises to prepare her student for such inevitable meetings.

Townsend slowly turned his body, arms lifting to cross, high on his chest, "What desires did she see in you?"

My irrational desire to look beautiful for a man who already desires me?

Margaret didn't say that thought, instead she answered with half a truth, "She appealed to my vanity, gave me a reason to leave my sidearm at home. Have you ever seen me *unarmed*?"

Shaking his head, Townsend needed no time to consider his answer. Gesturing toward the front door, towards command camp, he answered, "Why turn on *you*? Why turn on Amy?" In the time she'd known him, Margaret had never quite seen Townsend angry until now. It was an awesome show of fury, his eyes danced with fire and his voice bellowed around the room like a dog gone mad, knocking over chairs and tables.

Margaret smiled, enjoying the fury, "I'll ask her when I catch up with her."

"*She's heiress to this Empire!*" Townsend shouted, before biting down hard and regaining his cool. "She's heiress. And if we keep fighting like we did today, there won't even be an Empire." No matter how quietly he *spoke*, Margaret could hear his heart hammering at his chest, angry with almost every aspect of the world, save Margaret herself. It delighted her, and to some degree emboldened her beyond exhaustion. Lost for a moment in his rhythmic pulse, Margaret realized she was grinning at him, as desirous now as she'd been the night they first bedded.

I don't expect him to throw me on the table and fuck me with all that rage.

That was a lie. She *did* expect that.

"First thing," Margaret glared up under her fuzzy brows, "I want you to relocate your command to the home of Aurora Owens. Tell Aurora you're doing this *personally* and tell her that this came directly from *me*."

Townsend tipped his head, "*Alright,*" he said slowly.

"Second thing. I'm promoting you. *General* Townsend will command more respect. I also declare you *rightful* commander of all *loyal* 3rd Army soldiers. *Loyal to me.*"

Townsend chuckled, "I think General Bhatt will be disappointed to know he's been relieved of command."

"Bhatt went south with my brother," Margaret spat to the wooden floor, her sneer only turning nastier, more predatory, "and Bhatt isn't *fucking me*, so I'll invite him to go *fuck himself.*"

Townsend's anger had ebbed over the last few moments, and as clearly as if he'd spoken out loud, Margaret heard him think, *Bhatt would never shut up about it.*

"You have a bigger *dick* than Bhatt, if you're wondering," Margaret said.

Townsend answered, as smooth as a poured wine, "I wasn't."

A week ago, Margaret would have wrestled with the words she spoke next. Nothing had *really* changed in the days since, save her mind was occupied by storied betrayal and physical agony. She simply didn't have enough *mind left* to dwell on girlish anxiety. "It's much worse than what you see on my face. If you're wondering."

Exhaling, Townsend seemed relieved by this. It stood between them like a roughhewn statue, unvarnished and hideous, "You're going to lose that arm. I know."

Not today I won't, Margaret almost said it aloud, "I don't really know what to do when my paramour finds me revolting. I'm not *angry*. I can't even blame you."

There was a sincere silence between them, Townsend didn't dismiss her words, or defend himself. He knew his thoughts would never *truly* be private around her. When he finally answered, it was honest, "I don't know, either. But I know that you're alive, and I prayed to the gods for *that*. No favor is free, so perhaps Ares tests my dedication. I won't leave your side."

Ares would see my flesh ruined to test my paramour?

Margaret found that a very foreign idea. As a *witch* she'd grown used to being the *center of the world*, and as often as that was a truth of her condition, it was also an illusion that had damned her more than a few times. Margaret wasn't offended. If anything, it was an exotic notion, that she needed to offer her lover something *more* than simple lust, that she'd need to find new ways to seduce someone, ways not gifted to her at birth.

"Help me, please," Margaret gestured over to the rain cloak that Townsend had cast aside. "You'll have to pull it up my right arm without rotating my shoulder."

Crossing to the table, Townsend retrieved her cloak, turning the arms out properly, then placing it on Margaret as she stood up from her seat. It was a fumbled affair, though Townsend did better than Cyrus, avoiding her wounds. Aurora's coat nearly touched the dusted tavern floor and obscured *both* hands with cuffs and sterling silver buttons, measured for a taller woman. That was fine, because it also hid how badly her right shoulder was twisted.

"I need two escorts. Hard gunmen." Margaret said.

"You'd have had my best, regardless," Townsend replied, his pulse slowing as his big hands adjusted her hood.

"You won't much like where I'm going," Margaret looked at him, good hand placed, palm first, in the middle of his plate carrier.

"Don't imagine I will," Townsend shrugged.

"We need Duke Eric Owens," Margaret nodded, mostly for her own benefit, then lifted her hand from Townsend's chest, "We're not fighting the Dogs alone."

6:45pm March 1st, 39 Veilfall

Stockton, California

This wasn't the first time Margaret had strode the streets of a city under siege, but it was the first time she'd seen one so *vibrant* as fighting spread. Night was upon Stockton now, and her great walls cast deep shadows that obscured even the stars, a mother's cloak protecting her children from harsh winds.

The southern stretches of Stockton were mostly residential, pocketed with stores. Cargo and commercial traffic bound into the city's beating heart was routed along Boulevard 5th, garishly adorned with taverns and brothels, marketing to Stockton's inbound commerce. In better days it wasn't uncommon for the thoroughfare to be jammed, wagon-to-bumper, well past sundown. Townsend's temporary command quarter was located here, and he now controlled 5th.

Margaret and her escorts had to cross east, down narrow confines, of *Ateth Street*. Pre-Collapse homes, row by row, had become foundations for two- and three-story apartment complexes, sewn together tightly with narrow hovels built between. *Ateth* was mostly gouged dirt, paved in hammered feces and small stones. The air was cumbrous with rank sewage, where the upper-apartments dumped their bedpans at night, unconnected to the city's waterways. Most of these tenants had abandoned their homes as the day wore on, only a few derelicts held hostel. It reminded Margaret, quite intensely, of her childhood, walking empty streets with her mother and a small contingent of soldiers that would become the Antecedent Army.

At the easternmost end of *Ateth* was Grant Jail, a series of old townhomes that had been converted to house petty offenders and criminals scraped off back alleys and cellars. Pickpockets, thieves, thugs, and layabouts mostly occupied the grounds. Stockton sent her more violent offenders to the ruins of Sacramento where they worked in chain gangs, digging for the rest of their lives, or until radiation finally claimed them.

Grant Jail was also abandoned. Crossing to the rails, Margaret could hear bedlam, inmates crying out to guards who'd fled. Front gates standing wide open and guard towers left empty. Anyone could have walked into the place, ignoring high aluminum fences painted in extensive murals, a young boy stealing an onion, or a woman's overbag being ripped free of her shoulder. Unlike the other vivid walls of Stockton, these had been chipped and faded over the years, and often vandalized with simple black tags.

Margaret and her two companions could now head north along the rails, where multi-track yards and depots peppered the spine of Stockton. Feral dogs ran free, staying back, barking in impotent rage at the invaders who swept their territory.

It was at least *three miles* before Margaret and her escorts reached the Crosstown viaducts, fresh-water delivery for most of Stockton's plumbing. This had been one of Aurora's greatest achievements after the Collapse, a simple and effective means of providing running tap water, for drinking, cooking, and bathing. It was the first like it on the West Coast, Aurora had once explained to Margaret, a crown jewel second *only* to the city walls that kept her young state secure. It also leaked badly, and Margaret's companions waded through ankle-deep marshes, thick with high reeds, vibrant seedlings and mossy growth. People lived here in the shadow of Crosstown, collecting water that fell from the viaduct, selling it to the poor denizens of places like *Ateth* Street. Forgotten by Owens and Antecedents alike, these clever farmers, peddlers, and cobs watched from behind ramshackle abodes, made of rotted and soft wood, rusted iron, and dirty aluminum. They didn't surround themselves in vivid murals, but like most in House Owens, they wore vibrant colors, deep blue or yellow, that popped and flickered in their glowing fire light. They had no desire to disturb Margaret, their voices falling to hushed whispers and the gnashing of chew tobacco and spicy seeds. Margaret's mind washed across the swamp, a background tickle, hazy fear, a reminder that it was best to keep to themselves.

Past their huts, kicking through mud and morass, Margaret could feel the eyes of *other* things watching her. Not the scampering rat-creatures that fed on garbage and horse *shit* of a major city, this was more insubstantial. Hinkypunks, or *will-o'-the-wisps*. They weren't ghosts, there was no clicking and snapping of a human mind, these *felt* like a cat or weasel, inquisitive as they darted under the water and in the reeds. From time to time Margaret would see a soft glow pop up, reflections on wet stone, until she grew closer and only old bark looked back at her. Maggi had called them *luces del tesoro*, a goblin who might show a clever child where to find lost silver. Maggi had suggested that those children, lured deep into a swamp with sweet promises, would never return, but these little nixies seemed harmless. Every bit as curious as the occupants of Crosstown, and utterly without fear.

By the time they emerged from Crosstown's swamps, Margaret was weary beyond measure. For the first time in recent memory her face did *not* burn, but her body ached. Each joint strummed in a low and quiet pain, from her spine to knees and up into her neck. She needed rest, to sleep for a week or three. The idea of a bed was seductive beyond reason.

With one hand braced on a ponderous concrete support pillar, Margaret *had* to pause and rest. She could feel decaying cement, brittle and sandy at her fingertips and biting nails. One of her escorts strode up near, short and stocky, he was middle-aged with an ill-gotten beard that seemed too thin in all the wrong places. "If *ya'* need *ta'* sit boss, we gotcha."

Margaret couldn't place his accent, but she found his complete disregard for her title, *Lady*, to be charming. He was a Sarn't named Decklan Holloway, who had been passed over a thousand times for promotion due to an ill temper and a love of spirits, according to Townsend. However, his guncraft was some of the finest in the 3rd Army.

"For a moment," Margaret closed her eyes and turned to lean against the pillar, her eyes heavy and her knees weak. She pulled her right arm over her abdomen and allowed herself to slink down to the ground, in a crunchy well of gravel.

Deck's face and torso were illuminated by distant gas light, and an occasional glint of metal caught his rifle. He kept the weapon down, slung under one arm and inside a woolen coat of deep gray, though anyone paying attention would have seen it.

He withdrew a cigarette, and Margaret heard him strike a match, the smell of sulphur blazing for a moment. He held it between his thumb and index finger, burning cherry tipped up, inside his palm, to hide the extra light.

The road was ruin. Asphalt had become nothing more than a cadence of rocks and memories. Margaret turned south, inhaling burning tobacco, watching Stockton festooned by a fountain of murky red smoke illuminating streets, windows, signs and boards. Small arms fire could still be heard, popping, miles away. But *here*, in this one place, beyond Deck and rusted fences long bent and torn away, was peace. Total darkness. It beckoned Margaret close, tempted her with cool solace where she could lay, unknown and unseen, a place she could rest.

Margaret should have known sooner that there was *something* out there, summoning her close, but exhaustion and injury had blurred her mind. It wasn't until Deck turned away from her and took a few steps back, that she noticed. His cigarette smoke curled around Margaret's view, and in shades of dissipating tobacco, Margaret could see a figure watching her. Not wholly visible at one time. It might be legs one second, at another it could be arms. Fading and skeletal with bleached bones that shifted in hues of pale blue and cobalt, wrapped in tatters of old film, atrophied and crumbling, shifting and moving in a jerking dance, for a forgotten rhythm.

This was no ghost like Harvester, and certainly not a god squeezing a fraction of its consciousness into meat and bone. Margaret realized, *this thing,* it was attempting to manifest in her physical world, a display of terrifying power.

Margaret glanced over to her second companion, who'd been quiet. She was just a silhouette in the dark, but she seemed to be watching the same entity through Deck's smoke.

"Do you *see* that Erin?" Margaret asked, turning from the girl and back to the darkness.

"I can *feel* it," Erin answered, so softly that Margaret strained to hear.

"*See* what? *Feel* what?" Deck asked, his heels grinding up gravel. Soaked in anxiety, he tasted like bitter leaf, the kind you'd eat for a sour stomach.

Margaret had seen a great many things in her life, but nothing like that, nothing so non-corporal and powerful that it was ripping at physical air to manifest. When people discussed the fall of the Veil, what they really meant was the *weakening* of the Veil. If an uninclined saw a ghost, like Harvester, it tended to be powerful and full of rage. A witch who talked to gods, like Condatis, interacted with a physical shell. Spirits and hobgoblins from the beyond didn't walk unfettered and free, there was a price to pay.

"Are you inclined?" Margaret asked the small woman, named Erin, ignoring Deck's start and shudder.

The girl shrugged. She couldn't have been older than sixteen or seventeen, a former brassboy, she'd joined the 3rd Army somewhere in Nevada. Although she commanded no rank, Townsend promised she was an uncanny marksman. Margaret was, at this moment, numb to digging beyond Erin's skull. She needed this break.

Whatever held her gaze in the darkness was *still lurking here*, and Margaret's instincts suggested that leaving the darkness, *total darkness*, was the only way to be free of her.

Free of 'her?'

Margaret didn't second guess herself. Just because she couldn't focus enough to make full use of her abilities didn't mean that her senses were quiet.

"Help me up," Margaret asked, softly, as though Erin's quiet tone was a flu that she could catch by breathing too deeply. Deck offered a hand, and it seemed slightly too big for his frame. The muscles around his wrists and fingers had all the density of steel cables. "We should continue on. Pacific will be busy, at this time of night."

Margaret hadn't been wrong about this.

Pacific Avenue was the central hub and downtown furor of Stockton. A beating heart that infused all the city with frothing life. For the brokers and vendors that plied their trade under gaslamp and snapping fluorescents, there was no war being fought. They sold finely crafted leathers, clothing, and weapons both stylish and functional. Every kind of shotgun load that could be imagined, and unique daggers. There were a thousand types of cuisine, street cooks plied their sizzling meats and sweets on cobble's edge. From barbequed sausage to chicken marsala, smoked fish, *tacos a carne asada*, seaweed salted and dried, even crispy bacon fat, black with pepper, it was all here. Air was humid and foggy, with the tang of spice and curry, lard and skin, boiled with aromatic piquancy, filling lungs and wetting the tongues with esculent promises.

Clusters of men huddled up under street light to smoke and play dice, hushed whispers and angry growls just beyond earshot echoed off brick and plywood. "*The Antecedent Empire has gone mad, they're fighting each other,*" some whispered, others bit back, "*Fuck the Antecedents, long live Lady Owens!*"

There were also families marauding at the street's edge, children hugging their mother's legs close, full of fight and awe as they witnessed Pacific for the first time. Babies wept in their parents' arms, dreaming of home or a suckle at their mother's breasts. These were the southern Stockton residents, the poor who'd been displaced when Amy's Dogs seized their streets.

In this hustle, between the press of Pacific's garish neon temptations and cheerless dispossessed, Margaret could hear the traffic of a hundred other city-states. This was the reality that Margaret had grown up in, thrived in, listening to greasy innuendo of migration. How many times had she rode high on a big Abrams? Wrapped in goggles and shemagh, coughing at black carbon and watching a river of destitute souls leaving the fighting that she would soon join. Just like those men, women, and children, these residents clutched packs of valuables and rolls of bread or meat, small carts for the crippled, old grandmothers, and leashed dogs.

The difference was, Stockton had not known this kind of city-fighting since the first days of the Collapse, thanks to Aurora Owens.

"Where to, boss?" Margaret had paused outside a shuddered tannery, breathing heavy and fighting a new wave of exhaustion. Deck pressed his chest into her left arm, the upper receiver of his rifle swung up and bouncing soundlessly off her left breast and flak vest.

"Oxford Circle. A lot of the former Owens nobility moved there after we kicked them out of the palace." Margaret closed her eyes, feeling Deck's right arm steady her.

"*Ya'* sure it's a good time? *Ta'* have this talk? Talking with Lord Owens?"

"*No,*" Margaret laughed, her upper shoulder and clavicle spun a web of stiff discomfort and very real pain. It felt as though her bones wanted to rebel, pressing themselves out of her flesh, puncturing her skin, clawing at her from the inside out. A part of her *wanted* to panic at the sensation, but a wiser part of her realized that it was just a trick of imagination, "But, if we don't win the support of Eric Owens, I think none of us will like the outcome."

Deck Holloway laughed, the plate carrier he wore under cotton and wool vibrating with his deep chuckle, "Speak for *ya'self*, boss. When Alexander shows up, *Imma* out, droppin' gear, patches and armor. Netter Deck Holloway, that's *mah'* name. Better believe it."

Despite the grim subject, Margaret adored Deck's attitude. She couldn't *read* his joke, feel his thoughts, but it sounded about right for a man pinned down a hundred times in the Antecedent Empire. He'd only fight, or *die*, for Townsend.

"*Netter* Mayhem," Margaret exhaled hard, then straightened up as best she could. "I really doubt anyone will believe that."

"Boss, I'll get *ya'* over *ta'* Owens' house on Oxford. *Erin'll* book us rooms, up off Pacific, down *near'a* Red Light, Brothel Row."

"Thank you, Sarn't," Margaret exhaled.

It wasn't much further to walk. Oxford wasn't that far removed from Pacific, and it gave Margaret the time she needed to locate the last glowing embers of cynosure that she possessed in her soul. She was tired now and needed to expend all that was left of her will on wowing the heir of House Owens, convincing him to risk *his* life and limb for *her* life and limb.

11:05pm March 1st, 39 Veilfall

Stockton, California

"Lady Mayhem," Eric Owens smiled, green eyes the same shade of a flowing California river, "while I am grieved to hear of this dispute between your commanders, I fail to see what solutions I could offer to *Antecedent* problems."

Refusing the offer to sit in one of Eric's finely appointed leather chairs, Margaret leaned back, and tipped her chin up with the arrogance her position demanded. The stance was laborious, as her flesh stretched and pulled painfully at her side and abdomen, "I think what you fail to see, Lord Owens, is that these are *your* problems."

Eric speech was a raspy resonance from the back of his throat, almost certainly a souvenir of war, along with the jagged scar that marked his left brow. He was tall, slim, and wore a cashmere smoking robe, tattered at the collar and cuffs, a relic of a world that existed before the Collapse. It befitted a noble heir. Where the robe joined at his sternum, a clump of black chest hair, thick and glossy, jutted out, "There's very *little* I fail to see, Lady Mayhem. You're seeking my backing to make this schism legitimate. You stand before me, in one of my mother's old gowns, to beg the support of your *Antecedent auxiliary*. Support I should rightfully bring to bear on the side of a Lopez, like *Plague Dog*."

Margaret knew she cast a poor symbol of nobility. The gown that Aurora Owens had loaned her was stained at her ankles from Crosstown swamp and dusted finely in brick and plaster. When she answered, she forced total conviction into her voice, "*And yet,* you haven't. You've brought none of the former Owens troops to support the 9th Battalion."

Eric Owens clapped his palms together, leaning forward, directing real attention on Margaret, "Do you know why that is, *battlewitch?*"

Sneering, Margaret replied, "*No*, I don't. Because when my brother learns of your inaction, he'll fall upon Stockton with Plague Dog and burn your mother's city to ash."

"No," Eric held up a hand, separating his palms, then turning away from Margaret to a finely polished shelf of black and gray marble. Withdrawing a decanter of brown liquid, he poured drinks, "Your *fiat* brother will do nothing of the sort. He'll be short on supplies, returning from a long southern campaign."

Margaret stepped forward, closing the gap between her and Eric, balling her left fist, "If you think my brother's armies will be weak, you may be right, but he still commands *three* battlewitches, no less terrible than I am."

"Does he?" Eric paused, brows lifted, the scar tissue on his forehead creasing flesh at an odd angle, then looked back at two glass tumblers, free of cracks.

Why would you ask that, Eric?

Margaret swallowed hard and accepted one of the tumblers, two fingers of whiskey inside. She exhaled, then kicked back the glass, taking liquor at her throat, "You sound like a man who's too certain of things he has no right to be."

"I'm simply not interested in taking Stockton, or my soldiers, into an Antecedent civil war. Your masters are not *my* masters."

Margaret considered the whiskey smooth, smoky and even savory, but she felt no shame for downing it so quickly as Eric Owens nursed his tumbler, licking alcohol off his lips.

He's too certain, but he's never been an idiot, Margaret thought, *why would he so confidently disregard Alexander's rage?*

With that, Margaret remembered, "Ramona already visited you."

Eric crossed to the opposing side of the marble counter, so that it separated them. He wasn't grinning, his mouth didn't curl into a smile, but his eyes were *laughing* like a young boy who'd been told an especially dirty joke, "How many more burns does my mother's gown hide, I wonder? You've not lifted your right arm since you arrived. Witches can't focus if they're distracted."

Margaret sighed and slid her tumbler across the marble, shades of umber pockmarked with glints of gold and silver, "Pain is very distracting. *No*, I'm not listening to your mind."

Eric finally allowed his eyes to reach his lips, "So, we're *equals* tonight."

"Tell the truth, shame the devil," Margaret answered, dryly, her voice cracking as she spoke, "Pour another one, Lord Owens."

Eric filled Margaret's tumbler again from the same crystal decanter, then picked it up with index finger and thumb to sit it carefully down. "*Equals* then, Lady Mayhem. What do you think Ramona Lopez offered me?"

Margaret didn't hesitate to relieve him of the tumbler. She took a long sip this time, rather than emptying the glass, allowing whiskey to warm her throat and esophagus, coddling her tender nerves, "She seduced you. You said no at first, but she wouldn't relent. In bed, naked, she promised you the world. She explained the Antecedent disposition and offered to eliminate Alexander's battlewitches. When you asked her how, she explained that Plague Dog would kill me, and that my 3rd Army would break themselves on the Dogs of War in block-to-block fighting. She'd arrange the demise of each battlewitch at my brother's disposal, and you'd be free to negotiate an independent House Owens once more."

"Mostly true," Eric Owens shrugged, sipping again at his whiskey before placing it back on the marble, "I didn't tell Ramona *no at first*. I've never desired a woman so much, and I'll make her my *Queen* if she lets me."

Margaret made a sharp noise, something out of her throat that sounded like a screech and laugh, "Oh, *Lord Owens*, you poor fool man. I'm sure a *hundred* Lords and Ladies across the Antecedent Empire have said the same *stupid fucking thing*."

Lord Owens stood back, coming up to full height, cracking his thumb joints under each of his fists, "I know she wouldn't accept. I *can* dream, and I *will* dream, and that's the finest gift Ramona gave me."

Margaret shook her head, lips raised in disgust, *Long after we're all dead, that's what they'll say about Ramona. She gave so many fine gifts.*

"Unless, I kill her."

She'd said it under her breath, a whisper, a second of revulsion made manifest, wrapped up in a heady sack of anger, bloated with grief and exasperation. Eric Owens heard her regardless. He watched her for a moment, then finished his liquor, allowing the two to share his study in silence for several long moments.

This wasn't the first time that Margaret was deaf to the thoughts of another, and it made her feel as ruined as the burns across her body. *I'm not an idiot, I can still do this.*

"Ramona's offer is sound Lord Owens," Margaret spoke first, her mouth numb and soaked in stiff drink. When she blinked, each fall of her eyelids felt like cotton pressed into her eyeballs, dry, and stinging, "Allow me to make a counteroffer."

Lord Owens shrugged and tucked the two tumblers next to his chest, answering softly, "I'm listening."

For decades Margaret had stood next her brother, using brute force to negotiate what the Empire *would* and *would not* accept. Although Margaret understood that Lord Owens was not a fool, nor was he naive, she could not unsee him as just another hapless victim of the Lopez family. Her mother, her brother, and now her niece. She didn't have it in her to *take* what didn't belong to her, she *paid for all favors, in full.*

"Ramona has already schemed her way through my brother's command. Maybe you don't need to worry for his witches. You imagine that Alexander will fall east, defeated, allowing House Owens a chance to rise. I'll give you *better.* I'll give you the west *back.*" Margaret was only barely hiding her pain now, the whiskey had done little to take the edge off, and her cheeks were flushed, fevered as noonday sun, "We restore your mother, Lady Aurora *the first,* Heart of the House Owens. Your sister and her witches answer only to Modus Vivendi. I'll kneel at her throne and swear fealty, giving you a battlewitch. General Townsend and those loyal to him will also swear fealty. When my brother comes to demand your surrender, I'll end your Antecedent problem forever."

Lord Owens, leaning in now, watched Margaret carefully, gesturing slightly with his right hand, a gentle motion, barely perceivable.

I'll kill my brother. "I'll kill Alexander Lopez for you."

Margaret did not blink or look away from Lord Owens. She didn't want him to think this was lightly offered, or that she was lying. She *loved* Alexander, but she loved herself more.

Eric Owens was closer to Margaret now than was socially acceptable. His jaw was set and tendering nothing but gravest attention.

Imagine how much more awkward this would be if we'd actually fucked.

"*No,*" Lord Owens said, "This isn't enough."

Margaret almost slapped him. Her brother's life was on the table, as well as her own loyalty. She'd served the Antecedent Empire since they were nothing more than a band of hapless mercenaries and veterans, "The Antecedent Empire is my brother's dream. It was not Maggi's, or my own. What more could I possibly give you?"

For a second Margaret thought Lord Owens might kiss her, his eyes so full of passion. Without her senses to whisper all the hidden secrets, she could only estimate the situation on his body language.

"Give me Modus Vivendi," Eric Owens growled, and though he didn't kiss her, the tone was darker, *get on your knees, bitch.*

Margaret understood, "Kill your sister, you mean."

"My *sister* held this House hostage when your brother came. Modus Vivendi holds a dozen witches, and Aurora *Cuttersark* is a battlewitch no different from our mother. We could have stopped you, we could have fought you, if we held those witches in *our grasp*."

That was the cusp of it. Modus Vivendi held power separate from the Heart of House Owens, a purely *uninclined* role. Margaret remembered what Aurora Cuttersark had said, "*Because I once tried to master The Beast, when Alexander's army crossed the Sierra Nevada. I tried to harness the power of that monster to stop you all.*"

You'd stop Alexander's army for Modus Vivendi, Margaret knew, *not for House Owens.*

"I'm not an assassin," Margaret whispered, it was only a flirtation, she'd already promised to *assassinate* her own brother.

"No," Lord Owens shook his head, retreating back not an inch further, his voice rasping low, "But you'll make a *fine* Magnate of Modus Vivendi. I also think you'll manage the Bay Area Reach quite well as a *real* land-holding Lady."

Lord Owens asked the world of Margaret, demanding her loyalty, her service, and the lives of her men. To serve at his steed, the next Heart of House Owens, once his mother passed beyond the Veil. *In return he offers me wealth, power, and title.*

"As it pleases you," Margaret smiled, and she may as well have laid her ragged lips into his with a tone that defined her words.

Standing back, pulling away from her, the overtly seductive moment lost, Lord Owens stood erect and extended his right hand, "Do we have an accord?"

An accord to kill our siblings? Margaret shook his right hand with her left, an awkward gesture that she wouldn't pull away from even when Lord Owens tried to withdraw. She didn't want him to think, in this final moment, that she *belonged* to him. The handshake was a reminder that she'd do things *her way*, or no way.

"Your 3rd Army and my House soldiers won't be enough. My men haven't trained or drilled in two years." Finally, free of her grasp, Eric Owens shook his head, "We'll need support from the Maul. That may be a challenge."

"Oh?" Margaret replied. Feeling the fingers of her left hand begin to tremor as she groped for Lord Owens' decanter and removed the rounded top, "Am I also to be your errand girl? While you relax in silk and cashmere?"

"No," Eric reached for the decanter, but Margaret had already hefted it to her lips and was sucking at the sweet, warm whiskey, "The Maul are peculiar. They're a warrior caste. Their children are trained from birth to *fight*, but they won't respect an Owens, recalling them."

Margaret was at the very end of whatever fixity she'd reserved, her eyes didn't want to focus, and she feared she might even drop the decanter. A down payment on all the murder she would unleash in the name of Aurora's son.

"*Why?*" Margaret asked, lowering crystal behind the marble counter where Eric Owens could not reach for it.

"Because my mother and I capitulated. We *surrendered*. You command more respect in their eyes than we do." Lord Owens replied, shrugging.

"More *hatred* too," Margaret remembered The Metal Hammer, and the big man, Sammy, with all his boiling rage. Even memories of Sammy couldn't embolden her own willpower now, this conversation *needed* to end soon before she burnt it all to the ground by collapsing.

"I suppose," Lord Owens shrugged, resigned at the loss of his whiskey, "but you've promised me a great many deeds this evening, Lady Mayhem. I'm sure the least difficult will be persuading a fire-minded war-cult to fight next to you."

Sammy, your wish is as good as granted. Your Maul shall sing your deeds for a hundred years to come, Margaret smiled at the thought, almost giggling.

"Consider it done, Lord Owens."

Just a *few* more minutes, just a *few* more polite goodbyes, nodding and bowing and whatever scraping Eric Owens demanded. Margaret had nothing left to offer, her body was shutting down, pressed to its limits, she needed *sleep*.

12:15pm March 2nd, 39 Veilfall

Stockton, California

Thump-crack-crack.

Margaret was awake instantly, to a shotgun discharge, followed by a racked shell. With no clear picture of what had just happened, Margaret rolled out of bed, ignorant of any pain in her right shoulder or chest, tumbling to the floor. She was *sticky*, her sinuses full of copper and gunpowder. Although she'd fallen asleep with a pistol in her left hand, it was gone now.

A man was screaming, a guttural howl that was one part panic and two parts agony; the distinctive sound a man made when he'd lost a limb, his lungs and chest intact, but his extremities severed or burning. It was a noise she'd have recognized anywhere.

"Bitch! Bitch! Bitch!"

It sounded like Deck, his unplaceable accent muddled, as if repeating the expletive would summon forth a netherworld dwelling demon to visit upon his enemies.

"Lady Mayhem?" A girl asked, her voice soft and barely discernible over the shouting.

Warm viscidity blurred Margaret's vision as she worked to blink her eyes open. She wiped the back of her left hand across her eyes, and face, then looked down to see that her arm and chest were also covered in smeared cruor.

Is that my blood? Margaret thought in a panic. She clawed across her belly and chest, groping her neck, frantic fingers jabbed painfully at burns, but she found no evidence of carnage.

"Ya' fucking shoh' me! You shoh' me!" That *was* Deck that she heard. He was hyperventilating, gasping for air on the fall of each syllable.

"Lady Mayhem?" The second voice repeated, quiet as before.

I'm not shot, I'm not dead, so how bad could it be?

Margaret leveraged herself off the hotel floor, leaning forward and peering over her bed. The comforter was dingy and faded, pre-Collapse, and worse for the wear. It was coated in crimson sheen, save for where Margaret had been sleeping. Her pistol, an antique Austrian 9mm was resting where her left hand had been, untouched.

Sarn't Deck Holloway was pressed against an opposing wall of Margaret's hotel room. Free of his coat and plate carrier, his right arm missing just below the shoulder. Margaret could see tatterings of shirt, flesh, hanging loosely, and half-shattered bone, still covered with flecks of meat and muscle. Deck was clawing at his shoulder, *screaming*, at the ceiling, his face slick with salt and blood.

"Lady Mayhem?"

A third time Margaret heard the quiet voice. She turned to the hotel room's door to see Erin, still in kit, a shotgun braced against her shoulder. She leaned forward, eyes on Deck, unblinking. The girl wore her hair short, shaved close at the sides and rear, as many young Antecedents preferred. Her only omission to femininity were long bangs that fell in her face.

"I'm all right," Margaret said.

Erin replied, her dimpled lower lip moving, but Margaret couldn't hear her over Deck's garbled gibberish. The man was nearly frothing at the mouth, fat wads of phlegm and saliva rupturing over his lips like a waterfall.

"I'm all right, but I *can't hear you*," Margaret said, louder this time, clawing her way up and off the floor.

The room was merely a ten-by-ten square with one door, a wide bed, a paneless window and an old dresser made of particle board that sagged at the center. Bathrooms were down the hall, a community experience with no divided walls or tubs. This hotel was not meant for long term visits, and though clean, piles of dust and lint had huddled up by the room's four corners where brooms couldn't reach.

"Can you watch my back. In the hallway. Sir," Erin was louder this time, but only just, "I *mean* Lady."

Margaret moved around the foot of her bed and peered over the ledge. Deck's ruined arm was resting in a pool of clot. The hand was gripping an ugly, rust worn, .38 revolver, sporting a grip that seemed too small, even for a child.

"*What the shit?*" Margaret asked no one in particular.

"He came in your room. So, I followed him. No one can enter your room." Erin answered, unwavering in her stance, brow relaxed. None of the muscles in her neck tensed. Margaret turned away from Deck's bloody rapine to inspect Erin closer. She was only a few inches taller than Margaret, and leaning forward, they were almost eye to eye. She was pretty. She was *very pretty*, with thick lashes, eyebrows, and freckles that poured across her nose.

Margaret was too startled to be in pain yet, and the long sleep had done her good. She could focus again, and did so, jumping immediately into Erin's skull. The memories were fresh, drifting on the surface like antique plastic, bobbing on waves. She could watch the last few minutes unfold. Erin had studied a drab painting in her own room, sitting on the floor, listening. Someone was walking down the hall.

Big guy, heavy steps. Two-hundred pounds? Walking carefully, choosing their steps. Why are they choosing their steps?

Erin's internal monologue unfolded in Margaret's mind. She had stood, peaking out, watching as Sarn't Holloway opened the door across from Erin's room. Margaret's door.

He had a gun. This wasn't a memory. Erin was aware that she wasn't alone in her own head. She replied directly to Margaret.

I thought so. You are inclined, Margaret answered, for herself and Erin, as she turned back to the bleeding Sarn't in her room.

"*Holloway, look at me.*"

Margaret articulated her voice, resonating across aural spectrums that the uninclined could barely understand. She was using her voice to *command*, old, simple magic that endowed the very words she spoke with power. Maggi Lopez had taught her this when she was only twelve or thirteen, "*Stop bawling like a baby and tell me what happened here.*"

Deck Holloway bit at the air, his chest heaving so high it seemed his collar bones might snap against the hammering movement. He upchucked part of his breakfast, stomach contents, titian and lumpy. With eyes wide, he returned Margaret's scowl, his good hand shivering against the remains of his other arm.

"W-w-witches," Deck stuttered, then found his rhythm, "can't hurt *ya'* if *theys* asleep."

Margaret nodded, bracing her left hand to hip. Her mind was already cast about Deck's as she spoke, voice no longer her only means of compulsion, "*Is that right? Why would you be afraid of me, 'hurting ya?'*"

Deck snorted hard at the fetid torrent of mucus running out of his nose, his mind no longer his own. "Because I needed *ta'* kill *ya'*."

Deck Holloway hadn't been the first man to make an attempt on her life, and he'd certainly not be the last. She was, more than anything, disgusted at the trust she'd bestowed on Deck. Her amusement at his offhand and colorful remarks, a reminder of years long past.

"*Why? Why kill your battlewitch?*" Margaret's voice dropped down in octaves, almost masculine now. She could even sense *fear* on Erin's skin, sweating

With no stutter, Holloway answered, "The Plague Dog *'d* promote me for *ya'* head, I was sure of it. I was *sure* of it."

"Yes, she probably would have," Margaret retracted from Deck's simpering mind. The man *had* been a capable soldier, but his memories smelled like Maggi's breath a thousand times over, stale with liquor and rotting teeth. She could only conceal her anger for so long, *"The penalty for treason is death. You can take your own life, or Erin can execute you. Choose."*

Holloway nodded quick, his mind clouding again with pain, he stuttered once more, "I'll d-d-do it myself. No brassboy *'ll* show me the Veil."

Margaret smiled, then turned away from Holloway, to Erin, *"Blow his fucking head off, brassboy."*

Erin didn't hesitate. She punctuated Margaret's sentence with a trigger pull, and the discharge ripped Holloway's face open. Flesh was stripped away, and his skull shattered around the forehead and orbital sockets. The impact drove his vertex into faux wood panels and liquified eyeballs drained down his cheeks, along with whatever remained of his brain. It took a moment, but his body slumped down the wall, following grey and pink fluid that coated his clothing, before falling into a heap on the floor; a lifeless twist of elbow and knees.

Margaret exhaled hard, her voice regaining its natural tambour, "Do you have a last name, brassboy Erin?"

"Abid," Erin racked another shell into the 12 gauge, before lowering it and taking long, slow blinks.

"Did your parents know you were inclined? Did *anyone* know?"

Erin Abid shook her head, eyes fixed on Holloway's lifeless body where it had collapsed. He no longer seemed like a *person* who had once lived, only a collection of parts thrown together in a corner, forgotten and contemptible.

"You're no longer a brassboy," Margaret lifted her left hand and stowed it on Erin's shoulder. Under her fingers she could feel molle and chainmail, "Effective this moment, you're Corporal Erin Abid. You'll serve as my personal bodyguard, and servant, until such time as I release you to the command of General Townsend. Are we clear?"

Corporal Erin Abid nodded, silently.

"Fetch my pistol. Make sure it's clean. I need to wash up," Margaret turned and stepped out of the hallway. Several patrons at the edge of the walk rushed away, their prying eyes a known quality now, curiosity turned to fear. *Someone* would have called the Stockton guard by now and she'd need to deal with that soon.

Something itched at the back of Margaret's mind. It spoke in the voice of her mother, arms crossed, walking a wide circle around her. It was a voice of counsel, the tone Maggi used at lessons, stern, but not *unkind. Is that all you'll grant the girl? A promotion?*

Margaret didn't so much turn around as she took a step back and investigated her former hotel room. Erin was pulling the slide off Margaret's 9mm to inspect it.

"Corporal," Margaret started, waiting for Erin to look over her shoulder, "When things are calmer, and *if* General Townsend agrees, you can study with me. If you wish. You're inclined. You should learn about your gifts. *If you wish.*"

Erin didn't answer, she just *nodded*, the hint of a smile on her lips.

Giving her new Corporal a wink, Margaret turned back. The hallway was narrow, claustrophobic, impossible for two people to walk shoulders abreast. The carpet was an unremarkable blue patchwork, worn to slate at the center by years of traffic. Truncated at a washroom, the hall ended between two stairwells; one leading *up*, the other leading *down*.

Margaret felt her heart stop, skipping a beat, or two, then jumping forward again. The flesh at her throat pulsed for a moment and the burns under Aurora's gown felt *warm*, uncomfortably warm.

I have to pee, Margaret thought, *I don't need this right now.*

A door to her right opened. It made *no noise*, although Margaret could see a jitter in one of the hinges that should have whined. Beyond, a woman watched Margaret. Only a third of her face exposed, lips glistening with beeswax, paint shadowing her eyelids. Pupil and retina did not look out from the darkened room, instead a globe of swirling *blue sea* occupied the woman's eye socket. A window singing of lapping brine, nibbling at Margaret's ear, as a playful lover.

Fucking Aphrodite, Margaret thought, *I have to pee.*

"Do you think I care?"

Aphrodite jerked the door open and revealed the rest of her latest body. Margaret assumed it was a whore, but she couldn't genuinely tell beyond the heavy makeup, rouge and fussed hair. The woman was wearing a dress of blue, hewn from bright silks and Georgette, and likely the single most valuable prize in the entire hotel. Long lace gloves ran up past her elbows, crafted in symbols that Margaret could not recognize.

"Someone *just* tried to murder me, and you want to talk *now*?"

"Do you think I care?" Aphrodite repeated, her voice a husky contralto, dripping like sweet honey. Margaret almost bit her lower lip in response to the sensation.

The woman was a foot taller than Margaret, and *strong*. Aphrodite grabbed Margaret's left forearm, jerking her inside the room with presence and force she hadn't expected.

Against the wall of Aphrodite's hotel room, Margaret saw the door slammed shut without a finger laid upon it. The whore smelled like lavender and vanilla, a basic perfume for someone in such an expensive dress, but above that the room seemed to swim with an ocean scent so rich that Margaret suddenly lusted to walk barefoot in the cool tide pools.

"*You* smell like fire and sorrow, little Mar-gar-*et*," Aphrodite answered, pressing her body's firm breasts and abdomen against Margaret, who closed her eyes and head tilted back despite herself. It was rough, painful, and filled her sternum with a boiling sweet tea that almost choked her as she inhaled.

"I don't have time for sorrow," Margaret answered, softly. A whimper escaping the back of her throat. The burns across her body began to bite *less*, and the weight of Aphrodite's whore started to only *hurt* in the ways Margaret most adored.

"Do you wonder if Townsend will still *fuck* you? With those burns? Do you wonder if he still desires you? Or will his attention wane in the years to come*?*" Aphrodite stepped back, releasing Margaret to stand on her own, addled. "The libertine Mar-gar-*et*, sitting alone at a dinner table. Face full of scars, forgotten battlewitch of the Antecedent Empire."

Margaret exhaled hard and clenched her jaw, *angry* again, just as angry as when she'd realized Deck Holloway wasn't a man to be trusted.

"I'm not so cruel. I was merely repeating your *own* thoughts." Aphrodite grinned, teeth shimmering like rays cast on calm sea, straight and clean as antique pearls.

A noble woman's teeth. Who is she wearing?

Margaret's right cheek began to burn under the gaze of Aphrodite, "I'll worry about Townsend's desires. You seem plenty busy with *'a return to the good old days.'*"

When Aphrodite crossed her arms against her body's modest chest, Margaret could see more symbols woven into the lace of her opposing arm. "Watch your tone, Mar-gar-*et*. If you want to have *any* face left. I have no hand in the machinations of your nieces."

"*Your* Ramona started this!" Margaret leaned in, lips curled up until they hurt, flesh cracking and splitting under blisters.

Aphrodite nodded, and immaculate raven curls bounced across her body's forehead, "*Oh yes*, she did. *Divine* work. A *masterclass* in deception and manipulation. Ramona is *easily* my favorite since Clara Ward, Princesse de Caraman-Chimay."

Margaret pulled away from the flimsy wall, took one step forward, pinching her lips closed, refusing to wince, "Just tell me, what does Ramona want?"

Bound in a dress that Margaret herself coveted, Aphrodite's body laughed like two *cats copulating*, her whining yowl bounced around the room, "If I were to warn *you* of Ramona's deepest desires, how would you know that I didn't warn *her* of your plans to murder Alexander Lopez?"

Margaret reminded herself *who* she was talking to. Her powers meant *nothing* here, she stood prone, defenseless. "You and Ramona don't have the same goals?"

Aphrodite was *genuinely amused*, more so than Margaret had ever seen, "Ramona does as she *pleases*. I allow this until it interferes with what *I want*. You, on the other hand, *you do what I want*, and *only what I want*. Kneel at my feet, promise me your soul, your *love*. Then, *and only then*, we will discuss what I might *allow you to do*." Aphrodite stopped laughing and Margaret felt cold water drip down her spine. Aphrodite's face tilted, her jaw slowly fell open, and her tongue ran across perfect teeth, "If I wish it, you will fall to your knees, rip your tongue out and jam it into your *cunt*. Do you understand me? Do you *really* understand me?"

As if Margaret had found herself too close to a rattlesnake, she was facing a *bored god*. There was no angry ocean to churn and flash about in Aphrodite's eyes, only a low and hungry calm that quivered in the anticipation of seizing on a thing for no better reason than she *could*. Aphrodite would choose to strike, or *not* strike, based on desires that no mortal could fathom. Just as Margaret wove her tendrils of magic around the uninclined, Aphrodite's breath was power beyond imagining.

"I understand you," Margaret answered.

"Worship is worthless unless you do it of your own volition."

Aphrodite lunged toward Margaret. There was no time to reply, or even startle, no human could have moved that way. Her lips were across Margaret's, succulent venison, fire kissed and slippery, chattering with pepper and salt, kissing away the blisters and burns before they had a chance to cry out. It was a seduction of familiarity, a shift in odor, the dart of crisp air and whispers at the soft lobes of Margaret's ears.

Mar-gar-et, Mar-gar-et, worship me. Love me. I'll make you beautiful again, I'll give you back flesh. I'll make you the most beautiful woman on Earth. The ladies of Owens will weep at your glory. What will your new title be? I like Duchess. Or Grand Duchess!

The *true* voice of Aphrodite rippled and vibrated in the humidity of her mouth and mind. Tender and warm as her saliva, it dripped down Margaret's throat, turning her chest numb and igniting nerves in a bliss that biology had never designed them to endure. Margaret's ribcage cracked, an imbrued orgasm, she had never felt as defeated as that very second.

She *had been* a beautiful woman, despite her oddly large eyes and her misshapen shoulders. The scars she wore under clothes, her armor, they were private things shared with lovers, pressing them into open lips and needy teeth. What Amy had done, the destruction she'd wrought, was the fuel that burned hot in Margaret's nightmares. Her flesh was curled up, crusted, and black, just like her parents, bound before flame, as she was forced to watch them die.

Aphrodite had found her turn screw. This piece of Margaret had been bent up, pressed down, and manipulated once too often. It was now a broken, serrated edge, chewing on needles, *hungry and yearning*.

Between wakefulness and fantasy, Margaret found herself lost in a dream. Standing before Amihan, on the battlefield, dust sweeping and blinding them both. Guns, artillery, only an echo in the distance. Amihan was panting, her chest heaving under a tank top and plate carrier, her teeth full of blood and one eye swollen shut. Margaret could hear her voice crack as she said; "*I lit you on fire, how are you whole?*"

Margaret would have enjoyed that above pressing unmarred lips against Townsend's face. It was a more titillating fantasy than any other, even the notion of trusting someone to *hurt* her in the ways she liked to hurt, free of the marionette strings. Margaret *hated* Amihan to the edge of love, and it was beyond her will to say '*no.*'

If pressed; however, Margaret could not have explained *why* she didn't say '*yes.*'

Aphrodite withdrew, offering a wink, "The offer is on the table. Think about it, dream about it, scrub up in the bath with it."

It wouldn't be so bad, would it? To worship a god?

Margaret was aware that Aphrodite could hear her. She needed to collect her mind again, make it her own, forget impossible notions of bone marrow ejaculate, and center herself as any good witch would. As Maggi Lopez taught her.

Gasping, shoulders heaving as if she'd rolled out from under a lover, Margaret reached down, under her collar of lace and cotton. She pulled free the golden necklace, along with the *eye that does not see*. "You asked me to retrieve this, to return it to its rightful owner. You never said *who* that was."

Aphrodite reached forward and stroked a thumb against the *eye*. Each time she did, the veins under her body's flesh turned deep red. The air shifted from brine and venison to something like ozone and sweet flowers she'd never known and could not identify.

"I never said *return it*. I said *you* needed to be in possession of it."

Margaret's stomach turned. It was worse than starving, or any craving she could imagine. Aphrodite's voice didn't change, she wasn't *cruel* in a sneering or sadistic way. Her tone was one of affection, and the hint of a throat-weary lust that only demanded *love* from Margaret.

Love and worship.

Although Margaret had not known *fear* for decades, she was as mortal as in any in her desires. Part of her imagined Townsend distancing himself, ignoring her advances, just as she dreamed of Amihan's horror, in discovering her magic had been for naught. She envisioned herself a lonely old woman watching over the Bay Area Reach, hair white and face twisted up, eternally the shape of Plague Dog's hand.

Margaret *was* crying. Tears rolled down her face, relentless and warm.

"Well, I possess it now. What do *you* want me to do with it?"

Aphrodite leaned in toward Margaret, *the eye that does not see* vanishing into her balled fist, tendons clenching, knuckles pale, the very flesh of her hand translucent, showing bones and ligaments from within. When Aphrodite let go of the bobble, her hand was coated in white and blue enamel, she cast it to the floor with disgust and loathing,

"This was the *glamour of a god*. The eye was meant to be lost before your 'Collapse.'"

The eye fell back to Margaret's chest and milky paint dripped on her gown.

She scooped the artifact up with gentle fingertips. It had been an ovoid concave, roughly an inch across, polished glass with painted details of a pupil and retina. The jeweler had used tiny golden arms to hold it in place. Now, it was a dark brown, like cooked clay, and engraved in central circle from which extended golden threads like rays of sunlight.

Margaret pressed on, "Why hide the eye?"

Aphrodite's own strange eyes shifted, seas growing rough, tinged in white caps and great waves. She wasn't *angry* in any conventional sense, it was more like she was drawing herself up with pride and disgust, "Around your neck you wear the Eye of Shahr-i-Sokhta, the Burnt City. A place long dead for your people. Maggi Lopez was taught whispers of their language, she was the *last* who still rendered their words of power. She didn't find the Eye of Shahr-i-Sokhta, *it found her*," the deep voice Aphrodite borrowed made a rasping hiss, and she seemed lost in a distant place, "The Eye belonged to one of *my priestesses*. A powerful witch and oracle of her time. It bridged the gap between my side of the Veil and *yours*. The last of such relics, crafted by the fallen general of a dead god, in a time of *real* magic, when titans yet still walked."

When Aphrodite finished, Margaret was faint. Those words had stolen breath from her throat, "The creature we saw at Crosstown. You came to warn me for *that*. Didn't you?"

Aphrodite *never* blinked when she visited Margaret, but this time she closed her eyes, still, serene, calm hiding a much greater storm. There was power at the edges of her body's flesh that warped the very air, black curls lifting, along with her silver earrings and bits of loose lace. Margaret could feel the shift. The Eye of Shahr-i-Sokhta floated free from her fingers, along with her own greasy hair of auburn, and the tattered embroider at Aurora's gown, shaded in dried blood.

The creature who was promised this bobble, is ignorant and blind to its power.

The voice wasn't *in* the room, so much as it was *in* Margaret, under her skin, flowing in her veins and vibrating her organs. It was neither feminine, nor masculine. It had no gender. It was a power that had been molded to form ideas. Aphrodite opened her eyes again, speaking this time with her body's vocal chords, as if she'd somehow *lost control* of her physical bounds, her raw power breaking free for just a moment.

"Your mother made *bargains* with gods and spirits, and this creature believes it is owed the Eye of Shahr-i-Sokhta. You will *not* release it. You will *possess* it with all your might. You are now it's keeper in this world. Just as Maggi Lopez was before you."

Margaret's hair fell back to her neck and cheeks. There was no *payment* offered for this, and Margaret remembered the words from earlier, "*you do what I want, and only what I want.*"

"I'll guard it. From the spirit I saw, or any others." Margaret laid her palm gently on the Eye of Shahr-i-Sokhta. "May I *use* it? The way your priestess did?"

Aphrodite lifted her index finger and poked it *into* the window of her own right eye. It passed beyond the flesh eyelids and into distant oceans, "You *may*, but a sacrifice is required. You would need to lose an eye of your own. Just as Maggi did. What would it matter? You couldn't be any *uglier with one eye.*"

This made Margaret's flesh crawl, and she withdrew the Eye of Shahr-i-Sokhta, tucking the golden necklace, and trinket, back into her gown. A part of her was curious about the power such a thing must wield, and then she remembered Aurora Cuttersark.

She wonders what it is that an Antecedent whore like me possesses that she does not.

"The Eye of Shahr-i-Sokhta. It was *part* of what powered The Beast."

Margaret's words were barely a whisper.

A lascivious smile crept across Aphrodite's lips, "Mar-gar-*et*, Mar-gar-*et,* doesn't it feel good to exercise that beautiful mind you possess?"

Brassboy Erin Abid by LacticWanda

10:22am March 8th, 39 Veilfall

Fish Rock, California

Atop a series of rocks that created a westward overlook of gentle hills and cliffs, Margaret could see across the Pacific. Her eyes were fixed at the horizon where the two shades of blue met, a deep oblivion drawing her in, tugging at her hair like a child, demanding she come closer. She wondered where in those depths existed the waters that could be seen through Aphrodite's eyes.

It was a gorgeous afternoon north of the Marin Headlands. Clouds shifted across the sky, deep grey to the north and silken white above her, so vast and endless that if she had tilted her head back for a while, she'd have felt a sudden rush of *falling up*. Warm sunlight flowed across her skin; her face, neck, as well as her legs where she'd drawn up Aurora's gown to mid-thigh. The hem was ripped away now, much of the lace that had been carefully stitched to dark cotton was torn free and tattered. The once sable fabric was now muddled gray and alabaster.

Margaret felt *good* here, in this place. Running her bare feet through the salty sand, cool water kissing her ankles, free of tightly laced boots and cumbersome socks.

She was in pain, of course. If she twisted the wrong way, she could feel flesh pull and peel like fresh beef jerky, torn in narrow shreds. She could no longer move the fingers on her right arm, nor rotate her wrist. The skin was turning deep shades of purple, and her nails were now black. Margaret did her best to forget this. She knew the arm would need to come off, and likely soon.

Little anxieties nibbled at her mind, like a coyote on rotting carcass. *Can I still paint in charcoal with my left hand? Can I learn to write with my left hand? Or will I dictate letters?* She wondered how she'd comb her hair, or even pull on a blouse or jacket.

Will Townsend still want a one-arm witch as his paramour?

Disconnected from these thoughts that stirred deep in her heart and spine, Margaret could hear another man approach *before* she felt him. Only the most disciplined of uninclined minds could hide themselves that way. It required a man to spend *decades* learning to quiet his thoughts and calm the innate energy that could sully a person, making them noisy enough for a witch to detect.

Margaret did not turn. He approached from the left, and it would have pulled painfully against the ragged remains of flesh on her right shoulder. Instead, she simply tipped her chin down, looking away from the cobalt horizon, listening to him approach.

"You're the Antecedent witch?" He spoke first, his voice deep, certain, despite a tremor at the edge of his vowels, the kind of tremor that defied a man's nature, the curse of old age.

"Please, sit with me," Margaret gestured to the smooth boulder a few feet in front of her. It had been sanded down by a thousand years of wave and brine, protruding from the sand and surf below her feet.

His voice had betrayed him well. He was older, by far, than most people Margaret had met in her life. Lines etched deeply into his face, spots peppered his skin and wispy short hair undulated in the breeze, white like fresh snow. It seemed like his eyes had shrunk in their sockets, or perhaps that his brows had simply overtaken them. Despite that, Margaret could see a predator watching her. He took care to notice her bent and crooked shoulder, the way her back arched, lingering on her plum hand, and finally the line of her thighs.

Margaret smiled at him, as he sat.

"I wasn't told you were hurt," the old man grunted, "Curious that an Antecedent comes before me now, with a *dead* arm."

Margaret glanced to her fingers, swollen and unwelcome in their necrosis, "I'm no longer Antecedent. I come to you as a House Owens witch."

"Can't much trust someone who'll swap sides, like so much lunchmeat." The old man's accent was unknown to her, he used *very antique* slang, and dressed like an old-world soldier. Faded ACU's, the pre-Collapse kind, no longer manufactured.

"The choice was made for me." Margaret slid her left palm across the warm rocks. Calm, she felt as if she was looking upon a great marvel of her mother's time. The old man's white beard fell into a tan shemagh, as he worked his jaw, chewing.

"Not my place to calculate your loyalties, I suppose." He replied.

Margaret offered the man a smile, "Today, I have no secrets to keep. I've been told the Maul *hates* me, the witch who made Aurora Owens kneel."

The old man with a mind of granite grunted. There *was* anger there at the edges of his body, the light that escapes a solar eclipse. No matter how disciplined he was, she could still read him, "I suppose you're Mayhem, then?"

"Call me *Margaret,* please."

He watched Margaret for a while, then spit brown fluid to the moist sand at his boots. "Pretty face, Margaret, even with them burns. But those eyes seen some *ugly*. I suppose you do have secrets. How old are you, about, girl?"

Margaret didn't shift or really move her head. She couldn't place her finger on it, or even *define it*, but there was a familiarity to be found in the old man.

"I don't know. Older than I look? Probably in my forties, I guess. I'm a Collapse baby."

The old man nodded, looking down at dirty tobacco juice drying in the sand, "Bad times. *Ugly* times. Not a place for children, not a place for *anyone* who had a heart."

"So, you have no heart?" Margaret offered a chuckle, mildly flirting.

"Not since we shelled the Bay Area." The old man replied, somberly. She allowed him his silence, knowing full well the dark things that cascaded through his mind. They were at the edges of his eclipse too, scratching and nibbling at his disciplined walls. It was long minutes before he spoke again, "What's it like? To be a witch, I mean? I never had much opportunity to ask anyone else."

Margaret clicked her tongue, "How many witches have you known *to ask?*"

"*Ro Owens*, a few others. Never just shot the shit. I killed a witch once, but never just sat next to a pretty one with bare feet in the sand. Y'all normally is *flame and fear.*"

Shot the shit? What does that mean? Margaret skipped that thought and realized he'd also admitted to *killing* a witch. She answered, "Trade you. I'll tell you what it's like to be a witch, if you tell *me* about *killing a witch*. Good bargain?"

The old man nodded, before spitting again. "Good enough."

Margaret breathed a long sigh and closed her eyes. As she did, she allowed herself, her soul and energy, to unfurl and spread across Fish Rock. The Maul's camp, more like a town, was nearby, up the hillside and deep in the trees. "Imagine what it would be like to know *all* the secrets, *all the whispers* from ghosts and people around you. You're connected to the world, every moment, *every day*, and yet so *fucking lonely*. No one can really share it with you. Not even another witch. The uninclined make you a fetish, something to worship or rip apart depending on their mood. No one cares if you like the taste of *almonds* or *avocados*, they only make themselves *so* distant that you can forget them if you don't work at it."

Or fucked them, Margaret thought, remembering her sketches.

She had shared something deeply private, words never spoken out loud before. The old man reminded her most of her mother's men, the soldiers of her childhood. The ones who taught her how to skin a rabbit, breakdown and clean firearms. Margaret's father was long since dead, but she had been raised by *many* fathers, and the Maul warlord reflected those men.

He smiled at her, not unkind or mocking, showing off a mouthful of discolored and rotten teeth. The old man answered, taking his turn, "I didn't just *serve Ro Owens*, I fought with her, back before they built the walls up on Highway 5 and 99. We'd been fighting in Morada, maybe a *week*. We needed green grass to shake down Stockton. My spotter was *dee-oh-ayy* and *Ro* played the part for me. Well, she called a shot and I took it. That shot was a rival witch. Guess I expected a big explosion or that fire would shoot out of her mouth." The old man became hushed and squinted, "Her skull split open and she was just *dead*. The *end*."

There was roughness between the two and as the old man became more comfortable, so too did he begin using more pre-Collapse slang. Margaret struggled to understand.

"*Spotter?*" She asked.

"Scout Sniper team is two men. Sniper and *spotter*. They work together." The old man chewed at nothing again.

"*Ohh,*" Margaret knew exactly what this was. The Antecedent word '*sniper*' always meant a team of two, watchman and gunman. "Your watchman arrived, but *dee-oh-ayy*."

The old soldier pursed his lips, looked around, and offered a leering grin, "I can't even blame public schools for this shit anymore."

"*Public schools?*" She inquired, more curious than before.

"Don't worry about it, Sugarlips," the soldier waved her off, "Bottom line is, not much to tell. I put that witch in my crosshairs and she died like anyone else."

Sugarlips? Margaret wondered if he was implying that her lips were *sweet*, or if her lips were white and granular? Concerned, she wiped the back of her hand across her mouth and looked for dry skin or scabs. She decided that he was complimenting her and smiled back at the old man.

"What was Lady Owens like? In the old days?"

The soldier shrugged, leaned back, and watched the sky for a moment, "Ro had some boy up by old *SacTown*. Guess they knew each other on the *internets*, and she'd been by to *fuck* him the week it all fell apart. They nuked SacTown a day after she got out. Her, some engineers out of *Frisco,* and my team got isolated on Highway 5. Her boyfriend was a little bitch. *Died like a little bitch too.* So did the *faggot* engineers. But Ro? Not Ro. Any kid who can keep up with *fucking You-Es Marines*, that's no joke. She was a part of our family by the end of the year, and when she started *lighting shit on fire* with her mind, well, long story short."

Long story short? Was it a long story, or a short story? Margaret decided not to inquire. The old man's language was too distant from her own to understand everything.

"I came here today, to ask, or," Margaret narrowed her eyes, "*beg* you, to support Ro. I'm going to restore her to the throne of House Owens again."

"What about Eric?" The old soldier leaned forward again, "Is he at his mom's side? Good man, a fighter, just like Ro."

"Lord Owens is the one who told me you'd not come back."

The Maul warlord smirked with a wink, "He got his *dick* buried up your ass, Sugarlips?"

Margaret opened her mouth to reply, then realized that soldiers from *fifty years ago*, and soldiers from *today* had equally foul mouths and dirty minds. She answered the Marine the way she'd have answered one of her shield bearers or gunners: "Why? Are you *jealous*?"

"Marines don't get *jealous*, Sugarlips. Just need to know the score."

The score for what?

"I don't know anything about a *score*, but I know that my niece holds Stockton's eastern gate and a quarter of the city. She's waiting for her father to return, and when he does return, he'll pin down my garrison. That'll be the end of any *new* House Owens."

It was a *long* time that the warlord studied Margaret, long and decisively silent. His eyes ripped at her dress, and stabbed her in the heart, all at once. When he finally spoke, it was low in tone and his vocal tremor had vanished, "We are the children, *children's children,* of the 26th Marine Expeditionary Unit. We're not just some *jarheads* you send to die. We're family, blood and bone. We raise our own to live and die by the standards of the *goddamn* Corps. The Maul's support isn't *manpower*, Sugarlips. It's summoning God's own elements to earth. Just like a witch do it." The old warlord squinted and this time, when he spit, a gob of tobacco landed in the clear Pacific surf. "The Maul is *loyal to the side who fights hardest*. Ro Owens betrayed that loyalty. We'd have died for her, and you could have *zapped us* or *lit us on fire*, or whatever the *fuck* it is you do, but we'd have never surrendered."

A cool breeze snapped at Margaret's bare neck, warm sun now obscured by migrant clouds drifting across the coast, "I'm a *nightmare mirror*."

"*Out-fucking-standing!*" The old warlord barked, his grin genuine. There wasn't a hint of fear at the edges of his eclipse, if anything the notion of *fighting* Margaret only made him burn brighter. He offered a growl, "Never did answer my question about Eric, did you?"

Margaret broke eye contact and replied slowly, with an edge of embarrassment in her tone, "Eric turned me down, actually."

"No shit?" The old Marine coughed, "Eric ain't the man I assumed he was."

Margaret waved him off, "He just has no good taste in women. One of my garrison; however, has earned the right to call me *his*."

"Oh?" The old man gestured with his chin, "*One of your own*? One of your soldiers?"

"*Mm*," Margaret thought for a second, then answered, "We're joint commanders. In the Antecedent Empire, a General and a battlewitch work as a team. Just like your *sniper* and *spotter*."

The old warlord held his hands out wide, gesturing towards her. "Smart man, keeping a woman like you. Too bad, 'course. I was going to feed you some *bullshit line* about how the Maul seal every bargain in the Biblical approximation, eh?" He winked at Margaret, though she understood *none of what he just said*, only that it was a joke at her expense. He wasn't humiliating her, he was treating her like a peer, and *that* was exactly what she wanted.

"A woman like *me*?" Margaret replied.

The old warlord gestured at her hand, then her face, holding his fingers and thumb in a straight line, like a knife, "The way you sit, I'd wager most of your chest is burned up. Tell me I'm wrong." Margaret didn't answer him, so he continued, "Those are *fresh* burns, scabbed and nasty, something awful. But look at you, right? It's a long stage-ride up here, and you're trying to stitch me up with my old friend, Ro. Why? Just to *face-fuck whoever* did that to you?"

Just to face-fuck my brother, his daughters, and Aurora Cuttersark.

"Something like that."

"Look, Sugarlips," the old man was grinning, "you remind me of Ro when she was young and stupid. I liked Ro back then, liked her enough to be sad she married that Cuttersark *cunt*. A woman who'll fight, *fight hard*, why, ain't nothing in this life sexier."

Margaret had to blink hard to stave off a few tears. Although she was successful, the Maul warlord almost certainly noticed her efforts. Aphrodite's bargain had been loud in her ears these past few days, and until this moment she'd had no counter.

"Thank you," Margaret had said, grateful to the old Marine for his mercy and charm.

"The Maul will follow *you*, and *you alone*, Mayhem," The old man gave her a few minutes to collect herself. When their eyes reconnected, he spoke, "If that restores House Owens, that's fine too. But, Ro Owens, we're *done*."

"I'll deal with Ro Owens," Rubbing at her eyes with the back of her left hand, Margaret continued, "You help me deal with the Antecedent witch who burned me. We *aren't* done yet."

The old warlord whistled at Margaret, then crossed his arms, "*Fancy* like a pretty boy in a suit, making promises about the needs of God and Country." *Which god*? A brief spasm of loathing turned up her stomach. She could taste bile and acid in her chest as she lifted her left hand up to rest it on the Eye of Shahr-i-Sokhta, under her gown. "You fear her."

"*No*," Margaret shook her head, violently, ignoring any pain in her flesh, "Plague Dog and her sister are pawns in a game."

Margaret would have preferred to give the old man a scheme, something in stone that he could have charted. She had pieces of a puzzle, the Eye of Shahr-i-Sokhta, The Beast, Aphrodite's *ownership* of Ramona, and whatever machinations Ramona operated under; but how *each* of those things fit into a greater plan, she couldn't have guessed.

The old man tilted his head, eyes raising goose pimples on Margaret's arms and legs, the wind turning colder now; "Tell me, Sugarlips, who is this Plague Dog to you?"

Margaret's eyes *burned*, but she didn't look away. "She's my niece."

"*Damn!*" the old Warlord shouted in response, "you're *fine as fuck*, but I just dodged a bullet earlier. You'd have *froze my dick clean off*. That's *cold*."

Imagine what you'd think if I told you I planned to murder my brother.

Margaret answered, "General Townsend and the 3rd Army control Stockton's *southern gate*. Plague Dog's troops have dug in and hold the *eastern gate*. If the Maul attacks her there, combined with a southern push, her forces will collapse." *How could I possibly get close to Alexander?* Margaret thought, laying palm, above her thighs, *I don't want to fight the whole of the 1st and 2nd Armies.*

The old warlord's jest was gone for a moment, "We'll follow you back, push these kids out of Stockton. But we're going to need to do something first, little Sugarlips."

Margaret asked, with all seriousness, "Seal the bargain in a Biblical approximation?"

The old man's expression shifted, he started to laugh, thought better of it, and just stared at her for a moment, "I'm sorry Sugarlips, but we're going to need to *amputate* that arm. Maul has surgeons, *old world* surgeons, it'll be clean."

9:05pm March 8th, 39 Veilfall

Fish Rock, California

When Margaret woke up, she could see Erin at the corner of her room drawing down the wick in an oil-burning lamp, casting a flickering yellow glow. As it slowly faded, she was reminded of the creature from Crosstown, watching from total darkness.

"No, leave it on." Margaret's voice was hoarse when she spoke, a crack and fissure in her syllables. A bottle of bourbon had provided some comfort when the surgeon sawed her arm off, but not as much as it would have taken to silence her screams or alleviate wakefulness.

Erin mumbled something, then returned to Margaret's bedside, in dull light.

"I need you to speak louder. *I can't hear* the way I did when I was your age."

Margaret offered a smile, but it just looked sad. The Maul surgeon who'd removed her arm had also spoken to her of *fish skin* grafting, which now covered her ruined chest and shoulder. She'd been too drunk to ask questions. For now, the handprint on her face was covered in a silky black and silver crosshatch that caught lamp light, turning Margaret's cheek and lips a shade of gold.

"Because of the ghost?" Erin repeated herself, louder.

Margaret blinked slow, tired, "It wasn't a *ghost*. Listen to your intuition next time, don't make me correct you when you already know the right answer."

Erin sat down on a metal stool next to Margaret's bed, the legs scratching loudly across tile as it shuffled to one side under the girl's weight.

Margaret glanced at the layers of linen that were pinned up to her right shoulder, needles holding the bandages in place. The wound *ached* in a way that Margaret had never experienced, it was an empty, tugging sensation. She itched in places where a limb no longer existed.

I should ask the surgeon to boil the flesh off my bones, save them for me. A blacksmith could make me a prosthetic out of them.

It could never function the same way of course, but a good prosthetic could hold a pose, and with proper adjustment, she'd still be able to wear gowns and dresses without alteration. No one would believe her arm was real, but a prosthetic made from metal and bone would certainly remind them of *what she was*.

"*Talk* to me, Corporal Abid. Tell me *anything*."

Erin looked around the room, wheels and gears of her mind at work across her face. She had such delicate features, wearing her hair like a boy, elegantly androgynous.

"*Um*, well. I like the Maul."

"So, do I," Margaret gave her a slow nod. Unable to focus her mind she studied the girl with great attention. She was tired of this *pain*. It blurred much more than just her inclinations, it blurred her sanity. For a moment, a very strange moment, she felt as if *she herself* was Maggi Lopez, looking at a teenage *Mayy*, wondering what the future held for her, or what she would accomplish in her life.

"Did you ever care, mother?" Margaret let her lips loose without full control over what she would say.

Erin glanced away, leaned in, and then raised her brows, "Mother?"

Aware that her thoughts had roamed free in the air, Margaret waved off the younger woman, as if she'd bothered her with pointless trivia, "Tell me about your inclination. What do you *hear* and *see*?"

Margaret's eyes focused and unfocused around Erin, and the girl answered with thin lipped trepidation, "I've heard people's thoughts, forever," she leaned into her words, speaking faster than before, "I know when someone is *mad*, and when they're happy. I can hear lies. Or truth! *Oh*, and spiders."

Margaret wrinkled up her nose, never liking spiders particularly much.

"Spiders always seem to like me. There's some on me now. It's weird."

What the fuck?

"What the *fuck?*" Margaret withdrew a few inches from Erin. She'd never heard of such a thing in the inclined. Most animals favored witches, *but spiders?*

"I had a tarantula collection back in Nevada," Erin said, casually.

I want to think about spiders even less than I want to think about losing my arm.

"What about elements?" Margaret changed the subject, quickly, "Commanding fire is *very* common among us, as well as air, or perhaps water."

Erin shook her head, "I can't make fire. Unless I have some matches," it seemed very important to the girl to explain this. "You're the first one to call me *inclined*."

Margaret was just a child when Maggi Lopez asked her those questions. It was late at night and the old nightmares had come. She'd woke, *screaming*, and Maggi held the child to her chest, running fingers through Margaret's hair.

"It's okay," Margaret's ragged voice came out as a whisper, "I can't make tornados or any of that *shit* either. I wouldn't even be a battlewitch, if Maggi hadn't believed in me."

"Maggi?" Erin asked.

"*The Bruja*, Maggi Lopez, she was my mother." A look of awe and wonder crossed Erin's face, and her jaw clamped down on whatever else she may have said before freezing up for awkwardly long seconds. Watching her face, Margaret realized that the loss of her arm was a reminder of the day she learned of Maggi's passing. A part of her was gone, and there was no returning it, "She adopted me when I was still very young. She wasn't a very good mother, she was kind of terrible, actually."

Margaret laughed, and when she did, the tears ran down her face, and across her temples, from where she lay.

"She was a *shitty fucking mom*," Erin didn't interrupt as Margaret continued, wiping at her eyes with the fingers of her left hand, "but she was a *good teacher*. She loved magic, and I've come to realize that she was the *only* person I could connect to, that way."

Margaret was hardly even talking to Erin now, she was watching the plywood ceiling, stained with soot as she spoke, "Mom, she used to wake me up, with *spiders*. She'd enter my dreams and scatter images of them. I think it's because she knew what my *real* nightmares were. I think she didn't want to *really* hurt me. No other witch could walk in my dreams."

Margaret wasn't forgetting the bad times. They were there, they were *always* there, "But, I guess I did forget the *good* times over the years," she said, speaking her thoughts again, manifest and heard clearly by the younger woman.

Maggi had *understood* Margaret in a way that her own fingers understood the grease in her hair, and the crust at her eyes in young hours of the morning. Between them, they'd shared a unique bond in magic, touching and holding it close, a warm and breathing thing that suffered no fools and strode great islands of cruelty. It was *this* that kept Maggi close to Margaret's heart, a network of rusted wire and tattered tape that united them both.

Margaret could not bring Maggi back from the dead to share that connection any more than she could reattach the ruins of her right arm and run fingers over her own breasts and throat. Worst of all, Margaret would *never* be able to bear her own children, to share such a bond. She herself would only be *one witch*.

"I think maybe you'd like me to wait outside," Erin said, hesitantly.

Margaret could barely understand *what she herself* felt, let alone Erin, but the girl had a far better vantage point from which to read, even inexperienced.

"*Yeah*," Margaret nodded, "I think I just want to be alone."

2:34pm March 17th, 39 Veilfall

Rio Vista, California

The Maul was led, politically, socially, and strategically, by three warlords. All of them pre-Collapse members of the 26th Marine Expeditionary. They still maintained a martial society, training their children from a very young age to fight and defend themselves, as part of a life-long compulsory service that only ended in death. In yesteryear, they'd pledged their loyalty to the Heart of House Owens, while maintaining a remote state far north. A place that allowed them to continue their way of life. Owens law didn't interest them, nor did Owens politics. They chose to raise their children, and their families, without interference from the outside world. That city state, Fish Rock, was nearly *two-hundred miles* away from Stockton.

While the Maul rallied their assault and support personnel, Margaret had taken a few days to recover from surgery, and true to her request, she was given a small box containing the scrubbed bones that had once made up her right arm. The box had been carefully crafted from wood with notches at the corners and silver hinges, her name carved into the lid.

Margaret and Erin would leave Fish Rock for Stockton, nearly a day ahead of the Maul's main force. They were loaned a small, two-seat, 4x4 for the trip. The truck couldn't make more than twenty-five or thirty miles per hour, but that was far quicker than any stagecoach.

Margaret had favored Erin to drive, since she neither enjoyed motor vehicles, nor had she ever been much good at commanding them. The truck had been old before the Collapse, much of the body decaying, and it clattered so violently that it seemed like parts might fly off. The driver's side floor had rusted out so completely that the road below was clearly visible, and the engine choked from years of being fed poorly refined fuel. The little truck's engine was loud, a symphony of rattle and clamor, timing skewed and straight headers roaring. Words could not be traded without yelling back and forth.

Additionally, Corporal Erin Abid was a terrible driver.

The coastal road south had long ago been bulldozed, allowing for a smoother dirt highway that was maintained by local fishing villages and farms. The area was lightly populated, and there was no vandalism or burnt husks. Nor were there any new structures. Antique fuel depots had been converted into roadside taquerias or seafood grills, serving warm meals and hot tea to anyone traveling the coast. Several of *those* stations remained operational in their original capacity, previously run by House Owens. They had since fallen to private holders, offering fuel at varied prices.

Days off the coast, the dirt road would find tan and cracked asphalt again, just south of Santa Rosa. This had been one of the largest former city states that made up House Owens and was best avoided. A fat price on her skull made Margaret hesitant to learn if the large 3rd Army garrison stationed here had joined Townsend, or not.

The stretch of highway between Petaluma and Fairfield was a riskier run, however. This forty-mile stretch was harassed by freebooters who made their home on Skaggs Island, a hodgepodge of thieves, but few cutthroats. Crops and meat that could be resold at high prices in the north, and manufactured goods like lamp oil, beeswax, leather, and iron cookware could be sold *anywhere* in rural Owens territory. With the 3rd Army's attention divided in the south, and Owens guard absent, Margaret had been worried they'd find trouble.

There had been none, however. Just miles and miles of poor farmsteads checkering the landscape. Large structures half collapsed, ruined frames and entryways, even the occasional vineyards left to ramble free and wild, unkept and ignored for decades. People who lived here were sallow and sunken eyed, migrant workers rejected from larger Owens landholds, refugees from the Collapse who may once have lived in the Bay Area Reach or Sacramento. In these parts people still traded stories about Dread Harvester, sworn to the idea that San Francisco was, herself, a cursed place even now.

It would be many more miles before Margaret and Erin would cross into the silky, patchwork farmlands of outer Stockton. Static with crops, such as cabbage, potatoes, and tomatoes, or more exotic almond and walnut groves. Those farmlands altered the cuisine of Stockton and nearby towns. Almost all dishes included a smattering of chopped, salted, almonds, or ground walnut paste, a featured condiment with most local poultry dishes.

At last they were coming into Rio Vista, a farming hamlet a few hours from Stockton. Colorful banners waved in the wind, thick with humidity from the Sacramento river and farm manure. The town itself was pleasant enough, built around a fine collection of stores and depots, restored since the Collapse. Rio Vista even maintained a firehouse, complete with a rolling wagon and four-man pump.

That wasn't what caught Margaret's attention, however.

As welcoming as Rio Vista tried to be, it didn't feel like northern California. It felt like *ash and sorrow*. There was grit to it, like soot in the throat or dust in the eyes. Something that couldn't be shaken, the memory of a memory. It *felt* like Saint Louis for a moment, and Margaret's mood shifted accordingly, asking Corporal Erin Abid to pull off and park further up the river by a quarter mile. It was quiet there. Lightly wooded and shady, rocks peppered the sand and small birds skipped away from the clamoring truck as its engine finally silenced.

Margaret stepped out of the truck, as awkward as *that was*, twisting her hips right so she could unlatch the battered door with her *left* hand, then releasing her arm back to the seat to push off and out. She looked up, squinting, the unrelenting sun in the corner of her vision, nearly obscuring a big blue sky that stretched above.

"Did you need to rest?" Erin asked, softly, as she climbed out of the cab. Her driver's side door didn't close correctly, and when she slammed it, the door just bounced open with a noisy *crack*.

Margaret turned to Erin, watching, choosing her words. The young woman's Antecedent kit, molle and chainmail were in the truck. It was hot in the cab and she wore a tank top of mottled gray and black. It struck Margaret as odd that she hadn't ever come to *stink*, despite days of open road, and not once in their weeks together had Margaret ever seen the girl bathe, or even wash her hands. It wasn't worth further consideration, and she dismissed the thought before replying.

"What do you feel, here, in this place?"

Erin looked around for a moment, north toward the Sacramento river, then south. Relatively pain free, Margaret could feel Erin's mind, whipping about the air like a panicked animal, blind, and fearful.

"*Easy,*" Margaret resisted the urge to use her voice to calm the girl. "Take your time. It's hard at first. *Imagine* that your mind is full of snakes. *Imagine* that they fall free from you, slithering around the dirt and sand, into the water, up the trees and down by the reeds. Don't rush it, don't *force it*, like you'd hammer a nail. Just *listen*."

When Erin tried this, she lifted her hands, holding her index and middle fingers apart from her thumbs, as though she were painting in the air with her finger tips. Her chin moved slightly, and her brow twitched, but it *was* working. Margaret could *see* the tendrils of her energy spread out now, down the river, under the truck, and even past Margaret's feet. It was slower, *yes*, but if she paid attention, she'd learn more.

While Erin practiced, Margaret crossed down into the shaded riverbanks. It was a quick drop off to the water, no mud or beach to speak of. The river was beautiful, a clear and moving channel that caught sunlight and made it dance. Only the obstruction of limbs below created a soft trickling sound. Margaret could have relaxed in this place, perhaps even slept under sweet, humid air. Unfortunately, the itch at the back of her throat hadn't vanished.

"This place isn't *this place*. Does that make sense?" Erin spoke louder for Margaret.

"Yeah. *Yeah, it does.*"

Turning back, Margaret gestured her closer, waiting for Erin to enter earshot so she wouldn't need to yell, "That could be a lot of things. Maybe something is *hidden* nearby, or perhaps the place is *owned* by an old spirit."

Erin bit down on her dimpled lower lip, eyes narrowed for the sun, "It's like if you hold a magnifying glass up and look *at it*, not *through it*."

Margaret turned away from her, and back to the flowing Sacramento river, "That's not a bad way of describing it. In this case, I think I know why."

Aurora's gown was long since garbage, left behind in Fish Rock. Margaret had accepted a simple black dress made of smoked linen after her surgery. It was sleeveless and tied at the waist with a long chain of narrow links, smooth iron, turned a deep shade of rusted cerise. The garment was cool for long hours in their truck and allowed her wounds a chance to breath less painfully. She released the chain around her waist and the weight of the metal tugged part of the dress off.

"*Oh,*" She heard Erin cough, then shuffle, turning around.

Margaret almost laughed but thought better of embarrassing the girl. She wasn't naked, she still wore simple, high-cut pantaloons, corded above her knees so she could adjust them for comfort.

In memory of Saint Louis, Margaret looked below her left breast, at the jagged scar across her ribs and stomach. Exposed to the fetid Mississippi, the wound festered for nearly a day after Saint Louis. It had almost killed her more certainly than Amihan's flame.

True to the Maul surgeon's word, her flesh was now covered with *fish skin*, cut and placed like tiles across her shoulder, collar bone, breast, and ribs, obscuring the worst burns. It was Tilapia, a crosshatch of a silver that caught light and reflected it back in varied hues. The skin itself shifted colors with light or angle, shades of deep blue, malachite, and violet moving around her upper body like ferrets at play, darting, dodging, weaving.

The Tilapia skin had been stitched with care, fine thread holding it in place about her frame. It was ragged at the edges, curled up or twisted where her dress had worn on it. According to the surgeon, she'd need to wear the skin until her own flesh began to form scar tissue. It would reduce the disfigurement, and physical pain. It had turned her stomach at first, but *here* at river's edge with reflected sunlight prancing, she found an elegant beauty in it.

Margaret looked back, away from her colorful carapace, and let her eyes unfocus and drift in the river currents. There was a voice there, wordless and without language, an ebbing thing that politely demanded she come close, much closer than the river's edge. It was the key to what was shifting in this place, the division that tickled the back of her throat.

Condatis is here. The old river god from Saint Louis.

Margaret was fully in control of her person when she thrust her left arm behind her and allowed herself to fall, below, into the river. The water was a cold shock and she shrieked once, cursing, trying to acclimate. Her bare feet caught the river bottom, and she held herself up, surprised by the current strength. Once she habituated, she could allow herself to relax a second time, tilting her head back to the bright, rolling sky.

"Um," Margaret could hear Erin above, "What are you doing?"

Truly focused now, she didn't respond to the girl. Instead, she pressed her palm with care to the river's surface, *listening*. This wasn't her vocation, her métier, and it took many minutes to quiet her mind and synchronize with a simpler energy. Drab in so few shades, offering no sweet seductions for Margaret's spirit. She found no joy here, even her meditation was false, a spurious effort no different from a menial task, *doing dishes*, or *sweeping*.

The sort of thing she paid *servants* to do.

Margaret *and* the river finally reached an accord, and she was able to spread her mind wide, across the wetlands of Northern California. Part of her pressed past San Pablo Bay and kissed the salty ocean. Another part of her climbed up the narrow ship channels and into chilly Sierra Nevada run off. This connected, she could speak his name, *speak directly with him.*

"*Condatis.*"

Gods of the physical world were more disconnected from human condition than those vain creatures who could command flesh and visit beyond the Veil. They paid little heed to witches like Margaret, and Condatis didn't reply immediately. When he did; however, the Sacramento River slowed, and finally the current went still, wholly a giant puddle around her.

Margaret opened her eyes, allowing something like a disjointed smile, "Hello."

The water of the river pulled and twisted up, dark green and brown, giving way to bright reflections and shimmers. A shape, humanoid in form, coalesced up and out, head, neck, arms and torso, rising *many* feet above Margaret. So large was this arthropod that the river itself fell past Margaret's breasts, exposing most of her torso, and glistening fish vellum.

"*Little butcher, Bête Noire,*" the towering form gurgled, vowels and consonants were chirps and slaps of water, a pitter pat, leaking, *snap-snap-snap* noise.

"Why do you call me that? *Bête Noire*?" Margaret replied, calmly, her one arm stretched wide from her body.

"*Bête Noire is such that we name you. Such that you are.*"

Vividly aware of how cold she was now, a breeze dancing across her wet skin, Margaret shivered in reply, "Why do you swim in my rivers Condatis? You're far from the Mississippi."

The water darkened around her, turning a deep shade of blue, oily black where the light didn't catch, bold in refraction. "*Such as ourselves repay such as yourselves when we wish. How we wish. It's time to settle our debt.*"

Margaret was aware that Condatis was angry. More than *feeling* it, the river slid around her ankles and thighs, discontent, *agitated*. The concept that Condatis *owed* Margaret anything seemed to rile the very air and humidity she breathed, slicing at her lungs and eating away at her sinuses with sooty bite. "*Condatis*, you said you would owe me a favor. The favor of a god. You said, I *freed* you. I didn't *ask for this favor*."

Condatis didn't answer immediately, and Margaret could feel turmoil against her flesh. She supposed that he could simply drown her, if he so pleased. "*You paid dearly to kill the old Bête Noire.*" He answered, simply, in a ripple and slosh of syllables.

Margaret considered her reply, "I have thought warmly of you, over the years. If it can be done, I release you from any debts you think I'm owed."

Once more Condatis paused, neither moving, nor offering Margaret any sense that he heard her. When he finally spoke, he leaned over, dripping water across her face and eyes.

"*Little butcher, Bête Noire. You are at the center of a spiraling path. Other gods seek to use you. You're not free, you're crippled, hobbled.*"

Margaret licked her lips, water streaming down her face.

"This is true, river lord."

"*Little butcher, Bête Noire,*" Condatis continued, shrinking away, water churning about Margaret's belly and spine, "*I cannot return you an arm, but it is within my power to free you from your hobble, and make us equal. Without debt.*"

Condatis collapsed. The suspended form of water fell back into the river as though a giant bucket had released its contents across Margaret. That much water returning to the Sacramento was catastrophic. The force slammed Margaret back into the riverbank and pulled her down ten, perhaps twenty yards, from where she'd jumped in. An adequate swimmer with *two arms,* this departure was so violent that Margaret found herself *drowning*, unable to surface, with water filling her nose and mouth. She panicked, briefly, before realizing Condatis would wish her no harm, and she simply eased into the sensation. By the time she clamored up the bank, and onto the shore, she was coughing up water, and gasping hard. All the while, her mind was immersed in the cacophony of a thousand waterfalls spilling and splashing about.

He's laughing at me.

"Lady Mayhem?" Margaret could barely hear Erin above her own hacking cough as she spit up water, heaving, trying to regain her breath.

"I'm here." She replied, as loud as her throat granted.

Erin approached Margaret, taking her left hand, pulling her up from the sandy beach, south of where the two had parked.

"What did you do? *The whole river*, drained," Erin's voice changed pitch with awe.

To be fair, Margaret thought, *I've never seen anything like that either.*

"An old friend," Margaret coughed again, and looked over at Erin, eyes wide, "*'friend'* is maybe an exaggeration. An old river god who owed me a favor. A story I might never tell you."

"*River god*?" Margaret's Corporal was aflame in excitement over this notion, before she looked down, releasing Margaret's hand and taking a step back. "...your skin."

Still breathing hard, trying not to gasp, Margaret looked down to her naked torso. The fish skin that had been stitched across her ragged burns and tattered flesh was no longer a patchwork quilt of Tilapia. Rather, *all* her burns were now coated in a carapace of silver scale. Narrow threads were gone, so too was the bumped and rounded edges of where her fat boiled up. Flesh given at birth simply met fish skin somewhere in the middle, merging like a lifting fog in San Francisco, at noon day.

Margaret reached down with her left hand, running index and middle finger across her sternum and right breast. It *felt* like Tilapia skin, the colors shifted all the same, but meat and muscle underneath were firm, solidly *a part of her*. Applying pressure, then digging her nails in, there was no *pain* from the burns.

"*Gods be fucked*," Erin took one, two, and then a final step back, clutching her mouth closed with a palm, as if her words might bring down a lightning bolt.

Although her right arm was *missing*, Margaret's burns were *gone*. Wholly replaced. When she twisted her neck, rolled her shoulders, the Tilapia moved with her, no longer pulling or pinching, *flaying* her alive.

Margaret laughed out loud, as genuinely as Condatis had laughed at her. She'd been a great fool, not just today, but for a very long time. She'd believed the world to be a static and predictable place, governed by the laws of nature and magic. Within those laws, Margaret had done her finest, for decades, to avoid gods, and all their entanglements. It was, at this moment, that Margaret realized how little control she had. The power to bend matter around her had been so simple for the Mississippi river lord.

Words failed Margaret, she couldn't speak, couldn't summon words to answer this gift. Condatis wouldn't even remain to accept a *thank you*.

How would I thank a god for new skin?

Only in the shadow of mutilation had Margaret learned how much of her confidence kept rest in physical beauty. Only in the den of unending pain did she realize how much of her life she lived in the threaded glow of *magic*. This gift was beyond thanks, it was a distillery of hope, the chance to make good on her dreams.

Without word or warning, Margaret leapt forward, covering the paces between her and Erin, clutching the androgynous girl with one arm. The strange and glimmering skin *felt* the texture of Erin's tank top, the heat of her flesh, the movement of breeze at her shoulder. It was a freedom in the purest form, and Margaret could only giggle. A child again, holding her Corporal.

Holding, perhaps, her friend.

"Lady Mayhem," Erin squeaked, clearly uncomfortable with this unmitigated display of physical affection, "that's good enough."

Margaret pulled away, silver crosshatch on her lower lip stretching into a smile, "This *is* good enough, Corporal. Do you hear that? *Do you fucking hear that?*"

Erin's eyes jumped around, she was trying to *hear that,* "No?"

Laughing, Margaret ran her tongue in a full circle of her lips, "I can hear it. I can hear the sound of Amihan Lopez begging me for mercy."

4:04pm March 17th, 39 Veilfall

Thornton, California

From Rio Vista it was only about an hour to Thornton, one of the major land liege hubs north of Stockton, then a straight shot back into the capitol. Crossing Rio Vista put Margaret and Erin squarely in the rich heartland of House Owens. These barons had passed their land through family bloodlines since the Collapse. Their children and grandchildren now ruled landholds stretching across thousands of acres. Most of the hands that worked those fields also lived there, allowed free residence, safety, and security for their traded labor. Those families ate well but were essentially owned by the minor nobility of House Owens, who'd grown wealthy over the decades, supplying crops of every variety beyond Stockton, to the Nevada ranges and Central Valley waste.

A highway, rail, *and* river port, Thornton was ruled by the Leavitt Tillage, a trade hub with a ticking heart. Every building, every hotel and hostel, market, shoppe, tavern and diner belonged to the Leavitt family. Whether it was traffic guards or cooks, street cleaners or tanners, they *all* wore blue and yellow, groomed themselves to Leavitt standards, and spoke proper English as the Leavitts demanded.

Outside of the double-carrier diesel rigs that the Tillage owned to move crops and goods, the little 4x4 truck that Erin drove was the only petrol drinker in town. Most offices and keeps maintained tie and tack for horses. Indeed, much of the town smelled like boiled cabbage and the dusky aroma of horses. Blue and yellow banners flew on each street corner, and concrete sidewalks were lifted perhaps a foot above the street below. Two plumes of blackened coal smoke, further east of the highway, signaled freshly embarking or disembarking locomotives, along with the whine of their steam whistles.

As Erin drove into town it seemed far busier than would have been expected, walks thick with foot traffic. Much of the clamor seemed to be Stockton citizens, dressed to their own devices in the colorful hues of the capitol. Woven tapestries of lady's long skirts in shades of yellow and orange were dingy from soot and rail wear, blouses unlaced, and sleeves rolled, they were followed by men hauling crates of possessions, or parcels of food, while children drug their heels in somber dismay.

The solemn traffic only accelerated Margaret's desire to go home, back to Stockton. She wanted to make that last final dash, but she also wanted to *celebrate*. She wanted to show Townsend the strange gift that Condatis had bestowed, a twisted restoration that should never have been possible. Aphrodite offered *beauty*, but with a price, and not a price Margaret wanted to pay. She'd lived a long life, *free* of fetter and leash, enslaving herself to a god whose whims ran the gambit of horrific and *whorish* did not delight her.

"I guess the 9th Battalion is still fighting in Stockton," Erin said softly, pulling up next to a horse tack. She was parked perhaps a few hundred feet back from the arched platform that looked out on Thornton's train station, outside a tavern called *Golden Blue*.

Margaret kept her seat a moment, watching Stockton's evacuated families puzzle with glazed eyes and confusion. They pointed and gesticulated amongst each other, trading inquisitions. *Where are the hostels? Are they north or south? Is there a barter tax?*

Some of these families would sign on with the Leavitt Tillage to stay warm and fed, but there were only so many the landlord would accept before his cropper rosters were too swollen. Others would continue north, perhaps as far as the borders of the Antecedent Empire, up past Chico or maybe Redding, into the green lands beyond. A few could afford to abide by rents, hold up, and hope that the fighting in Stockton would end soon.

"People still need to keep the wolves away," Margaret finally answered. Weary of the grim spectacle, she looked over at Erin, "Have you ever drank? I mean, drank *liquor?* Not malts or ale, poorman lunch. I mean *real* drink?"

Erin smiled wide, eyelids dipping low, and she offered Margaret a shrug. That was enough of an answer, and Margaret was already planning how the next hour would go. The city of Stockton would *hold*, as would Amy Lopez. For now, Margaret wanted to twist her body, roll her neck, and maybe press her *fish breast* into a boney young farmhand's chest to remember what it was like to be whole.

Almost whole, she thought, and realized that the truck door wouldn't open because the arm she pulled at the handle with no longer existed.

Standing outside the cab, Margaret grabbed her 9mm off the dashboard and jammed it into the chain that bound up her black dress of cotton and smoky knit.

"I thought the signs said no weapons? When we drove into Thornton?" Erin saw Margaret holster the pistol, so she reached forward to grab her shotgun from behind tattered and faded backrest.

"*Oh,* Corporal Abid can *read*," Margaret winked, speaking in a sing-song rhyme, "Leavitt can *fuck themselves*, the last time I left a pistol behind I was nearly roasted alive."

Erin pulled her sling free, shouldered the weapon, then paused, "*Wait*, do you think my kit will get stolen?"

"*Maybe*? Don't risk it." Margaret walked forward, away from the 4x4's hood, her hand on beaten and warm metal, listening to radiator hiss. Erin squinted, annoyed, before resting her shotgun on the truck's hood. She withdrew a long sleeve blouse, glossy in duck oil with a stitched framework of chainmail and lowered it onto her body. Over that, Erin added an olive-gray molle vest with tattered chunks of old velcro, along with a hand stitched patch, "*3rd.*"

"Won't the *Leave-it* guards try to take our guns?" Erin inquired, pulling at her vest. Margaret shrugged with a smile. Tilapia skin on her face creased up and gave her a sinister glare under fading light.

With nothing more to add, Margaret turned, taking lead down a brick path that crossed onto gravel ride, and into the *Golden Blue's* entrance. Erin grabbed one of the two pine doors, lacquered a deep shade of amber and trussed with dark iron hinges, pulling it open quickly to allow Margaret entrance.

Turning to the right, alongside a bar of roughhewn wood, Margaret saw Ramona Lopez.

The younger woman wore a wide grin on cherry red lips as she turned away from the bartender. A low boat neck swept down across her shoulders on a deep blue dress of textured voile and linen. Fox fur, dyed teal, curved around her shoulders, crossing ample cleavage and back down to cover her hips. Her obsidian hair was pulled up and pinned tight under a high-crowned hat of black velvet, tilted over her forehead.

Both women's eyes met, in the exact same moment.

Ramona held her hands, palm on knuckles, at her corset. A look of amusement drew across her cheeks. Margaret's left hand was already drawing the pistol at her waist chain, finger sliding behind the trigger guard and taking aim for her niece.

When she had a *right arm*, the *right-handed* Margaret was more than respectable with a pistol. The 9mm felt *loose* and *undirected* in her left hand, like she was trying to walk backwards and chew on rail tar. Without slow or pause, her eyes focused to take aim and she simply decided, *I'll keep shooting until something hits her*.

For Erin, directly behind Margaret, it was like a flag shifting wide with the wind, appearing suddenly. The specter *wasn't* there, then he simply *was*, a smoky vision cast in shades of sepia. When the ghost shifted into sight directly between Margaret and Ramona, his head was up, clawing at the air, wrapped shirt like Erin's. The shade had intercepted Margaret's bullet in a brume of atomized lead, bright with orange sparks.

Ramona was still smiling.

I'll keep shooting until something hits her, Margaret repeated, to herself.

With one round in the chamber and *seventeen more* behind, Margaret unloaded the weapon, turning her frame to line up as closely as she could with her dominant eye. One foot in front of the next, closing the distance between the two, every round grouped closer and closer to Ramona's face. The sound was a litany of monotone hammer falls, a noise almost sentient in the bar as it rang on glass liquor bottles, brass cases kissing at Margaret's bare toes.

Every round discharged was met by a specter. They shifted like thick smoke, curled up and mutated into something unrecognizable, until only a blur of faded bronze and brick vapor jerked and popped in the unoccupied air between them. Ramona never shifted, flinched, or raised her palms. Instead, her smile grew to a wide and toothy grin, eyes twinkling.

Ignoring Margaret, Ramona shot a wink at Erin and the girl realized that a shade was standing right next to her, phantom firearm leveled to her skull, jaw bone hanging loose from his face, and battered ACH strapped to nothing in particular.

Margaret was less than a yard away from Ramona when the slide on her pistol locked back, her chest heaving, eyes stinging with gunpowder.

Ramona Lopez turned her eyes away from Erin, back to her aunt, then reached up with a hand wrapped in blue silk to flick dusted lead off her breasts.

"Quite an entrance, Mayy. Are you done?"

Margaret lowered the pistol, then glanced back to where Erin stood, a shade bodyguard looming over her. "Keep the scatt gun down and it won't hurt you."

"Unless I want it to," Ramona answered, "they're not quite as *automated* as I lead you to believe, when we met at the train station."

As she turned her head back to Ramona, Margaret unfurled part of her mind, whips uncoiling in the inches unoccupied between the two women, wrapping around Ramona's mind and spirit, digging with barbs to find grasp. Margaret didn't *expect* it to work, but if Ramona hadn't erected boundaries in the seconds it took to discharge Margaret's pistol, she *might* have a ledge to leap into her mind from.

There was a glimpse, *just for a second*, through Ramona's eyes, lashes fluttering, as she looked down on a newborn *baby boy*. His umbilical cord still hung from his stomach, eyes scrunched closed, covered in bloody viscous, and wailing like a banshee.

Ramona took a step in and threw her palm out fast, slapping Margaret across her face, the impact twisting her chin an inch or two, no more.

"You hit like a *girl*," Margaret licked her lips, head unmoving. There was a ripple of red and white in the air, as if someone had brushed the very oxygen around Ramona with paint, fading away a second later.

"*Ma'*am," from Ramona's right, behind the bar, a little man squawked like an angry bird, disappointed that a cat was too close, "*You want*, maybe I call the guard *cap'n*?"

Margaret didn't take her eyes off Ramona's, she was *ignoring* nearly everything in favor of drilling away at the younger woman's defenses, pressing, prodding, all over her mind for *any* weakness.

"*I want* you to *shut the fuck up* and *fuck yourself*." Ramona replied to the squawking man behind the bar.

"At least you're still a *real* witch, behind your phantoms and boy-toys," Margaret hissed, leaning back, relaxing her mind and withdrawing an offensive. There was no point, Ramona had done well, the barriers were nearly complete by the time Margaret attacked her. All she'd get was the vision of a baby covered in afterbirth.

I would rip your throat out if your goddamn ghosts would allow it, Margaret thought, hardly protecting or hushing her mind, easily audible to another witch.

"I believe you would, Mayy. Shall we *talk*?" Ramona's calm returned.

Margaret sighed, turning away from Ramona, looking at the bartender.

He was a buck-toothed little creature with tassels of hair on his shiny skull and eyes that seemed too small for his face. His right arm was stretched down, below the bar's edge, where he was *jerking* furiously.

"*Gods be fucked* Ramona. What the *fuck* is wrong with you?" Margaret sighed.

"Oh, we're *drinking*?" Ramona answered, snapping her fingers softly within her silk gloves and releasing the humiliated bar keep. He fell away from the bar, struggling with his pants and belt, a second later.

"*I'm* drinking. I came here for a *drink*, and now I need two." Margaret turned away from her niece and leaned up next to the bar. It looked to be a great old tree, cut cleanly down the middle and mounted on iron supports. Once the buck-toothed man had regained control of his pants and tucked away his genitalia, he scrambled back to face Margaret.

"*Bar's* closed, *ma'am*. Gunplay, scared off everyone." Margaret squinted then turned back to Ramona, who waited calmly, a hand on her hip.

"What the *fuck* did you do to him?" Margaret wrinkled her nose in disgust, then turned back to the little man, "*Just hand over a bottle of whisky and go somewhere else.*"

She changed the resonation in her voice and gave command, pressing at the barkeep, to do as she wished, if only for his own good. He needed to get away from Ramona and whatever wry controls she'd used to make the poor wretch dance like a puppet. It struck Margaret as cruel, like a cat torturing a grasshopper.

The keep turned and grabbed a bottle of blue glass off the shelf. He popped the cork out, backed up, and watched the two witches for a second. There were hundreds of candles illuminating the bar, reflecting and refracting through dozens of mirror carafes, creating a flicking wash of light, and countless shadows, projected in all directions.

"*Go,*" Margaret commanded the squawking man from his subjection.

He fled properly, managing to never stumble over his own feet. Once he was gone, Margaret turned her attention back to Erin, who still stood with a ghost soldier next to her, spun up in sepia vapor that shifted and blurred like static on a radio. "Stand outside, Corporal. If Leavitt guards come, show them the patch on your kit. Pull rank. Pretend you're an officer or something."

Erin opened her mouth, closed it, then opened it *again*, squinting at Margaret. She wanted to argue, or say something like *I can't,* or *I don't know how*, but she realized it was pointless. A look of unfettered anger crossed her face and she turned to pull one of the double doors open.

The specter who leveled a phantom pistol vanished as she did so.

Alone with her niece, Margaret picked up the bottle of blue glass and favored Ramona again, "Did Amihan and Alexander *ever* have those spook guards?"

Ramona, nodded, taking a step back, hand high on her hip, "Of course. We contracted with a British Bishop to create the poltergeists. Unfortunately, only the bones of *my* poltergeists survived my departure from Crafton."

"'*Bishop*?'" Margaret raised her brows, then shook her head, waving Ramona off an explanation, "Is there *anything* you didn't lie to me about?"

Ramona's face turned incredulous, one brow drawing up higher than the next, her lips parting in a crooked smile, "*Good witches lie.* Didn't you tell me that, *aunt* Mayy?"

Margaret genuinely lost whatever control she had of her emotions, "*Gods be fucked, Ramona!* I didn't tell you to betray your entire *fucking* family! A *good witch lies* because she holds the best cards in the deck. If you tell everyone *what the fuck you're holding*, there's not much point in being a witch, is there?" Margaret grabbed the nameless blue bottle off the bar with her left hand and upended it. She chugged the whiskey, none the wiser to whether it was smooth or burning, "I didn't *fucking* tell you to manipulate Amy. I didn't *fucking* claim I planned to *kill my brother*. I didn't *fucking* tell you to turn on me *or* Alexander. *You've probably single-handedly destroyed the Empire!*"

Margaret was yelling, her voice still sore and shrill. She cracked on a few vowels and her voice rasped over words, but the rage was undeniable. There was nothing but steel in her eyes when she looked at Ramona again, whiskey running down her lips.

Ramona nodded, calmly, "I'm sorry, I didn't think I could be honest."

Margaret gestured with her arms wide, forgetting there was no *right arm* to balance the expression, "What are you *possibly* getting out of this?"

Ramona laughed back, "That *salt bitch*, Cuttersark, back in San Francisco saw it. Why can't you? Magic doesn't serve my father, *he serves magic*. Maps *don't matte*r anymore."

So that's the game, Margaret fell quiet for a second, collecting her thoughts, then answered, "You've made deals with all the Antecedent auxiliary states. Haven't you?"

Ramona Lopez nodded, gently, "It's over *Aunt* Mayy. The Antecedent Empire will collapse by summer, and there's nothing you can do to stop it. I suppose you could go back and make counteroffers, but Stockton will burn without you. *Besides*, you must stay. You agreed to kill Aurora Cuttersark and my father. Didn't you?"

Margaret had been *okay* with the notion of assassination until she heard the words spoken out loud by her niece. The niece she *still* loved despite everything. "Lord Owens told you."

"He did," Ramona relaxed her shoulders, returning both her hands to the midsection of her corset, just a few feet from Margaret, "*You* outbid me, and that's fine. Honestly, Lady Manticore would kill my father, even if you didn't."

Margaret didn't hide her shock, "Geraldine is on this?"

"Geraldine never liked Dad. She was *your mother's* witch, a brawler and bruiser to the end. She wants to be queen of her own domain." Ramona was gentle with each word, talking the way she might have to a child who'd soon lose his gray, old dog to illness, "I'm *sorry* Margaret. In all of this I made *one* mistake."

Margaret put the blue whiskey bottle back on the bar and turned to face Ramona. Her shoulders tensed, and she clenched her jaw in something akin to rage. Every nerve in her hand wanted to wrap fingers into a fist and strike Ramona, then keep striking until the two sat in silence.

"I assumed you were *incorruptible*," Ramona shook her head, "I thought you were a true believer in this Antecedent scam. I didn't think I could offer you *anything* to make you turn on your brother. If I'd known a landhold in House Owens was all you needed, we could have avoided this." Ramona waved her hand at Margaret's missing arm, as if she was gesturing to an offensive mess in the kitchen sink.

"We shouldn't have crossed the Mississippi." Margaret sighed, looking away from Ramona, watching the dancing candles, "I never wanted to conquer the whole of North America. I only kept fighting for Mom. Magic and mud was all we had left between us. I could imagine how *proud* she'd be if I just kept following Alexander."

Ramona leaned over the bar to put her face between Margaret's eyes and whatever distant play she watched, "My dad has never loved anyone. Not you and not my mother. I'll miss him, but he's had his *day*. Now it's *mine*."

Margaret wanted to be *so much* angrier right now, she wanted to scream at her niece, slap her in the face, and make her *stop* this madness. She imagined how that would play out. Dramatic scenes of holding Ramona, tearfully convincing her to undo all the damage she'd wrought. A smile skipped across Margaret's face as she lost herself to the imaginary scenario, but it refused to end in a way that satisfied her. It was only a tale of Alexander Lopez and his pet battlewitch, forgotten in history, left to rot alone.

Margaret's smile curdled. Not out of *sadness* or *regret*, but because she could not bring herself to hate the future Ramona had so carefully crafted.

"The Antecedent Empire will shatter into a hundred city states. You'll be there to catch the pieces. You'll bed their warlords and kings, you'll bargain and deal, and every state in the Empire will answer *only* to you. Even House Owens."

Ramona nodded, then reached over for Margaret's blue bottle. She released it, allowing the other woman a chance to drink, "You're smarter than I ever gave you credit for, Mayy."

I don't feel smart.

Margaret continued, as if Ramona had never spoken, sweet poison like candied arsenic dripping from her lips, running down her throat, "You'll never have to worry about collecting taxes or water disputes. You'll never need to concern yourself with standing armies, conquests, defenses, or security. You will end up wielding more power than my brother dreamed possible."

Ramona was silent.

Margaret considered herself a clever observer of human emotion, but this left her rank and empty, this anger that refused to burn or grind at her bones. She wasn't even upset now at Ramona, but rather herself. Her greatest crime at this bar wasn't tolerating Ramona's schemes, but rather the shame that warmed her cheeks as she delighted in victory. That was the same glow that had become welts under Maggi's fists, a very young version of Margaret who just wanted to impress a woman who seemed larger than life.

I'm not a child anymore, Margaret seethed.

The silence between them was sticky like drying tears or salt residue, it tasted like half a hangover and sounded like a window that didn't shatter when hit by stone.

"I suppose, I have one last question," Margaret said, running only five fingers across the slick and lacquered bar, "Why not let me adopt your son?"

The mood shifted. It seemed to Margaret like the candles dimmed, shrinking. Ramona was no longer minding her barriers. There was a ghost of spoil in the air and a deep weight pulled at Margaret's stomach.

"I'm sorry for that too," Ramona answered, so quiet that Margaret had to watch her lips to understand.

"Where is he now?"

Ramona didn't answer with her voice, Margaret heard the words clearly enough in her mind, *I don't know.* The younger woman wasn't trying to be purposefully difficult, she genuinely didn't want to say that out loud. Margaret would never forgive Ramona her actions, though she would shamelessly profit from them. It was the *child* that Margaret was angry about now, the child that could have been her own to raise.

Silence separated the two for a while. The bar still smelled like turned milk, and perhaps half of the candles had died out when Margaret finally spoke again.

"You have a train to catch, don't you Ramona?"

"*Six-oh-five* to Reno." Ramona answered, her voice briny.

Margaret pulled away from the bar, "I need to get back to Stockton,"

"Mayy," Ramona looked away from the candles she'd lost herself in, reaching her right hand out for Margaret's right shoulder, "I really *am* sorry for your arm. If it's any consolation, I think the new skin is actually quite fetching."

Margaret pulled away from Ramona's touch, no matter how little she liked to. Behind a fiendishly clever young woman was a little girl who Margaret couldn't stop loving, who would always be saccharine sweet, and kind spoken. "Tell your sister how sorry you are. Before I kill her. She's the one you *fucked over,* worst of all."

"*Mayy*," Ramona blinked, and maybe she was about to cry, but Margaret couldn't tell, "I didn't lie to you about Amy, back in Stockton. She *loves you.* She's worshipped you her whole life. Sway her to *your* side, but don't kill her. Please try. Promise me that?"

Margaret bit back a laugh in her throat, unwilling to slap Ramona in the face with unbridled glee. Amy had chosen her own fate the moment she'd pressed Margaret's face to tarmac and reminded her what it was like to be a powerless little girl.

"*Sure*," Margaret shrugged, "I promise."

Good witches lie, Margaret thought, with no intention of sparing Amihan's life.

Ramona blinked again, a single tear racing down her cheek, running for her jawline, before falling, "We'll likely never meet again, Mayy. If we do, I suspect one of us will need to kill the other. Take care of yourself. I wish you a good life, here in the land of Owens."

Ramona tried to reach out for Margaret again, but she stepped back, avoiding the touch. For just a few moments the young woman's barriers softened, and there was a slip of sorrow at the tip of Margaret's tongue. It was a simple thing like an old wooden spoon, worn from use and left to heat on the stove, delivering a stew of rare bliss and awesome longing.

Margaret didn't know if it was *her* memory or Ramona's, but she was reminded of clutching the baby Lopez girl on her lap. Feeding her boiled carrots and beef broth, humming a melody for them both.

Margaret did not call after or clutch at Ramona as she left the bar, no matter how much she wished it, no matter how much her heart hurt.

11:18pm March 17th, 39 Veilfall

Stockton, California

"Did you hear about the man who couldn't juggle?" Arranged across the same upholstered sofa of red velvet and Cherrywood that Lady Owens had once kept court on, Margaret watched Townsend entering through the front door. "He just didn't have the balls."

Margaret couldn't even fake a laugh. Puns weren't *actually* funny.

Townsend held his breath, gawking at her with an open jaw. His face was smudged with carbon and he was dressed in ripstop trousers, with black plate carrier over a tan shroud shirt that looked a bit too small in the shoulders.

"I was never told that you'd returned."

Margaret tried to offer a clever grin, lifting fingers to her lips, attempting to cast herself in a seductive light. She hadn't changed from the road, and her bare feet were drawn up close to her thighs, "I had to sneak back into the city, around the Dogs, under Crosstown. I'm returning your brassboy, but I promoted her to Corporal."

The lemongrass and pine smoke of Aurora's old home was gone. Instead it was dominated by Townsend's aftershave and slithering gun oil. Across from the sofa was a mirror and tin basin that Townsend had used to shave, maps and gear sitting nearby.

"And *Sarn't* Holloway?" Townsend walked past the narrow vestibule and onto the deep red tile, kissed by veins of faux gold.

Margaret tipped her head back and forth like an old bobble toy glued to a dashboard, "He thought Plague Dog would promote him for my head."

Reaching down to unlace the sides of his plate carrier, Townsend growled in reply, "I'm *sorry*. I made him the same offer to watch over you."

Margaret eased out of her own mind a bit, allowing pieces of herself to flutter about the room, listening to Townsend's pulse. His nerves were sizzling, and there was a pull at his chest. Desire made tangible to such an extent that he hadn't even begun to question the silver crosshatch of her new skin.

"It was bound to happen. *Someone* would take a shot at me."

"You look," Townsend paused in study, tossing his carrier of molle and ceramic plate to the table, "*better.*"

Margaret reached over to her right shoulder and tugged her dress down to show him a rounded stump of Tilapia skin, "One arm poorer, but yes, I suppose."

Does he see my face? Margaret withdrew her mind from Townsend's neck and shoulders, avoiding what she *might* hear, or feel. *Only* her eyes ran across Townsend now, her tendrils, her very essence, withdrawn.

"Where did you grow up?" Margaret sat up, leaning on her left arm and lowering her eyelids, "Share that with me. With your *voice*. I want to hear you."

"New Castle," Townsend answered, his voice brisk, low. He sat down on the same chair that Margaret had kept when she brought Ramona to meet Aurora Owens. Painted oil lamps of ceramic and glass illuminated the room with a rolling banter of dim flame.

"My mother fought at New Castle," Margaret lifted her hand from velvet, letting her fingers trace across the soft fabric, to sit up straight, "They thought she died there. They *told me* she died there."

Townsend answered, hushed. "I was caught at the loading docks when the walls fell. Nothing but fire behind me and Antecedents in front. It was the first and last time that I believed I would die. I ran for the Antecedents. They shot at me, *of course*, assumed I was strapped with explosives like the other children. Not even a second or two passed before they died under New Castle mortars. They just floated there, for seconds, dancing, losing pieces of themselves."

Townsend was painting a vivid memory with his voice. It was certain, a thick brush, putting color to canvas, pressing in so deeply that when Margaret blinked, she could remember a scene she'd never witnessed. When she answered him, it was in memory of the first time she'd seen mortars kill a dozen men, and her words matched the melody of his own with succinct sorrow, "You couldn't believe how quiet it was."

"I never heard anything as quiet as that day," Townsend planted his big palms squarely on the knees of his ripstop. There was an openness between them, they were no longer trading greetings, talking about *how much better* Margaret looked, pretending that she'd never been doused in flame.

My turn, and she closed her eyes.

"My parents named me *Margaret*. I remember this. I can sometimes still hear my father singing my name, rocking me to sleep, promising to keep the monsters away, *promising* me the world. Let me hear my name, on your lips."

Does he know I'm not using magic? Can he feel it?

Townsend didn't blink as he watched her, his face betraying so little, save two hard swallows, and the slightest hint of a tremor at his thumbs.

"*Margaret*." Townsend answered.

Exhaling, Margaret bit on her lower lip. It was a trade of intimacy that went beyond anything she'd shared with Townsend prior. No slip of skin or touch of mind could have equaled his hesitation to speak, or hearing her *real* name suckling at her ears.

She stood up, slowly. Her bare feet slid along the cold and textured tile of Aurora's home, around the little table of wood and glass, and up close to the big man with his barrel chest.

"Does the 3rd Army still know I belong to their *General?* Do you brag with your officers what my breasts feel like in your hands?" Five fingers slid across his rough cheek and toward his jaw. She had *never* seduced a man without magic, and she was stumbling for what would appeal to Townsend, what would teach him her desire, with no tethers.

With his left knee between her legs, Margaret stood over Townsend, lifting her left leg up and gently wedging her foot under his inguen, the ripstop rough on her toes.

"I never assumed you *belonged* to anyone but yourself," she could *see* Townsend draw a deep breath, a part of him hesitating, just for a second, before he lifted his left hand up to her inner thigh.

I don't suppose a man would do that if he wasn't interested.

It was no different for Margaret than wearing a blindfold. She couldn't read Townsend's face no matter how hard she tried, and she *tried*, looking for any twitch of the eye or a shift of his brows. *Anything* that would tell his reaction. She *was* working for it and the very effort excited her further.

He was too gentle at first, and Margaret *almost* reached into his mind to nudge him.

Instead she spoke, "*Harder.*"

Margaret wasn't skinny, but she was small enough that Townsend's hand easily covered half of her leg, and when his fingers and thumbs retracted on her flesh, she tilted her head back, elated cry escaping her throat.

Margaret's hand reached to the smooth waist chain. She loosed the clasp, letting the wrap fall open. From here the fish skin was only somewhat visible near her sternum.

"I *like* that your moustache always smells like cigarettes, and I can never see your lips. I *like* how angry you always look, even when you're not. I *like* the way you don't flash your feelings around, and you make me *guess*. You make me *work for it*."

Townsend's left hand slid up her thigh as he reached for her dress with his right, fingers tracing up her unscarred breast, past her clavicle, to her left shoulder.

The fabric fell to the floor.

Now or never, you like Tilapia-woman, or you don't.

Her pantaloons were gone, cast off before she bathed in Aurora's ornate old clawfoot. She was naked before him. The Tilapia shimmered by lamp, malachite and violet writhing around each other, across ribs and breast, across her collar bone. The cross hatching was unable to decide between gold or silver, and at times it reflected *both*.

"*That's*," Townsend swallowed again, his eyes groping at her skin, "*beautiful*."

Margaret could now *feel* the awe that she heard at the back of his throat, but for a man who worked so hard to remain granite, it was a vivid tell that he'd been beguiled. Townsend removed his hand from between her legs and wrapped both big palms and fingers around her midsection, just above her waist. When his hands ambled up her body it was a uniquely different sensation on each side. His palms were *rougher*, *warmer* against her fish skin. She felt like she could feel every scar, every callous, every bit of torn cuticle. It wasn't unpleasant, it was just *different*.

This close, this intimate, with so much skin touching, Margaret lost her blindfold, and she was aware of every thought that jumped and sparked in Townsend's mind. She shrieked a giggle, and her own hand began crawling up Townsend's face, and onto his clean scalp.

I fucking missed those tits, Margaret heard. The thought was a firecracker tossed past her ear. He *was* relieved that her burns were gone and by no means did Margaret begrudge him that; the wounds had been grotesque and upturned her own stomach.

"Show me how much you missed them," Margaret replied to his thought, holding her tongue on her lower lip, a sing-song provocation. Townsend answered it with force, pressing her breasts together, thumbs riding up between them. The sensitivity of the fish skin was so different from her born skin that she found she was nearly *bored* by the clutching of her left breast in contrast.

I'll tell him to go harder on my old skin.

Except, Townsend did just *that*. On her left side, he dug in so hard with his fingertips she knew it'd raise bruises. She lost her balance, almost falling into him, letting a deep moan worm its way into his neck, where her face was now buried. She raked teeth against his weathered flesh, then pulled back, a trail of saliva running down chin, "You heard me? *You heard me?*"

Townsend shrugged, brows scrunched up, "Of course. You said, 'tell him to go harder on my old skin.'"

Despite herself, Margaret leapt onto Townsend's lap, grinding her bare flesh into intumescence of his trousers. She only regretted that she couldn't wrap *both* hands around his shoulders.

"I never *spoke*. We're touching, and my mind is *loud*. You heard my *thoughts*."

Townsend seemed confused by this, his breathing deep, and he shrugged, "You're a witch, doesn't that just happen?"

Margaret tossed her head back laughing, then swung in fast, planting her lips on Townsend's, "*No!* In fact, it's *never* happened! I don't even know how you did it. And I don't care, you big son of a bitch. *Fucking kiss me.*"

Townsend didn't hesitate to oblige her. She *liked* how small she felt in his arms, his fingers pressing so forcibly at her skin, behind her skull, locking her into the embrace. She could smell gunpowder on his sleeves and tobacco in his moustache. His breath hot in her mouth as she fought an elegant ballet with her tongue to gain dominance before finally submitting.

He released her head so she could lean back.

"You don't need to assume," she kept her lips close to his, so that when she spoke, she would feel his whiskers tickle her face, "I belong to *you*. Offer me your elbow and we command together. Ask me to drown a man in his nightmares and he'll wish for death. Put a collar on me and I'll walk on your leash. I'm *your*s."

The intensity traded between them now was magnitudes greater than the first time they met. Margaret forced herself to not claw at Townsend's skin, just to smell the blood, just to be closer to the moving cruor that powered him. There was no need to nudge him or command him, the game between them was out of control now, *chaos* that Margaret had never known intimately.

Townsend reached down, unbuttoning his trousers and Margaret grabbed a fist full of his cotton shirt in her little left hand, falling back, all her weight free.

She didn't care if she fell or not.

"Not here," Margaret panted, "I want you to *fuck the shit out of me* on Aurora's bed."

Townsend's hands moved to her hips, clutching around toward her buttocks and supporting her full weight as he stood up. Margaret couldn't feel his arms so much as tremble at her weight, but she fell into his chest regardless, her lips pressed into his neck.

For a moment Margaret almost whispered, *I love you.*

It would have been true. She could feel it crawling up her vertebrae, barbs wrapped around her mind and heart, tightening beyond all the joy she found in *physical* pain, burning her eyes and throat, a tidal emotion she'd never fathomed.

Those were tawdry and *stupid* words to Margaret. Her nieces used words like that, claiming they *loved* her, while they stabbed her in the back or lit her aflame. Telling Townsend that she loved him would devalue what she felt, steal away the heavy gold of this moment that drug down at flesh and wet her cunt against Townsend's dusted trousers.

Margaret wouldn't just *lie there* of course. She'd grind her hips at each penetration, bite at his face like a hungry dog, and claw at his back; but she was giving her paramour a sacrament that no other man had enjoyed before him. A gift far more special than a disgusting word like *love*. She was giving Townsend power. Control over his mind and body, as well as *her*. In this way, he was also the first man to make love to Margaret.

5:02am March 19th, 39 Veilfall

Stockton, California

Aurora Owens had kept an antique clawfoot tub in her personal bathroom. That clawfoot was one-quarter full of boiled, unslaked lime and linseed oil. Margaret was small enough that she could essentially bathe in the viscous and perilously slippery grease, warm on her skin. With one hand she slathered it across her face and neck, stroking it repeatedly through her hair, her auburn locks a deep umber and tangle, flattening out against her skull and dripping down her spine.

"Blacksmith grease?" Erin stood at the bathroom door, her back to the frame, arms up and crossed high as her eyes wandered off. It didn't bother Margaret to be naked in front of the girl, but it clearly bothered *her*, so she made a point of quickly dressing in the bath with undergarments soaked in tawny oil.

"Plague Dog is a fire eater." Margaret answered.

She shifted and drew up linen strips, then slid around so one leg hung over the clawfoot's polished edge. "Help me with this."

The black linen needed to be cross wrapped under Margaret's soles, around her ankles, then woven up legs and knees, to upper thighs. Erin turned, nervous she'd see more than her comfort would tolerate, and looked visibly relieved to see Margaret's pantaloons.

"Linen and cotton have to be soaked, and wrapped tightly," Margaret continued as she wound the dark fabric around her other foot and ankle, "it'll bind the fire retardant against my skin, even if the outer layers dry and burn."

Margaret wished she could reach her own home, procure her personal armor. She'd only be wearing modest ballistic protection over all this blacksmith grease, inferior to the modular gear that Janet had created with the help of a German armorer. It was layered support and protection that utilized linothorax and leather. She could swap out various pieces to support a wide array of climates and *opposing* witches. The German had also created a full over-bust corset and plate carrier, tailored to her frame and breasts, which could sustain direct rifle fire, called *rüstung sklaverei*.

The bathroom walls were tiled in cobalt and argent, brass rails mounted specifically for her to clutch and pull herself up and out of the bath, the tools of a woman long ago crippled. Grateful for Lady Owens' rails, Margaret used them to carefully retract herself from the tub. Erin didn't need to be instructed to begin wrapping her left arm, she had the good sense to know *why* she was here.

"You ever hear about *moose*? Big *fucking* deer-creatures, up by Canada." Margaret raised her brows, vision blurring as oil dripped into her eyes, "I've *seen* them. They're as big as an *em-wrap*, and twice as stubborn. Want to hear a joke?"

"Is it funny?" Erin answered, as she tied off the linen at Margaret's shoulder, turning to retrieve armor. Erin would need to lace rib plates from a full-size carrier across Margaret's chest and stomach, before wrapping those in another layer of soaked linen. A standard plate carrier would never have fit. It would be loose in all the wrong places, and a protruding *tit bulge* would only spray hot lead shards into Margaret's face, if hit.

Margaret raised her arm so Erin could work easier, "There's a captain newly assigned, up north, 4th Army. During inspection, he notices a moose tied up outside the barracks. He asks his lieutenant, 'Why is that moose there?' The lieutenant says; 'There are *four-hundred* men here and no women. Sometimes we get urges.' A month later the Captain gets some *urges*. He puts a ladder behind the moose, drops trousers and *fucks the moose*. His lieutenant happens by, giving him a weird look. So, he says, 'Is that how the men do it?' Lieutenant shakes his head and says, '*No sir, they usually ride it to the whorehouse!*'"

Silence.

"Was that all?" Erin asked, lacing a bound plate over Margaret's abdomen with soaked leather straps.

Yes, that was all!

"Did you get it? The Captain thought the moose was *for fucking*. Right? *Right?* So, he *fucked a moose!*" Margaret was grinning, stiff and still, but finally cracked up laughing at the idea. Her long chuckle ended in a gasping, low-throated wretch that made it sound as if she might even vomit.

"It's not really that funny," Erin shook her head, nose scrunched up, and eyes narrowed as she paused to wipe off her hands with a gray-green towel of supple cotton.

It's plenty funny, Margaret thought. Erin shook her head a second time, signaling that the young woman had *heard* this stray thought.

By the time Margaret was fully armored, they'd used *most* of the tub of blacksmith grease. Layers of woolen sock kept her feet from sliding around in boots a size too large, and a modified linothorax skirt donated by Lady Owens was glistening in the viscous gilt.

"Erin," Margaret summoned her Corporal back as she leaned over the sink, grinding a chunk of charcoal across her eyes. The grease and oil had turned the black carbon to a thick mud, "When we find my niece, I want you to *run*. Do you understand?"

Erin's kit was roughly the same as before, shotgun slung over her shoulder, barrel pointing skyward, "Why? She won't be paying attention to *me*."

With chunks of carbon dripping from her eyes and lips, the expression Margaret flashed couldn't have been more intimidating, "My *mother* could burn a man alive with a glance. Plague Dog suffers none of my mother's flare for the dramatic. She won't be waving her hands around, shouting '*burn.*' *You've never seen a fully trained battlewitch fight.*"

In her final words, Margaret allowed *power* to reverberate in her throat. She didn't do it to *force* or command the former brassboy. She was wielding her own theatrical flair, a manifestation of her very role since she was a teenager. Erin didn't need to assume that Margaret was a kind and harmless woman who offered fair trade for services rendered. She needed to know that she was standing in the company of *another* fully trained battlewitch.

Erin tilted her head, then looked away, one had clasping the door frame and her eyes focusing far away, "That's *strange*," she whispered, then lowered her eyelids as if she was falling asleep.

On the western wall of the bathroom, rays of the morning began to chip through painted glass. Lamp light flickered then faded, leaving only golden green-blue light cast across the waxed tile. Erin was cast in a shadow from Margaret's small frame, her head lowered, and shoulders sloped.

I know what this is.

Margaret exhaled, her breath a thick wisp of vapor.

Under wrap and oil, her flesh was *warm,* but the temperature dropped suddenly. There was a *bubbling fizz* beneath Margaret's nails, as if her fingers were alive with ants or ticks. Perspective no longer applied. The door frame could have been a dozen feet away, or so close to her that she'd have kissed Erin. The floor seemed a matte pallet, a limitless horizon. Vertigo rushed up Margaret's spine, clawing into her skull and pressing at her ears. She wanted nothing more than to *sit.*

When it *almost* seemed too much, *it was over.* Physics and sensation worked like they were meant to. Erin straightened up, shoulders rolling back, and her fingers running up the wooden frame like spiders. When her eyes opened, her lids betrayed golden orbs deep in her skull, reflecting aurelian light across ceramics.

"*Love* the fish-flesh, Margaret." Erin's lips parted for a smile too wide to fill her face.

Margaret took a step back to keep Eris's golden eyes from blinding her, "*Last* time you came to visit, my niece tried to burn me alive."

Eris was now soul-deep in Corporal Erin Abid. She waved her hand away, as if the idea was a humming gnat that had annoyed her, "Repercussions of *chaos*. With a taken-name like '*Mayhem*,' I would assume you were intimately acquainted."

Margaret hadn't appreciated Aphrodite borrowing Ramona's flesh any more than this, but there was *nothing* to be done for it. Erin was too inexperienced to keep one out of her mind.

"Are you here to tell me how *fucked* I'm about to be, or to tempt me as your creature?"

Eris held up Erin's hands, lifting and dropping them, *right to left*, "Little bit of *Choice A*, little bit of *Choice B*."

"*Fuck*," Margaret exhaled, aware that a clock was ticking. The assault on Amy's 9th Battalion would begin shortly.

"*Dite-Dite* doesn't understand *us*, does she Margaret?" Eris laughed, her hands reaching up the door frame, allowing Erin's body to lean in. Falling under shadow again, her golden eyes glowed, "Offering you *beauty*, as if you're such a simple ape. Didn't you ever dream of the Mississippi? After you killed that *old Missouri bitch*, didn't you wish you could just be swept downstream, to the ocean? No fighting, no blood, no more graves to dig, washed away where the universe commanded."

Of course, Margaret knew she had no secrets before a god, and she gave one stern nod to Eris, begrudging the loosed discretion.

"*Maybe*," Erin's voice drew the syllables out, long and low, "that wasn't a dream. *Maybe* that's your right. Ever think of *that*? You and *good ol'* Condatis holding hands in a river."

Margaret had *no idea* how to react to this. She'd never been a particularly structured woman, and for that matter neither was Maggi Lopez. Saint Louis had been unmitigated suffering and *chaos*, and until she quit trying to *control it*, the lessons she learned there had been painful.

Margaret tossed up her hands, "*And?*"

Eris cackled with Erin's head falling back to expose her pale throat. She snapped forward again, *clicking* her mouth shut. "Have you experimented with the *gift* I gave you?"

Thump-thump-thump.

Margaret glanced away from Erin's body, the familiar report of mortars going off behind her, eastward.

The Maul has started their siege of the eastern gate.

"The liquid charcoal? *No,* I was a little *busy*." Margaret twisted back.

Erin's arms dropped from the door frame, then snapped her fingers, pointing at Margaret with thumbs extended. "Too bad, little butcher. Remember that one time you met your arch-nemesis, Ramona, in a bar? And, you couldn't kill her? All you *witches* and your fancy *mind-walls*. That '*liquid-charcoal*' as you call it forms a bridge between *you* and *anyone else*. Their mind will belong to *you*."

Under the chunky, thick mask of soot that wept from Margaret's eyes and mouth, a sneer slowly twisted up her face. "You couldn't have told me that, *weeks ago?*"

Erin's head shook fast, then stopped, palms pressed together, "I *could* have. But it wouldn't have been *nearly* as funny."

"*Gods be fucked!*" Margaret screamed, forgetting she spoke with a god, "I could have slapped Amy in the face with that *inky-shit*! I could have already killed *both* of my brother's *fucking* twins. That's *funny* to you?"

Margaret's yelling bounced off the tile in Aurora's bathroom, reverberating and barking back at her with a quick, chirping echo. Just as before, with Ramona, her voice cracked and rasped through syllables.

The whole time *Eris* was laughing, Erin's face coiled up in uncontrollable glee, long past when Margaret's tirade was over. When she *stopped* laughing the room turned chilly, once more. Erin's face falling grim and starkly lit under painted glass and hammered umber.

"*Now you're annoying me*," Erin's voice turned low and metallic, pitch creating a painful echo off the bathroom tiles, "I thought *you*, above anyone, would get it. If Amihan wasn't allowed to burn you, how would we have *our* war, you and me? *Dite-Dite* is on about restoring an *age of gods*. *I just wanted to dance with you one more time*. I thought you'd understand that."

Margaret had no idea how to answer this either. Without thinking, Margaret asked, "We're friends. Aren't we?"

Eris nodded with Erin's chin, "I've been your *best* friend since you were a little girl. Do you remember the day we first met? You heard the *guns* outside, and you tasted the ash of a fire eater. They left you unchained, didn't they? Why did you decide to run?"

It was just a whisper, Margaret thought, *I thought I was whispering to myself.*

Margaret wasn't standing proud in Aurora's bathroom anymore. She was a little girl again. Dried tears on her face, raising hands, fingers releasing the clasp at the back of her neck, dog collar falling. All around was the grocery store that she lived, behind battered and empty beige shelves. Her mouth was dry, and she gnashed at ash, an effect that *Maggi Lopez* caused. It was midday, and the men who held the gutted building rushed for the exits, shouting as they heard the *popping* of guns.

Run away. Stand up and run.

Margaret was listening to a terrible hiss, vibrating deep in her chest. She tried to stand up, but her legs wobbled. How long had it been since she ran? Or stood under her own power? Weeks? *Months?*

Run away. Stand up and run.

Wearing nothing more than pajama bottoms covered in kittens and puppies, Margaret pulled on a big coat from the cubby she lived and *ran*. Her legs didn't want to move under her, and she had to focus on each step, each knee twist and footfall. The light outside was *blinding*, and there were rifle barrels pointed at her as she dove into the turned-up maze of broken cars and twisted metal.

"Whoah! Whoah! Barrels down, it's just a kid!"

A man from the lines ahead yelled. His voice was robust with command, as if his very words would arc like electricity and ignite the switches that could be turned in the minds of his subordinates.

Another man grabbed her and she almost toppled, face first into the ground. He was wearing gloves with armored knuckles, she remembered. Jamming them in her coat pockets, then up behind her back and down her pajamas finally. His heart was beating in her own chest, and he relaxed, thinking; *no explosives, thank god.*

Those hands were rough, but devoid of the lecherous sadism she's come to understand as part of her life. Saying nothing, he pointed at his eyes, then Margaret's, and finally back at a woman who carried the flank. She was slim, wearing blue jeans and a white tank top stained in hues of rust and ink.

Run to her, came the whisper from Eris, *run one more time.*

Margaret did as she was commanded.

"What's your name?" asked a young Maggi Lopez, offering a smile before twisting up her nose in a mix of horror and disdain. Her skin was hot to the touch and covered in embers when Margaret blinked. There was something *bright* and *magnificent* that beat in her chest, an ethereal power that Margaret didn't yet understand.

The memory cracked, and fell away like heavy chips of paint, leaden under the weight of years. Unceremoniously Margaret found herself still standing, where she had never left. In the bathroom of Aurora Owens, pressed against wooden foundations, supporting a tin basin, *sobbing*. If questioned on that moment, she'd have denied her own tears. There were some moments too intimate for Margaret to have *ever* shared, sacrosanct deep in her mind. This was one of them.

Erin stood over Margaret, fingers running through her oil slick hair, hushing her. Worms crawling under her fingernails promised Margaret that a *chaos god* still wore the young woman's skin.

"I never forgot what Maggi's soul looked like that day," Margaret whispered, sniffing hard at mucus demanding release.

You ushered chaos into Maggi's life that forged her into the steel everyone would come to remember, didn't you Margaret? Eris was in Margaret's mind, under her skin, flowing in veins and flexing with her tendons.

"Get out," Margaret ejected the words with no emotion.

"*As you wish it,*" Eris said, moving Erin's lips, "I told you, we've been friends a *long, long time*. It was just hard for us to share the *world* with you."

Thump-thump-thump.

Perhaps two seconds later, *thump-thump-thump.*

The Maul was getting ready to bring down the eastern walls of Stockton and assault the Dogs of War. Amihan's soldiers were about to meet an opponent more dangerous than any they'd known before.

"What do you want from me?" Margaret asked, refusing to meet the golden globes that seemed to hum like cicada this close.

"The others will offer you gifts. I've given you all the gifts you could *ever* need. *Now I just want your worship.*"

Margaret took a step toward the painted glass behind her, blinking her eyes clear. Erin's body lurched over, lips peeled away and teeth parting. Her muscles tensed, betraying neck, pulse hammering at her temples. Fingers curved in like claws. Elbows and shoulders twisting and jerking. The skin Eris wore was *human*, but it ceased to move like one. There was lust in her snarl and hate across her brows. Aurora's bathroom was turning as dark as it was cold.

"Gods be fucked, if I refused to worship Aphrodite, I will refuse to worship *you too*."

Margaret didn't retreat, she leaned in, and imagined Erin biting into her own flesh, ripping away skin and chewing down the meat of her face and neck like a starving dog.

Whatever remained of Erin's voice was traded for an uneven pallor, drifting from the girl's lips, into syllables, drawing nails on chalk. "Where was Aphrodite when you were a child? Did *she* help you?"

No.

The beautifully tiled bathroom turned claustrophobic for Margaret. A confine she only wanted to escape, a tight space she shared with something as mad as it was dangerous. Eris was all about her, gnawing and demanding for something Margaret could never give up. Finally, she closed her eyes for a dozen seconds, the scratching at her mind falling silent as she focused to speak.

"I won't worship *any* of you, and you can tell them I said that. This wasn't my mother's way and it won't be mine."

I saved you, Margaret.

Aurora Owens' bathroom ceased to exist. There was no dawn light or distant artillery wailing. Margaret and Erin ceased to have relevant bodies, nothing tactile in their wake, merely god-sliver souls coiled up in something like an embrace. There was no tidy little shelf that Margaret could display her feelings with an embossed docket.

I know, and I fed you chaos for twenty years, Eris.

Somewhere between the physical world and twining brambles beyond the Veil, Margaret and Eris embraced. With no sky and no ground, it felt like falling, a torrent of vertigo.

"Be careful, little butcher. You're not the only witch who the gods court."

Somewhere in this entanglement, Eris turned away, withdrew herself. Or the *fraction of herself* that stretched out and filled Corporal Erin Abid. It was casual and quick, and the young woman's body remained standing for a dozen seconds. Human eyes bolted to Aurora's painted glass as her marrow shivered and her jaw ticked, no bit to bite.

With only one arm, Margaret was neither strong enough, nor large enough, to keep the girl from collapsing. All that she could do was make sure that Erin's skull didn't impact on the wood basin. To her credit, Erin herself kept her mind square and clear, regardless the improbity her body had just sustained.

"*Hi*." Was the first word she spoke, looking up at Margaret's grim war paint.

"You okay, candy-striper?" Margaret asked, a smile lost somewhere in the chunky charcoal stew of her face.

"I think a *god* just borrowed my skin," Erin tried to move her arms, her fingers convulsing as she regained control of her own nerves.

"*Yeah*," replied Margaret, drawing her syllables out, "Good thing for you they always leave behind a favor, a *boon*, payment for your skin. With experience you'll learn how to keep them out, if you wish."

Erin shuddered, "I saw you, as a child."

You don't want to keep speaking, candy-striper.

Margaret didn't reply, the words wouldn't move. There was no shame to Margaret's mind in Erin's understanding, but the *look* that would come next, made her nauseated.

"They *raped* you. Tortured you, for *months*," Erin's voice fell flat and quiet, lips parted, and mind betraying her thoughts, *you were just a child.*

Margaret turned from Erin, to unsee her expression, no desire to witness her eyes. They would bleed for her, weep for her, a flood of empathy and regret. An act of contrition, as they wished for ignorance to the truth. No *sane* person wanted to know what had happened to Margaret, they liked her the way she was.

I'm sorry you know.

Spinning back to loom over the young woman, Margaret unleashed a vile grin, bloody with charcoal, a reminder of the woman who now wore that child's skin.

"It's not worth your words."

"I think *she* wanted me to warn *you* of something," Erin said.

Two drops of blacksmith grease fell from Margaret's sternum plate and tapped Erin on the chin, beyond her notice. "She told me. I'm not the *only* witch who the gods court."

"Not that," Erin scrunched up her nose, her habit when she didn't understand something that made her disquiet or uncomfortable, "she told me the *Lord of War* was coming."

9:09am March 19th, 39 Veilfall

Stockton, California

Thousands of core Antecedent infantry gathered in Lafayette Park, one of three staging arenas. They had been loosely organized by company, but the park was no parade ground, and the men pressed back and against each other, a piebald exhibit that would have made no sense to an outsider. Most of them wore fatigues, antique styles, a mix of camouflage. Some looked no different from the average denizen of Stockton, save the 3rd Army patches stitched to their shoulders or breasts.

Step by step, Margaret carried the awful visage of *Lady Mayhem*. Her dripping linens left clotted grease stains in her wake, and black soot bled from her eyes and mouth. Cobble by cobble, each mottled row of the 3rd Army dropped to one knee, elbow close to the ground, none of them averted their eyes. Their gazes like a deep ocean fog, tangible, edible to the likes of a battlewitch.

At Margaret's flank was Erin Abid, shotgun off her shoulder and braced on hip. From the receding companies of the 3rd Army, a man with a pencil moustache met the dread mistress of Stockton. A long scar ran across his brows, through his missing nose, and into the ruin of a cheek, exposing a half dozen blackened and rotting teeth. He squinted as if Margaret shone greater than the sun, with verminous eyes.

Margaret flashed a grin under her mess of charcoal. A hand wrapped in oil reached up and caressed the knotted scars of his face, "Badger."

"Your fireteam is reporting for duty boss," The man named Badger kissed the air and gave Margaret a wink, "Gamblers wouldn't have missed this, not ever. We heard *you 'se* was perched up here when Townsend called us from San Jose's garrison."

It seemed like Badger had more to say, but he paused as a full line of armor let loose a savage volley, a few streets over. The bellowing report shook Lafayette's cobbles, rattling Margaret's belly and spine.

She spoke again as concrete dust blew across her face.

"We're hunting a Lopez today. You feel good about that, Badger?"

When Badger smiled his face twisted up like a rabid muskrat, sneering and *leering* all at the same time, "*Fuck* the Lopez brat. Gamblers *only* serve Lady Mayhem."

Margaret's cackle filled her mouth with brick dust and sheetrock. "Then what are you waiting for? You want Amy Lopez to come to *us*?"

"*Sir! No sir!*"

Badger's fireteam, Gamblers, fell in behind Margaret. Counting Erin, it would be a total of five custodians following the 3rd Army's battlewitch. None of the fireteam looked genteel. The largest man, a brute Margaret knew as *Dirty Pete*, wore the cylinder of a six-shooter in his empty eye socket.

Entire city blocks of Stockton were consumed in flame. Black diesel vapor wrapped up streets as a wide and ragged cloak. Margaret marched in the lead of her troops, descending into the discord as another salvo of 120mm rounds flooded the air in dust and ash. She was no longer the pretty woman who stood under five-feet-tall. She was now the 3rd Army's manifest god, leading her vanguard. From the east came thunder and fury as Maul forces were loosed against Stockton's gates. To the south, Townsend was leading a smaller assault into the throat of Amy's command. From the north, the drumming antipathy of San Jose garrison's mortars. Nothing but hateful retorts and screeches echoed in Stockton's streets, a confused symphony, playing out of tune and off-key.

For Margaret and her vanguard, first contact came within a few city blocks.

Dozens of two-story apartments had collapsed under the weight of an initial armor assault. The gravel streets were soft and muddy with blood where camps had been crushed under falling stone and concrete. It was the quickest way to eliminate snipers and skirmishers who could have used these buildings for cover. 9th Battalion survivors ran south, their kit dusted the color of desert wind, faces slick in spittle and blood.

They were picked off, one by one, as they attempted to gain cover and engage.

Second contact came at a roadblock, *eight blocks* deep into occupied Stockton. Hundreds of men braced this street, behind windows, broken doors, or overturned carts. Margaret could see through their eyes, breath short, panting, sweat stinging. They *jerked* at triggers, little boys learning to masturbate as their throats welled up with belching cries. One by one, each man became aware that his brother nearby was going to *betray him*, all their sins and slights made manifest.

Lady Mayhem had already unleashed her terrible powers ahead of the vanguard. Her motor functions remained, bending knee, swiveling hips, overbite clamped down on blackened lips, but Margaret's *body* was nothing more than an automaton while her mind swept up and out, raging flood waters.

From a first-floor cottage someone shouted, *"Fucking die, Paulie!"*

Paulie knows I stole his fucking beans! He knows! He fucking knows!

The cry was followed by the clatter of semi-automatic rifle fire. The other 9th Battalion soldiers in the house turned on the man who stole Paulie's *fucking* beans, hammering his skull open with rifle butts, his brains emptied like a bedpan at morning, splashing survivors.

The carnage expanded, kindling for a greater fire as weapons chattered and sang to each other, entire sonatas performed in primer and powder. Lead and steel in percussion, howling and pleas crooned about from the wind, and finally strings followed with the shatter of broken wood and glass. Bones split by vibrating aluminum. Entire structures began imploding as grenades and nailbombs were deployed.

Behind Margaret came a single, giant, armored vehicle. It was an ancient Abrams tank, turbo diesel engines wailing out of time and tune, vomiting ink smoke along Stockton's burrows, some kind of sick and wounded demon ripped out of ancient tomes.

Under the blizzard of chaos, Lady Mayhem's light infantry poured into the streets. Fireteams broke off, huddled up single file; they kicked down doors and shattered windows made from colorful bottles and waxed sugar. Each survivor was executed, *one round to the chest, one round to the skull*, Margaret's men called out which buildings were *hot*, and which buildings were *clear*. All the while her Gamblers formed a protective line around the battlewitch herself, rifles on shoulders, eyes on scopes, rails clutched, breathing guarded and calm.

Margaret was *loosely* aware of the other strike points. Her mind could hear overtures in the distance, melodies gusting up and down streets, domiciles, taverns, cobblers and empty vegetable stands. It wasn't that she could *see* or *clearly understand* the progression of battle, it was like running blindly through the forest, *aware* of the largest trees. She could *feel* the savagery in this joint assault, she could *feel* the bloodlust of the Maul and the methodical focus from the San Jose garrison. It was a temperature at her palms, stuck to her fingers, tacky and saccharine like pulled sugar.

Racing east, the remaining soldiers from Stockton's southern urban area were in full retreat, Margaret's infantry chasing them down Charter Way. Those 9th Battalion combatants who hadn't gone mad under Lady Mayhem's hateful lust were insane with fear, weapons skittering across tarmac like cockroaches under lamp light. Some of them were screaming as they ran, every primal nightmare in the darkest recesses hot on their feet, *feral wild cats, venomous snakes, and giant spiders*. One by one they fell to the ground, their armor and flesh pulled open like a poorly made dress at the hands of a seamstress, hacking apart stitches, laying aside parcels of unwanted fabric. It was no longer a battle, it was a *route*, and Margaret's own soldiers were drunk on blood lust, feeding on fear no differently from their mistress.

It was a mile and a quarter into the vanguard assault that Plague Dog showed herself.

Margaret *tasted* her first. Much like Maggi Lopez, Amihan tasted of cold ashes and hot cinders, a bright, weaving vibration that showed her unique in this battle.

I need to get my men away from here, thought Margaret. This was her most nerve-racking responsibility. Evacuating her forces in the wake of another battlewitch.

"*Badger, pull back,*" Margaret spun to face the fireteam lead. Her voice cracked like a sputtering two-stroke, *commanding* him, "*North and south. Fall back to the mercados and hostels.*"

A sea of black oil began to fill Margaret's eyes, and whether Badger saw it or not, he didn't hesitate to follow orders. He'd been Margaret's *personal fireteam* leader since Saint Louis, the city that ruined his never-handsome face. He knew, two witches were about to fight.

The 3rd Army didn't scatter. They fell back into the surrounding structures, one team at a time, each covering the next. It had been two years since they'd engaged in this kind of combat, but their drilling remained true. The troops furthest east parted first, their flank supported, then repeating back to Margaret herself.

Charter Way was quickly becoming a ghost town.

"That means you too, candy-striper," Margaret glared at Erin Abid, nothing soft or friendly in her eyes.

"I can fight Plague Dog, with you." Erin's head dipped, but Margaret had no interest in arguing with a witch who couldn't even understand mortality. A young inclined offered no challenge, no danger for an experienced battlewitch.

"*I don't repeat myself, candy-striper.*" Margaret's voice resonated.

Erin's expression didn't change, but her physical body reacted like she'd been shot in the spine. Her chin twisted up to the sky and her shotgun fell free, dancing on roughhewn cement. She had no way of keeping Margaret out of her mind, swallowing nerve bridges whole, commanding every muscle in her body. She didn't turn or run. Her legs jerked up and back, thrusting about as a mad, wounded insect. She simply danced away, a puppet on a string, some kind of near-human abomination. Several of the vanguard grabbed her, pulling her inside a dingy cannery with low and wide windows. *They* knew what was coming, as well as the kindness Margaret offered this child.

Free of annoyance, Lady Mayhem turned to the east side of Charter Way.

A second figure was joining her. Wide in the hips and well-muscled. Her hair was a fiery wreck of bleach and henna, and a single line of ink ran across her face. The parts of Margaret that crawled and skulked, up and down these streets, peered out windows with the eyes of her soldiers. She could see Amihan just fine. Linen gauze wrapped her neck tight, but she labored through each breath. The second round from Townsend's gun had likely clipped a lung.

Margaret bit her lower lip, promising Townsend a sweet reward for his fine marksmanship. Even under duress, he'd delivered not one, but *two* near-fatal shots.

"I missed you at the front lines, Plague Dog."

Margaret's voice was gone, her throaty and feminine squeak was replaced with something else. Syllables and consonants were drawn up in a bow, taunt and broad, sound made corporeal in empty streets. Hunkered down, away from Amy Lopez, both witches could hear snickering from the 3rd Army. This wasn't so different from the scene that Margaret had fantasized about when Aphrodite tempted her with beauty.

"I don't want to fight you, Mayy." Amihan Lopez shouted in reply, horse and breathless. She wasn't armed as far as Margaret could see; a dozen eyes running across her from various angles. No pistols or knives to be seen.

"We're going to finish what you started at Stormair." Margaret's voice knocked rust off old road signs and battered bead hovels.

Slowly extending her hands, Amy held her palms forward, "Margaret, I *submit*. The 9th Battalion *submits*. You can parlay with my father, but we *submit*."

Behind Lady Mayhem's night sky eyes, Margaret remembered Amy's words from Stormair, "I *loved* you." Just as quickly, Margaret *also remembered* what it felt like when the skin blistered and ripped open on her face, under Amy's hand. Just as easily remembered was the *hiss* and *pop* of her own meat, boiling fat dripping to Stormair tarmac.

You burned me alive and now you want mercy?

The sun was turning the street bronze and red under a wreath of smoke. Margaret reached down for the 9mm pistol strapped under her bosom, unclasped the holster, and tossed the weapon to the pitted cement. There was a second pistol at her *left* hip. She unsnapped and discarded this as well.

"I know your poltergeists are gone. No guns. We finish this in the tradition of Maggi Lopez, my mother, your grandmother."

Amihan's chest heaved, and the smell of *fear* was all over her, pungent, calling out in the morning sun like a wailing cat in heat. "We don't need to fight! I *know* what Ramona did!"

The tawny fire retardant that covered Margaret glistened with a coat of rust, the remains of Stockton. Under golden sheen, Margaret began to perspire, black ink bubbling up from her pores, deep and viscous sweat, so dark it swallowed light, *only* reflecting flames that didn't exist in this world. A mirror into Margaret's mind.

Covered in liquid charcoal and nightmare infernos, Lady Mayhem charged Plague Dog as fast as her legs could hammer the street.

10:42am March 19th, 39 Veilfall

Stockton, California

Only about 300 feet separated Margaret from her quarry. At full sprint she could cover that range in *maybe* eighteen seconds.

Eighteen seconds was a long time between two witches.

The edges of Margaret's barriers lit up first, curving lines of yellow became visible to the naked eye of any 3rd Army observers, then blurred, curling. Fissures formed along the eroded, nodular concrete, rocks and broken sediment popped and shattered, scattering dust. Amihan was leaning in, fists balled tight, every muscle tensing. White linen wrapping her throat began to stain crimson. She was investing *all* her effort in some kind of kinetic attack, failing to split the very road on which Margaret was casting footfalls.

Fifteen seconds.

No different from Maggi Lopez, Amy needed to *borrow* flame. She couldn't simply manifest it. In a blazing city, this wasn't hard. Fire spun up and around *another* layer of Margaret's barriers. These were more complex, overlapping circles etched with what could have been writing or script, whispering to the wind that gusted against her ears at full stride. They burned hot, flashing white and sparking like an old transformer on rotted pole and line.

Twelve seconds.

The kind of barriers Margaret understood to protect her from fire were thousands of years old. Words of evocation passed down through the ages from a lifeless, more antique tongue. Maggi *herself* might have known the original words, teaching Margaret only half mouthfuls. In younger languages, like Latin, the *magic* didn't work as well. The barriers were soft and pliable, they bent and vanished not merely under the physical effects of *heat*, but also the onslaught of another witch's desire to *break something*.

Nine seconds.

With her left-hand Margaret ripped a strip of linen off her chestplate, pulling it across her nose and mouth. It was hard to draw breath through the oiled fabric and it smelled muddy, metallic. Her barriers would fail soon. The blacksmith grease coating nearly every inch of her flesh would protect her from *actual fire*, for a little while, but not if she inhaled it directly into her lungs.

Six seconds.

There was flame around her, deep orange, the kind of searing heat that gasoline could cast up. It moved about her physical body, independent of anything Amihan herself was commanding, a serpent with a mind of its own, weightless on her armor, making demands she couldn't understand. Her curas didn't ignite right away; the oil did its job, forbidding the blistering flame to come further. That wouldn't last forever, *especially* not against the heat that a battlewitch could summon.

Three seconds.

Amihan was now desperate. The fire osculated, yearning to burrow deeper under linen wraps with dreams of flesh below, a sweet delight, salty and supple. Somewhere in the final seconds between Margaret and her adversary crashing together in a rolling ball of oil and fire, she lost connection with the same reality that her 3rd Army observers understood.

It wasn't about Stormair. It was about watching her parents burn. She *saw* their skin peel off blackened bones. She *watched* her mother's breasts melt down her stomach, a deep, bisque sheen. She *watched* her father's skin curl off his face, and his eyes liquify. She *smelled* their hair and flesh turn to ashen smoke, the wind slapping her in the face with it as she wailed, *aware* that she was *breathing* her parents.

Let's see if you've more spine than your grandmother. She turned away the first time she glimpsed my memories.

Margaret was on fire when she crashed into the larger woman, full force. There was a *crack* in the air, blinding white. The physical world didn't react well to this kind of clashing magic. The Veil grew brittle in the wake of such exchange.

Fingers thick with midnight, one hand clutching her niece's face, Margaret dove into Amy's mind.

There were eight of them.

The men who'd broken into Margaret's childhood home. They didn't want flatscreen televisions or crystal chandeliers. They didn't want jewelry or gems. They built a bonfire in the street, made of her parent's furniture, lushly carved antiques piled high. Cabinets, a bed frame, chairs, *so many chairs*, tables, even a great clock made of glass and gold, bound in steel and rope. Margaret's parents were bound in chain to the wooden armada; naked, bloody, and beaten, their faces were a ruin of mud and bone. They were screaming.

At first, Margaret's father wept, begging them to *let his daughter go*. But that was abandoned when match struck gasoline. They didn't cry for Margaret's freedom anymore, they begged god for *a fast death*.

For the same reason that those eight men had wanted to smash her parents' home and burn them alive, they also had wanted a pet child to amuse themselves.

These were the nightmares that Margaret kept locked up, tucked away. Maggi *knew*.

So, will her granddaughter.

Margaret and Amihan clawed at each other, embracing so close that the blacksmith grease sizzling on the first layer of Margaret's armor coated Amy. Margaret could smell the clotted copper around Amihan's neck, *as well as* the diseased infection that was slowly killing her. Fire kissed them both, blistering Amy's finger tips.

Amy was panting and *wailing* a guttural cry that any who heard would most likely rather forget. She wasn't giving up, she was *striking* at the smaller witch who was now on top of her, landing hits with knuckle and fist. Margaret paid them no heed, no notice. She was leaning over Amihan, jamming her left hand into the girl's mouth, jerking her jaw open and clawing at her tongue. Black oil ran down Margaret's face and eyes, a cascade over her lips, thick and reflective, filling Amy's throat. She began to choke, all her strength focused on dislodging Margaret's hand, to no effect.

She was trying to scream, but it was only a gurgle. A dying horse in deep mud, braying for any mercy. Minutes ticked by in the physical world, but Amihan was shackled and locked to Margaret's mind. In that place, time ceased to exist.

"*This*," Margaret laughed, "is the Collapse!"

The two existed as a concept. A *view* of the world through shifting and disjointed memories, weightless and free. Around them *another* city burned, a city of the *old world*. Spires and steeples doused in molten smoke, painting the sky in shades foreign to modern eyes. Margaret could feel Amy's wonder at such a glorious monstrosity. The air was acrid, tangible. A kind of putty that could be touched, *manipulated*. The heat, the raw fury of such an inferno.

Total chaos was unleashed in all directions. Men were looting buildings while gangs beat young and old in the streets. With the Veil gone, all this anguish was escorted by the *old ones*, ghosts and devils, hobgoblins and demons who'd come to settle in *this* world.

They called us criminals, Margaret remembered, loud enough for Amihan to hear in her mind, *Criminals who had so much, when they had so little. They burnt my parents. And the little girl? She ought to be taught a lesson.*

"*Mayy,*" Maybe Amihan spoke, out loud, "*don't do this Mayy. I want to go home!*"

It wasn't little Margaret the eight men dragged away that night, it was Amy.

Dragged by a dog collar so tight she could barely breathe, Amihan experienced every sight and smell of the Collapse, through Margaret's eyes.

Amihan knew what it was like to be raped with a broom handle until she bled, and Margaret whispered in her mind.

Didn't you always wonder why I can't have children?

Amihan felt the big fist that slammed into her stomach and cracked her ribs when she refused to kneel. She smelled his unwashed, ripe genitals when it was stuffed into her mouth.

Didn't you always wonder why I refuse to kneel, not even for your father?

Amihan experienced every gang rape that Margaret had, including the one so violent that her right clavicle was broken. No matter how hard she screamed, they wouldn't stop. Her suffering only provoked them to greater forms of deprivation and violence.

Didn't you ever wonder why my right shoulder sloped? Not a problem anymore, my right arm is gone. Thanks to you.

In the real world, Margaret stood up.

Her burnt linens and linothorax were a matte black in contrast of the reflective and luminous charcoal that bled from every pore in her body. Margaret's face was cast like some kind of death mask, no *real* features, a clay model that had been molded by a sculpture. With her remaining arm, Margaret reached up and swept the sleek, umber butter off her face.

"*Badger!*" She shouted, using her ordinary voice, "Bring me your sidearm!"

She didn't want Erin's pistol for this. The Corporal was still young and simple in the ways of war. Margaret had done things with Badger that would turn hardened shock troops pale.

That's not even counting what we've done in the field.

"*You'se* hurt Lady? Feeling alright?" Badger's honey and gravel voice suckled at the back of Margaret's neck as she watched Plague Dog quiver and jerk. Her brain was still functioning, but she was in shock. Disconnected from her limbs, she whimpered like a child.

"*No, please, no.*"

She was speaking to memories of those eight men who'd tortured Margaret. Condemned in those months, the little girl would live shackled and bound, a toy praying that her pleading would be heard. It amused Lady Mayhem that Amy believed that *she* would be given different answers than Margaret had once known.

"Look at me," Margaret turned around, teeth coated in jet, "Right as *fucking* rain."

Badger nodded, his scruffy chin grinding at metal gorget. He reached down to his ribs, released a big 1911 .45 ACP, cocked the hammer, then spun it on his index finger to hand it over, grip first. It was corroded along the trigger guard, but mostly oiled and clean.

Margaret accepted the pistol with her one hand, then stepped off Amihan Lopez.

"In all the dirty taverns, where they mix vomit and beer, I want you to tell this story. You tell them. Antecedent, Owens, Maul. You tell *all of them* the same." Margaret's hand shook for a second, then she willed it steady with her voice and resolve.

Amihan's lips were moving, she was saying something else. Her face was covered in lurid charcoal and drying crimson.

"*You'se gonna* execute that Lopez, or what?" Badger snarled.

Blood from the prone woman's neck wound pooled on the ground with liquid midnight. Margaret leveled the pistol at Amihan's chest and spoke quietly.

"I'll tell your father that you fought to the end."

Just for a second Margaret could hear words on Amihan's lips. It raised gooseflesh across her body, and turned the humid pressure of her skin, ice cold.

"...*I give you my love, my worship.*"

Amy wasn't speaking to Margaret.

Margaret pulled the trigger, twice, on Badger's heavy .45 ACP. Two rounds discharged, directly into the chest of Amihan Lopez.

1:08pm March 19th, 39 Veilfall

Stockton, California

Just south of the Crosstown aqueduct, a block beyond the water servicing plant, was a five-story post-Collapse structure that housed logistics offices for the city. It was built in the style of old Victorian stonework, support pillars erected around several sets of wide and ornate wooden doors, carved with scenes of Stockton's fall and rise as a city.

Gambler fireteam, along with Badger and Erin Abid, escorted Margaret; who looked like a rabid animal drowning in a tar pit. She was caked in burnt linen and smudged with matte powder. Only her eyes gleamed ivory under flaking lashes. They walked, first up obsidian steps and onto the interior concourse which led to central office logistics. Two of the Gamblers dragged Amy Lopez's body with narrow chains and wooden handles. Her skull *thumped* rhythmically up each stair flight, rising and falling, until finally it grew soft and pudgelent. Blood painted across an enameled silver floor, her dead eyes unseen behind layers of black varnish that had leaked off Margaret's face.

The building was empty of pencil necks and bean counters, the engineers who maintained Crosstown, sewers, the power grid, and defensive walls. In their wake, former Owens royal guards stood watch, void of uniforms, dressed in whatever workwear saw them through new vocations and trades. A few were still kitted in plate or fatigues, those who'd become Antecedent bounty hunters or mercenary rangers since House Owen was dissolved. Margaret couldn't recognize any of them if she'd tried, but hard eyes and muted glares told her they *remembered* seeing her two years ago. Their minds whispered quiet anger, mixed with a healthy dose of fear.

Each floor had a narrow stairwell, not quite wide enough for two people to walk abreast. The inner rails were lacquered in dark beryl, across from opposing walls that had been painted in one of the most complex and detailed murals Margaret had ever seen. It was an endless canvas that wrapped up all five floors, depicting a serpentine map of pre-Antecedent House Owens. Flecks of gold or silver paint marked freeholds and baronies. Large portraits illustrated a dozen or more key members of House Owens' early days, and among them Margaret recognized a younger version of the Maul warlord she'd met in Fish Rock.

The magnificently painted stairwell led to the roof, out of two horizontal double doors, and directly facing Eric Owens and his mother. Eric stood tall in a cotton shirt the color of egg shells, with polished steel buttons reflecting golden sunlight. Next to him sat Aurora Owens in a thickly hewn chair of polished, red, oak. Hand carved in scenes of noble creatures holding her aloft. Margaret imagined what she would have looked like twenty years ago, when Maggi first stood at Aurora's court.

"Kneel before your queen. Heart of House Owens, Lady Aurora *the first*, protector of Stockton, Santa Rosa, San Jose, and San Francisco."

Corporal Erin Abid looked down at her diminutive mentor, face stained in soot and blood. When Margaret did not fall to one knee, she looked away, watching the Heart and her son. On her other side, Badger also refused to kneel, he simply spat chew tobacco, his face turned up in a defiant glare of loathing and disdain, something he couldn't control under such savage scars. If he wouldn't kneel, neither would the other Gamblers.

"*Mm*," Margaret made a simpering sound, then replied, "Probably not, Lord Owens."

Lady Owens raised her right hand, skinny and frail with age, her palm polished and smooth, fingers adorned in silver and gold rings, "It's fine, Eric. Lady Mayhem is not required to kneel. She *is*, however, required to swear an oath to me. Do we still have that accord, Lady Mayhem?"

A cool breeze drew up Aurora's white and gray hair, it twisted and twined around her simple crown of silver, measured to drop down on her forehead. It was new, and still bore smithing marks near curved edges.

"We do, Heart Owens," Margaret pulled herself up, as stiff and tall as she could stand, shadowed by her soldiers and escorts. She took a step to the side and gestured to the grisly remains of her brother's daughter. Her own *niece* crumpled up on the tar roof, "I bring you tribute to prove my loyalty to House Owens. This *was* the daughter of Emperor Lopez. Plague Dog, Amihan, 9th Battalion Commander of the Antecedent 1st Army."

For Margaret, the flowery prose of aristocracy did not come naturally. She'd stood in front of a hundred lords and ladies, captains of city states and kingdoms across North America. She talked to all of them the way *gods* had talked to her, casting off her tangible lusts and desires, imagining herself as mast on a tall ship, looking down on all she surveyed.

"I believe it was this witch who took your arm, Lady Mayhem," Aurora Owens answered, lowering her palm and tapping soft metal rings against the oak of her chair.

"It was," Margaret nodded once.

Even in her repose, Aurora Owens reminded Margaret of her mother. Though Maggi Lopez would never have sat at such gracious attention, nor would she have accorded herself this kind of opulence. Maggi was a brawler and Margaret supposed she was too.

"Tell me *how* this gift is an offering to the Heart of House Owens, and not *yourself?*"

The air smelled of burning wood and mortar. It could have been South Stockton, still ablaze, or it could have been Aurora herself. Margaret didn't know, but she found it soothing.

"I'd have killed Amihan Lopez for *myself*, but this betrayal now binds us. My brother will seek my head when this is done, and I will march with the armies of Stockton to confront him. If I bring you *his* head, will you find that less *selfish*?"

Aurora Owens chuckled to herself, the deep lines that frosted her mouth and lips creased as she did so. With her right hand she gestured Margaret forward, "Come here, Lady Mayhem."

Each step Margaret took was like swimming in thick mud. The linen and armor wrap had shrunk around her body, under Amihan's flame. Grease and charcoal leaked down her legs, creating inky footprints, glistening on the tar roof.

"You glowed such a deep red, that day in my palace. The day we met," Aurora's smile was as predatory as any Maggi had once offered, "Now, you drip pitch like a smudge pot. Do you know what happens to the brightest stars in morning light?"

Margaret's upper lip raised, showing a sooty half sneer.

"They fade, forgotten until the next night."

Nodding, Aurora's smile remained. She leaned in, hushing her tone, "Exactly. But pitch stains. It leaves a message, it *lasts*. Do you want to *last*, Margaret?"

I never thought much about it, Margaret hadn't expected that question.

The old woman wasn't spinning webs of magic, but she was building shackles with her words, leading and guiding the younger woman where she wished, for the result she *desired*. Margaret realized that this is what Lady Owens had done since their first meeting, and she ignored the question in favor of her own.

"You knew that I would turn on my brother one day. Didn't you?"

Aurora Owens shifted in her high-backed chair and lifted left hand to jaw, relaxing as she did so. "*Of course*. When your mother and I last spoke, I could see a future in her eyes that I did not understand. I knew a day would come that her son would force my House to kneel for him. I also knew a girl, aglow in red, would have trouble kneeling for *anyone*."

In the afternoon sun, Margaret wanted to be free of her oily bounds. She wanted to feel the breeze that played in Aurora's hair tickle her own neck. The cinders she was chewing on were *not* Stockton, they were a rich tapestry of flavor as she looked down on a witch who once rivaled even her mother. Their energies were mingling, and whether she wished to permit it or not, Aurora Owens was *reading visions* in Margaret's eyes. Just as she had once done for Maggi Lopez.

"I know what my *son* offered you," Lady Owens' eyes reflected more than just an atramentous witch, "and I am proud of him for holding *this* House, the House that *I* built, above all. I expect you to do the same. I'm *not* Maggi. I'm *not* going to adopt you or sing you little songs when you sleep. I'm not even going to *love* you, but I *am* going to give you your birthright."

Margaret didn't have to *ask* what she meant. Part of her already knew the answer. She was a clever woman, and while it was easy to imagine that the men who murdered her parents did so out of animal madness, swept up in Collapse chaos, it had never *quite* made sense. Those men had hated Margaret's home, her accommodations, every bit as much as they hated her mother and father. The memories she'd condemned Amy to before death remained an open wound. The odor of hate and resentment strong at the edges of her mind, gnawing like earwigs.

The little girl ought to be taught a lesson.

"I don't know *who* your parents were, Margaret. But, in your eyes I see reflections of great power. A husband and wife who stood tall in politics, industry. Wealthy and connected. If the Collapse had never come, you'd have attended private schools and had your choice of the finest universities. You would have worn *pencil skirts*, and silk blouses of cerulean, designed by men in Paris and Rome. With the razor-sharp mind you command, you could have been President one day. We would have never met. Your mother was a *chola thug* and I sold cheap furniture for a Persian. *You're not one of us* Margaret, and you never were."

Margaret didn't understand those words, 'pencil skirts' and 'Persian,' but as Lady Owens spoke, she composed swatches of her own memories. Grainy and dim, a thousand tiny boxes of *red, blue and yellow*, creating complex and beautiful photographs, moving frame by frame. They were crisp visions of a dead past, filled with metal sky-birds, and small radios in every hand. The streets filled with a thousand, *a million*, cars and trucks.

There was a place there for an alternative Margaret. She looked like *herself*, lines cutting her face a little deeper, standing taller, without misshapen shoulders or eyes that didn't fit her face. Her auburn hair was fashioned in wide curls, and her skin didn't fade into a crosshatch of Tilapia.

The smile and twinkle in her eye were the same; however. Playful, *dangerous*.

It wasn't as sophisticated as the nightmares Margaret had subjected her niece to, but it was an endless parade of wonder.

"Would you have hated me?" Margaret asked.

"*Of course not*," Aurora snapped back, louder, "My House never strapped bombs to children or enslaved the hungry and wretched. I never wanted to *punish* anyone for who or what they were. I only wanted to *build something* for myself, for my children."

"*Why* are we sharing all of this?" Margaret shook her head, aware that Aurora Owens was guiding them to a destination of her own design.

"Because *this* isn't over. If House Owens is to survive, I'll need the *nightmare mirror* loyal to *me*, and *me alone*." Lady Owens laughed, stuttering and wet, "In the dark, when you wonder why Aurora Owens is a worthy mistress, I want you to remember that I alone saw your *value*, your *birthright*, and offered it up to you on a golden platter."

Margaret found no seduction in Aurora's visions. It was easy to dismiss a future that never could be. A place and time that defied her comprehension; a future that didn't include Alexander Lopez, or the great shadow cast by his mother.

It was just as easy to imagine a world, as delicate and sweet as spun sugar, where a girl with no surname could rise as the most powerful landlady in House Owens.

Pitch stains, it leaves a message, it lasts. And, I want to last, thought Margaret.

Amihan & Ramona Lopez by Audia Pahlevi (Moonarc)

November 2nd, 20 Veilfall

Crafton, Pennsylvania.

Knock-knock-knock.

The small apartment had once been a hotel room, with bathroom and kitchenette set off to the side. Clothes were piled high in corners, along with a dozen kinds of mismatched plates and bowls, unwashed and peppered with food fragments. A few cockroaches darted from dish to abandoned shirt, to kitchen pots, and cracks for whatever paradise waited beyond. The walls were covered in smeared charcoal, sketches that started at the dingy carpet before leaping higher. The most prominent of these drawings was a man who clutched at his head, face twisting and unrecognizable, engulfed in flame.

Knock-knock-knock.

The queen mattress was biconcave and lumpy. On it was a man, easily in his forties. Layered pants pulled to knees, his pelvic bones sharp and ribs pried away at sallow skin below his muscular shoulders. The woman kneeling, splayed out across him, lifted her head, greasy hair of auburn falling across her face, as she cried out; "*Goddamnit, can't a woman fucking suck some cock in peace?*"

From the other side of the gated door came a muffled voice, "*Mayy*, it's Alexander."

"*Holy fucking shit! General Lopez!*" The man with sallow skin twitched and pulled away from the woman holding his genitals. Slick with saliva, he was free and falling onto the floor, jumping up and into his pants as quickly as he could.

The woman with auburn hair rolled onto her back, heaving a sigh that seemed to change the very atmosphere in the room. Light shifted and cockroaches fled in the blazing light of her direct attention. "My brother has no say over who I *fuck*."

Panic setting into his pulse, the man started to pull on a woman's shirt, stretchy and cotton, before realizing it didn't belong to him. His partner couldn't even remember the man's name. It was something luridly dull, like *Jack* or *Jacob*. "You're not even an officer, Joe, *relax. Alex* won't care."

"*What the fuck*, my name is *Jason*!"

Jason was vividly offended by this, and the auburn-haired woman rolled to her stomach, eyebrows drifting high, a playful smirk crossing her cheeks.

"We can pick up where we left off after Alex leaves. *Or* you can leave, and you'll always wonder what you missed."

It wasn't that Mayy wanted to *humiliate* Jason, she just wanted to see what would happen if she made the man sit at her bed while she interfaced with the ranking Antecedent State officer.

That's a lie, I do want to humiliate him and see what he tastes like for it.

Standing, Mayy revealed black cotton shorts and a thickly boned bra that did little to flatter her bosom, but quite a lot to support her chest. She was small, with crooked shoulders and eyes that seemed a bit too large for her head. She'd already begun to ignore Jason. The part of her mind she needed to shut down his motor functions was already coiled up around his spine. She could have just as easily whispered inside his skull, *you don't really want to leave, do you?*

Knock-knock-knock. Alexander *hammered* on the door this time, a closed fist rattling the gate, tangible rage drifting through woodwork.

"*Learn some fucking patience!*" Mayy shouted, grabbing the first long coat near her kitchenette. It was black polyester, puffy on the inside, with yellow, blue and green stripes down one shoulder, stained in grease or blood, or maybe both.

When Mayy opened the door, it was snowing outside. Chill air cut in and across her bare knees like little knives. She was smiling when she unlocked the gate, a slick and canny grin, her lower lip falling away, showing her front teeth. "You couldn't wait until *morning*?"

Alexander Lopez was taller, by far, than the woman and her greasy hair. Whiskers had begun to pelt his dimpled chin, and his thick brown hair was only a few shades darker than the same tan skin his mother wore. Alexander looked past her shoulder, to the gaunt man sitting on Mayy's thin mattress, "You're *fucking* one of *mine* again?"

Stepping back to allow the tall man entrance, Mayy rolled her eyes and offered a hand to gesture inside. Alexander smelled like road and gasoline, burning oil and the bite of winter. His heavy jacket was lined in down and chainmail and gave the appearance of even greater shoulders than he may have possessed.

"They're not *yours*, Alex. They're just people." Mayy replied.

Alexander elbowed the door closed as flurries of snow gamboled through the gate, to the floor below. Her apartment smelled of sweat and sour food.

"You probably shouldn't *lecture* me on possession," Alexander pointed at the Antecedent soldier seated where Mayy had lain seconds before. His eyes twitched, side to side, like he was reading a book quickly. He didn't even stand to salute.

"I'll let him go *later*," Mayy said, her tone a pitched whine. She wrinkled her nose, as if the very sound of her own voice offended her.

"*Whatever*," Alexander held up a hand, to stop her from making further faces, "I'm in no mood to argue."

Mayy put her hands to hips. She hadn't buttoned the snow coat closed, so her sternum and belly button were visible as she arched her head back to match Alexander's stare. She exhaled slowly, feeling her body spinning up to *fight*, something her brother always brought out in her. "*All right*, fine. What are you in the mood to talk about?"

Alexander's voice was low, serious. He wasn't playing anymore.

"There's a morning meeting. Lorne, Chandless, myself, and *you*. Maybe a few other vice officers. It's time you stepped up. Into my mother's shoes."

To Mayy's reckoning, it felt as if her stomach had fallen out of her skin, sliding down her pelvis and knees, exploding at her feet in a wash of bile and half-digested turkey fat.

She snapped the fingers on her left hand, one of Maggi's habits. A habit she had tried to break. The gaunt and muscular man on her bed fell asleep, his eyes calming, his brain shutting down. The weight of his day, his entire *week,* just too much to withstand. He fell backward onto the drool stained pillows behind him.

"Mom is dead?" Mayy replied, the bite in her tone gone, the playful ease of her frame replaced with stiff shoulders and neck.

It took a moment, but Alexander broke eye contact and turned away from the smaller woman. He was working his hands into fists, then releasing them, over and over. It struck Mayy that he was more *frustrated* than sad, or angry.

"Her team returned from California, without her."

Mayy lifted right hand to face, casting off a tear that decided to leap forward. She held the hand at her lips, as if Alexander would never notice. Her fingers smelled like saliva and *cock*.

"I suppose you want to carve up the States, then. Decide *who* takes *what*. You don't need me there, I don't want *any* of it."

Alexander glanced at her once, then held his gaze elsewhere. Under grinding teeth and tensing fingers, he *was* sad. She could feel it drift past her ears like the echo of a pretty melody, played on a piano, slightly off-key. "The Federals will realize Maggi is dead. They'll think us weak, and we'll face more attacks. We need to *drop the hammer* now, show them all who the dominant power in the *east* is."

We need to drop the hammer, Mayy thought to herself. A bitter hollow opened in her chest, a hole that all of Crafton's snow couldn't fill.

"I won't kneel for you Alex. I hope you know that,"

Alexander's tone turned condescending, as when he arrived, gesturing at the man on Mayy's mattress, "*Everyone* knows you'll go down on your knees. You'd *best* kneel for someone who has *earned the respect*."

"Alex," Mayy turned her head, blinking long and hard for a moment, "My mother believed you were some *goddamn* super-man who'd save the world. I don't know if you are, I don't even *really* care. It should be enough for you that I'll abide the final desires of *Maggi Lopez*. You'll see me at this meeting tomorrow, you'll see me on the front lines, and *gods be fucked*, you'll see me take a bullet for you if that's what it takes."

But you'll never see me kneel for you.

Alexander Lopez had been a *cute* baby, a handsome boy, and a lady-killer in the glory of manhood. His brows were set and serious like he was reading beautiful poetry, eyes under them full of unrelenting confidence, as well as *unrequited arrogance*. The girls of Crafton had always liked that about him. They liked his beauty, but that was only because they never heard the ugly things he thought.

I'm stuck with a half-size slut to replace my mother.

Mayy heard the thought, loud and clear. The voice was as bold in her mind as if he'd turned and yelled, uvula flapping. Above the distant echo of sadness, there was nothing now, save anger that Maggi was dead, and unable to relieve him of these grievances.

Grievances like me, thought Mayy.

"*Fine.*" Alexander answered after watching the much smaller woman for at least a minute; as if he could read her mind as well.

As he turned to reach for the door, Mayy called after him, "You know, if you ever wanted to talk, about *her* death, I'm here."

I'm going to regret that, Mayy thought, and she shed another tear in front of her brother. Her lie was too obtuse, and they both knew what she'd really told him.

Can we talk about this? About her? Please?

"Of course," Alexander nodded, withdrawing from the door again, pressing his left shoulder into the frame. He offered up the same smile he gave his mother's soldiers and the single ladies of Crafton, "We'll talk about it soon."

She knew he'd brushed her off, just in tone. It was the curse of her nature that she could hear his final parting remark.

Only one of us is her child. Go fuck yourself, witch.

Mayy didn't have the experience, or self-discipline, to hide her reaction. She coughed and felt a painful buzzing between her eyes as if he'd stabbed her.

The door fell closed, the metal gate along with it, deaf to Mayy's sobbing.

10:45am March 25th, 39 Veilfall

Stockton, California

"The first bath I ever took was in the Ohio River." Margaret was slipping in and out of foot traffic across the blocks surrounding Pacific Street, speaking over her shoulder, "I'd been with Maggi for about a week. I stayed *so* close to her, I don't think I ate or slept. She finally woke up one morning yelling about *that stinking little girl* and hauled me down to the river."

Margaret laughed, despite herself, when her Corporal didn't reply, "I couldn't swim. I ended up nearly drowning myself. Maggi *lost her shit*, and she was trying to drag me out of the water, but she was wearing boots and *she* couldn't swim either. By the time we were back on dry ground we were both laughing. *Very few* ever heard The Bruja laugh."

Margaret could still smell the Ohio River, and the way Maggi's narrow fingers had felt on her shoulders.

"How is that funny?" Erin Abid replied, and Margaret stopped, between rolling carriages and busy men with fresh leather hides slung in packs.

"How is that *not* funny?" Margaret hadn't even considered a better retort, "That's *fucking funny*. We almost drowned."

Erin looked serious, shaking her head.

Stockton wasn't a place to sleep or wait for permission to breathe. With a full *one-fifth* of the city burned to foundations, many of the residents who could return already had, by steam engine or horse, to rebuild their homes. One of the first decrees that Heart Owens made, a day after reclaiming her throne, was sanctioning a government buyout of supplies. She was offering discounted rates in exchange for using House blueprints, power grids and water tables. The fetid squalor of Stockton's poorest neighborhoods would not be returning under the Heart's oversight.

As the streets curved to the north, they became too narrow for carriage or cart, and the press of flowing humans reduced. The air here was earthen and smoky, sweet, and just a few degrees warmer than a block earlier. There was a clamor of steel hammering, and the huffing of kilns and forges alike, the slumber of a long-forgotten beast. Most of the smiths kept open-front shops, while others managed cement shacks for finer jewelry work.

Margaret didn't answer Erin right away as they continued past smitheries. There were certain things she didn't wish to share, namely why a near-death experience in the Ohio was *such* an improvement on the six months prior, "You had to have met Maggi, I suppose."

"So, *who* was Maggi Lopez?" Margaret could see Erin shrug in the corner of her eye, as she sidestepped a smith patron.

In the middle of the street, Margaret stilled, inhaling sweet grease. "I can't answer that easily," she began slowly, holding her tongue on the ledge of her lower lip, then facing Erin and meeting her eyes, "Maggi coined the phrase *battlewitch*, but she never wanted to be that. She was uneasy in her magic, not like any witch I've ever known. A long time ago, before I met her, *before* the Collapse, I think she would have been kinder. Before she hated herself."

Erin wrinkled up her nose, a habit she had when confused, almost clockwork predictable, "How could anyone hate themselves?"

I don't know, Margaret thought, and decided to be honest with the girl, "I can't answer that, because I never have. I *never* will. But, for Maggi it was like breathing air. It's easier to forgive her when I remember that."

"Forgive her, for what?" Erin answered, curious.

Margaret didn't *want* to reply. It would have swept away her affectionate glow at the wonder of *good* memories.

"Come on then," Margaret's silence ate up long minutes, to the point that Erin had become visibly uncomfortable, "Let's go get me a new arm."

Out of a dozen or so shops, only *one* of them was helmed by a woman. She was tall with shoulders as broad as her bust and hips, wearing a thick apron of brown leather, coated with a grease not unlike Margaret's own fire retardant. Under the apron she wore layered wool skirts that fell to her boots, and a white shirt cuffed to elbows.

"Lady Mayhem," the woman nodded, stepping away from a dark, metal anvil.

"I brought the cast and bones," Margaret turned, gesturing to her Corporal. The younger woman sat down two wooden boxes at a steel hemmed table.

"And a sketch?" the bigger woman grabbed a tawny cloth, scrubbing at her hands and wrists. As she did so, her forearms and shoulders flexed with thick sinew.

Margaret withdrew a piece of paper from the right side of her black, suede jacket. "I'm no artist, but I hope this'll do."

The blacksmith reached for Margaret's slip and unfolded it. The paper was thick, swart, and the sketch on the inside was painted in shades of charcoal. It was a collection of bones, arranged in the shape of an arm, from upper humerus down to each of the metacarpals and phalanges that collectively created *fingers*. Extending from the bones were delicate mounts, curved metal that outlined exterior skin.

"You're a *helluva'* artist, actually," the blacksmith looked it over. "These sigils here, you want that etched into the silver? *Magic*, isn't it?"

Margaret didn't nod or blink, she simply replied, "Yes."

"My husband will see to that. He's the gunsmith and engraver. I'll see to it that the bones are drilled with steel, and that the hinges and springs twist and lock." The blacksmith walked past

Margaret to open the little wooden cases. One of them housed a collection of Margaret's arm bones, still stained crimson and hazel with bits of torrid meat that hadn't been cleaned. The second box contained a wax cast of her good arm, giving an example of how her skin curved around muscle. "That'll do."

"How long, smith mistress?" Margaret asked, her body still facing the forge and anvil, but her head twisted so the big woman could hear.

"Mayhaps *three* months. Four months, most."

Margaret's head shook slowly, and she reached into the same jacket pocket her sketch had been withdrawn from, "*One month*, no 'maybes.' One month."

The coin that she retrieved from that pocket was easily as wide as her palm. It was solid gold, covered in tarnished grime and scratches, with a contour relief of a much younger Heart Aurora Owens on either side.

The blacksmith took a step away, watching the big coin, "That's an old Owens Promise."

"I figure that's a *year's* profit, for a master blacksmith." Margaret's voice was steady, cool, she had no intention of using magic to force the issue. She wanted the work *fast*, not stinking of fear.

"*More*," the blacksmith said, "a Promise is rare *nowadays*, since the Antecedents."

Pinned to Margaret's right shoulder was a cotton sash of argent trim and tassel, printed in silver poppies, a gift from Heart Owens. The silver caught shifts of forge light and turned shades of orange and red.

"Maybe not so rare anymore," Margaret lifted her hand to the silver poppies, the traditional House Owens badge, a smile creeping across her face.

The blacksmith's eyes were blue, pale and warm, that smiled as easily as her pink lips. "I think *one month* won't be a problem for my husband and I."

Margaret could feel *nothing* but a sense of pride rising in the blacksmith. She probably didn't *trust* the little witch, but the Promise said that Heart Owens did. When she accepted the Promise, it was no different than accepting payment from Lady Owens herself.

"I'll see you in exactly *one month*. Good day, smith mistress."

1:28pm March 25th, 39 Veilfall

Antioch Queen Sunrise Special, California

Badger tugged at his collar, thrusting four fingers under the white shirt biting at his fatty jowls. A black star was tattooed across each of his knuckles. Faded, block ink on his finger joints read '*FIST*' on one hand and '*FUCK*' on the other.

"Boss, you *ain't never* made me wear no Antecedent uniform. Now I'm crammed in this Owens sack of *shit?*"

Grinning, Margaret crossed her legs, aware that the skirt's slit rode up at just the right angle for Badger to be captivated by a preview of her inner thigh. The gray skirt was dyed a shade of oiled gun rail, and embroidered with polished metal in complex, spindling patterns. Vines wrapped up and around human skulls from her knee to hip, each skull uniquely stitched with impeccable detail.

"*Zip your bitching*. You'll be glad I made you wear it when we get to San Francisco."

"What's your rank?" Erin Abid asked, sitting next to Margaret, "Should I salute you?"

Badger pulled his hand away from the shirt collar, "I tell *ya* what, *you'se* probably *should*. Gamblers *gota'* special *sorta'* salute *you'se* kids *gotta* have an observance for."

Turning away from Badger, Margaret lifted the back of her left hand over her lips so Erin wouldn't see her smiling. It was hard to stifle the laughter that threatened to choke her.

Corporal Erin Abid leaned in, "Of *course*," sincere as the day she was born.

"All right. You *salute my dick with your face.*" Badger, sitting across from the two, punched himself in the crotch, and Erin nearly jumped out of her skin, sliding away from Margaret on the lacquered wooden benches.

The southbound locomotive had departed Stockton at a little after *noon-thirty* and was hauling a half-dozen passenger cars, along with postal cargo and cattle freight. The coach cars themselves were made from wood and creaked like waves at a beach as they jarred rhythmically over miles of rail.

"Badger's *truncheon and balls* got shot off in Denver," Margaret gestured at Badger's crotch, "but he's never let it slow him down."

"*Gods be fucked, Mayy,*" Badger rolled his eyes, "Don't *tell* everyone. I get up behind her tonight, do a little *cunt* dance with my right hand and she'd never be the wiser!"

Margaret's upper chest shuddered with laughter, then she looked over at Erin.

"Are you *blushing*?"

Erin answered fast, biting at the air, "*No.* I just, *I just*, don't know how to answer that. I thought I needed to salute him."

"Forget this saluting *shit*," Margaret shook her head. For a moment she *thought* she was holding both hands up, palms out, but only *one* hand raised, "All you do is tell the enemy who to *shoot.*"

"Boss is right," Badger nodded fiercely, "I *ain't* got no formal rank neither. I'm the Gambler fireteam leader, and *that's that*. I don't answer to anyone but our Lady here."

"Erin," Margaret lowered her hand, neck bobbing with the rails, a rolling current, "*I'm* your boss, but if Badger tells you to do something, you do it. He's been Antecedent special forces for as long as I've been a battlewitch."

Badger wrinkled up what remained of his upper nose, it twisted the scars away from beneath his eyes, showing off what teeth he still had under his cheeks. "She *lemme fuck 'er* once, and now she can't be rid of me. I'm like a puppy. I followed her home."

"He's not *entirely* full of *shit,*" Margaret's tone turned more vulgar around the small man with a ruined face. Badger was roughly Margaret's age, also a Collapse baby; he'd never grown too tall, and he'd never been too healthy.

"Little *babs* here," Badger gestured at Erin, "*You'se* had your first *period* yet?"

Margaret could feel her younger escort starting to respond, *sincerely*, to the provocation. As she leaned in and her mind snapped back on the words, reality of the jest now clear.

"I don't know. Did your *mom* have her first period yet?" Erin replied.

Badger, in response, turned his head and reviewed Erin with an uncommon expression of disbelief. Margaret couldn't help but laugh again.

As the coach car swayed side to side, Margaret could hear a boy on a fiddle, a few rows up, toward the engine. She couldn't *see* him, but she knew his age, as she perched herself at the edge of his mind. He was playing a few classic jigs, but as he skipped away from familiar melodies, he began to improvise. He was paying close attention to his fingers, twitching along the fiddle neck, feeling the instrument vibrate against his collarbone, whittling away with his right hand.

As her companions continued to banter, Margaret simply stopped listening. Her eyes focused on horizons that didn't exist, part of her drifting *into* the boy. He had no clue she was there, but as his right arm worked a bow, so too did she imagine her own in his place. She *could* play some on a fiddle. Soldiers had taught her over the years, at bonfire's ledge, as she grew weary of dance. *Swallowtail Jig* had been one of her favorites, and she began to tap her left hand in time to the tune in her head.

The boy began to fiddle *Swallowtail Jig*.

"Don't mind the boss. It's what she does," Badger said, hushed now, as several other passengers softly tapped their fingers to palm, in tune with the boy. Erin realized that this wasn't an accident. She could either sense or *see* the tendrils of Margaret's mind.

The melody did not change or alternate as Margaret reached into a small satchel of leather, to withdraw a tin. She popped it open with one hand, and pulled a twig free, freshly rolled in brown paper, sticky with mint oil.

As she lifted the cigarette to her lips, Badger leaned into Margaret and lit her cigarette with an old lighter of scuffed silver.

"I've never seen you smoke," Erin said, her voice hushed, as if she was afraid to disrupt the fiddle tempo, or wake the mind that Margaret was controlling.

"You've never seen me do a *great many things*." Margaret shrugged, exhaling from her nose, much the same way that Townsend smoked, "You never saw me execute someone until I killed Amy Lopez."

Badger nodded to *Swallowtail Jig* as he leaned back in his seat, his tone a little more serious, "*Boss'll* always surprise, kid. She can be *sweeter'n* sugar, or nastier than steel in *you'se* kidney."

Margaret pressed her right side onto the coach's wall. The glass next to her shoulder looked like clear water caught in a breeze, curves warbling up the window, comfortable under the rail sway. She was investing only the *slightest* inspiration to the passengers of this car and had plenty of focus left to weigh heavy on Erin's mind, *prodding her* for an answer.

"Did you *see* me do it? Did you *see* me put two rounds in her chest?" The young Corporal blinked, her gifts telling her this was a test. She was *right*, but just as Erin was about to answer, Margaret stopped her. "*Don't lie to me.*"

Slumped over with chin in the folds of his woolen coat, Badger watched in silence. Margaret could hear Erin's chattered thoughts in the back of her skull.

She was begging her to stop. Why did she do this to her?

Margaret inhaled her cigarette again, gently this time, almost smiling, "How did that make you feel, Corporal?"

Eyes lost on the same window Margaret had watched, Badger leaned in and held his fingers out to borrow the cigarette. Margaret released the twig, listening to Erin.

It made me sick.

"What did you do to her? With the ink?"

There was no loyalty for the dead Lopez, only an empty regret, oozing empathy. It made perfect sense, Margaret knew. They were about the same age, children of a new world. It was hardly a stretch to smell the hints of fear that stuck behind her ears like soap from a hurried bath.

"I showed her *real* terror. Nothing more," Margaret answered, quietly, taking back her twig as Badger exhaled tobacco.

Nothing less.

Erin's anxiety abated enough that she could speak, though she continued to tweak and tug on her fingers, harder and harder for each word spoken, "Why do *that*? Why torture her that way? Why not just *kill* her and be done with it?"

Margaret didn't reply, rather she took her own drag. The cherry tip had now eaten halfway down the sticky paper, waiting for a particularly violent jostle to toss it asunder.

"May I, boss?" Badger's voice sounded like a rusted shovel cutting into a pile of wet gravel. Margaret nodded to him, once, still not speaking.

"Boss is a Collapse baby. *You'se* kids *gotta* know that's ugly times. Her parents got barbecued, *'front* of her, when she's a kid. *You'se* like to take a guess how she reacted? What with getting burned up by Plague Dog?"

Erin didn't hesitate, "*Oh*,"

"I knew that *shit'd* be bad for the Lopez kid. *I knew it.*"

Badger was one of the few people who knew about Margaret's parents. Only Maggi and the Antecedents present the day Margaret escaped, *guessed* how much worse it had been.

Margaret spoke for Badger, "It wasn't vengeance or torture. I just wanted to Amy to know what it was she did to me. I wanted her to *really* know."

None of this seemed to comfort Erin. She was still nervously working her fingers, only now she fidgeted in time to the boy's fiddle.

"If I killed my brother's daughter, *what's to stop me from killing a no-name Corporal?*"

Erin nodded without replying or making eye contact.

Exhaling tobacco, Margaret closed her eyes and the rhythm of the coach car fell silent, along with the boy and his fiddle. She didn't *will* them quiet, but even the uninclined could pick up on the moods of a room.

When Margaret opened her eyes again, she spoke, "I was a poor aunt to Amihan. She reminded me of my mother's worst traits. I spent years treating her the way I wanted to treat someone who was *dead*. This doesn't give her a *free pass*," *Nor does the fact she was lied to,* Margaret didn't mention. "I'll mourn her until the day I die. But the moment she turned on *me*, called *me* a traitor, and declared *me* her enemy? That was the moment she forfeited her life."

The moment she lit me on fire, Margaret's face turned from sad to sour.

It took Corporal Erin Abid a long time to answer, "I guess it's the same with Deck." Her lips spoke, but her mind didn't quite agree.

Deck was holding a gun to your head.

The odor of fear didn't vanish, and Margaret finished the oiled cigarette. Her eyes narrowed on the pretty girl with short hair, "*Never* betray me. I can be *sweeter 'n sugar* for those who give me love." Margaret borrowed Badger's jargon and gave him a sidelong wink. "You still love me. Don't you Badger?"

Badger crossed his arms, lifting his shoulders up high and creasing the shirt at his biceps, "Margaret done right by me, all these years in. I been *recompens-erated* good. I got no regrets. *'Cept* maybe getting my *cock* shot off. That was *shit*."

Erin seemed to relax a little. Margaret suspected she was listening behind words, reaching as far into his mind as she dared taste. Whatever affection he offered to Margaret proved itself genuine.

Closing her eyes, Margaret reached for her shoulder stump and tugged it back so her hips could twist into the corner seat, "You should try and nap. It'll be long hours before we reach San Francisco, and tonight will run late."

8:03pm March 25th, 39 Veilfall

San Francisco, California

Having grown up on the east coast, Margaret could confidently say that the wind which gusted off San Francisco Bay was one of the coldest experiences of her life. When it came up off the water, it cut through her skirt and gnawed past her corset and short-heel boots of leather. It was a pinch at first, before the flesh began to smart, unrelenting as any cut or bruise. This wind simply had no boundaries, no sense of privacy, she may as well have been naked astride the Wave Organ.

This narrow peninsula had been manufactured from old world gravestones. A keenly morbid relic of pre-Collapse antiquity. Storm and rain had eaten away at the sandbanks, revealing carved granite and marble, where they'd been lain. The Organ itself was just a collection of softly abraded stones, roughly cast seats and stairs, which worked hard to swallow the long pipes built into the odd cathedral. As the bay spat up at the Organ, seawater whipped around those pipes, creating an echoing hymn, a gush and gurgle of waves, spun into long, haunting notes. This was a musical instrument that the very ocean herself plucked absently, as if bored by sluggish eons. It didn't fill Margaret with comfort, or charming memories of lifted skirts and jigs. Rather, it set her on edge, teeth grinding, left to wonder why the old world had built this thing of aberrant beauty.

"*Aubriana*, I don't know where else to find you. I seek your company."

Margaret spoke so softly that her voice was carried up by ice clad wind, threaded through the Organ, and spat back as whines. Left shoulder shifting, she was hefting the weight of a brass lantern, an octagonal cage of burnt mirror and glass, kicking away hues of firelight, infected with sickly rainbows, as motor oil spilled to pristine pond.

Margaret heard a soft hum first, followed by down tempo song.

"She died of a fever,

And no one could save her,

And that was the end of sweet Molly Malone.

But her ghost wheels her barrow,

Through streets broad and narrow,

Crying, 'Cockles and mussels, alive, alive, oh!'"

A hard gust knocked into Margaret's lantern, rocking it to one side on a ring of leather, creaking. When the light swung back it illuminated henna and auburn tones of the woman they had once called Dread Harvester.

Harvester wore a thick leather bustier, pulled up and over her shoulders with braids of rusted steel cable. Without her grim mask of broken blades and rusted knives, thick sepia lips smiled back at Margaret. She was opaque, when sea spray scrolled up it scattered through her.

"Do you still speak with who you please?" Harvester asked. Her voice harmonized with the Organ, almost singing. Her visage blurred and froze for a moment, before she tipped her head to the side.

"*I do,*" Margaret smiled, standing before the Bay's great, chilling hatred.

The ghost of Aubriana was unmoving, "You know, this is where I stood, before your mother and I fought. I was sick. *Twenty years* in a state of slow decay. Do you know what it's like to *eat* without a jaw? *It's disgusting.*"

Margaret knew very well where they were standing. She'd heard those stories for years.

"I'm here to *parlay*. I can't trust the living tonight."

Aubriana smirked, and her eyes grew dark, windows of night, "The daughter of Maggi Lopez summons up the ghost of Dread Harvester to explain how *untrustworthy* the living might be. You should retire as a witch. Be a *stand-up comic.*"

What's a stand-up comic?

Aubriana began to slowly pace around Margaret. She'd vanish behind her, out of view, and the hairs at her neck would stand at attention, before Aubriana materialized again.

"You're exiled here. Aren't you?"

"*No one outruns death forever,*" Against the salty bite of ocean air, Margaret could smell wormwood, orchid, and ginger every now and again as Aubriana moved, "I broke my bargain with a god, to save a young girl. My fledgling. That girl was named Aniceta, and if allowed to live, her children would change the world that Maggi Lopez built. A fire god told me this on the streets of San Jose, wearing the skin of a dying man."

Now I know the score, Margaret rolled her eyes, sucking salty air in through her teeth.

Aubriana paused in front of Margaret, twisting her neck and examining the woman whose hair was soused and shaded black. "No, I didn't *hear* your mind. Just because I'm dead doesn't mean I can't read another woman's face."

Margaret peered up. Even with blocky two-inch heels, Aubriana had stood taller than her in life, and still did in death.

"Your fire god's prophecy was *true*. Aniceta had *twin* daughters, one of them named *Ramona Lopez*. You met her at my side, on The Beast. She set into motion a sequence of events that will destroy the Antecedent Empire."

Eyes of dull sepia began to shift into shades of ivory and deep beryl, just as last time. No ghost Margaret knew had eyes so beautiful. "You're going to kill Alexander. Aren't you?"

Margaret considered lying, then cast off that thought, "*I will*, yes."

"I held that baby in my arms, you know." Aubriana's eyes shifted back to faded chestnut, her lids unblinking as she paused, "But, we all die someday."

Another great wave assaulted the Organ. Without a *right hand* to wipe her face Margaret could only blink hard, several times, "Before that happens, I need to kill a very dangerous witch. I need the help only a *ghost* can offer. Maybe, only Dread Harvester can offer."

Aubriana took a step back, leaning down to study Margaret. Her lips didn't move, nor did her face offer expression. She simply blurred and sharpened around the diseased flames, *waiting*. Even for Margaret, it was *unsettling*.

"I need you to move undetected, unseen by the inclined. I'm going to *give* you a body tonight, and loan you something of *great* power. In return, you may keep the body."

Aubriana reached up to her face with both hands, fingers running down her jaw, and she answered with a smile, "*Ghosts* can only control a living body if the person *consents*. Or if their mind has been rendered feeble. A *witch,* even a *feeble witch,* would never allow it."

The storm that had merely plied at Margaret's comforts was now commanding more power, and waves grew angrier by the minute. "I'll take care of the *mind.* Are you familiar with Aurora Cuttersark?"

While Margaret shivered like a baby bird, Aubriana's apparition only came into sharper focus. Her voice was *visible* in the physical air around Margaret, creating slender, salton strands that evaporated after only a second.

"I know her. *Aurora Owens'* child. She's *czarina* of Modus Vivendi."

Margaret's brows furrowed, "I'm *giving* you her body tonight. Her brother wants her dead and imagines me as *Magnate* of that order. An order of *witches* whose loyalty she's cultivated for years."

Aubriana answered with a mean and toothless grin, "He wants you stabbed in the back. With clean hands. *Disgusting.*"

Margaret nodded fast, her toes numb, "I kill his sister, give him the power of Vivendi witches, and his sister's followers kill me. *Easy*. But that's not how I plan to die. If I give *you* Cuttersark's body, you will keep them *in check*. I'll be Magnate in name only. You'll be the boss of that cult until the day Cuttersark's body dies."

"*I'll amuse myself, somehow*," Aubriana answered, a noise that seemed to vibrate the very stone under Margaret's feet. There was a deep echo in those words, something living inside the storm, something in the waves that even Margaret couldn't understand.

"Tonight isn't just about assassination. You'll have access to something far more valuable than Cuttersark, or Modus Vivendi. Can I *trust you* to freely return this power?"

Margaret had spoken with and seen ghosts her entire life. They flickered about in the shadows and walked empty hotel lobbies. Some, no more than memories, others manifest. Mad with years, but capable of careful reason. In all that time, she'd never once seen a ghost pull itself out of the drained and hollow sepia tones where they existed. Aubriana's color returned for a few seconds, the dusted black of her leathers seemed solid enough to touch. Her auburn hair was almost the same shade as Margaret's, with gray streaking her temples.

At her breast, stitched into the flesh, was an old name patch: *HARVESTER.*

She flickered as she pressed into this more physical manifestation, as if Margaret had looked at the sun for seconds too long, stuttering her eyelids in a quick succession of blinks.

"You want me to wear the flesh of Aurora's daughter like a cheap suit. I told that *bitch* to never return, and look at this city. *She did return.* I'm *far* too amused to betray you, little Margaret. You have a deal, and maybe a *friend*."

When Aubriana leaned in to say '*friend*,' there was an unspoken threat. The emotional response of the specter was strong enough to create a physical imprint on the world.

Yes, Aubriana, if I betray you the way Maggi Lopez did, I'll live to regret it.

"When you have flesh again," Margaret nodded, looking across Aubriana's vibrantly colorful form, "we'll shake hands."

Margaret had no intention of lying to the Dread Harvester's ghost.

10:13pm March 25th, 39 Veilfall

San Francisco, California

A short walk from the Wave Organ, where Margaret's mother had once fought and *killed* Dread Harvester, Modus Vivendi sat on a flourishing knuckle of land. Before the Collapse, the elegantly garnished structure was known as The Palace of Fine Arts.

While the neighborhoods surrounding it were lit only in dim and flickering gas lamps, the majesty of Modus Vivendi was illuminated by San Francisco's young power grid. Manicured gardens, looming trees, and a freshwater lagoon turned shades of coral and orange under buzzing bulbs. Directly across the shallow lagoon was a wooden pedestrian bridge, built over the water on low trusses and painted a deep shade of mahogany, caked in decades of wax. Hundreds of candles burned, sizzling under the very first trickles of a soft rain.

The bridge truncated at an enormous stone rotunda, around one hundred and sixty feet tall. One of the tallest features of old San Francisco remaining since the Collapse. Held aloft by eight enormous pillars, and frosted with old world frieze and modern stone carvings, statues of the influential witches had been added to the structure. Lady Owens and Lord Cuttersark greeted Margaret as she descended the trussed gradient. The stone was painted in enamel, bringing to life the House Owens founders in vivid detail that fell into shades of apricot under high pressure sodium. The wind had pelted their faces slick, giving an appearance of tears.

Under the great dome stood Corporal Erin Abid, nose tucked under her black woolen coat, buttoned up past her collar. Next to her was Badger, striking a formidable pose in Owens black and silver; a shade of death, his nose missing, creating the implication of skull under his deep-set eyes.

"*You'se* didn't tell me this city was so *ass fucking cold*," Badger shouted, his hands buried deep in the pockets of his coat.

The air was still in the rotunda interior, a massive arena tiled in polished black granite and dull steel slabs. Arranged in one-foot-by-one-foot plates, the ground was stained in a thousand shades of dried blood. From flaccid pink slivers to deep black gashes, bits of bone and dried marrow remained. Toward the exterior pillars were many more candles in blue, green and red wax, spindling stalagmites sprouting up from a substantial bone collection. The ribs of cattle and goats were clean, hewn free of meat. Pyramids of skulls had been stacked, from all manner of animal *and* human alike. Some had been etched with stone or blade to contain various arcane symbols from dead languages, while others had been painted with sticky polymers that reflected coral light. This was a place *of power*. Margaret could feel it needle at her feet, *tickling at first*, almost driving her to giggle, then clutching at her thighs and groin, a greedy and demanding lover, ascending into her chest, spine turning into a warm glow that bound her close in a sense of awe and familiarity.

At some moments it smelled of *blood* or tannery chemicals. At others, was the heady aroma of burning grasses. Margaret swore a few times she could see, *and feel,* cinders kiss her face. This was a place of sacrifice, and worship. Even in the inception of a sea storm, the odors held their dominance. Each of the tall arches between rotunda pillars represented a gate. Each gate was *idling*, whispering in *Latin*, *Sanskrit*, and even *Sumerian*. One, Margaret could only see out the side of her eye, the hint of movement, rats and vermin clawing about for purchase. Another seemed to blur air like a mirage in hottest summer, promising water where none existed.

"Do you know where we're standing?" Margaret favored Erin with her eyes, boots tapping against the stone and marble floor, creating two distinct echoes as she did so.

Erin pulled her nose out of the long coat, sniffing, "There's nothing *burning*, but I can smell it. It feels like we're in the middle of a road. It makes me feel like I have a fever."

"Makes me have to *piss*," Badger said, mostly to himself.

"*Eight* roads, to be exact. Eight pillars, and eight roads." Margaret reached for her cigarette tin and tossed it to Badger. He relieved her of a twig and lit up as she pulled off the cotton sash of silver poppies and suede jacket underneath. "My mother would have called them *huacas*, or *ley lines*. You can call this a *crossroads*. A place to offer gifts and ask favors."

Erin visibly shivered, and Margaret thought she could hear her teeth chatter, "Modus Vivendi makes *all* their guests walk through a crossroads?"

Margaret's jacket and sash fell to the smeared floor, sticky at her heels. Underneath she wore a simple black waistcoat made from thick linen. It wasn't tailored *for* her, and was too tight across her chest to look attractive. It took her a moment to release each button of bone, and toss this atop the pile. "They're reminding us who has all the power."

Badger shrugged, exhaling mint oil and tobacco, his eyes taking in the great columns, "Just a place like any other."

"That's because you understand fear about as well as I do, Badger."

Last to come off was Margaret's skirt of gray, embroidered in metal beads. This, she'd miss most, since it *had* been tailored for her. Custom made in fact, years earlier in Denver. It was probably the sincerest sacrifice she offered.

Sticking his lower lip out, intentionally creating the vision of a pensive man, before breaking a rough laugh, Badger replied, "*Yeah*, there's always that."

Under her clothes, Margaret wore a sweetheart overbust corset with embroidery work at her hips. Roses and thorns twisted and crawled up her stomach and spine on matte, black, cotton. Flowered scallop and lace pulled her bust together under boned support, before clustering at her throat. An asymmetrical slip of garish, red, silk fell over her legs, barely touching one knee.

"I guess I'm undressing?" Erin looked around, unbuttoning her coat.

"Only I need to sacrifice. I'm the only mature witch here. You both left your pistols back at the hotel?" Margaret slid a sharp object out of her corset spine, where a thick support bone had been. It was a narrow piece of razor, thin as a knitting needle.

"*Yeah,*" Erin seemed unhappy, but not nearly as annoyed as Badger.

"As *you'se* say, boss." He nodded once, hard, suckling at his cigarette again.

Margaret leaned over, and ran the narrow razor down the inside of her right thigh, closer to the knee, careful to avoid her femoral artery. It didn't hurt nearly as much as the unrelenting cold. Replacing the razor, she had to slap her thigh several times before blood would let slip.

"*Fuck*, boss, *you'se* didn't say we had to do foreplay *too.*"

Badger laughed, before flicking the remains of his twig across the rotunda, between middle finger and thumb.

"Twig," Margaret replied, satisfied with the blood. Badger opened her tin and retrieved another brown roll of tobacco. With one hand, and with great care, Margaret worked the cigarette in her bloody fingers and palm until it glistened. She leaned over the pile of her clothes, toward Badger, "*Light a lady.*"

Badger obliged, and Margaret took a few puffs off the twig before dropping it to the ground with her beloved skirt. Though he was uninclined, this wasn't the first time Badger had helped Lady Mayhem in ritual. He handed her a metal lighter and she crouched down to catch the clothing aflame.

The wind didn't seem welcome in this place. The air was still, cavernous, and it certainly wasn't wet. Margaret's raiment was ablaze in moments.

"You've sacrificed something, you made payment." Erin spoke as Margaret remained close to the flame.

One by one, metal beads were falling free, bouncing on the tile and rolling free to whatever safe harbor they understood. Margaret whispered, not in English, but *Español*. The words a gift that her mother had taught. She didn't understand the whole prayer, but enough that she could recite it with clear intention.

Standing, Margaret looked directly at Erin, then past her, *right through her*, far into a gate where swirls of green and blue swept up and danced with each other like quarreling dust devils on the Great Salt Lake.

"You have *two* choices, Erin," Margaret said, and for a moment she bit into her vowels just like Maggi used to, "You can walk away now, sleep in your room tonight. In the morning you can catch a Peninsula bound train and return to Stockton. General Townsend will accept you into any branch of the 3rd Army you please. My gift to you, for your service."

Margaret corrected her voice, shaking off her mother's accent and then speaking low from her throat, "*Or* you enter Modus Vivendi with Badger and me. You will spend the night fighting *fear* and you will do *as you are told*. No less, no more. If you hesitate, if you *risk our lives*, Badger will kill you. Consider this a *real* test, if you want to study with me."

Badger knew Margaret well enough to inquire no further. He simply pocketed her twig tin and tilted his head down to the tile, watching little beads flee Margaret's sacrifice.

As Erin's face grew more focused and her brows lowered further, so too did the smoke between them turn black and ashen with bits of fabric, caught in updraft. *Spiders* crested Erin's shoulders, crawled down her shirt, and even scampered in her short hair. It could have been a dozen, or two dozen, large and small, migrating on paths only they understood.

Fucking spiders, is this her only gift? Margaret thought before Erin finally replied.

"I'll go in with you."

Badger turned, looking Erin over. He saw the spiders as well, though it seemed like he didn't care. The fire was beginning to die, and Margaret's clothes were now retreating cinders.

There were no further words to be spoken, and no reply escaped Margaret's lips.

She wasn't dressed in the fashion of House Owens, nor the witches of San Francisco. She wore no gloves to bar herself from those inside Modus Vivendi and she made no attempts to hide her Tilapia skin. The fish flesh of her lower lip felt cool and smooth at the tip of her tongue, ridgeless and erotic. It glistened coral, as if part of her had been at sea, swimming in the ebb and wave of coming storm.

Crossing out of the rotunda, Margaret stepped out of another quiet gate. In slumber this one contained a shimmering fog made of gold dust, drifting lazily. The closer she got, the fewer particles appeared, until finally, she walked out and there had been nothing after all.

For just a moment, Margaret caught the glimpse of sepia at stride, a few paces up and to the right. Wide in the hip, thick hair spilling down shoulders. It was for less than a second, just the outlines of movement, then it was gone.

Dread Harvester was true to her word.

Black and steel tile simply lead up to three enormous double doors. The stone frames were painted in overlapping symbols that had either faded into cast shadow or glowed in soft yellows and vibrant reds, arcane evocations. Some of them Margaret recognized, variations would be etched into the silver of her new arm. Others she had last seen decades before, inked into her mother's skin.

Some, she'd never known before this night.

"Do any of these forbid the dead?" Margaret whispered low, her lips unmoving.

In reply, three identical sigils across the upper frames dimmed and died until they seemed little more than wet paint. If Margaret blinked fast enough, and paid attention, she could see the after impressions of many more evocations, visions beyond the physical eye.

"*Of course,*" Margaret heard at her left ear, the sensation of moth wings skipping past her skin, "*but these were designed to keep wandering spirits away. None bar me, a guest at your own request.*" The flicker moved to her right ear, along with the susurration.

Margaret ran her left hand through damp hair. It had begun to curl and crimp, "Stay in the shadows, you'll know when it's time."

Aubriana did not reply, she was simply gone, vanished between worlds in the places that even a witch could not see.

Whatever remained of the outside world began to evaporate. There was no more storm, no more San Francisco. This was the edge of the map, and Margaret willingly plunged off.

10:34pm March 25th, 39 Veilfall

San Francisco, California

A new world foyer met Margaret and her companions.

Sleek onyx tile reflected orange gas lamps, and walls of matte pitch seemed to absorb light rather than refract color. Under low wattage bulbs were mannequins carved from wood and stained in rich auburns, posed with gestures of open arms and regality. Margaret could recognize one of the wooden frames wearing white and silver linothorax as Heart Owens, from her youth. Emblazoned with poppies on the breast guard and stitched with ceramic plate, it was similar to the one Margaret had borrowed. A sibling mannequin bore less regal fatigues, none more elegant than Townsend's own battle rattle. A brass plaque identified it as the former field dress for Lord Cuttersark himself.

Separate from the witches who founded House Owens were several other outfits, and one caught Margaret's eye. She left her companions, approaching a woman's mannequin which wore dingy green slacks and dusted boots, as well as a shemagh that Margaret *knew*. The clothes were tattered and dirty, stained with blood, and singed with fire.

"Before you is notorious Antecedent battlewitch, *The Bruja*. In life she was better known as Maggi Lopez, a California native who fled east during the Collapse. She's known as a friend of House Owens for dispatching two dangerous *Ifrit* in Carbondale."

Margaret's jaw fell open, genuine shock foaming in her sternum. A *ghost* in pre-Collapse regalia manifested from nothing next to her. He wore a rumpled jacket with ridiculously excessive golden epaulets, and a tall hat adorned in various feathers and trinkets. This ghost held more clarity than others, though he still blurred and washed out like Aubriana, as he moved and gesticulated with life.

"*Who the fuck are you?*" Margaret asked, unable to contain her disquiet.

"Welcome, weary traveler. My name is *Emperor Norton*. I'll be your guide through the history of Modus Vivendi, the birth of House Owens, and the advent of magic in our time." The ghost answered, taking no notice of her shock, or disdain.

More perplexed, Margaret decided to engage the ghost, "Who *were* you in life?"

Norton smiled big, showing the most handsome set of teeth Margaret had ever seen, his face shifting through an opaque spectrum of puce and rust, "My name is *Emperor Norton*."

Margaret understood aspects of old-world technology. Simple battery-powered devices continued to function for a few years into her childhood. Her mother once found a doll with pink and blue dress, and a string connected to its spine. If the string was pulled, the doll repeated a recorded message. It had made Margaret sad after a while because no matter how many times it repeated those messages, they would never change, never evolve. It could never answer questions or engage with her. That same sad feeling leaked down Margaret's throat now, clutching her windpipe, making her short of breath for a second.

"Tell me again, who was this."

Emperor Norton resurrected his smile, "Before you is notorious Antecedent battlewitch, *The Bruja*." The ghost repeated, word for word, the same tambour, the same cheerful exuberance that promised he would be just as interested in this *as you wanted him to be*.

Ghosts could emote the same as any living person, but their existence was tied beyond the Veil, so there was no mind to dig around in. No drawers to search, no secrets to be found. This *thing* had been mutilated into the same kind of awful carcass, no different from Margaret's doll with a blue and pink dress.

"Do you like him?"

Margaret turned from Norton as he finished his speech to see Lady Cuttersark approach. Her face was thick at the jawline, and she was wearing a form fitting dress that ran from a copper choker at her neck, made of white leather. She was *full bodied*, and her stomach was divided into two bulbous segments under mounds that made up her bosom. It gave Margaret the impression of a sausage tied in knots, underneath a long coat of black, dyed, fox fur.

"He's just a recording," Margaret *almost* crossed her arms before realizing she could no longer do that.

"Of course, he's just a recording. We found his ghost wandering the streets, *sweeping* them as if he expected that they'd grow cleaner. He *claimed himself* to be Emperor of the United States and Protector of Mexico. Utterly mad, of course." Lady Cuttersark stepped past Margaret, waving her hand through Norton, then snapping chubby fingers to vanish his manifestation.

"How would you *do* that? Make him this way?"

"*Easy*. We contracted with a former Bishop. She calls herself '*hexengeist*,' and she specializes in the control of spectral manifestations."

The same as their last meeting, Margaret could taste salt in Aurora Cuttersark's wake. Her dark coat of fur powdered with fine dust.

"I keep hearing that word. *Bishop?*"

Lady Cuttersark's lips pursed as she walked around Margaret, then stood next to her, eyes focused on Erin and Badger who still waited in the dimly lit foyer, "It's what the British call their witches. Who are your *little friends*? I liked Ramona Lopez better than these two *creatures*."

"The girl is Corporal Erin Abid, my personal escort. The *gentleman* is a member of my combat fireteam." Margaret thought better than to introduce Badger as '*Badger*.' She could *feel* Lady Cuttersark examining them, probing, winding around their spinal columns and listening to the sound and echo of their mood, all but pressing them for their thoughts.

"Have you come here for my head, Lady Mayhem?" Aurora Cuttersark answered, cool and quiet. Margaret's own skin was *drying* out, and she suddenly wanted to scratch at her throat and chest.

"If I wanted your head, why would I come to your home? I doubt you're the *only* witch to reside here." Margaret licked her lips, realizing even her Tilapia skin was parched, and took a step away from Aurora Cuttersark.

"*Home*?" Aurora Cuttersark laughed, "I don't *live* here. No one *lives* here. This is merely a *capitol building*. We have a social lounge, the largest arcane library in old America, offices, and public halls for conducting contractual business."

For Margaret's part, she'd had *no idea* what to expect upon entering. Seeing her mother's old clothes from the journey west didn't set her at ease, and the idea of a ghost who'd been enslaved to become nothing more than a recording unsettled her stomach.

What will your hexengeist do with my bones when I die?

"Let's call this *business*, Magnate."

Aurora Cuttersark turned away from Erin and Badger. As she stepped into motion, a fine powder drifted off her shoulders, stinging Margaret's sinuses when inhaled, "Join me in the lounge then, Lady Mayhem. Your *friends* can mingle as they please, however the *uninclined* have no rights here. No more than a house pet would. If one of them *shits on the rug*, we won't politely ask them to leave. We'll slit their throat."

Margaret followed Aurora Cuttersark with enough distance that her eyes didn't itch, and her lips wouldn't crack. Her energy *stung* the edges of Margaret's mind, like whiskey poured on a bullet wound. Her emotions were locked up and guarded behind gates and doors, no different from the moment Margaret had stepped foot in a place like this.

The *lounge*, if it could be called that, was equal parts abomination and paradise.

Down a curving hallway, behind two sets of steel-framed oak doors, was a large open space. New world tables and chairs of iron cluttered the floor, created from ornate molds, enameled with ruby highlights. Beyond the seated area was a small dance floor below a raised stage, under the glow of colored electric lights that shifted between gold and blue.

In the center of the lights, on stage, was a woman in a wide, baroque gown of green velvet. She was belting lyrics in an unfamiliar language. Her projection was remarkable, singing directly from her throat, lips curling around each word and note as though it were a particularly savory slice of lamb. The melody itself was soaked in sorrow and loss, a heartbreak that washed out across the room and changed how the air *tasted*. At least, for a witch.

Her eyelids had been sewn shut. Dried blood cracked and flaked off her cheeks, and her hands were wrapped in white linen, stained almost black, where her fingers should have been.

Aurora Cuttersark looked over her shoulder, grinning, "A Bellini aria is *best* performed when you have something to cry about. Don't you think?"

The woman's pain was a tangible river, undulating and rising, falling as mist through Margaret's hair and across her face. It was a thing of unspeakable beauty, divine in every meaning of the word.

You've cut a woman's fingers off and sewn her eyes shut to harvest this divinity.

Margaret did not answer, and Aurora Cuttersark turned, leading her to a long and narrow bar set against the room's northern wall. A collection of shattered mirrors, painted in what appeared to be pitch and rubicund, were mounted behind a vast store of liquor bottles. Some were dusted, dark, labels ripped off and forgotten. Others were new decanters of glass and crystal, housing a thousand shades of liquor: clear, ecru, and even pitch black.

A man strolled up from a few yards distant, wearing a waistcoat of red and purple stripes, each as wide as a finger, over a white cravat that looked like Georgette. His accent was rhotic and unfamiliar to Margaret's ears, "*Yer* usual, Lady Cuttersark? What about *yer pretty floop*?"

Aurora nodded, sniffing at the air as Margaret stayed a few steps back, "Pretty? You have an unusual opinion of *pretty,* Edgar. She has only *one* arm."

Margaret worked her jaw, ignoring the comment, "Whisky, top of the tumbler."

Edgar, the man with a Georgette cravat, grabbed two short glasses and began pouring drinks. Whatever Aurora Cuttersark *usually* drank was a more complicated concoction than a simple whiskey. When he produced the drinks, he tipped his head down and tried to walk away quickly before Aurora Cuttersark could speak further, but he was too slow.

"Edgar? *Hang on,* don't you wish to ask Lady Mayhem a question?"

The bartender, who'd maintained a wall of neutral emotion, now turned moist, clammy. Margaret imagined she could taste the sweat that ran down the back of his neck.

Or maybe that's just Lady Cuttersark I taste.

"I think not, no questions." Edgar did *not* allow his eyes to meet Margaret's, but his knuckles were flexing and turning white as they kneaded the rag in his hands like an anxious baker.

"Edgar, don't be shy. *You* wanted to ask her if she'd step behind the bar and *suckle at your dick*. You could keep making drinks. No one would be the wiser. Lady Mayhem wouldn't even charge you, from what I hear. What do you say Edgar? Go ahead. Ask her."

The very tone and tempo of Lady Cuttersark's voice ground away the edges of Margaret's patience. She sneered as she spoke, showing her fine and shiny teeth, tilting her head back and forth as the words fell out of her mouth like unchewed crackers.

In the back of her mind, Margaret scolded herself for not considering *how many* witches held the room. Most of these people were *uninclined*, vaguely sensitive, people who liked to play with fire. The same sort of individuals who liked to walk feral neighborhoods at night, unarmed, drunk on risk. Praying for the satisfaction of violence to follow. No one here was *blind*, or stupid, they were simply sadists and *masochists*. Margaret considered skipping inside the bartender's skull, promising him safety, but the little rat didn't *want* or *need* that. He *wanted* to go home after his shift. Jerk off into one of his socks, dreaming of the witch in fish skin who *might* of have killed him with the snap of her fingers.

"*Aurora the Younger,*" Margaret's eyes never came close to Edgar the barkeep, focusing on her host, "I came here to do business, not be insulted."

Lady Cuttersark laughed. It was shrill and nasal, just like her voice, "You came here to ask for help defeating your brother. I *know* you killed Amihan Lopez, and I know you're hardly in condition to take on other Antecedent battlewitches."

Margaret leaned forward, clutching her glass tumbler tight, the sound of Lady Cuttersark's voice pulling her nerves taut as fiddle strings.

"It was my understanding that Modus Vivendi witches were for *hire*."

Lady Cuttersark sipped her drink, and Margaret wondered what part of Aurora Owens lived on in those dark eyes, "Last time we met I *asked* you; *what do you possess* that I do not? Now you come before me, possessing nothing. You're an Antecedent turncoat, and you've installed my mother as Heart. A temporary effort to legitimize your treachery. You're missing an arm and your face looks like a freakshow. I don't want your *money*. It's even less valuable than your begging, in this place."

Margaret grinned, her lips separating at the center of her mouth to show her own, crooked and yellow teeth. She jerked the whisky tumbler toward her face and upended it to open lips, letting liquor fall back, down her throat. To the credit of Modus Vivendi, the drink was real quality and her chest turned warm in contentment.

Margaret gestured the tumbler, heavy in her hand, base pressed to palm, "I don't want to hear your voice anymore. I don't want to be called an *Alviso whore*. I don't want your petty humiliations. Do you know what I want the least of all?"

Lady Cuttersark glanced to the glass tumbler and noticed Margaret's hand turning black. Silver chandeliers offered dim, shifting light that swayed slowly. It made the onyx hard to *see*, such a simple thing at first, as though her skin was misted in a fine residue of motor oil from stuttering exhaust. The thick, obsidian coat spread around her fingers like tiny rings, hiding her knuckles, swallowing her short nails, and flowing *up* her arm like water.

Cuttersark was so fixated, she never saw the single drop of liquid charcoal fall off Margaret's lower lip, landing on red scallop lace.

"I don't want you to display my mother's clothes in this *fucked off* place."

Margaret never took her eyes of Lady Cuttersark, nor did she stop smiling when she slammed the glass tumbler into copper plate. It shattered with a resonate *pop*.

I hope you're proud of me for this, mom, thought Margaret, as she slashed one slender shard of glass across Lady Cuttersark's face. It cut to the bone when Margaret stepped in, ripping a gouge across the other woman's lower temple, straight between her eyelid, and across the bridge of her nose. Cuttersark's eyeball shrank away and spilled open like a cheap whore's diseased cunt, fluid falling, a hint of the blood that would pour free.

The broken tumbler flew away, bouncing off table and tile. Margaret heard a woman *shriek*, then another, then a man swear, "*Gods be fucked!*"

Lady Cuttersark fell to her knees, efforts at barriers vanished, silent and impotent. Margaret could *feel* her spinning up something else, whatever arcane powers she could manifest.

Her left hand, closest to the bar, swept wide, fingers spread and shaking. Liquor spun up in decanters, a blurry cyclone, cutting away at the inside of crystal and glass.

Every bottle exploded in a mist as fine as sand.

There's salt in liquor. So, you're a battlewitch after all.

Margaret moved away, shifting quickly to avoid what Cuttersark had summoned. At a glance it looked like solid fluid, blurred and wound about, moving, salt and glass shards in flight. The lash gouged away chunks of the floor, splinter and nail torn apart in an even grind that looked like beavers had been unleashed. Even wrought iron bent and frayed under the savage saline assault.

Margaret had no desire to find out how badly Cuttersark's *salt storm* could injure human flesh. She had one hand of ink pressed into Cuttersark's face, running from her chin and lips, up past her nose and eyes, clumsily groping, a young boy grabbing his first breast, unsure whether he should rejoice in the prize, or ask *what next?*

She was inside Lady Cuttersark's mind, *everywhere*, spreading like flood waters out a broken levy. Locking down the other woman's physical nerves, removing her command of hands and fingers, driving her down. The rational thought needed to command weapons given to a witch also began to shutdown, along with her reason and problem-solving skills.

Entire sections of Cuttersark's brain simply went dark in the wash of Margaret's will.

The salt storm cast off a thousand liquor bottles died, shattering like snow and spreading wide across hardwood floor. The lounge smelled of whisky and rum, vodka and gin, so pungent and certain that Margaret imagined how drunk she could get just breathing in the bitter fumes.

Holding Cuttersark's face in one hand, Margaret looked out over the lounge.

The blind vocalist with no fingers kept crooning. Men and women gathered at iron tables around the room stood, *watching*, seduced by this savage command over blood and magic. Margaret could hear their pulses skipping, pounding, hot and urgent in their veins. They had been afraid tonight would be *uneventful*. The alcohol flood was servile considering this starvation, this hunger. Beyond her physical senses Margaret could smell labia dripping in arousal and erect cocks commanding an ovation. This was the brutal sport that these uninclined so desperately desired, each one of them fantasizing about the one-armed-witch and her liquid charcoal. Part of Margaret found this notion thrilling, but it was *her* little secret that she shared in private. Nothing so *vulgar* as to display at court.

This made her *sick*.

There were *three* witches in this room, she could *hear* them thinking. They were *afraid* and *confused*. Their energy was dim and cool compared to what Lady Cuttersark could wield if her brain functioned.

Doesn't mean anything. Mom wouldn't have taken the risk, and neither will I.

Margaret gave the locations of all three witches to Badger and Erin, offering them a picture in their minds of the lounge she commanded in gruesome dominance. Those locations came with a clear understanding of *which tables they sat*, and an odor that even an uninclined could pick up on.

It was like pointing to a crowd, in the mirror, whispering, "*The man in blue, that's him.*"

Kill them, they're witches, Margaret's voice hissed in their minds, a memory of a shout, the hint of her lips at their ears. Badger would know exactly how to handle this. It's what he did, unleashing murder upon an unsuspecting world.

Erin would either follow orders, or fail, there was no middle ground.

Margaret turned back to Lady Cuttersark, her face covered in oil and cruor, her breath bubbled through thick coat across her nose.

"I *know* you can still hear me in there, Aurora," Margaret stepped back, hand free, watching the charcoal and blood drip down her tailored dress of leather. "I'm not a sadist, I don't get *my* thrills like you do. I'm just an *Alviso whore*, remember?"

Kneeling, Lady Cuttersark was still much larger than Margaret. Wrapping her left hand around the other woman's face, Margaret moved behind her and pressed Cuttersark's skull into her corset front. She stroked Cuttersark's face, and fell back into her mind. Part of the big woman was locked away, *screaming* in anger and pain, clawing to free herself. Margaret truly had no interest in that part of Lady Cuttersark. It was an ugly and drooling creature that had lost possession of sanity in the wake of such a simple horror. Margaret wasn't *really* hurting the other witch, she wasn't raping her with a broom handle or putting lit cigarettes out on her skin. She wasn't showing her *any* horrors.

This was *nothing* by Margaret's calculations, except a little payback.

Margaret followed Lady Cuttersark along for her adventures in life, watching her study at her father's side. Listening intently as he explained a hundred medical terms the child could never grasp, gesturing at a microscope and forgetting about her. She didn't hate him for that, she understood the importance of his work, but she *was* lonely. Her mother granted her even less attention, shushing her when she spoke, refusing to answer her questions, and some days pretending she never existed at all. She nipped a bit at Lady Owens for that, always looking to anger her, rebel against her, give her a *reason* to yell.

In this, Margaret found a degree of warmth, caressing Lady Cuttersark's bloody and swollen face. Maggi Lopez had never forgiven Margaret for *existing* on the day that her lover died. She also *had* loved her blood son more than Margaret.

But, she never treated little Margaret with indifference.

Margaret decided, here and now, that she could accept that; accept her mother's love for what it was, not what she wished it could have been.

"I'm sorry. This *will* hurt."

Margaret slid her left hand over to Aurora's ruined eye and pressed her fingertips into the wound slush. Her eyeball was still intact, simply separated, cut like a grape. Margaret pushed her fingers in deeper, middle and ring, behind the eyeball, until it slid out and flopped into her palm. Gelatinous meat rolled up against her flesh, mixing with thick oil, dripping off fingers. It reminded her of throwing up into one hand, all the soggy food and bile pressing between fingers, ejaculating down her chest.

The optic nerve and blood vessels didn't want to wrestle free at first, but with a quick jerk, they let go and a second round of warmth fell.

For a moment, Margaret examined her palm, nerve stem drooping down like a freshly shorn umbilical cord. Lady Cuttersark's eye curved in on itself and split across the retina where broken glass had cut so smoothly.

Margaret tossed it behind the bar where it hit something with a wet *plop*.

Hand still covered in a thick placenta of ink and blood, she reached inside the top of her lace scallop, to the underside of her right breast. The sensation of a slick warmth crossing her nipple made her giggle for a second before she focused on retrieving the hidden trinket.

The Eye of Shahr-i-Sokhta.

Turning it over in her hand, the curved eye was free of its golden housing. Margaret reached back for Lady Cuttersark's face and began forcing it into the socket where her old eye had lived. It required some force, pulling and twisting away eyelids, but it wedged into place.

"I'm going to grant you mercy, now. I'm going to turn you *off*, wipe away any part of you left in this mind. You won't feel any more pain. Before we say our goodbyes though," Margaret leaned down and nuzzled at Lady Cuttersark's right ear, whispering, "Your mother *and* brother commissioned your death. I assumed it was just *cold* political maneuvers. Now, I think they just *never* loved you. *My mother* would beat me until my eyes were swollen shut. But you know what? She never ordered me killed."

With that Margaret stood up and stripped away any part of Lady Cuttersark's mind that made her a sentient person. It was like scooping out a melon, memories *gone* first, followed by her favorite alcohol and the fact she preferred lamb over beef. Every book she ever read, and her understanding of magic. Her favorite color had been *light blue,* and she really did *love* Bellini. She had always wanted to pierce her nipples and she dreamed one day of visiting Britain, on the other side of an ocean.

These things were pared away, cut free, and cored out, until only the *meat* of her brain remained. All the electrical triggers and processing functions, the command network that allowed her toes to curl and eyes to focus.

"*Aubriana!*"

Margaret yelled, tossing her head back to the ceiling's dark framework above, breathing deep, and exhaling even harder, "I've made good on my bargain."

11:20pm March 25th, 39 Veilfall

San Francisco, California

"All right *you'se fucking cunts*, get the *fuck* out of here!"

Badger shouted from the floor, forward of Vivendi's lounge. He was wielding a broken liquor bottle like a hatchet, three-quarters of the square glass sheared away, leaving one jagged side as a weapon.

Margaret looked around for Erin, then noticed a figure jerk upwards suddenly away from a table. It *was* Erin. She was bleeding from ears and eyes, her pomade-slick hair a scattered mess, and jacket half pulled off. She jumped away from a table, grabbed one of the wrought iron chairs, hefted the back above her shoulder, and tossed it down to the floor with all her force.

"*Badger!*" Margaret stepped away from Cuttersark's kneeling body and pointed toward Erin once Badger made eye contact.

The lounge was mostly empty by now. Skulking denizens stumbling out of their chairs, rushing for rearward exits. They'd been close enough to smell the blood that percolated out of Lady Cuttersark's face, holding their breath *and* their cocks while Margaret ripped an eyeball out. Now, they could thank the gods above and below that they wouldn't find themselves covered in liquid charcoal.

"*Whoah! Whoah!* She's dead, little tomato!" Badger was yelling as he stumbled over another chair and rushed to the left of Erin, prying her back.

"*Fuck you! And fuck this bitch!*" Erin shouted, raising her fists high and stomping down on something. At this angle Margaret could only make out tables which still had white china scattered about them and stacks of candles hanging from steeple hooks.

"You didn't tell me that you'd *take her fucking eye*."

It was Lady Cuttersark's voice, but she was speaking slower, not enunciating words with the same precision. She rolled her neck, slowly, three-hundred-and-sixty degrees at her shoulders, before her body stood up again.

Margaret grabbed two napkins off the closest table, white linen, thick and folded. She whipped one, like a wet towel, to her hip, then started cleaning Cuttersark's face. The Eye of Shahr-i-Sokhta was firmly lodged in her skull, golden starburst obscured by viscous blood and threads of meat.

"You and I are square." Margaret nodded, once, for her own benefit.

Lady Cuttersark's surviving eyeball strolled to Margaret's face, offering a grin caught between a mad giggle and a genuinely *angry* grimace, "*Square?*"

Margaret stopped, tossed the first napkin away, covered in thick crimson and night.

"Story was, you stabbed my mom in the *eye*. I told you, whatever you two had going on didn't include me. But, if someone stabbed *your* mom in the eye, what would *you* do?"

When Cuttersark had sneered or smiled, it had pulled at her thick and supple skin, giving the impression of a *fat baby* who'd found breast milk sour. In contrast, Aubriana Harvester brought dread to her expressions, a flat, undeniable loathing for everything she surveyed.

Aubriana shrugged her new shoulders, "*Fair enough.*"

Margaret turned her head back to Badger and Erin. Commotion continued, and now a table was tossed over.

"Quit *fucking off*! Kill every candle in this place and find me the chandelier controls!"

Margaret pointed up, but it seemed mostly for her own benefit since neither Badger nor Erin bothered to glance over.

"This is *fantastic*." Aubriana growled with her new voice, left hand reaching up for her face, flexing her fingers and clawing at the air.

"*Um*," Margaret turned away from her escorts. Badger was now screaming something she couldn't understand.

"I haven't felt *anything* in decades. This is *fucking exquisite*." Aubriana stumbled forward, moving her legs with clumsy starts and stops. Once she found her footing, she rushed toward the closest table, where she grabbed a handful of mashed potatoes and peas, shoving it all into her mouth with a wet gagging sound. "I *fucking* hate peas!"

Aubriana grabbed another handful, the green pods turning to slop between her fingers, leaking down her chin, mixed with blood and ink. She was chewing wildly, her jaw working in exaggerated mastication.

"*Lady*," Badger shouted, "I think we need help!"

Gods be fucked.

Margaret bit her lower lip and turned away from Aubriana. She had shoveled another handful of food into her face. Talking through the food, unintelligible, she spit clumps of mashed potatoes.

Turning, Margaret rushed between the wrought iron tables and chairs. By the time she reached Corporal Erin Abid, the girl was sitting on the floor, next to the remains of a witch that Margaret had called out for execution. Any details of that woman were now spread across lacquered floor. Her forehead was bent in, drawing a deep plum hue. Her sockets languished with clabbered claret, behind eyeballs that jutted out like curious rabbits from a hovel. The remains of a nose bent off to one side, and her front teeth concaved. Deep blue layers of cotton bound her cooling body, embroidered with golden thread in the shape of doves or pigeons, Margaret couldn't say. In death, the witch had pissed herself and smelled strongly of urine and sandalwood.

Kneeling next to Erin, Margaret watched her eyes despite dim light. Her sclera had turned bloody, and ruby tears traced her face from ducts, bruising a garish shade of purple.

"*Calm*," Margaret commanded, sticky left palm pressed to Erin's scalp, reaching into the girl's mind. She throttled down adrenaline, worming her way through the terror and shushing it to sleep, a familiar beast that Margaret could tame.

Margaret glanced to Badger, his silver and black uniform glistening sanguine, reflecting candlelight, "I've got this. I want *every* light in this room off, save the chandeliers. Bar the doors."

Badger seemed happy to accept an assignment he *understood*. Whatever happened to the little Corporal was beyond his comprehension or his desire to deal with. The man was a savage artist of murder, *not* a counselor of comfort.

Removing her hand from Erin's head, Margaret hiked up the side of her slip so she could sit down next to the young Corporal.

"*Talk to me*," Margaret used her command voice, low and soft, but resonation crawling along the triggers in Erin's mind that would oblige her beyond any limits of trauma, "*I can't help if you don't tell me what happened*."

Erin's lips moved with easy calm, even though her hands were shaking, index fingers tapping rapidly along trouser knees. "I thought she blinded me. I couldn't see. I tried to break her neck with my hands, but I don't know how."

"You did *good*, kid," Margaret nodded, reaching to wipe some of the blood off Erin's ears, "Don't worry about it."

"I know," Erin replied, "that was stupid. I never broke someone's neck before."

What?

That was a disjointed answer, and for the moment Margaret chalked it up to trauma.

"Can you see now, candy striper?"

"I can see. I just don't *want* to see."

Erin's shoulders trembled as she spoke, and more blood escaped her eyes. Her upper lip was glossy with mucus and this close Margaret could smell her breath, stale and rancid from a half-finished lunch.

Pausing, Margaret listened to the room around her. Aubriana was shouting something, but she decided to ignore her, "I'm going to step into your mind, I want to see what you see and hear what you hear. This will be intimate, okay? You'll *feel* me in there."

Erin nodded, eyes wide, blood drying in her lashes, crusted. Her hair was thick with pomade, and a spider crawled up, out of her locks, skittering across Margaret's middle finger and stopping on her knuckle. It was a black widow.

Fucking girl and her fucking spiders.

Margaret gritted her teeth, ignoring the arachnid. She stepped into Erin's mind with ease, windows and doors wide open. She could hear the ticking of a pulse and remember the smell of a hot engine burning sage brush as it crawled dirt roads. It wasn't like prying apart Lady Cuttersark, there were no sophisticated passions or disgusting diversions here. The girl worried about her dog, *Gertrude,* who was back in Nevada. She lusted after a fight for the *sake of the fight,* it boiled in her blood and made her feel vitally alive. Her father had taught her kata, a martial art that served little in a real war. She kept red wax candles in her satchel of personal effects, lighting them on a high full moon to pray to Ares, Lord of War. *If you want to play with fire, you'll get burnt,* someone repeated inside her skull, a memory she'd held as a mantra.

There was no *fear* in here, no terror. Whatever the witch with bulging eyeballs had done to Erin was a different kind of magic, and not something Margaret had ever seen.

"Look at me," Margaret said softly, listening with Erin's ears to the sound of her own voice.

Under fluttering candlelight Margaret was looking at a scrawny girl with misshapen shoulders, perhaps fourteen. Her auburn-red hair was tied back in a ponytail. She was *smiling*, though Margaret was *not*. The handprint of Tilapia was nowhere to be seen.

Margaret recoiled. *That's me as a child. What the fuck is wrong here?*

"You wore paracord, in your hair, didn't you? As a child?"

Erin seemed to find comfort in the startle. Tied close to the older witch now, there's no reason she couldn't hear the percolation of Margaret's thoughts.

"I did. What did Badger look like to you?"

Erin was genuinely more relaxed now, and she scrunched her nose in reply, "Uglier than normal. It seemed like his skin was shriveled. His teeth looked like a dog's."

Badger had *never* been balanced. His past wasn't much better than Margaret's. He had been recovered somewhere in Ohio, a child caged and forced to fight feral *dogs* and *other* children. Margaret had been in his mind often enough, over the years, to know that part of him still lived in that damp and feculent pit, ripping animals apart with his bare hands while they clawed flesh from his chest and stomach.

"That's basically what the *real* Badger looks like."

Margaret withdrew her mind, and her hand, leaving Erin to her privacy. She cast the black widow off her knuckle with a quick brush.

I'm still that little girl with her hair tied up in paracord?

"*Why?*" Erin pressed her elbow under one side so she could sit up.

"I don't *entirely* know. I don't know if this will wear off or not. At a guess? I think maybe you tangled with a *scourge-tongue*. They're curse witches. Maybe you're a *cypher*, and all she did was damn you to *only* see and hear the truth."

Or, maybe she damned you with that power.

Erin was licking the back of her wrists and smearing away the blood on her face, "I don't understand. *Everything* I see is the truth now?"

Margaret's lips parted, her teeth still blackened with charcoal, and she bobbed her head back and forth, "*Maybe*? I don't know yet. I *won't* know for a while."

Erin blinked, as if she was still blind, then stood up with the ease of a young woman not even yet twenty, "You think I'm damned."

"I don't honestly know for sure," Margaret spoke quietly, her voice carried no further than Erin's ears and she chose each word carefully, knowing the girl would *only* hear the truth. "But, yeah. You're probably *cursed*. I don't know if that can be *reversed*. I don't know *anything*. I'm a *nightmare mirror*, I don't know the first thing about curses."

Erin looked down at Margaret as she shifted, placing knees under her, kneeling. There was a sense of flavorless calm around her, the taste of a sunny morning hangover or the hum in your ears that summoned when the plains were *too* quiet.

She's in shock.

"Will you help me?"

Margaret offered a hand, and Erin accepted it to pull her off the ground. No matter how many years separated the two, Margaret could *only* look up at the girl, even with her short, block heels. "I'll help you as much as I can, candy striper."

Margaret didn't *quite* mean that, and she wondered what Erin *actually* heard. She wasn't electing to abandon the girl, but she also had no idea how she could teach a cursed witch.

This place steals everything, Margaret thought, sourly.

Aware that the hour would not wait, Margaret pulled Erin toward the bar. She spoke as honestly as she could, "We're running out of time. It's almost *midnight*, and I've given the most terrifying witch in history a body so that she can help me draw out an ancient spirit whose power I barely understand better than yours."

11:48pm March 25th, 39 Veilfall

San Francisco, California

"Vodka is a disinfectant!"

Aubriana was pouring clear liquor into Lady Cuttersark's empty eye socket.

The dress of white leather was now smeared in umber and crimson, a shifting palette of colors that reminded Margaret of the Collapse. It wasn't the aesthetic, it was the dusty way her liquid charcoal had dried and cracked, like a sky of smoke and fire.

Tilting her chin down, Aubriana's face was cleaner, despite a spate of blood still oozing out of her eye. She glared after Badger, lower lip pulled down like a predator who couldn't decide *which* prey to seize first. Lady Cuttersark had drawn herself up tall, shoulders squared back and head held high, but Aubriana Harvester was hunched forward, her head swiveling on her neck, and her legs separated, waiting for spring and *strike*.

"Now you're flammable," Margaret said flatly, reaching for the bottle of liquor. Aubriana didn't release it easily, but persistence paid off, "In a few minutes I'm going to try and summon *something* into this room. A *spirit*, I think. An old one."

The golden Eye of Shahr-i-Sokhta was visible, sans blood, and a flicker of saffron sparkled across the ancient disk. Aubriana ignored Badger and Erin, wallowing her good eye on Margaret, "Your old 'spirit' is already here. *She* didn't even notice the finger-paint at the door."

Margaret drank from the vodka, as if it was a field canteen, up ending the glass bottle and letting it fall past her tongue. "How do you know?"

Aubriana twisted to move away, *watching*, skulking, a predatory animal choosing each step with care, silken and noiseless.

"This eye can *see*, it's *alive*. It's talking to my *bones* with *real* power."

Erin stepped up behind Margaret's right, watching the body of Lady Cuttersark with intense focus. Margaret glanced to her, much of the blood had wiped away from her face, but she was quivering in a grimace, "You should get behind the bar. Stay low. There's *nothing* else you can do but watch."

As if Margaret had never spoken, Erin opened her mouth and started to speak, but no words would follow. She tried a second time, "She's all bloated up and rotting, and she's leaking water. She has *no jaw*; her tongue is just hanging there. Like a rope."

A smile parted Aubriana's lips and she made a hissing chuckle that started at the back of her throat and worked its way up like food poisoning, "*Aww,* you don't know who I am? This is *my* city."

Gods be fucked, what have I done?

"*Gods be fucked,* Erin, get behind the bar!"

Margaret tried to snap the fingers of her left hand and failed. Erin tipped her head down and scurried for the bar, a moment before the spotlights around the abandoned stage went dark. With all the candles cold, and wall stanchions lowered, only the chandeliers overhead remained. They were pre-Collapse, electric, and set on dimmers.

"I'm betting it can only manifest in absolute darkness."

"You're right," Aubriana growled, stealing back the vodka for herself, drinking it this time, instead of washing her eye with it.

"*Badger!*" Margaret shouted up to the stage, holding a hand to the side of her lips, "Did you find the switch for those overheads?"

"Sure did boss," Badger replied, his voice projecting.

Margaret nodded to him once, lifted her chin up high, then made a cutting gesture across her throat. Badger gave a thumbs up and leapt down off the stage.

It was an old habit, and probably didn't help, but Margaret licked her palm once and slapped it to her bare chest, pressing in. She'd licked some of the dusted charcoal, and her saliva burned like whiskey and sung like honey. She pressed on her sternum and began to whisper some of the old words. Words that her mother had taught her. Her mind drawing in, around manifest barriers. First, she would create an outline, a basic idea of what she wanted, and layer by layer would come the details, the shading, until it was wholly what she imagined it could be.

"You've said it wrong," Aubriana spoke, as Margaret opened her eyes once more, "you're speaking Elamite, a dead Bronze Age language."

"It's what my mother taught me," Margaret replied softly, aware that her barriers were spun up and as ready as they could be.

Aubriana shook her head, a look on her face like she'd sipped at sour milk.

"Who do you think taught her?"

Without drawing her eyes off Margaret's, Aubriana repeated the same phrase, using a different accent, a more focused speech pattern, pausing and stopping at different times, expelling new words to Margaret's ears. When Badger killed the lights, a series of spheres hung around Aubriana, each one a deep shade of dead roses, dimming by the second, and bleeding rubies, crystalline cruor.

Margaret had never seen Maggi manifest *that*.

When the last of the broken roses fell to Aubriana's feet, there was no more light of any kind. Not one candle flickered, no glass reflected, there was simply *no more illumination*. Margaret could no longer hear Aubriana's husky breath or Badger's footfalls. It was as if sound had become mortified in the absence of light.

"You're not Maria. No, that's not right. She didn't like that." The voice shifted around the room like a child's toy, shattered, and bouncing across furniture. There was a gasping urgency in the words, a woman near climax, biting for *more*, and *still more*, bound up in parcel ties, mad giggles. *"Magdalena. She liked Maggi. You're not Maggi."*

"My name is Margaret, and I'm now the Eye's owner. Who are you?"

The voice shifted and moved close to Margaret, a chill gust of wind rustled her hair, colder by far than any ocean breeze, *"Marinette Bras Cheche."*

"Her Lady of the Dry Arms," Aubriana answered a question that had never been asked, somewhere to Margaret's left. She'd been *moving* this whole time, in silence. "I know you, *lwa.*"

That's good, because I have no idea what I'm dealing with.

Margaret turned away from the icy air and took a step toward Aubriana's voice.

"You've been following me for the Eye of Shahr-i-Sokhta. Haven't you? The eye that Maggi promised you."

Between where Margaret and Aubriana stood, a *third* person was moving, shifting, a sound like sashes caught in the wind, hands underwater, groping at smooth skipping stones. Beyond seeing, Margaret could *feel* the physical world curvilinear; it tugged at her scallop lace and slip, taunt at her skin, *almost* painful.

"The eye that does not see. I want that eye, one last gift."

When Aubriana spoke, using Lady Cuttersark's voice, the pitched whine of her tone was gone, and although she didn't *sound* different, every word contained a grim determination that the younger woman had never learned in life.

"Maggi is *dead*. If you paid her *before* she produced your *gift*, that's only your folly."

Margaret could see something emerging from the darkness. At first it was simply *more* darkness, afterimages glancing, for a second or two. Impressions behind the eyes, creating a brief, *splitting pain* in Margaret's optic nerves, running up through temples and into her neck.

Marinette Bras Cheche was manifesting in this world.

"You're wearing my eye. You will give it to me."

There was no more *giggling*, when Marinette spoke it sounded like a never-ending *inhale*, ragged and *angry*.

She can't take it, Margaret considered, *it must be given.*

"Aubriana, let me see through your eyes, I need in."

Margaret could imagine the dim look Aubriana might have given her in the full blossom of daylight, holding glare under brows, unblinking as she processed disgust. Regardless of that disgust, this was *why* she'd jammed the Eye of Shahr-i-Sokhta into Lady Cuttersark's skull, and Aubriana was clever enough to know that.

Aubriana was frantic, struggling, pulling needles from her arms when she realized that her head jerked sideways, and something tugged at her throat. Not merely her throat, but deeper into her esophagus. That's a breathing tube.

The memory was simply *there*, lying on the kitchen counter like a half-eaten sandwich, attracting flies. Margaret was groping for her own jaw, her throat, gagging on a recollection that didn't belong to her. She regurgitated the vodka onto her hand, unaware of what the bile smelled like; she was too distracted, choking on the smoke filling her hospital room.

Aubriana's hospital room.

Blind now, Margaret was looking out of Aubriana's eyes, the Eye of Shahr-i-Sokhta superimposing it's strange and disjointed images across her field of view. Marinette appeared as both a squirming stain of intense energy dyed in glow that splattered and illuminated the chairs as tables; but also, as a misshapen skeleton, hovering a foot off the floor. Her jaw was too large for her skull, and moved absently of speech, chewing undercooked meat for eternity. Her spine was a woven rope, caught in a breeze, scoliosis eternal and lost in music that no one else could hear. Margaret had cultivated her skill at *mind diving* since she was a child, and over decades she'd done it with *and without* the consent of her target countless times. In all those years, she'd never experienced anything like this.

Say what I say, Margaret was rapidly losing any sense of her own body, forgetting that she had *one* arm. In another body, she felt oddly whole.

"Next you'll want to braid my *fucking hair*," Aubriana said that out loud, *or she didn't*, Margaret couldn't fathom that. She was more than herself now, and certainly less.

Tell her she can't have it. Tell her she can make a new bargain.

Aubriana leaned forward, fists balled up, and immediately shot into colorful, old world vernacular, "If you wanted it so bad, you should have taken it off Maggi's corpse. Your deal *died* with her. Now, you need to make a new deal."

That's not what I had hoped you'd say.

Marinette drew back in something like loathing, her spine wriggling, "*I followed Maggi, when the pit grew cold and dark. She did not have my eye, the eye that she promised.*"

Carbondale, the birth of The Beast, Margaret thought more for herself than Aubriana.

Aubriana looked back to Margaret and Margaret could see herself cast aglow in shades of crimson and rust, a shimmering pond outlined in the shape of a one-armed woman.

"If the current owner is willing to pay that debt with something of equal or greater value, will you consider Maggi's bargain kept?"

The sashes and shawls of Marinette whipped back and around her skeletal form, revealing only a spindling, illuminated fabric, woven of a thousand fibers.

She replied with a choleric disdain, "*I will make no bargain with you, oathbreaker.*"

Oathbreaker?

Withdrawing much of her mind from Aubriana, only barely able to visualize the ancient spirit, she fell back to her own voice and tempo, "Bargain with me then, *Marinette Bras Cheche*. What is the eye worth to *you*?"

How much could she possibly demand for its ransom?

Beyond her eyes, Margaret could feel Marinette Bras Cheche turn her attention, pulling at the lounge air, the very physical bounds of this place. Near such power, Margaret was intimately aware that the Veil wasn't *completely* gone. Tethers survived, and a wall remained.

"*You'll grant me any treasure I desire?*" Marinette spoke on inhale once more, her voice chilling Margaret deep, past her sternum, to parts of her that could resonate, "*I need not share?*"

Margaret wasn't sure why, but she held her hand out, fingers turning numb, and the skitter of rats clawing up her arm, pulling at flesh with hooked claws.

"Any treasure you wish, *Marinette Bras Cheche*. But I will keep the eye that belonged to Maggi Lopez. Do we have a bargain?"

Although she was fairly certain that no physical harm had come to her limb, holding it in the space occupied by such a powerful Veil creature required discipline and focus. It was blurring realities around her, making her blind to some things and consumed by others.

When Marinette answered, it was without pause or delay, as if she had a special wish list scrawled in a hidden place, behind stone and ledge, that she could recall at any time.

"The brass and leaden carapace; that killed a royal king. Two hearts pledged together, bound by golden rings. A snake of bloodied leather; whose bite will burn flesh with icy knell."

What in the fuck?

"Deal. I will trade these things for *the eye that does not see*." Margaret did not delay her answer, she jumped on the bargain without more than a second or two of pause.

"You have until this day, one year from now, to make good on this bargain."

Time was Margaret's most valuable resource. She couldn't earn or steal more, but she could always solve Marinette Bras Cheche's riddles. One was, of course, *wedding rings*. The others would become clear enough when they needed to be. Objects trussed up in sky blue silk, darkened at the edges by her own blood.

"Keep your word, little Bête Noire."

Marinette Bras Cheche's final words reminded Margaret of Condatis. The Veil's wrenching twist released, and Margaret felt as if she could breathe easily again, free of an incessant tugging. Warmth ran down her left arm, and fingers, blood flowing free under acquittance, whole and part of her again.

She didn't need to borrow Aubriana's mind to know that the ancient spirit was gone, vanished from the Modus Vivendi. Only in her wake did Margaret realize the raw and sour stench of this place, meat yearning for the vultures.

12:18am March 26th, 39 Veilfall

San Francisco, California

"Give us light, Badger," Margaret shouted, exhaling hard.

Badger did not shout back, but after long seconds the electric chandeliers slowly began to illuminate once more. Nothing had changed. Even the sticky vomit that dribbled off Margaret's fingers, down her cleavage, was a restorative when compared to this blighted, blubbering place that threatened to violate souls.

Margaret wondered what would happen to the mutilated vocalist now that she could no longer croon for Lady Cuttersark. Would Dread Harvester have such perverse tastes?

With thumb and forefinger, Aubriana pulled the Eye of Shahr-i-Sokhta from her skull, tugging hard after it refused to let go immediately. She never whimpered, nor cast note of pain, and Margaret could taste no suffering. As immune to agony as Margaret was to fear, Aubriana would have been a fearsome brawler, a witch whose focus could not be broken.

I can see why you loved my mother.

Margaret accepted the bobble from Aubriana's pudgy fingers. The empty eye socket began to bleed once more, all the exposed meat and gristle twisting at the air, gently, rhythmically.

"I've made good on my bargain," Aubriana said softly.

Margaret accepted the Eye of Shahr-i-Sokhta. "I've never taken something without payment. I will not start today. I'm sorry you'll wear one eye in this body."

Aubriana shrugged, thick juice of ruby, slowly clotting on her face, "It's fine."

Margaret tipped her head to one side, considering Marinette Bras Cheche's words, and replied; *"Oathbreaker?"*

"I've been cheating death a *long time*." Aubriana smiled. She answered the question with no vitriol, as evenly as one might explain their plans to eat a nice lunch, "At the dawn of the Collapse I made a bargain with *Styx*, Lady of the River. I make no apologies, and I have no regrets for breaking that bargain. If all that Maggi built falls into the sea, *dead and forgotten*, then we can consider ourselves *even-steven*".

Even-steven? Margaret wondered, before ignoring the antique slang.

"Candy-striper! *Get over here*."

Erin rose from behind the bar, watching the two women talk of dark times and vibrant vendettas. She looked almost a decade older. Dark lines carved up, under her eyes and lips, as if she didn't know how to smile anymore. Her fingers were shaking, and she said nothing, favoring the side closer to Margaret.

"*Candy-striper*," Aubriana twisted her new face into a look of bemused glee, lips curled in a hungry grin, "She's a nurse?"

Someone confused by my slang for once, Margaret almost smiled, answering, "A candy-striper is just a young girl who's accepted apprenticeship."

With her right hand Aubriana reached out, grabbing Erin's chin and twisting her head side to side as if she needed to peer around her face, and into whatever secrets sat behind bone and marrow.

Uncomfortably, Erin answered, "Why?" As if that word alone would sum up her confusion.

"Aubriana, this is Erin. She's been my escort. She saved my life in Stockton, and I promoted her to Corporal in my 3rd Army. She's one of us now, though. She can hear and see the truth of things. *Only* the truth. She sees us *both* for what we really are."

"Anathema," Aubriana jerked Erin's head side to side, "She's cursed."

Margaret once more attempted to cross her arms, before realizing it was no longer possible, and settled on groping up the right side of her chest.

"I've never seen *that* before. I'm not even sure if it can be *fixed*."

Aubriana thrust aside the girl, almost violently, tossing a glance back to Margaret, "All curses can be lifted. This one will kill your *candy-striper* in due time. She'll go mad first, slowly, over many years. Then a day will come that she can't lift her fingers to hold a spoon, her knees will stop working, and her lungs will forget to breathe."

How much do you know?

Margaret wasn't in the habit of feeling inerudite, and few living witches possessed as much arcane wisdom as she'd accumulated. Aubriana, however, had been older than Maggi in life, and spent the last two-decades only learning more as a ghost.

"Can that *not* happen?" Erin's voice turned meek, cracking on the final syllable.

With her left hand Margaret began to replace the Eye of Shahr-i-Sokhta under her top of embroidered scallop lace, low on her chest, above her cleavage. It wasn't very tight, but Aubriana's drying blood would cement it in place. "I don't know what your price is, Harvester, but I'll pay it. I've shown you, I'm a woman of my word."

Aubriana clasped her hands behind her back and stepped to the right of Erin, walking around her, before coming full circle and watching Margaret.

A heavily puffed sigh escaped her lips, "Before the Collapse, I trained your mother, free of price. Because, it was what she *needed*. I would have saved your pet *candy-striper* from this curse too, but," Aubriana smiled, "since you've offered to pay me, what fool would I be to turn that down?"

Margaret glanced away, ready to laugh at herself, and unable to hide a smile. It was a somber moment, but Aubriana's grace was lushly painted canvas that defied indifference.

"What would you like in return, Harvester?"

Aubriana shifted weight, along with her chin and neck, a great albatross considering what savory organs might undulate behind Margaret's fish flesh, "I'm not pretending to be someone else. I'll be myself, or no one at all."

Margaret considered the Modus Vivendi lounge, and found herself delighted at the idea of *Dread Harvester* cleansing this place of ill-gotten depravity, "You *realize,* Heart Owens is still alive. And, she hasn't forgotten what you did to her."

"Good lessons are hard to forget," Aubriana bared her teeth, in nothing that could have been mistaken for a smile.

What's the worst that could happen? Margaret shook her head, half smiling, and offered a hand to Aubriana, "As you wish it, *Dread Harvester.*"

Aubriana lifted her right hand first, realized that was incorrect, then favored her left for the one-armed woman, stepping away from Erin's shoulder slightly.

"Do you fear me, child?" Erin gave up her answer to Aubriana, easily, with just a simple expression, "If you only hear *truth,* then let me make myself plain. I would enjoy a witch at my side with your gifts. I would also enjoy a *friend.* I won't be able to save you, not right away, but cheating death is my specialty."

Margaret watched Erin as she listened to the other witch, her face a ruck of trepidation. It was within Margaret's power to *command* the girl to serve Aubriana. Even with a 3rd Army rank, a brassboy had little voice in her own future. "You have a good opportunity here with Aubriana Harvester. She *was,* and *is,* one of the most powerful witches who ever lived. A clever and loyal friend could earn a seat at Modus Vivendi's table."

Both older witches could *feel* the girl boil up in a brine of anxiety and terror. It was within Margaret's power to hush those nerves once more, calm her with a whispered lullaby, but it seemed like coddling now. Had she been born uninclined, she could have taken a smoother, easier path, but between her gifts and the parting curse of a dead witch, she had little choice now.

Besides, Margaret thought, *Erin may temper Harvester enough that she doesn't burn the whole city to the ground.*

"I'll stay with Aubriana," Erin said, voice ajar with lamentation, loss pressing down deep behind her eyeballs and at the bottom of her throat, somewhere near the pit of her stomach.

Margaret glanced past Erin, her eyes unfocused, resigned, and saw Badger grabbing a bottle of liquor from behind the bar. "*Hey*, you going to grab one for me too, *selfish-sally*?"

"I was going to grab *two* for me, and *one* for *you'se*, boss," Badger laughed, skin sliding along visible teeth at the side.

Chuckling, Margaret didn't turn to Erin immediately, "I promise you this is the right choice. You're one of *us* now, you're a *witch*." With a nod and no eye contact, Erin acknowledged that she'd *heard*. Margaret turned toward Aubriana and her skulking glare.

"I'll be in Stockton for the next few months. Should you need me."

Aubriana lifted a hand, laying it gently on Erin's shoulder. It didn't seem like any magic was at play, just kindness for a child who'd been told she was going to *die from madness*, "You're alright, Margaret Lopez. I might like working with you. If you don't die."

Margaret smirked, stepping back a few feet closer to where Badger stood.

"I'm not a Lopez. Maggi never let me take that name. I'm just *Margaret*."

There was little else that Margaret needed to say. Aubriana didn't need to know the mosaic of emotions and theater that had been her life with Maggi, or the long years she'd spent missing and *hating* her mother in equal parts.

On her way out, leaving Modus Vivendi, Margaret stopped by the wooden mannequin meant to represent *The Bruja*. The old clothes had become faded and thin, but when Margaret ran her fingers across them, she could vividly remember the smell of her mother's hair and the sharp accent she spoke in.

Margaret untied Maggi's tan shemagh, kissed by fire and stained with blood. Woven fiber pressed against her heart, it left the building with her.

9:08pm March 26th, 39 Veilfall

Stockton, California

I'm waiting on someone, thought Margaret, *have I ever waited on anyone before?*

She considered, briefly, and the answer was rattling. *Maggi, I waited for Maggi a hundred times to return from the field or campaign.*

Maggi had *known* that she'd never return when she left for California. She even wrote a goodbye for Margaret in an old book.

"Be a better woman than me, be a better witch. I'll always be proud of you, Margaret."

It had been scrawled in Maggi's terrible handwriting. Margaret recited the words from memory, and as she did, her voice cracked along levees that kept tears from running down her cheeks.

What remained of Heart Owens' home-in-exile was an opulent husk. Black and white marble still presented a stately atmosphere, as did thick curtains of jacquard, low over windows, depicting High Sierra scenes. With nothing *to make it a home*, Margaret lit candles around the floor, near the vestibule. The orange and yellow flicker easily kissed every corner of the room, casting shadows from thick lint balls.

Margaret took her time removing the embroidered corset at her waist, casting it to red and gold tile, along with her bra and Maggi's old shemagh. She considered those things, then sat down with her legs crossed. She remained in her slip of cotton and scallop lace, a chill leaving her nipples erect and visible under a narrow margin top.

Burns on one corner of the shemagh had blackened into a chainmail crosshatch. The kind that Maggi had worn inside her jacket. Another corner was stiff and saturated in dried blood.

Margaret didn't need to run her fingers across it to know that it wasn't Aubriana's. With care she folded it first into a broad triangle, and again diagonally before pressing the damaged edges underneath until it was only a small square. Handling the fabric like a living thing, she laid it next to her and curled up on cold tile, her face resting in the shemagh. She could still smell road dust and diesel soot, along with glancing memories of a thousand miles that Maggi crossed coming to California. At times she could taste liquor or rain, at other moments the musky scent of Maggi's unwashed hair. For Margaret it was a vibrant thing, a second skin, not so different from her own Tilapia, something that her mother had lived and fought in, saturated deep in her emotions.

She could never explain this to anyone else, not even Townsend. It was a private experience that required her lonely attentions. She imagined herself surrounded by merciless gale, whispering eons and soulless ghosts that existed somewhere within the cracks of history.

I can be angry at Maggi for everything she wasn't, or I can be thankful for everything that she was.

Margaret didn't absolve Maggi of her abuses, but she did understand them better now. Maggi had been too young to adopt a fragile little girl and too young to process the loss of her lover, Alexander's father. She was thrust into the painful undulations of change, a violent and unrelenting world. Maybe a better person would have acted with greater kindness, or maybe they would have shuddered under the weight of those days as well. It didn't *really* matter.

At some point Margaret fell asleep on her mother's folded shemagh. She didn't dream, only languished in the black of sleep, eyes closed and lost. It was the clicking and fumbling of a lock that woke her, and she stirred to watch Townsend enter.

"Margaret?" He asked, his voice as soft as his big lungs would allow.

In reply Margaret blinked several times and sat up, "You ought to move in with me. I have furniture, and servants, and a bed."

Townsend stepped across the red and gold tile, his boots muculent with grime and oil. He wasn't in full kit, but he wore fatigues faded from black to a silver gray, under molle vest. Dark rings circled eyes a deep shade of charred steak, his jaw and skull heavy with stubble. She could see his balding zenith, sides still thick in follicles.

"I haven't slept much these last few weeks. Not sure how much good a bed would do."

Margaret smirked and glared, "Beds aren't *just* for sleeping, I'd remind the General."

Since their first night together, a narrow, but deep canyon had separated them both. It wasn't a lack of attraction or tenderness, it was an understanding that stood between them. It felt to Margaret that when Townsend watched her, he was waiting to lose her. She could hear it at the edge of his thoughts, feel the prickle of anxiety. He *wanted* something, and it was a thick vine that choked him in her company, a hidden desire that Margaret *did* understand.

She simply wanted him to *ask*. Prone to intimate dominance, Margaret enjoyed the strength of Townsend's resolve, and though she had every intention of *giving him exactly what he wanted*, she'd delight in hearing him speak it.

"Sit with me, General," Margaret said, folding legs under her, crossed. One elbow on her left knee and leaning forward, picayune before Townsend's full height. He did as she requested, though she giggled as he attempted to sit on the floor, joints popping.

"Twig?" Townsend asked.

"Let's share one," Margaret nodded once, smiling, "I'd like to taste your lips."

Townsend's case of cigarettes was simple, folded aluminum, dented at the edges. He withdrew a twig wrapped in red paper, and lit it with a silver lighter kept in a molle pocket.

Margaret tipped her head back, auburn hair falling away from her ears.

"Tell me what you want most in this world."

Townsend exhaled smoke through his nose and offered the red twig to Margaret. It smelled sweet and ashen between them. "I never much considered that. Never much saw the value in *things*. You can't take them with you after you're dead. Spent my whole life marching through *oceans of things*. Just rust and rot."

Margaret accepted his cigarette and ran it along her lips. A part of him was painted on the parchment. His adoration of puns just lurking at the edge of her mind, with the sound he made the moment he first entered her body, "I can have *anything* I want, but I'd trade all my velvet and silk for a right hand. *Or*, perhaps, teach this body to make do. A night where my right arm doesn't *itch*, or my fingers stop aching."

I won't prompt you, Townsend. You'll need to ask me for it, of your own will.

Margaret kept her tendrils close, whatever Townsend may have felt in her company was just ambient power, bleeding at her pores and pooling around his dirty boots. She even kept her mind *still* and *quiet*.

When Margaret handed him back the ruby twig, he accepted, but didn't lift it to his lips. Rather, he watched the tile for a moment as the paper and tobacco slowly burned, then answered her with sullen puissant, "I guess if I wanted anything, I always imagined a woman at my side. Not a *whore* or *battle buddy*. A companion who'd stand with me, ready to live forever in the death of a worthy enemy." When he finally inhaled the cigarette, his eyes rolled up and locked on Margaret, "Truth be told, since Saint Louis, I always wanted that woman to be *you*."

Margaret wished she could tell him the same. Townsend had been nothing more than a warm body the night they first shared a bed. A handsome and powerful man who she could play her games with, and forget the sting of Duke Owens' insult. What had separated Townsend from all the other men she'd known, was his *understanding* of who Margaret was.

I think some days you know me better than I know myself.

"You don't call me 'witch.' You've always called me a woman." Margaret spoke to herself, matching his stare, "I can't give you children. Would *land* do? I'm about to be *Duchess* of the Bay Area Reach. I assume I can ride a horse wherever I please in that case. *Really*, I could do that already."

It was jest, and Margaret laughed as she spoke, still leaning forward, bridging the gap between them. He didn't answer with words, rather his cigarette fell away to the tile and Margaret *knew* there was a shift in the room, but without pouring through Townsend's mind, she was at a loss to *what* he was feeling.

This was a moment of critical intimacy that Margaret had no experience with, and before she could fidget further, she fell forward on her thighs, reaching for Townsend's groin in an aggressive seizure of his trouser inseam.

Townsend froze, one of his eyebrows starting to arch up, and his lips parting.

"What just happened? What are you doing?"

I have no idea, Margaret lowered her eyelids and smirked, with no answer.

"Margaret, you don't need to grab my *dick* to show me how you feel."

Margaret's face flushed a shade of spring cherry. The *nightmare mirror* knew nothing of fear, but understood much of embarrassment in this moment.

"What am I supposed to do?"

"Just *say* how you feel." Townsend withdrew the slender hand from his genitalia, leaning down to look closer at Margaret's face, "Tell *me* what *you* want most in this world."

I am a witch, and all that comes with that, Margaret almost laughed, but it was a kiss of salt on her cheeks that came instead. She knew nothing of *affection*, and she barely understood the kind of power exchange that Townsend was initiating.

Pressing the heel of her left hand to tears, Margaret answered, "I want to *share* my lands, and my wealth, and everything I paid for with an *arm* and my own *skin*. I don't want to be *just* *Margaret* forever, and sometimes I sit around and think about what it would be like if I heard people say '*Margaret Townsend*.'"

This was the closest that Margaret could ever be to the word '*love,*' a word reserved for her real parents and the last time she'd given *them* that gift.

Does he know that's what I just told him?

"I would be *your* husband, even if you were a poor brassboy. I would offer you my name and as many years as the gods will grant me."

Townsend leaned forward, pressing Margaret backward and down, flat under his weight and strength. When he kissed her there was a static snap on her lips and she favored a soft giggle. There was no magic in that, just charged ozone. She didn't wrap her mind around him to elicit any particular response, she just wanted to be closer than flesh could allow, listening to his pulse and tasting his memories.

As their lips parted, a trail of saliva linked them briefly, "I would own your name, and your years, but I have *always* paid for the things I took."

Townsend ran his fingers through Margaret's hair with one hand, the other pressing him off the floor enough to not crush her. She met that hand with her left, palm pressed to his tendons and knuckles, rough edges of his fingers biting at her fingertips.

"You can't take something that's freely offered."

When he bit at her neck, he took no care to be gentle, and the gnashing elicited spasms of electric glee. Margaret realized as Townsend pulled at her skirt, that she could never *give* herself to a god the way Ramona had, because a god would never have seen her any differently than a mortal. She was an object, a key to turn a lock, to open a door, a clever puppy. Margaret would *never* see herself that way, and she'd never tolerate another to *own* her if they didn't have a full understanding of the soul that powered her flesh and bone.

An understanding that beat hot in Townsend's blood.

Under her breath, true to her warning, Margaret whispered her debts to the ceiling of Aurora's old home. Her chin curved up and her back arched under Townsend's ungracious entry, in litany and song that blurred language. Syllables became weak, crippled, folding into the mire and wetlands of her soused desire. Her legs had wrapped around Townsend, and she met every thrust with indigent counterassault, unsatisfied with any hammer fall that didn't bruise her pelvis.

All of it was dedicated, *gifted*, in a keenly honed tribute. Every time a shriek left her lips, every time her throat or stomach spasmed, each time her body exploded in unvarnished reply to Townsend's focused brutality. She didn't need to be a witch to experience this protracted kingdom, it was a place any could enter if they shared something with another mortal that Margaret shared with Townsend. Inclination only made the world vanish, until it seemed like Aurora's cold tile had ceased, and the candlelight gave way to blinding sun. It wasn't even possible for her to perceive Townsend beyond the parts of him that contused and confused her.

When it was all over, he didn't withdraw or roll off, he remained, pressing down to her excitation and labored breath, still inside of her.

She ran her left hand across the back of his skull, forehead pressed at the ledge of her breasts, breathing ragged.

Consider this my gift to you, Aphrodite.

10:20am April 15th, 39 Veilfall

Manteca Reach, California

"How *fucking* hard is it to lace a corset?"

Margaret turned; ready to backhand the steward that had been provided by the 3rd Army's command. She was twenty or so, with a head full of hair cut like straw, falling across her brow and ears. A brassboy, same as Erin had been, this steward was gangly, tall, and moved like a poorly animated marionette.

"Two *over* two, and keep it tight near the bottom." Margaret couldn't release her anger, nor could she unwind the knots in her stomach. Every time the wind hammered her tent, or the crack of distant thunder echoed, she found her fingers taping absently on her left knee.

"*Nada, nada,* Lady," the steward mumbled, a mouth full of marbles, words blending into each other like overflowing rivers, spilling across the causeways of grammar, "*She'cha sorsay.*" The girl's r's rolled uncomfortably long, a hallmark of California *low-English*.

There were six carrier pockets under Margaret's breasts. She'd placed each plate herself. They were a little under an inch thick, held in place by laces and clasps that pulled taut between steel bones. Unlike Margaret's other corsets, garnished in brightly dyed laces, this particular beast was a flat front overbust that climbed all the way to her throat. Reinforced metal was sewn up behind her neck, and webbed across her shoulders. Another plate would be fitted and bound in clasps over her chest, three more at her upper back.

Rüstung sklaverei.

The armor was one of a kind, and required a hundred feet or more of cord. The leather and molle were dyed black and chainmail curtains hung over her flexible joints, fixed rondels that hung like Spanish moss. It smelled like stale sweat and pungent copper, old hide and gun oil.

"*Vey-hey, vey-hey, ask'a* Lady," Margaret felt the laces tighten more agreeably this time.

"*Ask'a,*" Margaret replied, her pronunciation clear. She had no intention of dropping syllables like an overburdened boat tossing off passengers.

"*Nada, ehn'verno, gust'a, gust'a nada ease?*"

The steward wished to know how wind blew from the east.

Margaret spoke *some* low-English. A prerequisite to military command. However, the dialects evolved throughout most regions. California low-English was a mottled mop water mess of *bad* Spanish and *bad* English, shoved into a sour cake. Rather than trying to decipher the illiterate languages, she listened to the *mood* and *emotion* of the words. Not going so far as to unwind her senses and swallow the steward's mind whole, just paying attention to intent.

"It *doesn't* blow from the east, *chil'a. Como-ya, chil'a?*" Margaret answered, flatly, her breath labored. It had been a few years since she'd worn *rüstung sklaverei,* and Stockton had added a few inches to her stomach.

"*Leena,*" the girl drew out the first syllable a second longer than anyone should have, and Margaret wondered if that was how her name was *actually* pronounced, or if she was merely impregnating the word with sing-song grace.

"*Leena,*" Margaret didn't overcomplicate the name, "there's a *battlewitch on'a* enemy lines, *a'ma brutalla. Wind-witch.* worry-worry, *nada.*"

Did I just tell this poor girl that a battlewitch who commands storm-wind is nothing she needs to fear? Margaret tried not to laugh, her anxiety abating.

She lifted fingers from her knee and rested her elbow at a table to her left. Here sat tasset and cuisse, waiting for Leena to strap her into the hip and lower leg armor. Next to her seat was a small, wooden, hassock that she kicked closer to herself and lifted bare feet to rest on, ankles crossed. She was wearing bindings of black linen over her arches and tarsus. Knees and feet would remain unarmored to favor speed and agility.

Leena made a deep gasp, "*Ay-ah! Vey-hey, vey-hey. No brutalla.*"

No matter what language she spoke, she was the same as most people; the *unknown* frightened her beyond most things. This business of battlewitches, *brutalla,* was more than she wanted in her life. Margaret could hear her yearning for a mending tent, fixing fatigues, or fabricating rucks.

"*Get out,*" At Margaret's back, was a loud, direct voice, meant to convey a message that could not be misunderstood; even if Leena didn't speak high English.

Leena's mind scattered like cockroaches caught at torch light, gasping, she dropped Margaret's laces.

Margaret twisted back to see Leena flee past Lord Owens.

He was wearing a leather and molle carapace, painted and tanned in a deep shade of ecru over dark wool sark, his shoulders decorated with *real* silver epaulets, along with a high and rigid collar

"Good morning, Eric. Have you come to lace up my linothorax?"

He was *upset* enough that he was blocking none of his thoughts, yarn wound up in an ugly ball, tresses hanging about, rolling loose and free, "Don't *fuck* with me Mayhem," Lord Owns cornered Margaret's right side, boots falling as hard as he could possibly muster on carpeted dirt. The sound was impotent, "You know *why* I'm here."

Margaret pursed her lips, glancing down to her undergarments. Simple briefs made from dark linen, wrapped around her hips, below the armor line of her tasset straps, "I'm sorry, you missed your chance a few months ago. *But*, there's nothing wrong with a good forebattle *fuck*. Be a *sweetie* and summon General Townsend, would you?"

Eric's face was drawn up in a very serious scowl, warping scars with withering abandon as his nostrils heaved under the weight of climatic oxygen expulsion. "You shoved *that thing* into my sister's corpse. You brought back *Dread Harvester* and gave her flesh. *Flesh!*" When Eric Owens yelled, a thin, yet consistent expulsion of spittle departed his lips. "That was *never* part of the deal we made!"

Margaret looked up, snapping her tongue behind front teeth, "You seem unhappy."

Lord Owens opened his mouth to speak, squinting, then began a calmer parlance.

"You need to relieve Harvester of my sister's corpse, and return her body to my mother for burial. Otherwise, you can expect no land, no title, and no Modus Vivendi."

For his part, Lord Owens maintained a steady demeanor. She could *feel* his pulse racing like the wind that beat Margaret's tent, but he kept his expression blank.

"*Eric*," Margaret had never offered her brother his due appellation, and Eric Owens would enjoy a similar experience, "You knew when you came to my tent that you'd have no leverage. You can't *threaten* or *intimidate* me. What do you hope for?"

Very clearly, Margaret's imagination filled with Lord Owens' hands wrapped around her throat, squeezing, harder and harder, until his muscles twitched with exhaustion and her face turned a shade of dusk. He was projecting the image as loudly as a gunshot.

"We *helped* you. My mother called you *friend*. Yet, my sister's body now contains one of the most *ruinous* witches who ever lived. You know that Dread Harvester used to talk through her victims, *right*? She butchered *anyone* who came to San Francisco, and made *puppets* of them."

Margaret frowned in reply, "I think she didn't have a *jaw* to speak with."

"That doesn't change the fact that she crippled my mother for *life*." Lord Owens answered in a snap, his anger peeking through curtains, a curious child.

Margaret leaned forward, lifting her feet off the wooden hassock, "Your mother was never my friend. I wanted to *believe* she was, I liked pretending that maybe she was *my* mother. But she's not, she's the Heart of House Owens, and she'll do anything to preserve her family and her city. Amihan *woke me from that delusion of loyalty*. Don't tower over me, fantasize after my death, and pretend all you ever wanted was *good and shiny* things for little Lady Mayhem. You sent me to Modus Vivendi to die."

For a moment Margaret thought that Lord Owens might lunge forward, his neck tensed, and she could *hear* the weight of his thoughts as he considered what it would take to kill a battlewitch. Margaret only grinned, gesturing with her left hand, as if San Francisco was a piece of armor that rested near her, "Witches who served Aurora Cuttersark since her father's death would simply just throw up their hands to follow *me*? After I *murdered* her? You knew they'd turn on me, and you knew they'd kill me. Modus Vivendi would belong to you."

When Eric Owens replied, his voice dripped vitriol, "I think, these last few months, I underestimated you."

Margaret shrugged, for his benefit alone, "I've never been *stupid*, Eric. If you assumed I was, you'll be ill-suited as Heart. Dread Harvester will control Modus Vivendi on my behalf, *you'll* give me the Bay Area Reach, and the title of *Duchess*. You'll need to work with me, and you'll need to find a way to calm your mother. Small price to pay for the restoration of House Owens."

What are you hoping for? Margaret had already won this argument, or any version of it that Eric Owens could have brought.

"Even if I consent, my mother will find a way to kill Dread Harvester," Lord Owens turned away from Margaret, eyes groping the tent interior, tan and green canvas, waterproofed and odious with cooked fat, reminiscent of stale bacon.

"That's Aubriana's problem, not *mine*."

It didn't offend Margaret to be so clearly filled with the vision of her own violent demise. Under other circumstances she might have found it deeply erotic. However, Lord Owens couldn't leave her tent with a false sense of safety in that fantasy, "Major Grace commanded *one-third* of General Townsend's forces. When he took Santa Rosa and named himself king, he positioned himself to threaten Stockton. What do you think my 3rd Army will do if I'm dead? What do you think the *Maul* will do? Your mother's golden city won't just fall, they'll burn it down fighting with each other."

Decades will pass before the Owens Army can rebuild, Margaret thought, smile spreading across her cheeks. Just as Lord Owens had subjected her to a reverie of strangulation, Margaret now offered the visage of Stockton drowning in blackened smoke behind her noble walls.

"What do you want?" Eric Owens asked, his back still turned.

I want my arm back, Margaret thought, and offered a chuckle. "I want *only* what I was promised. I'm not here to extort you, I'm here to *retire*. I've been good to my word, I've killed Amy Lopez, as well as your sister. In a few hours I'll kill my brother, too. You *will* be Heart one day, and I'm *more than happy* to leave real responsibility to *you*."

Ramona's words girded Margaret's mind, "*Magic doesn't serve my father, he serves magic. His dream to unify North America is a joke, maps don't matter anymore.*"

Ramona Lopez had taught her aunt much more than just the nature of betrayal. As much as it felt like a beetle clawing its way up Margaret's throat, she had to admit that the young woman was correct. After Maggi Lopez had weaponized magic, the chimerical concept of nations had already begun to obsolesce.

Lord Owens turned away from the undulating canvas, his eyes falling short of Margaret's, and his jaw tensing, "You've only killed *one* of your three."

One? Margaret genuinely didn't understand, "I killed Amy *and* Aurora."

A smirk crossed Eric Owens' smooth face, "*That's* why you thought I was here to achieve something? I'm here because your promises are in doubt."

Margaret stood, left arm pressing her up, corset laces falling, leather tapping and skipping on the chair, "I put *two* rounds in Amy's chest. Her blood was in my mouth. *You and your mother saw the body.* Amihan Lopez is *dead.*"

The look Lord Owens delivered was like sand across Margaret's eyelids, but she could smell nothing like deception. She knew her face was flushing, her cheeks warm, and her chest tight. "She's not. Our scouts saw her with Emperor Lopez a few hours ago."

Margaret's nails were pressed into palms, and she realized she was holding her breath so that Lord Owens wouldn't see her exhale hard.

That's what he wanted, Margaret realized, *for us to be equals in this.*

"Please leave me, Eric," was all she said.

"Of course, *Lady Mayhem,*" Lord Owens offered up the honorific with ease and tidy respect, "I'll see you on the line."

Alone, Margaret returned to her seat, hand covering her mouth.

She could no longer hear the flogging wind or smell cooked fat, boiled leather, and the grease of steel. She was lost in the final moments she'd shared with Amy, her face covered in liquid charcoal, the wound Townsend had placed on her neck swelling up, black as the oil that coated her eyeballs.

"*...I give you my love, my worship.*"

Could a god return her to life?

"*Fucking* Lopez twins."

Margaret spit on the bice carpet, before summoning Leena to return, her voice shrill and furious. The corset laces needed to be finished, along with mounts for the tasset and cuisse.

Quickly, Margaret had somewhere to be.

12:08pm April 15th, 39 Veilfall

Manteca Reach, California

The valley sky reminded Margaret of Aphrodite's eyes.

Layered in mare's tail, clouds moved faster than was wholly natural, curling and billowing waves on a great ocean. Angry as any sea storm, it created an unsettling landscape, with Owens' farms splayed before a briny deep in the heavens above. The air smelled like moist soil, ozone, and the cool mist of tempest waiting at the precipice, eager to pounce and lay liquid upon the soft earth below.

"Mayhem Actual, *check, check*." Margaret spoke into her headset, elastic band across her forehead, microphone pressed close to her lips like a ripe plum waiting to be slurped up whole.

"*Check, check,* loud and clear Mayhem Actual." The response in her ears was ragged, a distorted voice that could have been anyone on channel command.

Margaret handed Badger her helmet, "Help me with the chin straps, please."

Just like at the Battle of Stockton, Badger wore interceptor armor, heavy gear, an antique from a bygone era. Throat, groin, and bicep protection tattered and dusty from years of wear. Round impacts on his ceramic plate had been stitched up in tan and black thread.

Standing at the center of such a large army, there was a din that resonated off the ground, reflecting back thousands of minds locked in one central mantle, a collective vibration of fear, clammy with excitement, pawing, and clawing at nerves. Her right eye twitched beyond any control she could afford, a physical symptom of being drawn down deep into the mires of anticipation. It tugged at her bare toes, pressed on her lips and demanded her attention like a starving animal or hungry lover.

Badger didn't reply, he simply accepted Margaret's high profile, ballistic helmet, and secured it on her head. Her auburn-red hair was slicked back with engine grease, and Badger snapped up the straps which held the helmet in place. He was a cool spring pond, undisturbed, in the wake of 3rd Army's anxiety.

"I hope *you'se* got the 2nd Army right," Badger wrapped his knuckles on her helmet to make sure it was secure.

Margaret smiled, the handprint on her face dark silver and steel without direct sunlight to ignite the blue and green of her Tilapia flesh, "I'm more worried about Plague Dog. We didn't equip to take on a *fire eater* today."

Badger's disjointed grin looked like an angry possum's rectum, "With permission, boss, I'll unload a magazine in her face."

Margaret had already enjoyed her personal revenge in Stockton, condemning Amy to the horrors of the Collapse. It didn't matter to her now, "Permission granted."

Badger cackled, laying a hand at the back of Margaret's neck and crouching down. He smacked her helmet into his own, the ballistic material *cracking* loudly, "The world would be a *piss-poor* place if *you'se* got those *tits burned off.*"

One of them already got burned off.

Margaret's grin was more of a leer, and when Badger released her, she turned to grab her horse's reins. A mustang, painted in hues of cherry and tan, she had once been wild in northern Nevada. Now, she was saddled and wearing her own light armor. She towered over Margaret with raw strength that defied imagination, an old world tale, a monster returned to life, impossibly tangible. Badger helped her mount the animal, and much to Margaret's surprise, he did *not* use this opportunity to grope at her buttocks, either out of respect for General Townsend, or some newfound propriety incurred from a head trauma.

Respect for Townsend, Margaret thought.

Once squarely settled in the saddle, Margaret began to erect barriers.

Bare skin on her finger tips stroked at the mustang's mane and hide, coarse and warm under her flesh. She stepped a part of herself into the animal's mind. The horse didn't *think* like a person, she was more connected with her instincts and the same senses that Margaret had been gifted at birth. Much like her mistress, she was comfortable at the rattle and din of an army. It was the storm that set her disquiet, an *unnatural* thing that didn't belong in this world, and Margaret offered calm, just as she would a person. It was easier with animals, no doubt or hissing noise to get in the way. Simply the clay of urge and desire to be molded.

Once the connection was made, Margaret slid her fingers away from the mustang and exhaled slowly, part of her mind watching through a second set of eyes. Commanding her horse forward only required the simplest breath of will. It was no different than stepping forward with her own feet, and the mustang was happy to oblige, *aware* that Margaret would keep her safe.

"I'm behind *you'se*, boss," Badger shouted, mounting his own steed at her flank.

Margaret would need to ride through 3rd Army lines to reach the front, facing east on the far side of Manteca Reach. The land here was incredibly flat, farms being ground up and pressed down by thousands of soldiers, vehicles, horses, and heavy armor. Without any kind of cover or variations in the terrain, the 3rd Army had been arranged behind narrow company columns with the largest tanks as vanguard. Those monsters would block the worst incoming fire, each row of men no more than twelve feet wide, shoulder to shoulder, with technicals and armed 4x4s abreast. It was an imperfect formation, and the men at line's edge knew their lives would be forfeited by any leaden breach. Cavalry companies set up on north and south flanks reported directly to General Townsend, while his senior staff kept direct command over their primary columns.

The allied center was all Maul armor and mechanized infantry, flanked by the weaker, less experienced Owens army. The Maul *felt* like a granite core, unmovable, a thing of ancient solidity around which soldiers could form, layer by layer, supreme in their confidence at foundations where they stood. Of the Maul's collective focus, Margaret could not have been more impressed, and a part of her found their discipline titillating.

Had I these men at my back in the last decade, Margaret thought desirously. She also wondered if Sammy, the bull of a man from San Francisco, had joined his brothers here.

As Margaret's mustang strode down the hammered and creased dirt, she passed by company commanders, also on horseback. Each one nodding as she passed. They wore a mottled combination of plate armor or simple leather, a few bound up in linothorax. She knew some by name, others by reputation, but none were strangers. They had shared much with her over the years, may it be drink, foxhole, or bed.

Captain Drake's company would have been lost in Nebraska, pinned down under mortars, if she had not arrived with her fireteam to press back on the enemy.

Captain Murashige had been trapped behind enemy lines in the block-to-block fighting during the Battle of Denver. With no radio to call for help, he and his men would have died without Margaret's rescue.

Before he was promoted, Captain Reyes was the sole survivor of an annihilated unit crossing into Saint Louis. Despite her exhaustion, Margaret had pulled him back to the Antecedent lines under fire.

None of them had forgotten the decades, or campaigns. When Townsend had called upon the 3rd Army to support their battlewitch one last time, they had answered.

They lowered their heads for her now, dropping to one knee. Quiet was expanding across the ranks. Margaret felt like a scythe weaving through barley, the anxious din of their minds cooling, finding a center soundlessly. This wasn't *just* her barriers, it was a shadow she cast, the confidence she offered, a testament to *faith* in one small witch.

This was the *last* time she'd ride to the front as *Lady Mayhem*. The last time she'd hear the quiet traipse and bite at her flanks, young pups eager to earn her affection. This was the last time she'd breathe the bitter carbon of a *thousand* idling engines mixed with sour alfalfa and horse shit. This was the last time she'd see the dust rise and fall like keys on a piano, companies moved and arranged, Sarn'ts shouting orders, and men moving as one fluid entity. This was the last time she'd watch the guidons raise, one by one, a mess of color and waving fabric. This was the last time she'd ride past monstrous armored vehicles, lead vanguard, their tan and green plate pockmarked, chewed and chipped from a hundred battles since the Collapse, diesel turbines spooling and whining like tortured animals and midnight banshees; old world magic cranking alive under the doctors of gear and oil.

This was the last time she'd ever sit *quite* so high, her spine arched, her misshapen shoulders rolled back in pride.

At the front, the 3rd Army's line, formed north to south, was nearly perfect. Heavy tank cannons protruding the ledge, elderly roots hanging off a cliff face. Glancing to her left and right it looked that the 3rd Army and Maul were spread down a road berm, an old highway that had been ground down and broken up years before, now a smooth mottle of gravel and dirt that was battered flat. Wagons and trucks would haul crops into the central of Manteca and indentured servants would likely keep the highway maintained through any rain-heavy months.

Margaret glanced over to Badger as his horse strode up next to her own. His mount was larger and mottled in shades of cream and tan, a long mane of blonde hair under crownpiece and browband.

"What are you going to do with yourself, after today?"

Badger wrinkled up his nose, and shook his head abruptly, "Never much think ahead of *today. You'se oughta'* know that."

Margaret *did* know that, "I won't have much need for a fireteam."

"Probably, I'll join the 3rd," Badger reached over his shoulder, pulling at the sling for his rifle so that it would rest at his right leg. It was painted in a mottled biscuit, chipped and scraped, matte black underneath, "*there'll* always be need for men like me. *Shitkickers*, who only exist to *fuck up everyone else's day*."

If she'd still owned her right *arm*, Margaret would have reached out, and laid a hand on Badger's shoulder. He was a drowning pool, waiting to consume anyone foolish enough to step near, "I think you should go to San Francisco. I *think* Aubriana Harvester could use a man of your *shitkicking* talents."

Badger looked away from the road, poking his tongue at intact cheek, "*Dunno, boss*. I never much liked fat girls. At least when we ride together, *you'se* make *me* look good. I'm at least *seventy-five-percent sexier* just standing close to *you'se*."

Margaret cracked up, laughing. So did her horse, with gusted winnie, although the mustang couldn't have known why.

Facing her forces, their own idling engines choking the horizon in a veil of onyx smoke, was the 1st Army. To the north, with a diagonal line, was the 2nd Army. A combined mass of easily double that of the allied House Owens forces at Margaret's rear. In all her life she'd never seen this many Antecedent troops gathered in one place, against each other, or shoulder by shoulder. It was a site full of both awe and alarm.

Her composure regained, Margaret glanced up at the undulating sky, a spatter of rain stroking her face and eyes, "We better get going. It'll rain soon."

*The 3rd Amy Captains prepare for war, by **SapFire***

12:41pm April 15th, 39 Veilfall

Manteca Reach, California

The crossroads of Yosemite and Murphy is where all three armies would meet.

First to arrive were Lord Owens, General Townsend, and Warlord Meyer, all three on horseback just like Margaret and Badger.

Eric Owens' steed was a purebred, black as dirty motor oil and twice as glossy. Rippling with muscle and light ballistic weave, great eyes of liquid night watching Margaret and her smaller mustang, twitterpated, both afraid and aroused. Townsend was kitted up much like Badger, bicep and shoulder plate shrouded in ripstop and camouflage, face a mask of stone and granite. His moustache was waxed down and obscured his mouth so thoroughly that even a tooth-wide grin would have been shrouded. Meyer wore no uniform, his thick arms naked in misting wind, covered in degrees of faded ink, a colorful mottling of art slowly accumulated over decades. He was older, though not as elderly as the old Warlord who Margaret had met to parlay with months earlier.

Reaching under the pistol strapped to her corset armor, Margaret withdrew folded fabric, old and tattered, a deep shade of dust, patterned in a complex weave of dark brown. She began to unfold her mother's shemagh. It was difficult to tie at her neck with only one hand. The fabric knotted at the back of her neck, under ducktail of auburn hair, her fingers cold in the chill wind. Townsend watched her, unblinking, and she could feel a similar pool of calm behind his skull. In his heart a warm desert wind kissed Margaret's cheeks, turning her lips rosy and her toes red.

"Your brother approaches from the east. Lady Manticore from the north," Townsend gestured down each road with a single hand, fingers held straight and thumb resting rigid.

Meyer's horse, annoyed, turned sideways, rotating on all four legs as he spoke, "On behalf of the Maul, Lady Mayhem, I want to thank you for this day."

Margaret glanced at Meyer. He didn't wear a helmet like herself or Townsend, and his face was covered in ginger and salt stubble. His forehead seemed a little too big, and his nose had been broken directly between his eyes, "I'm thinking *none* of us will die today, Warlord."

"*Ha!*" Meyer barked, his neck easily as wide as his skull, "It doesn't matter. We shall meet in no man's land. This is a holy place, and the *Lord of War* smiles upon us."

Perhaps he does, Margaret thought.

The air had fallen still in the crossroads, only smatterings of rain still hinted at the black skies overhead. Toward the 1st Army sat a series of large concrete warehouses, painted in vibrant murals, showing Manteca Reach farmers tilling and harvesting under blue skies. That seemed like a broken promise. Besides that, the ground was flat in *every* direction, only interrupted by road brim. She could see riders approaching, just as Townsend had promised, and she held her hand to the mustang to keep her fingers warm.

The northern riders arrived first.

Both were women. The first on a gray and white steed, unarmored, quick in the haunches and mean in spirit. *Lady Manticore* was more than a decade older than Margaret, with wide shoulders, hips, and an ample bosom under ballistic pauldrons and black corset, not all that dissimilar to Margaret's. Her hair was mostly a puree of white and gray, braided at the sides of her skull, back to the edges of her shoulders, waxed and greasy with silver ribbons and a crown of bronze chain and onyx beads across her scalp.

"*Little Mayy, yuh'* filthy *cunt*, you ain't died of syphilis yet?"

Margaret twisted her horse away from Townsend and Meyer, her hand still resting on the mustang's neck, keeping the animal calm. *Two* more witches in this proximity would make her jumpy. Meyer's mount reared up once, then backed away while he hollered for his animal to calm.

More accustomed to *this* kind of magic, Lord Owens and Townsend maintained better control of their mounts.

"*Fuckin'* come over here," Margaret's eyes welled up with salt and she drew her horse along Lady Manticore's, leaning across the divide and wrapping her left arm around the bigger woman.

Manticore came from the same school of magic as Maggi Lopez and Aubriana Harvester, with a strong embrace and arms that clutched like binds of rebar. Barriers spun in Margaret's mind to be so close, gusts no one else could feel crawled up and under her skin, tugging away from her bones and marrow.

"*Yuh'* got one arm, kid. How in the *fuck, yuh'* only got one arm? *Who 'ina fuck did that* to *yuh'*, little Mayy?" Lady Manticore's eyes bulged, as she backed out of the embrace, waving her hands as she spoke, the conductor of a symphony only she could hear.

"*Alex's* kid, Amy. I shot her in the chest for it, but I guess she's back," Margaret was intensely comfortable with the older woman, and it showed as her voice relaxed.

"Long time no *see,* Mayy," the second witch rode up on Manticore's right, dressed in white linen and black leather around her shoulders and sleeves. She was a little younger than her cousin, Geraldine Bianchi, and wore narrow spectacles of smoked glass, spherical and bound in golden wire. Valerie Fazio, better known as Lady Cuir de Cordoue, had been blind since birth. "You still *look blood-red* to me."

"Val," Geraldine faced away, "the girl is missing an *arm*. Her *fuckin' arm* is gone."

"Have you *seen* Amy Lopez since the 2nd Army arrived?" Margaret asked, intently.

Geraldine turned back to Margaret, gesturing to the eastern road with one hand, her eyes still wide, "I saw her. *Bitch ain't* right. White eyes, chalky skin, *yuh'* wouldn't believe it. *Bitch* feels like a *fuckin'* cemetery in winter. Like, when *yuh'* go to bed with a *fuckin'* sore throat. Val and I want *nothin'* to do with that *shit circus*."

Looking over Geraldine's broad shoulders, Valerie spoke to the dirt with a soft tone, brown hair dropping past freckles, "Her skin and bones, they're not part of the world anymore. They're connected to *something* else, something *old*."

"When *yuh'* brother shows, I'm *tellin'* him. *We'ya out. Yuh'* know that, right? *We'ya* not *fightin'* here today for you, or him, or the Antecedency." Geraldine's accent stayed as broad as her chest, but her voice fell low as she looked over a shoulder at the three commanders with Margaret. She was reading them, glancing through their minds, figuring them out.

"Ramona told me," Margaret answered, "you're taking the southwest for yourself."

Geraldine barked a laugh and held up both her hands, palms facing each other, as if she was holding a loaf of bread, "I'll call it *Angelise! Get it? 'Cause* Los Angeles! *'Cept* that name is stupid. *Gonna'* rename that whole *shiteating* city, build me a palace *onna' fuckin'* water where it's *warm*."

Margaret reached for Geraldine's hand, wrapped up in faded mint leather, "If anyone says I turned on Alexander, just know I didn't. I was *pushed* to this. I want you to know *that*, at least."

Something in Geraldine's gray eyes, or at the corners of her lips, would always be matronly for Margaret's senses. It was the same glimmer that had kept her so close to Aurora Owens and had commanded her to chase Maggi's *love* like a starving mongrel.

"*Yuh'* didn't need to tell me, little Mayy. I know *whatcha' woulda'* done. I'm *fuckin' thrilled* that *yuh'* didn't make me *hafta'* kill *yuh.*'"

Nothing in Geraldine's tone suggested she was kidding.

"Geri," Margaret lifted her head, tilting like a child who was about to ask for a second helping of dessert, "I need a favor before you leave."

"*Whatcha'* need *kiddo*?" Geraldine laughed.

"Alexander is almost here," Townsend shouted from behind Margaret, and she was thankful for the warning. She wasn't paying attention to much past Lady Manticore.

"I need that whip you *always* carry. I need to pay off one of Maggi's debts, and I think an old spirit demanded *it*."

Hanging off Geraldine's saddle was the very whip Margaret needed.

It was buttoned on with a narrow leather strap, just left of the pommel. It didn't *seem* like much. It was thick with a hammered steel hilt and notches carved and cut through leather rope. Age had polished the black edges, and barbs wound into the weapon with narrow cuffs of battered steel. It had been carved in such a way that when Geraldine cracked it, air would dart in and out of the notches, making a howling sound.

"*Screamer*?" Geraldine looked honestly shocked, "*Whatdya'* need *Screamer* for? Can't *yuh' fuckin'* negotiate a new *fuckin'* bargain for Maggi's debt?"

Margaret shook her head, "This *is* the new bargain," without thinking about it, Margaret lifted her left hand to sternum, exactly where the Eye of Shahr-i-Sokhta was resting against her skin.

"*Fuck!*" Geraldine shouted, looking away, up and to the sky around her, wind turning up fast, a violent bellow that died as quickly as it started.

"I'll *owe you*." Margaret said, ghosts of whispers at the edges of a gust tugging her shemagh and unsettling the horses.

"*Fuckin'* right, *yuh'll* owe me," Geraldine was watching past Margaret and ice tumbled down her spine. She couldn't precisely *feel* her brother, but she could *see* him in the face of Lady

Manticore. A moment of respect for what was about to happen skittered across her face. "They say *yuh'* the new Owens' mistress. *Yuh'* better *fuckin'* believe I'll come to *fuckin'* claim *yuh'* debt to *me.*"

With her left hand, Geraldine unsnapped the whip, *Screamer,* handing it over to Margaret in something closer to a toss. The weapon felt like *water* under Margaret's fingers, cool across her skin, turning warm quickly. There were memories embedded in the ragged leather. The sky was growing darker by the minute and the rumble of distant thunder strode across Manteca Reach, a giant immune to the hopes and nightmares of mere mortals.

"They're here, aren't they?" Margaret didn't look at Geraldine; instead her eyes were fixed on the plumes of diesel smoke climbing off 2nd Army's lines, perhaps a mile distant.

"*Yup,*" Geraldine said, "we *doin'* this or what, little Mayy?"

Margaret laid the coiled whip to rest at her pommel and urged her mustang to turn and face both her brother *and* Amy Lopez.

It was starting to rain now in earnest.

1:04pm April 15th, 39 Veilfall

Manteca Reach, California

While Margaret still looked ten years her junior, she'd have guessed that Alexander had aged a decade prematurely.

The weight of command burdened his brow, chipping away and cutting deep lines across his face. He was squinting, eyes against a flurry of rain that sometimes whipped across his face or shifted to spatter the back of his coat. He didn't wear the chrome plated armor of previous years. Useless, it simply cast him as a larger than life figure, reflecting the very sun on earth, polished and pristine in a messy and cruel world.

Instead, he wore black wool and heavily pocketed slacks, boots easy at his stirrups, a half-hearted endeavor to lace them. His coat had a wide hood that started at the shoulders and was stitched under two gunmetal epaulettes, falling at his neck. He had a dimpled chin and a face full of scruff that would swell to become a thick beard if left unchecked.

For possibly the *first* time in his adult life, Alexander wasn't radiating a supreme confidence. Against Margaret's mind he felt steadfast, *consistent*, but his throat was full of humility and his shoulders tensed with trepidation and *worry*.

Margaret tensed her own jaw in reaction to his coiled emotions. It was a seed of doubt that bumbled around her chest. Seconds at a time, she wondered if this was *right*, if committing murder in no man's land was the *only* solution. There was a wave of numb that crossed her fingers, buzzed at her lips, and the tops of her ears.

As Margaret approached, she lifted her hand to the Owens commanders, cautioning them to approach no further. This conversation was not *for them*, it was a private moment that would not be etched into history books, subject of conjecture for a century to come.

Alexander Lopez did not speak first, instead his daughter cast the line.

"Mayy, I'm *so sorry.*"

Her voice was a rattle. It sounded like a cicada caught in her throat. Amy's lips didn't move *quite* right, as if someone else's voice was filling in for her own. Her flesh was sallow, gray, burdened with veins of blue, and eyes that wouldn't focus directly on Margaret, instead falling somewhere to her left knee. Amy's hands were *shaking* at the wrist, palsy and frail, fingernails peeling and broken. The tattoo ink that crossed her face even seemed less crisp, fading at the edges and blending into her dull skin.

Margaret's lips curled up, and she let the weight of her helmet tip her head sideways as she spoke, "*Shut up,* Amy. I didn't come here to parlay with a *ghost.*"

Although Margaret's bitter disgust was *real*, she was actively hiding a gnawing sensation at the back of her skull. It felt as if rats had burrowed past her hair and skin, scraping their teeth against bone and spine. Amihan was *not* the woman she'd been at Stormair, she wasn't even the pitiful creature begging for mercy under Margaret's nightmares. The *thing* that rode on an auburn horse next to her father was a husk. A toy that didn't work right. There was no flash or spark, no burning cinders at Amy's lips, no bite under her skin. None of the *fire* that flickered so deep inside Aurora Owens or Maggi Lopez.

She was cold. *Cold* like a winter morning in Crafton, just after snowfall, before the shops and merchants opened for business. Plague Dog was easy to hate. *This thing* was hard to pity.

"Amy told me everything," Alexander spoke with a deep tone, free of his mother's clipped accent, still as a stone, "She told me about Ramona, and what she did to you."

Margaret moved up closer to Alexander's horse, facing his left side, still far enough away that when he spoke, he was raising his voice over the den of rainfall. It was heavy enough now that Margaret could feel the cool seeping through joints and chinks in her armor, under molle and straps, down her chest and singing at Tilapia flesh. The helmet's brim shaded her eyes against the wet unless the wind shifted, then it spit directly in her face.

Lifting her left hand up, Margaret groped her right shoulder, "Ramona didn't light me on fire. Ramona didn't take my arm, or scar my face. Ramona didn't command the Antecedent forces who fought *my* 3rd Army," without shifting her eyes from Alexander, Margaret's left hand fell away and lifted lazily to favor Amy with a stiff and angry index finger, "That's on Amy."

Margaret was joined on the right by Geraldine and her cousin.

Lady Manticore leaned over her horse's neck, wrists crossed on reigns, and shoulders hunched down. She was sneering when she spoke.

"*Yuh've* lost control, *Alex.* I know it. Little Mayy here, *she* knows. *Yuh'* kids kicked *all'yuh* china over. *Ain't* no *kinda'* glue fixes this *shit circus,* Alex. No *kinda'* glue."

He has no idea, Margaret thought, reading her brother as well as any book. He *honestly* believed that he'd *fix* everything with a rousing speech, an embattled sales pitch.

"Geri, we *can* fix this. Ramona Lopez has turned on the Empire, *turned* on all that *we* built. *All that we built*," Alexander's words were just as strong as a shot of gasoline to the throat. His fist was clenched so tight that the knuckles turned white, "She lied to all of us. We can hold Stockton here today. The 1st and 2nd Armies will force House Owens to surrender, and then we'll turn east. We will chase down my daughter like a dog, for the Empire."

Alexander summoned his *own* kind of strange magic. His ability to connect with others. Margaret could hear Maggi's voice whispering at the back of his words, a cloying righteousness that had seduced Margaret since she was a child. It was the illusion of morality, the suggestion that what he wanted to do was *right* for the sole purpose that *he* wished to do it.

He even dared to smile, and that shook Margaret to her core.

He's talking about killing his daughter. How can he summon that much conviction?

He was wholly avoiding those emotions, to such an extent that only the familiarity of his mind made Margaret smell the sorrow that was leaking from wrapped pipes in his soul.

"*Yuh'* already heard? Reno seceded. Reno *and* Omaha. How many others, Alex? How many others we *ain't* heard? *Bitches* that didn't *send a dear-john*? How many, Alex?" Geraldine lifted her hands up, gesturing east, past where Margaret sat, "*Yuh'* Empire is *dead* Alex. *Go home. Go back to Crafton. It's ov'ah.*"

With his right ankle, Alexander spurred his horse closer, between Margaret and Geraldine, his chin lifted, his chest tightening to unleash another sustained volley of direct inspiration, "The Empire is *not* dead. You served my mother, now you serve me. We can *take back* everything Ramona stole, we'll cement our foundations. *We can do this!*"

Margaret looked away from her brother, eyes skittering across Amy's quivering body, across the road and into the brown puddles that bounced under rainfall. No one was likely to notice that she *was* crying. There was something inherently cruel in all this. Allowing Alexander to *believe* he could win here today, that he could simply talk his dream back to life.

That's the problem, Margaret grimaced, *we all shared the dream until Saint Louis. We should have just turned around, we should have called it done.*

"*We* can't," Margaret heard Geraldine say, "because *we* don't *wanna.*"

"What are you saying?" Alexander answered, his voice prying into the cold snap, his mind a wall, *pushing and pushing*, just like it had always done, even when he stood only as high as Margaret's hip.

Margaret couldn't watch, and she didn't. She only listened.

"*Alex,* the 2nd *Ahmy form'lly* says *fuck off.* I'm *takin'* the Southwest, too. *Los Angeles, an' Phoenix*, all of it. *Yuh' ain't* no Emperor there. Unless *yuh'* march an *ahmy.*"

A dish fell somewhere in Alexander's mind. Margaret heard it. Old bone china, hand painted, a relic of his mother's time. It was something he'd taken for granted, even ignored, long since retired from the kitchen. It now sat somewhere on a shelf, displayed for his tender graces on the occasion that he was bored.

"Does she speak for you, Valerie?" Margaret could hear him ask Lady Cuir de Cordoue. The quiet told Margaret that Val had simply *nodded,* and every nerve in Alexander's body turned chill and prickly.

He was too stunned to be *angry.*

Margaret wished that Geraldine would do it *now.* Draw a sidearm, and just take the man out of his misery. *I'm lying to myself,* Margaret realized a second later as her own hand began to tremble, *I simply don't want to kill him.*

"Manticore Actual," Margaret turned away from the mud, reflecting dreams of ashen cloud and dull light back to the heavens. Geraldine thumped on the chest microphone, "All 2nd *Ahmy* Captains, *yuh'* ordered to *stand down.* Repeat, repeat, *repeat.* All 2nd *Ahmy* Captains, *yuh'* ordered to *stand down. Roll it up, we'yuh headin' home.*"

"Ramona got to you." Alexander said for no one's benefit.

Val turned her horse first, pulling away from her cousin and Margaret.

Geraldine turned away from the Antecedent Emperor, favoring Margaret with a smile, her shoulders squared back, "Be good, little Mayy. See *yuh'* in the funny pages."

Why are the pages funny?

Geraldine gave Margaret a wink but did not favor Alexander's eyes again. It was as if he'd simply ceased to exist in her world.

Margaret's brother didn't turn to watch them leave. His eyes were falling to the wet road, just as hers had, and she wondered if this was a behavior he'd learned from *her*, or she'd learned from *him*. It surprised her to think that a time had existed where they'd been so close.

"We still have Mayy," Amy said, her voice as broken as before, head swiveling at the chin each time she bumped a syllable.

"*No,*" Alexander looked up from the mud, facing Margaret, his eyes narrow and jaw clenched as Lady Manticore and her cousin road toward their 2nd Army. "I don't think we have Mayy, either."

There were a hundred things Margaret wanted to tell him, each one wrapped up like a bundle of kindling, bursting into flame. Her muscles ached, her mouth was parched, despite soaked armor. She wanted to yell at him, berate him for all the times he'd denied her a surname, all the times he'd mocked her, ridiculed her, or laughed at her. For the first time in his life, Alexander was watching Margaret as an equal and that might have been the kindest gift he could give.

"Do you want to enjoy the rain for a few moments, Alex?" Margaret said, her voice soft.

To the end, Alexander fought, just as he had his whole life.

"Name your price, Mayy. Name it, *name anything*, and it's yours. I'll accept you as a Lopez, grant you land, grant you power, grant you *anything.*"

Margaret blinked, unable to reply. She could recall when he was too young to take on Maggi's worst habits, when he had been a baby, and then a toddler with mischievous eyes and a daring grin. His hair was slicked down, just as it was now, promising her things he couldn't even understand the value of.

"*Emperor Lopez,*" Lord Owens shouted, separating from the other commanders, his horse lifting spindly and muscled legs as he approached. All the pride he'd been denied these last few years was released in the rain like a new kind of flood, "Stand down your army, or the *independent* House Owens *will* defend themselves."

"What would Maggi say?" Alexander's mouth fell open, "You're an *Owens* witch now?"

Margaret's expression changed and she could feel her fingers and toes again.

A hundred more replies swept up through her mind, just as dry and brittle as the last batch of kindling. Her left hand lifted, halfway between her pommel and the pistol under her breasts. It would be so easy just now, to thumb the weapon free, draw, and *shoot*. There'd be no more words, no more fake goodbyes, and certainly no more moments left where Alexander could pretend he still held authority.

"I don't care what she'd say," Margaret shrugged, "she's dead."

I've missed you, and I will always miss you.

She *wanted,* more than anything at this very second, to be afraid. She wanted to fear her brother's death, fear the way her heart would split, fear the agony of his loss, but it couldn't be summoned. The weapon she'd forged of her mind since she was a child was nothing more than cold steel at the pulse of her nerves now.

I'm sorry, Margaret considered saying, but that was a lie. She *wasn't* sorry.

You don't deserve this, she thought next, but she didn't *care*. She didn't deserve to be set on fire, she didn't deserve to lose her arm, or wear fish skin on her face, but it didn't take those things away.

I wish things had turned out differently. That was *also* a lie. Townsend, the Bay Area Reach, all of this was something that she craved. A belonging that she'd never found with Maggi or Alexander, regardless of whatever love she felt for them.

In this, Margaret found the words that she wanted to speak, here at the end.

"Thank you," Margaret said, "for being my brother."

It was *now* that she realized, they'd both simply accompanied her through this life. They'd *never* been her family, and she'd always been foolish in her attempts to make them so.

I don't need to belong.

"Thank you?"

Alexander Lopez asked, eyes dark and hard against the rain, turning from Lord Owens. He never saw Margaret's left hand move up another few inches and thumb the snap on her pistol, nor did he see her draw, fingers clutching grip.

All he saw was the shadowed interior of a 9mm barrel leveled at his face.

The next few minutes were a blur for Margaret. She had no time to *feel* anything, only to act and react. The first round from her pistol penetrated her brother's left eye, snapping his head back, causing his body to shift on the horse. She squeezed the trigger again, allowing her arm to shift *up* by a millimeter, and placing the second bullet in his forehead, just above the brow. Both impacts caused a sputter of thick crimson, spit up from an infant, no longer able to hold breast milk. The caliber was too small to shatter her brother's skull, or pull apart the flesh of his face. There was a stark moment, frozen, for just half a second when he still sat upright on the horse, *fighting until his final breath*. Remaining eye focused on some distant horizon, that only the dead could see.

Alexander's horse reared up, kicking back the body of Margaret's brother, losing it from the saddle, ankles caught in stirrups. There was no time for Margaret to calm the animal, it bolted for its life, hammering metal shoes into the soft road, fleeing the unknown.

Alexander's body was drug under the animal's haunches.

Amy *screamed* next. Something vile and bloody churning up from her throat, the projection of agony so foreign and strange to Margaret's senses that she barely recognized it as human. It bent and pressed at the air, startled her horse first, then Eric Owens' mount. The very rain that pelted them seemed to consider flight.

With 9mm still drawn, Margaret's eyes were wide, mind open, *aware*, as everything around her began to fall into a whirlpool.

"*Why?*" Amy's cry bellowed, the syllable drawing out, hands clutching her face, clawing at the skin, ripping loose membrane, but no blood would wash free.

"All Captains, *hold!* All Captains, *hold!*"

If Amy's howling was acidic and loathsome, Townsend's voice pouring through Margaret's headphones made her feel like she was asphyxiating in molasses.

"*Kill her Mayy! That's a goddamn order!*" Eric hammered in a bellow, fighting his horse, gesturing wildly toward Amy.

"*Why?*" Amy demanded again.

Her fingers pulling at the skin around her mouth, bloody spittle running down her chin, the very vibration of her voice was driving Margaret's mustang mad, the animal *actively trying* to break free of Margaret's control, pulling so hard that Margaret fell forward for a moment without a second hand to keep her balance.

From the direction of the 1st Army line, one of the big Antecedent guns fired. The whine of a shell cutting through the rain and wind met Margaret's ears before the *thump* of ejaculation, chasing a *wump* of impact, one-hundred meters away.

Margaret took a shot on Amihan Lopez, but the first round went wide. She was easily twice the distance that Alexander had been, and Margaret's left hand *was not* dominant. The second round found her throat, punching through Amy's windpipe and out the back of her neck, silencing the grinding revulsion of her cries, and calming the horses for a moment.

"*Movement, five-by-eight. Enemy forces are moving! Repeat, enemy is moving.*" Margaret couldn't recognize the voice in her ear, metallic noise pressed like a beetle looking to burrow inside her skull.

"*Confirm, 1st Army is advancing.*" A second voice cut in, a calculated squawk that made her head turn, watching Townsend's response. Lord Owens struggled to stay upright, Meyer was retreating, and Townsend had clutched his headsets to better understand whatever channels had come across.

"*Boss!*" In all the chaos, Margaret had lost sight of Badger. He was now on her left side, voice projected in a cry above the radio traffic that filled Margaret's mind, "We need to go! *We need to go now!*"

Two more shrill songs played across the sky, a siren of thunder, trapped in a cage between *thump* and *wump*. These explosions were *much* closer, pelting the road in chunks of wet soil and stone. The air smelled like sulfur and petrichor, humidity braying at Margaret's sinuses and lips.

It was then that she caught a glimpse to her right, away from Badger, and realized that Amihan Lopez hadn't toppled from her horse. Instead she stood stiff on the animal, onyx cruor fell across her pauldron and plate carrier, her lips spread and teeth smeared with glistening black.

Badger saw Margaret's eyes shift away, back to Amy's horse. He couldn't help but sneer against his own scars, watching, and *refusing to believe.*

Amihan was *still alive.*

Throat perforated, her arms were lifting, fingers jittering like a spider's legs before they realized they were dead. The air was curling up around her wrists. This wasn't the simmering blur of *heat* under a fire eater's command. It was as if clear pustules bobbed and popped the world inside out. The very core of this energy made Margaret's eyes *ache*, a savage tugging at the back of her sockets, where nerves were tethered. Margaret's stomach turned, and beyond her control, clear liquid was summoned up and out of her throat, running down her lips, warm against the rain, splattering on her saddle and crotch.

"*You* need to leave Badger," Margaret coughed, her chin quivering, "I'm not going anywhere until this bitch is finally dead."

1:28pm April 15th, 39 Veilfall

Manteca Reach, California

Pistol still drawn, Margaret held it level and unloaded the remaining rounds in her magazine on Amihan Lopez. It was a total of *thirteen shots*, each jerk of her trigger finger, each hammer strike on the primer, tossing back the slide, muzzle flash as clear as the sun.

Not every shot hit, but she watched as they split open Amy's plate carrier fabric, exploded chainmail, and blistered her right arm. Two bullets hit the other witch in the face, one shearing open her cheek, shattering teeth in a mist of enamel, another cleanly taking her ear off.

Amy didn't *move*, her body didn't shift, or pry away from the saddle. She simply leaned in with eyes that had turned the color of dirty paint thinner. Thick fluid fell out of her mouth, chunky, full of broken teeth, dragging her uvula and tonsils as if her entire mouth had turned to a ragged, frothing soup.

You should be dead, Margaret raged past the bile that burned her gums, *you should be dead!* In impotent anger she even tossed the 9mm at Amy, slide locked back.

Somewhere in that rage, Margaret's mount *finally* freed herself, mind rendered aloft, falling prey to panic, a feeling Margaret had never known from an animal in her entire life.

Because, Margaret realized, the mustang's hide and skin were *melting* off.

The animal reared up on two legs, kicking back at Amihan, clawing with hooves, as cherry and tan meat curled and fell to the ground with a surfeiting slap and flop. Muscles fell free like burned rope, loose and greasy, bubbling in ruby smears. The bit fell from her mare's mouth, then armor at her haunches, leather and steel along her neck, all of it falling to saturated earth. Ligament and cartilage, even the poor creature's eyeballs, melted and ran down cherry hide, exposing bone stained a deep ecru and sour crimson.

It had been only *seconds* and the animal smelled like it had been left to putrefy in the Nevada sun for days. Caught in shock and tangled in the last bastions of a dying animal's terror, all Margaret could do was lean forward and exhibit some kind of *control* on the beast. Some part of the mustang was *still* alive in her last moments, wild and pleading, listening to Margaret's retching command.

Get me close to the bitch and I'll avenge you.

The dying beast launched herself into stride, covering long yards between both witches, as it swole over itself on a wave of rolling gore. Her intestines fell from underbelly, along with her stomach, half-digested alfalfa and carrots withered up in a blend of rank feces and stale urine to press the animal in a sliding gush. Her bones began to snap under their weight, under *Margaret's weight*, disintegrating in a rain of slender shards.

It wasn't a majestic assault on Amihan, and when she struck the ground, the horse's fracturing skull was driven into the abdomen of her armored corset. She was close enough to grab Amy's left leg with one arm, craning downward, pulling Amy off to one side, unbalancing her mount.

"All allied Captains, advance! Weapons free! Weapons free!"

Townsend's voice was kissing at her ears, even as he shouted orders. His voice level, smooth, as though he was pouring coffee with care, to avoid a splatter or spill.

Margaret pressed her mind close to that voice as she rolled back, her knee sliding out from under her as a flood of bubbling intestines and shit slid under, knocking Margaret to the mud, the back of her helmet grinding small stones.

She was staring up at Amihan's horse, its limp penis flapping as it tried to *back away*, to free itself of this gelatinous nightmare.

"Vanguard-five and ten! Tick-tick-tick! Tick-tick-tick!"

Troops in contact, Margaret thought, a 3rd Army Captain shouting into her headphones, just as Amy's horse shifted up and stomped a metal shoe down a few inches from Margaret's helmet. The splatter of mud and rot hit her in the face and she could feel Amy jerking at the horse's right shoulder to push him forward.

The horse turned, pulling Amy away from Margaret's groping hands, as she attempted to claw out from under the animal. It was too late, and she felt an impact at the back of her helmet. One of the animal's hooves landed square against her head, driving helmet to mud. The front of Margaret's chin strap broke, and her radio gave a final crackle before headphones were torn out.

I'm going to be trampled by a horse, Margaret thought, gasping at the rotting carnage and sludge under her, remembering Saint Louis.

Blind, Margaret could only hear something like a shrieking upchuck from Amihan's direction, followed by *howling* from the air above.

Thump-wump, thump-wump, two shells hit.

So close, that Margaret could feel a wash of heat and change in pressure.

It felt like physics had been switched off, the gods hammering an emergency *stop* button, and Margaret was weightless as the world was suddenly upside down.

For a moment Margaret could see flame, then the sky, *then the horizon,* followed by the sky again. The world had no weight or frame of reference. Even Amy's horse was caught in this strange swimming lesson through summer air that dried her lips and kissed her eyelids shut.

It's not summer, Margaret thought, just before she hit the ground.

1:34pm April 15th, 39 Veilfall

Manteca Reach, California

Margaret hadn't been *fully* knocked out by the impact, but her head swam loose and free just like contents of her mustang's stomach.

The sky was once again *up*, coating her face in cool nips and nibbles of rain. The world was free of *sound*, and a long-pitched whine was digging into her skull like a pack of earwigs intent on tunneling through her brain.

This is fine, Margaret decided, *this is all fine.*

Pulling herself up, she appraised her body. Her one arm was working, bones and joints moving as they were meant to. The same could be said for her legs. Her helmet was long gone, but if she was wounded, it wasn't anything that would kill her.

The rain had accelerated, now falling at a sustained rate across the mud below. She couldn't orient herself, and she was no longer sure *where* the 3rd Army lines were. As she rolled into a kneel, Margaret realized Amy's horse was still alive, jerking wildly with broken legs bent and bobbed at obtuse angles. The younger woman was *under* the animal and struggling to get free, silt and rocks tossed in all directions.

Stumbling up to her feet, Margaret tripped once and almost fell, planting her bare toes on the wet earth, grinding in her heels, and trying to reorient herself beyond the spiral that seemed to pull her down.

My neck hurts, she thought, *so does my head.*

She reached into the surviving horse's mind and clamped down on all its fear and panic. She couldn't *take away* the animal's pain, couldn't heal the wounds, she could only whisper a lullaby and convince the great beast that it'd be okay.

Margaret fell forward, over the animal's stomach, gashes and cuts exposed bright claret along his hide. It didn't smell of boiling rot, not the decay of a creature left to die, slagging off skin and hobbling bones. No, it smelled like *blood*, and the rain smelled of ozone. In *this* violence Margaret found something familiar to grasp onto, something to make her forget the last few minutes.

Margaret was face to face with Amy Lopez. Her throat was a pool of black wine, thick, and gurgling with bubbles that snapped and popped. Her jaw flopped wildly, eyes wild enough to pause Margaret. They weren't the dim, matte milk from earlier, these were eyes of *little Amihan*, the angry girl who'd rallied against bedtime, vegetables, and all the terrible injustices of childhood. Amihan was there, *somewhere*, in this twisted body that refused death.

She was there and she was raging back at Margaret.

This pause allowed Amy the time she needed to ball a fist and punch back at Margaret's face. A solid blow, enough to make Margaret's teeth *click* together loudly and drop her sideways off the still horse.

I need to rest a moment, anyway, Margaret thought, sliding off the animal, then struggling back up to her feet. She couldn't shake the spinning in her head, and she wanted to throw up again. She hadn't *hurt* earlier, but now there was a dull ache at one of her ankles, and her ribs had begun to chirp in dismay.

Struggling back to her feet, Margaret ran fingers through her wet hair. They came back bloody. As she studied those fingers, rain cleansing her cruor, more than anything Margaret just wanted to lay down. Close her eyes. Maybe take a nap.

Blinking hard, more for her sake than any need to hide from the rain, Margaret twisted and turned back to see Amihan standing, out from under her calmed horse.

She wasn't quite *standing*. Her left knee was bent to one side and the leg of her trousers were black and swollen. Much of her weight was shifted against her good leg, and her hands were clenched fists that still shook at the wrists.

You killed my father, Amy whispered, her lips clamped shut, her throat tattered, she was projecting a sound into Margaret's mind. Just as the eyes *looked* like a young Amihan, so too did her voice, a sing-song tambour, the same as when she was eight or nine years old. Begging for flan before bed, leaning across every syllable she thought might gain her the slightest favor.

You killed my father, Amy repeated in Margaret's mind.

"I'm sorry," Margaret said, her words an echo in her own mind, lips moving, speaking. She remembered *what* an apology was, after all.

Just a selfish act to relieve a person of their own guilt.

I loved you, Mayy, did you ever know that?

Margaret watched part of Amihan's chest separate, just above her plate carrier. The dark fabric tattered out, and something zipped through her, trailing a long stream of dark mist, before impacting into one of Margaret's plates. The force pushed her back. Most of the impact was absorbed across ceramic armor, buried beneath a layer of molle and leather. The *smack* seemed to reverberate through her body and Margaret could hear her *teeth* grind.

The tracer fire looked like stuttering flame. Extruded, dripping horizontally, molten hot. A dozen more rounds whistling past Amy *and* Margaret.

This is no man's land, Margaret remembered. *How could I have forgotten?*

Head still spinning, ears ringing, her lips cracked and dry, Margaret set into stride. Each foot fall planned and coordinated as she rushed Amihan. They could talk all day about their *feelings*, or Margaret could finally end the witch who had traded flame for rot.

She could feel the warmth of Amy's dying horse under her toes as she lifted up and past the prone animal, wet gravel digging into her heels, rain sweeping her face, the bitter smell of sulfur around her. Margaret leaped at the zenith of her lunge, throwing all her weight into Amihan, thrusting her back into the dirt, the vibration of the impact sending shivers up Margaret's arm, past her shoulder, and rattling her mind to the point where she almost blacked out. There was no time for this. She didn't have a *knife,* she didn't have another *pistol,* but she did have her *teeth.*

They killed The Missouri Witch, and they would be plenty fine to kill Plague Dog.

Amihan's skin had turned rough, collapsing under Margaret's teeth like gristle. Her thick and languid blood was a vile taste of copper and spoiled milk, mixed up in chalk and bitter roots, spilling around the edges of Margaret's lips. Once more she turned *her own magic* on herself, allowing proto-human instincts to seize her mind, clutch her throat and *fight* Amihan harder than logic pled reasonable.

She ate mouthfuls of Plague Dog, raw.

Amihan didn't go without a fight. Her fists pried and pressed the smaller woman away from her, punching at her face, her temple, her skull where she bled across auburn hair turned dark. She quaked, blood no longer drawing close to her skull, ceasing to power her body. Death *should* have claimed her when she was shot in the throat, *death should have claimed her now,* but the body simply kept plowing ahead, more crippled by the second.

There was no more thought between the two.

Margaret's primal madness had reached out and spread across Amy's oyster skin, shriveling in the mud. One of Margaret's molars tore clean from her jaw, around Amy's neck, suckled deep inside, swallowed whole, and lost to twisted tendons, fetid and blossoming in pure black sludge.

In her final moments, Amy was able to slip to one side, twist her weight over and roll away from Margaret. Heaving herself up, she pulled herself over the smaller woman's chest. Grabbing her one, flailing arm, Margaret's knuckles were forced back into soused mud. Amy's neck was no longer straight, it fell to one side, cartilage and trachea flopping forward to her chest and tattered armor. Her eyes didn't work right anymore, her jaw was open, and her tongue fell like a snake cut in half by a wide shovel.

Seconds passed, and Margaret *screamed* into the bile and ruin that disgorged from her lips, down her cheeks and throat, threatening to suffocate her. She saw Amihan withdraw the knife from her side, right hand clutching it like a monkey would hold a foreign tool. Her fist dropped, hard, hammering the fixed edge directly into Margaret's sternum. The first strike was caught in molle and leather, no plates to protect her.

The second strike *penetrated* Margaret's armor, but didn't bite skin.

The impact was stopped by the Eye of Shahr-i-Sokhta. It cracked under Amy's force.

Releasing Margaret's left arm, Amihan lifted the blade high, both fists clutching it in a mottled array of ill-placed fingers and slick gore. The tip curved up, and a glint of tracer fire made it sparkle for a fraction of a second.

Amy brought the knife down, a third and final time, into Margaret's chest.

Rüstung sklaverei gave way, and the Eye of Shahr-i-Sokhta shattered into a hundred pieces, turning hot for a second, then ashen. As the knife plunged down, ten, eleven inches, it didn't break through Margaret's sternum. The metal grew soft and powdered, the grain disintegrating.

Margaret was overwrought with rage and nausea. The world was silent and still. Amy was collapsing forward, her fists pressed together at Margaret's sternum, their foreheads meeting and Amy's muddy drool flowing across Margaret's lips. Amihan's eyes fixed on Margaret's.

I still love you, Mayy.

It was all Margaret heard before an unmitigated beam of light shot up, erupting from where the Eye of Shahr-i-Sokhta had shattered. It thrust Amy up and off Margaret, bathing her ruined throat in blinding syrup, a thick and malleable thing that reached for the storm, and past the clouds. The glow was blinding as it spread, a complex network of roots that divided, multiplied and dimmed.

It looked like the very world around Amihan had fractured. A fracture that flowed in all directions, far above Margaret, stabbing her deep in the throat and mind, washing away her disorientated vertigo.

Something was happening. Margaret could feel it under her flesh, yanking at her eyelashes, twisting her nipples, sawing against flesh and melting her teeth where they sat inside of her jaw. It was an uncensored glimpse of the world *beyond the Veil*, something a human mind wasn't engineered to understand. That Margaret could lay under the Veil fracture and watch it *consume reality*, without losing her mind, was an act of endurance beyond imagination.

The veins of liquid gold soon faded around her, and so too did the strength of Amihan's body. Her eyeballs had washed milky, and her skull tipped down, dead, before falling.

All Margaret could do was lie on the ground, clutching at her sternum with one good head, *screaming*. She screamed until her voice turned raw and fell silent. The fractures and cracks in the world were dim now, and everything felt quiet. She didn't know how much time had passed, she couldn't fathom a measurement like that. She had no physical connection to the universe. Reality had become a concept so distant and foreign, that the notion of *sky, ground, and rain*, almost terrified Margaret to apoplectic frothing.

Forcing back the symphony of madness, Margaret braced herself on an elbow, rolling to face the ground. She tugged thick and ragged gallimaufry free from her lips. Skin had lodged itself in her throat, tendons and cartilage. She ejected *all* of what had once been Amihan from her mouth, throat, even her stomach. Her breathing was desultory, broken, and she was blind with tears and blood.

What the fuck? What in the fuck? She repeated, a quaking mantra, each word deconstructed until she could remember *language* and what it was to *think like a human.*

Covered in carnage and dire entrails, Margaret stood up and away from Amihan's cold corpse. Around her a battle was raging in a strange kind of slow motion ballet. She could see the blurs, wisps of motion, flame, expulsed dirt, and engorged organs. It was a whipped spiral of color, dark and intense, jerking across a spectrum of understanding.

This was *reality,* but it was not the reality Margaret stood in.

Every inch of her body shook. Her auburn-red hair had fallen across her face, and part of her armor *glowed* with the residual energy.

Was that all it took? To shatter the eye? It couldn't be so simple.

Bordering on madness, Margaret laughed at herself, a fragile cackle that steadied her mind and whispered things at her ears she couldn't possibly understand.

With her left hand outstretched, just as she'd held the pistol earlier, Margaret pressed her thumb, index, and middle fingers together and did the only thing that seemed prudent.

She snapped her fingers.

2:02pm April 15th, 39 Veilfall

Manteca Reach, California

Snap.

Less than fifty-feet away from Margaret, an armored vehicle from the 1st Army struck one of her own heavy tanks at something close to full speed. Part of its opposing treads caught the other vehicle head on, ripped free, and unwound across the field in spinning pieces. The impact launched a sixty-five-ton monster up and over the ground, shearing off the 3rd Army tank's main gun. Mud, sparks, shattering plate, gear and equipment, expulsed up before the first tank rolled to one side in clamorous ruin. The sound was a deep belly-punch, a noise that could only exist between two unbreakable objects meeting each other. Cheap toys, painted in acrylic, torn asunder at the hands of gods.

Gods.

Margaret could *see* and *hear* clearly again, though the battlefield around her had become a vociferous curtain of bedlam. She could *sometimes* catch the staccato pop of small arms fire, but it would melt into the heavier reports, tank-killing guns, and artillery. Men were shouting commands from both sides, but that bled into screams of the dying.

Against all logic, she simply stood in the center of the fray under a cool rain, pelted by falling lumps of earth.

This isn't the same. This isn't right.

There was a boundary to existence, at least as the mind could observe. When the Veil first collapsed, many boundaries had been lifted, creating something like a *ledge* that could not be crossed. Beyond that border, past the waking world, *things* existed beyond the Veil. Some had names, gods possessing flesh, djinn powered mechanisms, and skulking creatures at city foundations. Language had never expanded to understand others, and every witch knew that there was still a wall staving off the unknown.

What was the story, mother? The story of the dark?

A round smacked into Margaret's corset, shattering one of her ceramic plates, and likely fracturing a rib. She didn't wince, she could barely feel the pain now, her mind was so far removed that the battlefield ceased to matter.

"When man discovered fire, he would never let it grow cold."

Margaret could hear her mother's voice, remember her face illuminated by the dancing flames over crisscrossed twigs, the kiss of wood smoke and warmth at her fingers and toes.

"He kept that fire burning, as he traveled, as he migrated. He slept by that fire, with his back to the darkness. He knew for a fact that if the light would ever go out, should the shadows rule, he may never wake."

Another round caught Margaret on her largest back plate. This one shoved her forward but didn't penetrate.

Margaret spoke to a ghost, or perhaps simply herself. *I think the Veil is gone.*

"Lady Mayhem!" Someone shouted into Margaret's ear, close, so close that she could feel their spittle coat her cheek, hands on her arm, jerking her back to a physical body, the sounds of battle winding up around her, *louder and louder*, until she wanted to claw her own ears off just for a hint of silence.

When she spun, Margaret was looking up at a painted face, deeply shaded around the eyes and nose, with stripes down his lips, redolent of a skull. Brows were set low and his eyes were tiny, *angry*, and familiar to her.

"Sammy?" Margaret asked, her voice a shriek in melee.

"You can't just stand here, we *hav'ta get'cha* behind cover!"

Sammy's booming voice didn't ooze nearly as much rage as those *tiny* eyes and Margaret imagined tugging them from his skull, suckling them in her mouth, past her lips and tongue, like skinned grapes.

Glancing past her, Sammy lifted his lips in a snarl, then shoved Margaret to one side, so hard that she lost her footing and fell to the mud once more. Amy's horse, now dead, was next to her, but the young woman's body was gone.

A soldier from the 1st Army, wearing muted sage and dark tan, with animal skins across his shoulders had launched directly for Sammy. He was a foot shorter than the big man, but his eyes were drunk with lust, an antique AK-47 clutched with no magazine. The bayonet hilt and barrel were caught in Sammy's right hand, a curling hunk of flesh colored steel, jerking the 1st Army man forward. Sammy's left hand laid into the Antecedent with *one and two* hammer strikes, and Margaret saw the smaller man's nose shatter like a rotten apple.

Rifle protruding from the ground, bayonet buried deep in mud, Sammy lunged, hands wrapped around the Antecedent's helmet, jerking him forward and slamming his face into the butt of the AK-47. Rain caressing her face, Margaret could see the man's skull collapse like a paper mache doll, skin taunt at his cheeks, eyes bulging free, and teeth expunged. The man was dead before Sammy tossed him to the earth.

I'm so glad we fucked, Margaret thought in a penultimate gasp, a momentary distraction from the real danger she and Sammy were in.

"You still ain't no Owens daughter," Sammy shouted down to the prone woman below him, offering her one of those big, strong hands, "*but yer' all we got!*"

Margaret accepted Sammy's hand. The large man tugged her up with one, effortless jerk. He was wearing a single plate carrier strapped up with two knives and a rifle dangling off his chest. In Maul fashion, his shoulders and arms were bare, painted in mottled charcoal patterns.

Margaret rapped knuckles against her chest plate, focusing herself, preparing to join the fight. "*If you walk with me to hell, I will give you such a glorious death that your Maul shall sing of your deeds for a hundred years to come.*"

Sammy remembered that promise. Something at the edge of his jaw told Margaret that he hoped *she* wouldn't forget. She also suspected he'd cut his way through the battle in search of the little witch he'd met in San Francisco, who once offered him *glory*.

Chin tipped up and tiny eyes lifted, something akin to awe ran across the muscles in Sammy's face. Margaret didn't follow right away. She could feel something tighten in her spine, pulling her close to the ground, as if every vertebra was being tugged apart. It was physically painful and made her aware of every nerve in her body. The twisted ankle, cracked ribs, and the blood that didn't dry on her scalp. *All of it* burned bright, magnified for a brief second of agony.

With her face gnarled up like a dying olive tree, Margaret finally let herself turn toward the gaze that captivated Sammy.

A hundred feet or more above the 1st Army lines, the very air and wind pulled back on themselves, twisting into a gouge that glimmered golden light and bled liquid night across burning vehicles. The anomaly *hurt* to watch, like needles pressed into Margaret's irises, pushing deeper and deeper until she began to weep.

"*Gods be fucked,*" Margaret whispered.

The light ebbed and warped around something that resembled labia, then burst out in a violent quake, blurring air in jarring shimmers. From the eruption came a *physical form*, impossibly feminine. She was twice the height of Sammy and proportioned like a child's drawing, neck extended, arms twisted, and bosom curved at the *wrong angles*. All of her was *wrong,* undeniably impossible, and entrancingly *erotic*. Her flesh was *golden*, shimmering liquid, as bright and true as any polished coin, flowing like water, lighter than air, and granite solid.

Margaret had seen gold like this before. The *apple* Eris had offered at Stormair. She already knew who this was, she remembered it all.

"Do you know what I look like free of this flesh and bone I wear, free of costumes and lies? Those are my terrible wings."

Those wings spread up from Eris' spine, unfolding, piece by piece, extending *hundreds of feet* in either direction, midnight cuneiform, a thousand feathers, drooling void and weeping night. In her wings, Margaret could see night skies of untold eons, a million whispered dreams, falling abandoned.

Eris *screamed*.

It was noise beyond imagination, and perhaps *hearing*. It was a howl of ultimate satisfaction, as if every orgasm Margaret had known in life were bound up in a heavy ball of clay and projected into her mind, *every mind,* around her. Chattering clatter, uncontrolled anxiety, something *like* fear and adulation.

Uncontrolled and unsustainable chaos.

Margaret closed her mouth suddenly, aware that she too howled in unison. It was only now, under the anodyne of her own self-control, that Margaret looked down to see the liquid gold running off Eris's legs, breasts, and hands. It was *burning* through tank armor, falling upon the 1st Army, molten and glowing, so hot that the air bled. Men were screaming and running in all directions, begging for their lives, *begging for death*, hot metal scalding their arms and legs, blinding them, crippling them, pooling on the ground, an inglorious beauty.

"That's impossible," Margaret heard Sammy say, as she watched men boil alive.

Not anymore, Margaret thought, "The Veil is *gone.*"

Eris flew across the battlefield, turning away from Margaret and Sammy. Her wings moved like a great condor, leaking onyx. The downforce created dust devils and gusting wind that slapped and pawed about Margaret's face and sticky hair. Both armies were cast into total chaos, platoons turning on each other, several squads on both sides running free of cover and charging their opponents with bayonets and knives. Some were driven so mad that they placed a sidearm to their own skulls.

There was no more order, no survival or flight, there was only an altar on which wholesale death was being offered to the heavens.

"What do we do now?" Sammy asked quietly, his voice a rattle, something like joy cracking his vowels and something like terror leaking down his throat.

I don't know, resigned, Margaret spoke it. A lifetime as a witch counted for naught.

"I don't know."

One of the 1st Army Abrams was dead, directly in front of where Margaret and Sammy stood. It had been cover for advancing companies, and if it had kept rolling earlier, it would have crushed Margaret. She'd have been bent up and pushed deep into the mud, bones shattered, and internal organs exploded. Now it sat quiet, coated in gold, burning metal creeping over every inch of its armor, across carbon smears. Slowly, almost imperceivably at first, the gold began to shift and turn chrome in a deep shade of fetid urination, whispering, holding Margaret's heart, a great magnet.

We're not done yet.

She knew it in her marrow. Her fingers trembled and her throat groaned no differently from when Townsend savagely penetrated her in the most intimate of moments.

Sammy wasn't *afraid,* standing at her side. He was only *angry.* Angry that he was babysitting a *witch* when he should have been at his brothers' side. Angry that he didn't understand these awesome and terrible sights. Angry that he had not yet killed enough of the enemy. Angry that he couldn't simply *fuck* Margaret right now, and even angrier that he couldn't *fuck* Margaret *and* kill Antecedents at the same time. Margaret could hear it, pouring off him, a raging waterfall.

Margaret was entertaining Sammy's fantasy when she realized *who,* or *what* was here.

She told me the Lord of War was coming.

The tank, rigid and chilly chrome, was bending and breaking under its own weight. Thick plate armor and metal folding, clipping back like rice paper, pulling itself apart. The sound of *ripping steel* was something Margaret could never have fathomed. Piece by piece, something in the shape of a person tugged and heaved lose, freeing itself from the tank, a manifest entity, some kind of ingot creature that moved with a jerking twist of legs and arms. Melting, curving, and binding with iron tendons and muscle. Step by step, it approached, fingers rolled, arms next, layer by layer, growing. Biceps, triceps, brachioradialis, and deltoids formed and pulsed with a vibration of solid metal.

At times it seemed like veins of brass wrapped up around ligaments. Jagged and broken iron, almost ore, fell off and heaped to the earth. Sometimes it would shimmer and reflect fire light. Other times it was dull and dusted in deep grooves, moist in oil and flexing beyond any reality metal could achieve.

Less than ten feet away, the monstrosity was shoulders above Sammy, dwarfing Margaret as if she was a small cat, feral and wet in the rain, nothing of consequence.

Sammy dropped to his knees. *He knew* who this was.

"Ares, *lord of war.*"

Armor plate, god of hate, Margaret remembered The Beast.

Somehow this sculpted creature of steel, brass, and chrome was more defiantly *powerful* than a five-hundred-foot-tall golem, commanding unambiguous authority and palpable brutality. Margaret was clenching her teeth so tight that her gums bled, her heart forcing its way free of her chest, and for brief moments she could feel *both of her fists* balled up.

"When the Eye of Shahr-i-Sokhta shattered, the remains of the Veil did too," Margaret spoke, her mouth open, a strained gasp forming syllables. She wanted to *turn* on Sammy now, she wanted to *strike him*, straddle him, and *fuck him until she bled*.

Each step Ares took rattled the ground under Margaret's feet, and when he spoke it was a bass growl that brooked no quarter, no doubt, no challenge.

"The Eye couldn't *simply* be shattered. It had to be destroyed in cold murder by one whose heart bled *love*. Amihan loved you more than anyone else when she drove that knife into you, right through the Eye."

Margaret was suspended in a state of *aggression* and *lust*. She understood *everything*. Aphrodite had already told her the secret.

"*We only offer kindness when the sweet scent of your soul is required to make the magic work, and we only offer suffering when your terror makes the lock turn.*"

Margaret reached her hand up to her chin, fingers up to her lips, digging her nails in, the kind of pain she begged Townsend for. "This was all you wanted. The Veil shattered, to *walk among us again.*"

Ares shrugged, hues of bronze, silver, and grey twisting with his form, "You didn't *really* think this was about you. *Did you*? That we somehow had your best interest at heart? The gifts from Eris and Aphrodite were only meant to keep you alive long enough to reach this day, to *die* under Amy's knife."

Aphrodite didn't give me a gift, Margaret thought, and as the metal lips of Ares curled into a grin, listening to her mind, she knew the answer.

"Townsend," Margaret whispered.

I never loved a man until the night I met Aphrodite.

Though she was small, smaller than almost every adult she'd known in life, and though she was used to looking *up* at almost everyone, Margaret had never felt as diminutive, as irrelevant, and powerless as she did under the shadow of a war god.

"You were supposed to die," Ares nodded to himself, the tendons in his neck shifting colors of mottled tan and gunmetal as he clenched one great fist. The snap and crackle of his knuckles sounded like solid axles snapping, and the twist of his muscles reminded Margaret of singing railroad steel. "So, you *will* die."

2:34pm April 15th, 39 Veilfall

Manteca Reach, California

Margaret *wanted* this death.

As much as her pulse quickened, the idea of falling before a god, *this god in particular,* was intoxicating, seductive, and dreadful. She didn't want to defend herself, there was no magic to summon, no tricks or schemes. It only mattered *how* she passed. The woman who refused to kneel would die *proudly*, Margaret knew this for certain.

"*No,*" Sammy said. His voice seemed meek and childish against the deep rumble of a war god, but his conviction was no less. One boot forward in the mud, a cascade of rain washing off his tiny eyes, Sammy of the Maul shouldered his antique rifle, leaned in and set his jaw. "I can't *let'cha* do that."

Ares, towering above them, unclenched his fist and swung both hands together in a clapping motion. It sounded like iron thunder and tornadoes, sparking light behind a rumbling belch of laughter.

"You'll 'let' me do *nothing.*"

Another step forward, forearms tense, Sammy lifted the rifle high, and did not flinch, "I serve warlords of *th'Maul*, and *th'Maul* serves Lady Mayhem. I can't allow an Antecedent, or *anyone* else to harm her. Not even you."

The grave metal face of Ares turned serious, his smile collapsing, his brow a terrible doubt upon the world. "I've heard your prayers, Sammy of the Maul. You would cast aside *your own* god for this *witch cunt?*"

Sammy took a third step forward, voice steady, "Lady Mayhem gave us our pride back. She gave us our glory back, and I *love her*, as I *love you*."

Margaret turned away from the titanic silhouette cast by Ares to look at Sammy's profile. She didn't imagine that she'd have such an impact on the boy's world. He was just an angry *hatefuck*, and she'd never taken anything in her life that wasn't paid for. To imagine Sammy so loyal to her for such a simple gift rattled her own pride, in the face of death.

"You are no Diomedes. You *will* die."

Sammy answered this with rifle fire.

Beyond where Margaret's toes curled down into mud, she could smell the blood clotting at her skull. Sammy's teeth clenched, his finger jerked against the trigger, and the rifle's muzzle flashed. He didn't just loose lead into the face of a war god, he charged forward. He crossed foot after foot, and when his rifle emptied, he tore it from the shoulder strap and swung it with all the fury that a fragile mortal of meat and marrow could muster.

Each shard of metal that his rifle belched hit Ares in neck and face, burning hot, flattening into his own carapace, consumed wholly by the god's form. Each falling brass case turned to water on the dirt below, and when the rifle struck Ares it *shattered* like falling icicles. The hardened steel of the barrel tore apart; magazine, rail, and sights pulled up and were swallowed by bubbling gold and silver muscles.

Sammy died instantly.

Ares raised a mighty fist and struck down. The force and speed created a wake that shoved Margaret back, stumbling. Sammy's spine collapsed, his knees broke, the very skin of his body rippled like waves under gusting wind. His head split open, five ways, a ripe cantaloupe falling free. His hair parted and gray fluid erupted from within. His blood coated the armor of Ares, and it too was absorbed like the lead and rifle, welcomed into a warm embrace.

Margaret was close enough that some of Sammy's blood coated her face and chest, in her eyes, and on her lips. One last time she could smell his semen and sweat, remember what it was like when he forced her face to a sticky bar, hammering her pelvis with his erect cock.

You have the glorious death I promised you, Sammy, Margaret thought.

"I will make sure your Maul sings of this for a hundred years to come."

The body of Sammy crumbled. His boots and ankles had been driven into the mud, holding up his hips and lower back. Blood and brains leaked down his body, and his arms slowly drifted under the weight of gravity. He was frozen in a strike, a statue dedicated to unmitigated aggression and rage.

Ares lifted his eyes, liquified metal turning solid. No emotion could be read on the steel statue, "I've heard his prayers since he was a boy."

There was regret in his voice, a humming drone of steel, something like sorrow. With her lonely hand, Margaret reached up and ran index and middle fingers down her face. She drew cruor and tears, depositing the sweet salt against her tongue and lips, "He just died at the hands of a war god for his *mistress*. This was the glory he desired, and you *know it*."

Ares stood, a perfect specimen of masculinity. An unobtainable example of humanity: wide hands, long fingers, and dangling phallus. When he answered, his voice echoed in total pride, "All these years, and you *never* prayed to me. A *wretched cow* so consumed with war, so in love with *my boys*, and yet all of my altars you *ignored*."

Margaret had been called *plenty of things* in her life. Some kind, others cruel, or crude, but up until this second, *'wretched cow'* had never been one.

"I've never feared death, Ares," Margaret smirked, "Let's get this over with."

Turning from Sammy's corpse, headless and broken, standing eternal, Ares began to shift in color and shape. His height seemed to pull and ebb back like a falling tide, his metal flesh and muscle paled and turned a shade of mist, veined, and wholly human in deception. Leather grew upwards and wrapped around his thick calves as knee-high boots. The dread clamber of his footfalls were no less heavy, bouncing rock and stone, thumping at pooled water, chasing rain and sending a biting vibration up Margaret's legs and hips, chewing angrily at her clitoris.

"Without *fear*, what value does this world hold for you?"

Standing before her, every bit as real as Sammy was, Ares cast a shadow of unbridled brutality and beauty. Margaret's eyes fluttered beyond her control and as much as she tried to focus on the metamorphosis of a steel god, her vision blurred and she bit her lower lip, choking on a whimper that sprang free.

The world holds no value.

"There's only *fighting* and *fucking*."

While pandemonium reigned in all directions, Ares met Margaret in this holiest of places. His chest was inches from her chin and his eyes burned with flame reflected through marbled glass. He smelled of musk and oil, and an intoxicating weight of copper, prompting total avidity in Margaret. She raised her one palm and pressed into the chest of Ares, heavy in boiled leather and notched metal. It may as well have been a mountain that her hand trembled before.

A witch until her last breath, Margaret *saw* things beyond reason. Colors and sounds, glimpses into worlds unlike any she'd imagined. Gods moved about her for a fraction of a second, spoke in languages no human could learn, and felt emotions magnified by untold power. She was drowning, and breathing, all at once. Parts of her mind switched off in total disbelief of what they witnessed.

Pulling her wrist away from his chest, Ares' hand wrapped around much of her forearm with such pressure that Margaret imagined her bones snapping like twigs. No physical act could have replicated it, as painful as it was pleasurable.

"Are you going to kill me, or do I have to *beg* for it?" Margaret looked up at him.

Crouching low and leaning forward, Ares kissed Margaret. For a few seconds, she knew what it was like to be a *god.*

His lips burned and his tongue bored into her mouth like a bullet through flesh. This was nothing as simple as *lust.* She was greater than herself, Valkyrie incarnate, an echo of every dying breath, the cry of victory and the howl of defeat. She was the *winner* and the *loser*, the *living* and the *dead,* over and over again. She was the ghost on a radio frequency, witness to the shelling of the Bay Area Reach, and Sacramento's atomic fire. She was cluster munitions coating the enemy in flame and hate, the succulent taffy of napalm as men and women and children burned alive. In this moment, Margaret knew what it was like to not merely fight a war, but what it meant to *be the war.*

Let me stay, let me stay, let me stay here forever.

It was also a whisper. She was *begging* as his unyielding form tightened around her, dense beyond imagining, stronger than a thousand tanks and burning so very hot. She wanted to *die* here, she wanted him to consume her. Just the same as Sammy's blood.

Let me stay here forever.

Ares released her, drawing back, and Margaret heard herself beg for him with a cracking and broken voice, sizzling on her own tongue.

His appearance had shifted, and now Ares stood before her in a coat of onyx leather and shimmering blood, a uniform that she'd never seen. Wide lapels and wool jacket bore metal pins, a strap crossed his chest, neck tie clutched with white linen collar. His cap bore a single skull at the pinnacle, and below the brim his eyes blazed the heat of burning cities.

Margaret realized she had never loved a man before Townsend because no *single man* could have compared to the maul of *war* itself. Her favorite lover above all others.

"*I love you,*" Margaret wept as Ares growled. One hand clutched her shoulder, the other her twisted collarbone.

The battlefield around her was quiet, frozen in time. Margaret could see tracers hanging in the air, Antecedent, Owens, and Maul soldiers alike, charging each other. Rifles held high, bayonets fixed, caught under cold explosions, the mist of burning diesel and evaporating rain.

Her place was *out there.*

"It's *frozen,*" Margaret spat in wonder.

Ares answered, his voice no less broad than before, "We are caught between seconds. We are standing in the place that gods walk, between the moments that you believe are so important. We watch you live, your blood running fast and hot. So afraid. You seem as ants to us. Do you *understand* now? Why we did this? *Why* we manipulated you?"

You love this world, Margaret thought, aware that Ares heard her, "You wanted to return to this place. To walk with us again."

She couldn't focus on Ares now. His eyes blurred the very air that made her heart stop. She could smell the gunpowder and blood and *fire, all the fire, all of the cities burning.* She wanted to be loosed into this fray, tossed free and discarded. She wanted the wind to lift her high like leaves, she wanted to unleash terrible dread on these armies.

I must help my men, they need me.

"*No, Margaret,*" Ares answered, and something about his words pulled her back to his smoldering eyes, reflecting millennia and devastation. "Your soldiers *will* die, and there will be no witches to hasten this end. They will fight. They will not run or retreat. It will be a symphony of death not seen by your kind since the world was two-thousand years younger. You will not deprive me of my feast."

She didn't *want* to accept this, but there was no room for negotiation. The fingers that held her were stronger than falling mountains. It was now that Margaret understood, she'd *never* had a voice. This outcome was decided *long* ago. She was just an actor in a play. The illusion of her control, the deeds she'd accomplished, the pain she'd felt, all her hardships, had simply been a part of a greater scheme.

"They'll die," Margaret replied, crying.

"Yes, *many* of them will die. I don't know who will be victor. The two sides are equally matched, equally skilled, and equally brave."

I can't protect them anymore, Margaret realized.

"No, you can't. But this is how it shall be."

The air was so thick, Margaret imagined she'd gag on wet and smoke. Her heart detached from her chest, a thing drawn up and out of her, beating free of her body, a living creature with its own dreams and desires.

"I can't give you the freedom to command this battle, but I *can* give you the *one thing* you wanted above *all others* in this life."

What?

Margaret's eyes unfocused, and she remembered so many dreams she'd never had.

"A *child*." Ares answered.

Long after she'd worked so hard to forget, decades had passed. She'd spoken her eulogies. She never stopped being *angry*, every bit as angry as Sammy had been. The part of her born a witch *knew* she'd been robbed of her ability to create life. She didn't need a doc or medic to grope her cervix, she *knew* what had been stolen, the one thing that could never be given back. The price *they* believed she had to pay.

    Just because I was born to wealth and power.

    "Damn you," Margaret's anger was a balloon filling her chest and stomach.

    Ares seemed to feast on her rage, and he smiled, "You'll have *one* child before you're too old. *One* chance at this. If Townsend survives today, perhaps he can be the father. If he falls, I could always be persuaded to provide *my services.*"

    "*Damn you!*" Margaret shrieked, her left arm lifted high, hammering down into Ares' chest, hitting hard enough to numb her nerves, no different from punching a tree or slapping a tank carapace.

    With his right hand, Ares pulled Margaret close to him once more.

    Margaret knew on some level what would come next. She *knew* this would hurt.

    Ares *punched* Margaret in the stomach.

    Tons, perhaps *hundreds of tons*, hammered into her skin, and she knew the damage was very real. Her spine shattered, her ribs snapped, crumpled, and peeled back. Her pelvis disintegrated, and intestines spilled free of the gaping punctures that emptied her stomach. It was agony beyond description, far above the pain of being *shot* or *stabbed*. Even the flames of Amihan Lopez were *nothing* compared the sudden fury of this savage malady. If she could have killed herself at this moment, Margaret *would have*, just to free herself, to depart her body of screaming nerves, the very meat that powered her, a betrayer.

    Somewhere in this pain, Margaret's body *died*. It couldn't help but to do so under the weight of such physical trauma. Somewhere in her death she was *flying*, weightless, tossed asunder like a broken toy that no longer served a purpose.

In that moment of death, Margaret was also reborn.

Her body was pulling itself back together, unfolding bones and growing marrow, tugging and pulling tendons tight, unfurling yards of blood veins. Somewhere in that reconstruction, the parts of her that had been wounded were mended. *She could feel it.*

Margaret didn't know how long it *hurt*, or how long she slept. She didn't know if she was dwelling in the moment between seconds, or if she was bleeding to death and being reborn in her own time. She stopped understanding pain, her own existence, and simply ceased to be aware, passing beyond sleep, into a reality that had never been documented.

8:22am April 16th, 39 Veilfall

Manteca Reach, California

"Is you a witch?"

The voice belonged to a child. When Margaret turned to face him, he couldn't have been older than five or six. His hair was blonde mixed with platinum and had been slicked down against his head with whispers of rain. His eyes were dark blue, and he bore a scratch at his cheek. The kind of wound likely inflicted by learning a lesson.

"*Yeah,*" Margaret croaked, her voice sounded like a series of twigs snapping rhythmically with her syllables.

"We *suppos'd* to report a witch. A one-arm witch, *no-slack.*" The boy answered, stumbling across the phrase *one-arm*. It came out a syrupy mumble. He wore woolen packs over his shoulders, crossing at his narrow chest, each loaded with brass casings, soaked at their bellies with moisture and mud, hugging his burlap pants.

"I guess you'd best help me up," Margaret stuttered for a second, rolling to her right side. The stones at her ribs pressed past broken ceramic plate, making her wince, "because you just found *a one-arm witch.*"

The boy agreed, dutifully holding her wrist with both hands as she brought her weight up and off saturated earth. Her ankle buzzed with sharp ache. She glanced down at the armor around her abdomen and pelvis. The corset was still intact, but she could see where bullets had struck. If any one of those rounds had slipped between plates, she'd easily be dead by now.

There was no evidence of the wound, the impact, gifted by Ares.

Was that real? Is that how my mind processed it?

It seemed real. So literal in pain, a string tugged and pulled along a rotten, old sweater. When she pulled her hand from the little boy's fingers, she pressed at her stomach, between the corset bones and her armor.

"You going to have a baby?" The child asked her.

Margaret had paid no attention when she touched the little brassboy. Nor had she listened to his mind, but now she took a step back in both wonder and shock. He couldn't have known what she was thinking, it *had* to just be a logic bridge.

Probably.

"What's your name, brassboy?" Margaret asked, coughing. Her throat was defiantly dry, despite clothes being soaked to the skin as she shivered.

"Poul," the boy nodded, his voice small.

Margaret looked away from his blue eyes and brass bags, up and over the battlefield remains. A flood of black and sooty smoke promised fires. It looked like *most* of the larger armored vanguard were wrecked, painted an ugly shade of night in scorches.

The *bodies*, however, the *bodies* seemed to go on forever.

The chill and rain had kept rot close to the ground, but if the sun darted out to warm the ocean of carcasses it would surely raise a foul odor. For now it only smelled like *blood*, cold and copper, sharp and stinging, mixed with the loose bowels and bladders where men had fallen in heaps. Tangled, frozen in moments of unadulterated violence. Knives clutched in blackened knuckles, twisted fingers on throats, eyeless rage caught in death. It reminded Margaret of the white caps that she'd seen in Aphrodite's eyes after the *first night* with Townsend.

There was also pooled gold. Lumps of yellow metal, clinging to the mud, or melted across skeletons, exposing rib cages and spinal columns.

So, Eris had been real.

"Poul," Margaret didn't look at the brassboy, "what army do you serve?"

"3rd Army, ma'am." The boy replied.

Margaret closed her eyes and tilted her head back so that mist would stroke her face.

At the very least, we won.

Ares had been right, of course. A battle of this magnitude, without witches, was a slaughter. As her adulation over the victory grew, so too did her sorrow. There was no way to count the dead, and she wondered how many faces would she recognize? How many other Daniel Hasgards would look back at her, their chests opened and engorged, trailing their intestines, clawing until their fingers broke and their nails tore free?

Fuck, Margaret laughed and her knees shuddered, *what about Townsend?*

He was the allied commander, Maul and Owens units had placed themselves under his jurisdiction. It was *unlikely* that he'd been fighting at the very front lines, but in the wake of the endless carnage she now witnessed, *anything* was possible.

Her voice stilled a frantic giggle, the closest she might know of fear, and Margaret looked back to the brassboy, "Can you lead me to 3rd Army's command?"

The boy seemed perplexed. *A brassboy would have no clue about army command.*

"I can try?" The answer came out as a question, "But, *no-slack* on brass, I *gots* more pick up, ma'am."

Margaret considered assuming control of the boy's mind, then decided against it. He was young and she could take the extra moment to convince him.

"Take me to the one who told you, about a *one-arm witch*. Then you can return to picking up brass, *yeah*?"

Little Poul seemed to find this more satisfying, "Yeah."

Running a hand across her face, Margaret sloughed off mud and dried cruor. She also pressed at lumps around her eye and temple, even her jaw, face swollen. She wondered how many days had passed since she'd shot her brother in the face.

Margaret did her best to not trip over the dead. The uniforms and armor mottled up in shades of black and ashen gray, coated in scorch and varied shades of erubescent. Under coats of butchery, they all seemed the same. One after another, a twin to the next. If she stopped to study one, or two, she could tell them apart, some were taller, others wore beards or had green eyes, but at a glance it was simply a carpet of death.

The closer to the active camps, the more bodies had been drug away, stacked and sorted for burning or burial. Rifles had been collected, forming vertical piles, jagged edges where bayonets protruded. Plate carriers, armor, and helmets were also stripped, forming smaller pyramids.

Older brassboys sorted the dead, looking for unspent ammunition, supplies, and food to be collected. A few of them were girls, like Erin, wet hair pulled back, quick fingers drawing out pockets and unlacing boots. Some of these soldiers would have notes or letters, to be consigned to their loved ones, wrapped around a single coin. Payment for the brassboy who located it and saw it delivered beyond death.

This was, Margaret always believed, one of the most important jobs of a brassboy. Collecting memories, ghosts of the fallen. Those letters were normally handed off to flywheels and runners, mercenaries and freebooters, of various ages who specialized in deliveries at great distance. Some had no taste for war, others were simply too feeble of body or mind to become infantry. A hundred opportunities awaited them between city-states, harbingers of information.

Deeper, canvas tents had been placed around old plastic tables arranged as a brassboy hub. Older teenagers organized and directed their operations here. The one who Poul introduced her to was a man-grown, easily twenty or twenty-one years old, his chin peppered in a charade of beard, lips chapped and eyes watering.

"*Bossboy,*" Poul said, pointing at Margaret with narrow fingers, blackened by powder residue, "I found a *one-arm witch.*"

Smacking at chew tobacco, the older *bossboy* glared at Margaret in nervous disdain. He was afraid of her. Something crawled at the back of his mind, like the shadow of spiders caught in candlelight. Without a touch, or diving deeper, she'd never have imagined *what* caused this, but it made him hesitant near *any* inclined person.

"No-slack here, *pity-pity,*" he said, looking away from Margaret, back to Poul, "*Break bulk,* and quick with it. Eat, *yeah?* Eat and no-slack."

The brassboy gave a weird half-salute, as serious as the grave; "No-slack!"

Looking away from little Poul, the bossboy spat a wad of brown chew, "Lady Mayhem. *We's* ordered to seek you, no-slack. *We's* told it was a-number-one, highest priority." The older lad raised his hand, fingers flat, well above his own head, rising on tiptoes to demonstrate the importance of his orders.

"*Who* ordered it, bossboy? *A-number-one* priority?"

"Cap'n *Raises,*" the bossboy stumbled over the name *Reyes,* and Margaret heaved a sigh of relief, for any to notice. That was at least *one* that had survived the meat grinder.

Margaret's smile was genuine, "Escort me to Captain Reyes, *please.*"

The bossboy nodded, clapping his hands together twice and gesturing with his chin to follow him. Further north, away from pustulant smoke. Margaret did her best to ignore *that* smell, to not wrinkle her nose or cup her face with a dingy palm. It wasn't the *same* as fresh skin and muscle ablaze, but it was close enough that her memories threaten to capsize against rising tambour of anxiety.

What if Townsend was killed?

It was strange to consider. Would she be able to live her remaining years, happily, in the absence of the only person who had not only *understood*, but *accepted* her? Could she *replace him*? Or would they just be a warm body pressed against her back and buttocks when she slept, a smile at breakfast, an even tone reading books to her? The winged horror of Eris and the strength of Ares couldn't teach her fear. But, with each step, she knew *something* like terror. It forced her throat closed, labored her breathing and hissed at her ears like a venomous serpent.

Is this fear? Or some kind of new love? Margaret was illiterate to the answer.

Maul soldiers limped past her on crutches made of broken rifles. Wrapped in beige and red bandages, stained dark in the rain, threatening to turn putrid. Men screamed in medical tents, howling, pleading and praying to the gods as their wounds were closed or limbs amputated. Agony flowed around Margaret like flood water, broken pieces of dreams drifting by her mind, each one a *question.*

How will I make a wage, no legs at all?

Will she still love me, will she still think me handsome?

I was right handed. How will I write? I can't write with my left hand!

That very last one cut deepest for Margaret. She'd not even tried to bring pen to paper, and she wondered if she'd ever offer herself up to that foul humiliation. She could imagine scrambling with the weaker wrist, unable to grip quill, forming ugly and misshapen words, unwanted and unloved, a stillborn child at her fingers.

The thought disgusted Margaret.

When they finally found Captain Reyes, he ignored the brassboy and embraced Margaret like a lost lover, pulling her up, off the ground. Her back cracked under the strength of his arms, where armor plates separated.

"We *really* thought you were dead, Lady," Reyes placed Margaret down, back on her feet, where the mud was firm. She had run the back of her hand across the Captain's neck, gritty with soil and salt, she didn't want to *wait*, she didn't care to ask the officer.

Townsend was still alive, Margaret thought, slipping through Captain Reyes' memories, wandering around early morning when all fighting finally ceased. Townsend's armor was spattered in ink and blood, his helmet gone, still wearing his headset and microphone like the one Margaret had lost. His eyes were heavy, and his brow beaded with furor and dread. He smelled like an ashtray, chain smoking, his hands quivering from adrenaline and something close to anger. Reyes was talking in the memory, his teeth clicking as he spoke, but Margaret paid little heed. She simply watched the big General nod in sullen loathing, moving in and out of lantern shadow.

He thinks I'm dead, Margaret realized, in horror.

He didn't suffer her immunity to fear, all the muscles in his face clenched and twisted as emotions crossed his eyes. He was the king of a black day. Somewhere beyond the duties he'd resigned himself to, was a man who believed a very small woman, who he loved, had fallen in his black day.

"I'm sorry," Margaret shook her head, withdrawing from the memory, leaving Captain Reyes to rest in his mind, alone, "I'm sorry for *everything*. I'm sorry I wasn't on the front lines, and I'm sorry you fought without a *witch*."

Reyes pursed his lips, eyes focusing far away, "No one survived the front lines. *No one.* We assumed you'd fallen in the crossfire when you didn't pick up on radio."

The look Reyes offered to only the gods, told Margaret a multitude of details. The carnage of this fight wasn't something Reyes could wrap his mind around. Not *yet*. Just as Margaret had her own demons to tame, Captain Reyes would one day need to domesticate the horror he'd just taken part in.

"The 1st Army?" Margaret questioned, her voice trailing off.

"*Dead*. To the man. They wouldn't surrender. Or run. *Dead*, to the last man."

Ares hadn't lied. "*They will not run or retreat, it will be a symphony of death not seen by your kind since the world was two-thousand years younger.*"

I can send Townsend a message that I'm safe, Margaret had work to do now.

"Nothing to be done. Fetch me a brassboy who can help with my armor. I'll attend the wounded."

Captain Reyes didn't respond right away. His dark eyes fell off a ledge that Margaret couldn't see or sense. When he regained composure, he lifted one dirty hand to his jaw, running a palm against stubble so thick that she could hear sandpaper scratch.

"*Lady*, I can't really allow that. Not this time."

Rankled, Margaret withdrew, body pulling away from the Captain and mind recoiling, "No one *allows* me to do anything, Commander."

Reyes shook his head, fast, dragging his gaze across the mud at Margaret's bare toes, crusted and stained black, "*No, no,* Lady. That's not how I meant it. I know you've always tended the wounded, the dying. But, this is different. General Townsend and Lord Owens have both summoned for you. *If* we found you alive. Townsend left express orders that you be brought to northern command immediately."

In his terror of displeasing Lady Mayhem, Captain Reyes let slip something that she should have already known. *He doesn't see me as a battlewitch anymore. He doesn't see me as mistress of the 3rd Army.*

"Because I'm not. Not anymore." Margaret whispered the reply, her eyes closing.

"*Lady?*" Reyes answered her, tensely.

Margaret shook off the notion like a bad dream. She was left with a mouth of cotton and the lonely, disconnected sense of no longer belonging.

"It's *fine*. Take me to the command post."

Somewhere in their walk, between the flapping tents of the wounded and the guarded fortifications of field command, Lady Mayhem blew away in the wind.

She was a dry and dangerous tumbleweed whose time was now past, caught in flurry and gust, a memory to be held by anyone who witnessed her.

Only Duchess Margaret of the Bay Area Reach remained.

11:44pm December 4th, 39 Veilfall

Santa Cruz, California

"We're here, Duchess."

Margaret couldn't see her driver in the dark. Her name was Bixby and she was the daughter of Townsend's steward. A tall woman with bony knees, elbows, and a clavicle that extended itself unnaturally far from her chest. When she laughed it sounded like a pigeon dying, but her eyes were just a bit too big for her face, the same as Margaret, and she found this endearing.

"Turn off the lights," Margaret answered.

The road had twisted up and around the proper reach of Santa Cruz. Asphalt had been eaten away by rain and time, crumbling in chunks down moist mountain soil, riddled with weeds and wildflowers. Back the way they had come, the road crossed a pre-Collapse cemetery, surrounded by a well-kept fence of wooden pickets, wound in dark ivy. Stones near the center looked to be easily two centuries old, while recent burials swept out beyond the central bounds. The further they drove, the darker it became. A young moon was swallowed by thick clouds, heavy with rain, and scented in ozone. The forest opened up for them, and quickly closed with weighted canopies, fluttering in a breeze and sprinkling the 4x4's cracked windshield with droplets of water.

Margaret and Bixby sat together for a while, air so quiet that it became a low-pitched ringing in Margaret's ears. A never ending note, the sound time made as it died.

The night was total, luring the human eye forward until optic nerves began to manifest their own hallucinations, gimmicks to keep the brain sharp, spurring adrenaline and whispering primal tales of *what lurked in the shadows*.

Of course, *things actually did lurk in the shadows*.

"Are you scared?" Margaret asked softly, as minutes passed.

"Hard to be scared, here. With a *witch*, Duchess." Bixby's voice cracked and changed pitch. She was invisible and her words seemed to float around the cab of their truck, fish caught in an old aquarium.

Margaret sighed. The noise may as well have been a firecracker. With her left hand, she reached over her lap and opened the passenger door by pulling an old, plastic latch. It creaked once, then snapped, before swinging open. This triggered an overhead light, yellow and dim, sick like a dying animal. It blinded Margaret briefly, but she blinked hard and looked down in her lap.

In front of her wide, taunt, stomach was a square box, hewn of wood and bound with tin and silver. It was no more than a few inches deep, and had been lacquered a shade of cerise, still tacky under Margaret's fingers. Her thumb had left deep creases, curving and twisting. Across the box, trussed up in a floppy oversized bow, was a narrow strip of blue silk, bound tight. Along the edges, the silk was marked with black and deep crimson, dried blood from Margaret's own skin. She'd carved at her right thigh, holding a narrow dagger, making the offering sincere.

My mother would have packaged this gift in the forest, Margaret smiled to herself, *but she had two good hands to use.*

Meticulously sorted items filled Margaret's box of wood and tacky lacquer. There were two metal buttons, a copper coil twisted to look like a dragon, rusted tacks and silver earrings that didn't match. There was also a flattened piece of lead, two wedding rings of soft, simple gold, and a large whip that could scream when cracked by a certain witch.

This was the debt Maggi Lopez owed Marinette Bras Cheche.

"The brass and leaden carapace; that killed a royal king. Two hearts pledged together, bound by golden rings. A snake of bloodied leather; whose bite will burn flesh with icy knell."

Considering the box, Margaret gasped, in both surprise and pain.

"Duchess?" Bixby inquired, turning sideways, offering a hand with chewed nails.

Margaret shook her head fast, dropping her right leg out of the truck's cab and glancing over at the steward's daughter. Her face was long and gaunt, and she had no need of rouge to color her cheeks and flushed nose, "Barrett just kicked, nothing to fret."

Wrinkling her nose, Bixby inquired, "You're *sure* it's a boy, then?"

Exhaustion crossed Margaret's face, but her smile was sincere, "I *know* he's a boy, because he told me. He won't be so tall as my husband. That's my fault, but he'll be strong all the same."

Bixby seemed amazed by this tale, her large eyes growing as her jaw began to slack. It seemed to Margaret as though she was listening to an old story about ghosts or haunted houses. Afraid as she was in love with things that seemed so impossible. Margaret didn't bother to read her mind. There was little that Bixby didn't freely share with her mouth.

"Take care then, Duchess."

Turning away, and letting her wooden box, trussed with blue silk, fall to the warm seat, Margaret slid out of the truck and stood upright. Under a jacket of cotton and duck oil, a metal hand poked from beneath her right sleeve. The silver plates caught bisque light, shimmering briefly.

"Pray to your gods, child," Margaret leaned in, grabbing the package with her functioning left hand. Shadow turned her auburn-red hair *black* and made her eyes depthless pools of night, "They'll watch over you when I'm gone."

Stepping back, Margaret kicked the 4x4's passenger door closed.

Total darkness returned as easily as it had been chased away. Imprints of the cab and Bixby's face blinked across Margaret's field of view, each time her lashes fluttered. With great care she slowly stepped around the truck to begin her walk across the decayed road, stone and pebble biting the arches of her bare feet, demanding she offer *them* just the smallest drop of blood in payment for her toll.

Santa Cruz was a river below her. A strange mix of old and new energy, intense power that lurked between hills and trees, *watching* her. An ancient god, awake just enough to be interested in the little witch and her large belly.

Margaret kept walking, into the darkness.

Darkness was key, she imagined her mother saying, *the right kind of darkness. A place where trees were so thick that the moon couldn't penetrate.*

The further she went, the more limbs tugged at Margaret. She was careful with her footing, unwilling to risk tripping. An inconvenience that would risk an already risky pregnancy. This was, however, part of her payment toward Maggi's debt, some of the interest owed.

When she understood she'd gone *far enough*, Margaret carefully knelt down in the cool, damp soil, placing her wooden box to the side. She took a moment to hike up her skirt, just enough that her knees laid bare on earth. The song of the world could vibrate up through her spine, a memory of the land itself.

This sort of digging needed to be rhythmic, pulsing, you must let your hindbrain take over and set your breathing in time with the movements.

Maggi, or perhaps the memory of Maggi, whispered in Margaret's mind as she withdrew a small, iron trowel from her jacket. With one hand she stabbed into the soft earth. Over and over again, dragging soil up to her knees, past her thighs, and even kissing her swollen belly. The artificial arm hung at her side, frozen halfway between motion and illusion, hinges locked tight, silver plates of her fake fingers clicking as she leaned forward.

Finally, pleased that this was deep enough, Margaret replaced the filthy trowel and reached for her box of tacky lacquer, carefully placing it in her miniature pit.

"Maggi's debt is now paid," Margaret whispered, her neck tilted back, hip cramping. She wanted to take a second longer, to listen to the silence of the forest, to stretch her mind out and feel the shadow creatures that skulked among the trees. Something pushed back, however, something told her *no*.

Accepting of this, Margaret used her left hand to scoop the freshly damp soil back over her offering, palm pressing and patting the earth until she was satisfied.

It was a challenge to stand up. Barrett was a bigger child than her tiny frame could accommodate, and she only had one hand to steady her, but Margaret returned to her feet.

"*For me?*" The voice was feminine, distant, and muffled. "*I need not share?*"

The syllables moved around Margaret, gasping for air. Skipping stones clattered around, dry bones hinging against each other, clicking like insects and then shifting with a breeze that didn't blow. The world was curving around her. Not as violent as it had been in San Francisco, nowhere near painful. It simply felt like a door had opened, beckoning into distant hallways.

Maggi's voice whispered close to Margaret's ear, *My Lady of the Dry Arms, I'd never ask you to share your treasure.*

"This treasure is *only* for you. The debt I promised, paid. An answer to your riddle."

Sifting sashes caught a light that didn't glow in the forest, and Margaret could see afterimages moving close. Bones and fingers, ribs and spine, silhouetted against nothing more than the darkness, "*Maggi wished for flames on her fingers, a kiss of agony. Her debt is now paid, but perhaps we can do business?*"

Margaret smiled, easily. A clever witch, she could never be lured into such a trap. Marinette Bras Cheche was a kind of lovely parasite, a necessity of the *old world*, a broker in dreams and wishes.

Then again, Margaret considered, clearing Maggi's credit, *stealing* the Eye of Shahr-i-Sokhta, it had all been easy enough.

Easy enough for a clever witch.

"I have no more trinkets to pay you, *Lady of the Dry Arms*."

Marinette Bras Cheche's shawls and scarves fell across Margaret, cold and perhaps wet, beyond a winter kiss or flurry of snow. This was a cutting algid, a reminder that this world had little in common with any beyond the Veil.

"You've proven a witch of means, with a word like iron," Marinette whispered close to Margaret's ear, a tickle across her lobe, against her neck. She could hear the same giggling orgasm that Townsend gifted, the night they'd made Barrett.

"*Mmm*," Margaret thought, toying with this idea, "What could I ask for?"

"*My lovely,*" the brumal murmur sweetened, "*you can ask for anything.*"

Margaret expected the memory of her mother to argue, in her mind. To demand she leave this place and make no more bargains beyond the Veil. But the memory was silent, just as silent as the grave of Maggi Lopez. This was Margaret's choice, and if she told Marinette that she wanted *nothing*, it would have been a lie.

Few things were beyond a battlewitch; fewer still, Duchess of the Bay Area Reach.

"I'm with child, a *boy*. It's rare that boys inherit magic, but it *can* happen. It *has* happened. I want this child to know the world as I know it. I want him to hear the sound of dreams and taste love and anger as I have. I want him to be a *witch*."

Marinette cackled close to Margaret, the sound undulating past her skin, raising hairs at the back of her neck, and pouring lascivious desire into the very marrow of Margaret's bones.

It was so long before Marinette replied, that Margaret wondered if perhaps she had found *something* not on offer for a wish-broker.

"Oh yes, little witch. We shall do business together."

8:32 pm January 8th, 40 Veilfall

San Francisco, California

A man, in plaid pants sat at the corner of this restaurant. His face was narrow, ill shaven, with thick bangs that fell past his eyes as he leaned over a wide, wooden instrument. A hurdy gurdy. His right hand moved the crank with rhythmic stops and starts, fingers of his left hand spasming across the keys, hammering on the strings. The instrument was freshly lacquered in black, painted in the silver blossoms of House Owens, and smelled of oil. Behind him was a dowdy woman with crooked bangs and tobacco stained lips, her elbow to bow. Raking across the strings of a less cared for violin, battered and scratched, her chin tucked low.

The couple weaved melody like a fine tapestry of thick woolen twine; it covered empty tables and chairs like a warm blanket and echoed off the wooden floor and plaster walls. Tangible as the white smoke rising off incense decanters, at wall's edge.

"Mistress, *you'se* have a visitor."

Aubriana Harvester turned away from the music, a deep strum pulling at her chest, behind the sternum. Yellow chicken fat ran down her chin and she leaned over to run her jaw along the black velvet of her coat shoulder. "A visitor? At this hour?"

The man standing over her was small, with scars efflorescent. Yellow teeth were visible past a lumpy, ruined cheek, and his nose was long absent giving him a skeletal appearance with rat eyes. "It's a *fucking shit-show*, Mistress."

Aubriana smirked. Badger's voice of saccharine gravel delighted her. "*It?*"

Badger shrugged, the tendons in his neck taunt, "Could be a *she*."

The chicken leg in Aubriana's right hand was tossed to plate, rolling through a sauce of grease, melted fat, and thick curry. She ran her fingers across the mauve table cloth until they were clean, leaving dark stains. Cuffs of finely spun, golden chainmail whispered around her wrists, then draped down past her knuckles when she kicked the wooden chair back.

"I'm game," Aubriana's smirk became a smile. Her voice was husky, slippery, like warm batter and chilled lard.

Badger didn't acknowledge this, nor did he scrape, as he turned on a heel to leave. It seemed to Aubriana that he moved with a hitch in his step, an old wound at the knee or hip.

Running her tongue along teeth, picking out fragments of meat and spices, Aubriana turned her head and spit. One of her eyes was a pool of splattered ink, the other covered with a thick patch of umber leather that had been stitched into her flesh with thick twine of burgundy. When she drew breath it came deeply and heaved her chest in, as if she savored the air.

Badger returned in several moments with something *like* a person.

It *did* seem feminine. A clearly defined bust above stomach, wrapped in narrow strips of tattered wool, each dyed a different shade of gray or jet. When *it* walked, *it* drug a left leg as if it was a dead animal, brought to ground, fresh for the stew. There was nothing natural in how *it* moved, a lurching half-stumble that almost matched the hurdy gurdy rhythm, arms shifting for balance with graceless jerking, fingers drawn up and tensed.

Aubriana did not turn away from the *thing* as it approached. Her pulse quickened with something adjacent to adoration.

"*It's* a *she*, Badger," Aubriana said, turning her head with a shout back to the man with no nose, "and she's *lovely*. Take your leave."

Badger wrinkled up the remains of his face and mouthed the words '*take your leave*' to the table closest, before stepping back to the restaurant lobby.

The closer Aubriana's guest came, the more fetid her stench of rotten flesh and wet wool became. A raucous odor that left Aubriana's smile undeterred.

With her left foot, Aubriana kicked out a wooden chair at her table, extending it for the wretched husk, hand gesturing slowly, with gentle ease.

When the ragged woman sat, it was with great difficulty. Her left knee would not bend and stuck out past her chair, like a nail that had been abused at its neck by hammer, rusted beyond repair. Lines around her eyes cut deep. Shaded darker than colorless and tattered lips, every bit as gruesome as the scars that exposed Badger's teeth.

Her eyes, however, were milk white. A drawing fog that invited chills down Aubriana's spine despite her affection. Beyond the mask of ripped flesh and molding burlap, Aubriana could feel *nothing* about her guest. She was a void, a place where the hurdy gurdy and violin wail did not penetrate. A cut in the room, that opulence found impenetrable.

"You have a name?" Aubriana inquired, tilting her head down, one good eye in her skull offering a kinder gaze than *anyone* had known in countless years.

Plague Dog.

The woman calling herself Plague Dog didn't project the words into Aubriana's mind, so much as she flooded the room with a stain of sorrow and pain, painted in syllables and vowels. It was so intense that Aubriana heard the violin player flummox several notes.

"You can't speak?" Aubriana ignored the groping sadness that pulled at her velvet coat.

Plague Dog did not answer.

Undeterred, Aubriana pressed on, but leaned in closer to whisper, "You're Amihan Lopez, then? Daughter of Aniceta Lopez?"

Again, Plague Dog did not answer.

Exhaling slowly, Aubriana chose her words carefully. "Aniceta was in my care, a *long* time ago. She tended my wounds, and we had a secret. *I* was the one in *her* care."

My mother died when we were young.

Once more the hollow swoop of weary sadness flooded. Aubriana glanced to the stage as her violinist dropped instrument and bow, swallowing hard. It was thick in the air, a feeling that painted the tables and chairs in swatches of dolor.

Aubriana's smile did not falter and after a brief pause she said, "It's amazing what you can do when you refuse to die. *Isn't it, Amy?*"

It was only now that Aubriana noticed the table at Plague Dog's side was beginning to *decay*. Bright green enamel was peeling up, powdering, revealing grayed wood that turned bleached and brittle. The chair under was no different, twisting and crumpling under Plague Dog's weight as years ticked by, faster and faster, in unchecked *entropy*.

Every nerve in Aubriana's mind told her to *run*, to get away, to flee this *thing* whose very touch was caustic. Her body was a gift from Lady Mayhem, a treasure of unimaginable worth, young enough to move without pain, graced with a lovely *jaw that hinged and slurped at the delights of this world, teeth and tongue wholly intact.*

Aubriana, however, did not run.

Plague Dog's chair shattered, centuries rotten and frail. Flecks of green paint were spirited away, dust as whispers. As dread the visage of Plague Dog was, so too was the intensity of her piteous collapse. She wept, her mouth open and silent in the room, fingers clawing at her face in a baseless rage that threatened to rend off what remained of her pallor. Her shoulders heaved, ghostly sobs, silent as a graveyard.

Rattled to her very core, Aubriana stood, kicking away her own chair. The hurdy gurdy player ceased performance, nearly dropping his instrument, and clutched the hand of his partner. They fled, as fast as legs would carry, boots and shoes scuffing, gasping at air to fuel their labor.

Aubriana had once stood in flesh given to her at birth. Not a stolen corpse, but bones that grew and held her high from infant to woman. She could still hear the hum of a sodium street light, and remember how jeans moved against her hips, the arch of her feet, bend of her ankles in heels, and salton balm of bay air. Plague Dog's cry was a familiar old melody that Aubriana kept in tune for *decades*. It was a kind of loneliness that peeled flesh from muscle and hollowed out the mind until something like madness was left in its wake. To *fear*, one had to possess something that could be lost. Aubriana *feared* to lose her body, a return to her exile, a colorless specter bound to San Francisco for eternity.

"I know what you feel," Aubriana growled, watching the pathetic creature writhe. She was in *pain*, madness threatened to drown her where she lay.

The wooden floor under her spine and shoulders was starting to warp, with age.

What am I?

Her thoughts shrieked, no longer a torrent of sorrow, rather a crash of rage, hammering old rocks and seagull shit.

"You're a monster. A *beautiful* monster."

Aubriana Harvester knelt, her knees pressing up against Plague Dog. Her arms reaching for shoulders, one hand cradling the creature's face. Energy that beat with her pulse could crack like a whip when commanded, or it could unravel, draping a hundred hooks below the angry swells. Each hook dug into Plague Dog, found purchase and tugged at her mind, her body, the ruins of her knee and face. Jerking at the ivory bulbs that jittered below sallow eyelids. The very fabric of Plague Dog was pulled asunder, collected up and categorized, pressed against the most intimate reaches of

Aubriana's soul. For a few brief seconds, Plague Dog would remember the sound of a sodium street light humming and the kiss of warm water in a shower.

She'd also remember the day that Aubriana woke with no jaw.

The sad and desperate creature's entropy began to slow, tighten, like a bolt about to break, then finally *freeze*. The only living *necromancer* could as easily halt entropy as she would rend a body apart with it. Whatever province stuck to Plague Dog, killing the world around her, was a thing that Aubriana *herself* could command.

Just as Plague Dog remembered glimpses of a life she never led, Aubriana caught memories on the young woman's breath. She saw Plague Dog's father *die*, and felt the sting of a twin sister who cast her to sea, a total betrayal. For a second, Aubriana also felt a profound love well up in her throat. The *need* that a child felt for mother's breast, unvarnished affection for her aunt, a woman who strode the world a titan at less than five-feet-tall.

"*Oh*, Amy," Aubriana leaned in, inhaling canker and putrefaction, "I'm so sorry."

She *was* sorry too. Aubriana Harvester knew a great deal of what it felt like to be murdered by someone she loved.

Plague Dog still quaked under sobs, shivered and twitched as though exposed to the winds of ice, but Aubriana did not let go of her. No matter the stench of death that flooded across her clothes, no matter the way her bones popped, or her skin shirked beneath touch.

Somewhere in that embrace, Plague Dog finally grew still, and her mind silent. A thing like sleep spreading through her decaying marrow.

Aubriana sang a song to the woman who couldn't die.

"*In Dublin's fair city,*

Where the girls are so pretty,

I first set my eyes on sweet Molly Malone,

As she wheeled her wheel-barrow,

Through streets broad and narrow,

Crying, 'Cockles and mussels, alive, alive, oh!'"

Dread Harvester by LacticWanda.

(END)

The world of Veilfall will return in *"Battery Acid,"* a full-length sequel to *"Mayhem."* Keep your eyes open for the anthology *"Veilfall,"* and novella, *"A Day in the Life of a Dead Whore."*

Learn more about Maggi Lopez in *"The Bruja,"* (available in softcover & eBook,) and Aubriana in *"Dread Harvester,"* (e-reader only). Order your copies now & follow author Michael Molisani on Facebook, Twitter, and Goodreads!

www.michaelmolisani.com

ABOUT THE AUTHOR & ARTISTS

Michael Molisani has had a mind full of terrible horror and bewildering beauty his entire life. Unable to exorcise these visions of worlds beyond imagining, he set out to become a writer. Having no idea what a terrible decision this was, he soon went mad, burrowing into the unspoken mysteries of how to tell a story worth reading in a style both pleasing and entertaining. When he's not hard at work writing, Michael Molisani can be found falling backward in time on the sidewalks of Virginia City, Nevada; or exploring the remote mysteries of The Great Basin. Michael and his wife, Kimberly, reside in Northern Nevada.

Nan Fe can be followed on DeviantArt
(https://www.deviantart.com/nanfe), or Instagram
(https://www.instagram.com/nanfe1789/)

Karolina Jędrzejak (RinRinDaishi) can be followed on DeviantArt
(https://www.deviantart.com/rinrindaishi), or Instagram
(https://www.instagram.com/rinrindaishi/)

Audia Pahlevi (Moonarc) can be followed on DeviantArt
(https://www.deviantart.com/moonarc)

LacticWanda can be followed on DeviantArt
(https://www.deviantart.com/lacticwanda)